Hurricane Season

Time Spent in Key West.

By Doug Miller and John Pugh

ISBN 978-1-4357-1588-2

We only had to turn the bend before we would be able to see the intersection of A1A and US-1. I remember looking at Reno and wondering if my face was as ashen-colored as his was when we came around the curve. Because it was at that moment that the world seemed to be moving in slow motion as our worst fears came true. There were two ambulances parked diagonally across the intersection, along with more police cars than I cared to count. Red, blue, yellow and white emergency lights were flashing everywhere. There was absolutely no sound. The only sense in my body functioning was my eyesight, and I didn't like what I was seeing. I didn't even know Key West had a police department, but apparently the entire force had convened on this intersection. Both of the westbound lanes had been blocked off. Amidst the broken glass and yellow plastic fragments, the highway was lined with burning flares as three police officers directed the westbound traffic into the far left eastbound lane. There was a definite haze in the air from the flares and the humidity seemed to hold the smoke hovering above us.

Suddenly, my ears were filled with the sounds of traffic, burning flares, wailing ambulance sirens, and the police officer's whistles that screeched intermittently as they barked out orders. By this time, both ambulances had sped off in the opposite direction, followed closely by a couple of police cars. We had no clue who was inside. But, from the sight of the two yellow scooters that lay smashed in the middle of the road, I feared the worst. "I hope those weren't Lew and Phil's scooters." Reno said, his voice cracking a bit.

I didn't respond.

PROLOGUE

The scheme began to take shape in early February.

About three weeks after he'd moved his family into their new house, Phil invited us over for a drink. We'd been meaning to get over to see the place and this was as good an excuse as any to get together and knock back a couple of beers. So Lew and I loaded into his truck and made the long trek across the train tracks to the other end of town. Upon our arrival, it became obvious from the debris strewn around the house, that Phil had just finished repainting the walls upstairs. When I asked him what would possess a person to repaint the walls of a brand new house, he just chuckled and started folding up a paint tarp that was lying in the hallway. "No, really. What happened?" I repeated. Little prompting was needed. Apparently that morning, he and his wife had been babysitting a little boy from the neighborhood. It seemed that after he woke up from his nap, he found it fun to smear the poop from his soiled diaper onto the walls.
"No way" I laughed.
"Dude, did you go crazy, or what?" Lew asked.
Phil rolled his eyes. "Hey, I just grabbed a bucket and sponge and started cleaning up." Unfortunately his builder's grade paint wasn't very thick, and when he rubbed the walls, all the paint came off. "Oh, well. What are ya gonna do?" Phil sighed. With the folded paint tarp under his arm, Phil brushed past us on his way down the stairs. Trying to change the subject, he asked, "Hey, you guys hungry? I've got some meat on the grill."

Phil Kappell has got to be the most laid back guy I've ever met. Nothing fazes him. Lew and I met him three years ago at a party. Not much for conversation at first. I think he said about six monosyllabic words the entire night. But like an old mole, he kind of grows on you. As time passed, Lew and I started hanging out with him more and more. Nowadays, he may actually string together an entire sentence in response to one of our questions.

Being a tall guy, at six foot ten, Phil is consequentially very methodical and deliberate in his movements. Yet despite his best efforts, his eight-foot wingspan renders his appearance a bit gangly and awkward. With dark brown hair and brown eyes, he could be described as tall, dark and handsome. But looks can be deceiving. Back in the day, he was never real smooth with the ladies, but he always dated some of the better-looking girls because he was a ball player. Even to this day, Phil is still an exceptional athlete and as a high school senior was one of the most recruited centers in the entire nation. Every college wanted him. He decided on The University of Kansas, since it was close to home. Unfortunately, in his freshman season, a career ending knee injury canceled all dreams of turning pro. He was that good. The university honored his scholarship though, and he obtained a degree in Finance four years later. He is a good friend to many and is always in a good mood. Phil is the kind of guy that will help a neighbor mow his yard or shovel his drive with a smile on his face and no requests for thanks. He's an excellent husband and a wonderful father to his kids. Because of his naturally good demeanor, he often retracts himself from negative situations. Phil can usually be found far in the back of any large crowd, 'just taking it all in'. To sum him up: Phil is on island time all the time.

A twenty-pound bag of charcoal in a ten gallon Weber Grill, doused with an entire bottle of lighter fluid. This is what Phil decided was required to cook eight polish sausages that night. A little while later, after experiencing Phil's unique grilling style, the three of us escaped downstairs for a nightcap. I remember making fun of his wife's gargantuan tropical plants sitting underneath the black light as he showed Lew and I the plans he had for remodeling his basement. It must have been the tropical scent in the air that started my creative juices flowing - either that or the two extremely well done sausages Phil had scorched on his grill, mixed with the numerous Miller Lites I'd consumed throughout the evening.

"Hey, what in the hell are we going to do for Reno's bachelor party?" asked Phil.

Reno is Phil's best friend. They've known each other since college and have traded favors for just as long. As a result of this friendship, Phil was slated to be Reno's best man in the upcoming wedding. It came as no shock that he was at a total loss for his sole responsibility - the bachelor party. Reno comes from a small town in Western Kansas where literally everybody knows everyone else in town. He grew up on a wheat farm, and is no stranger to the hard work ethic that comes from a rural lifestyle. However, early on in his life, he decided that five in the morning wake up calls to feed the pigs and milk the cows was not what he wanted to do for a living. Plus, his brothers were oxen of men, with Reno being the runt of the family. As a result, he moved to the city after college. Reno is wiry and fast paced. He has light brown, almost blonde, hair and green eyes. He weighs maybe a buck forty with his shoes on, but he's a pistol. He's always got a grin on his face - reminds me of that damn cat from *Alice in Wonderland*. His real name is Kevin Jones, but he prefers the name Reno. He's an aggressive gambler to say the least, and is always playing around with a pair of dice. Before I knew him, he lost a lot of money in Las Vegas one weekend and vowed never to return. He makes his quarterly trip now to Reno, Nevada, hence the nickname, Reno. I don't know if it was his upbringing or what, but Reno is crazy. Reno's the guy that people will talk about after a party is over, saying things like, "could you believe what that guy did". He's the kind of guy that will antagonize a person until a fight breaks out and then step aside to let the bigger boys finish it up for him. Needless to say, Reno and Phil make quite a pair.

Lew and I were introduced to him shortly after we got to know Phil. Since that time, the four of us have become quite close. Mostly, we end up just wasting away the summer weekend evenings. Despite all of the time we had spent together, we had never traveled or vacationed anywhere as a group. All of that was about to change.

As soon as Phil had asked the question, I began formulating a plan in my head. "Phil, I'm not even sure what date they settled on."

"Dude" Lew interjected. "I heard the wedding is sometime this fall - apparently after a mere ten years of dating, he decided it was time to propose last month. He did it when they were on that cruise."

"Hey, you heard what his fiancé is doing for her bachelorette party didn't ya?" asked Phil.

Lew and I shook our heads.

"They decided to take a trip - to either Las Vegas or along the West coast somewhere." Phil replied.

"Vegas?" Lew laughed, "I bet that'll burn Reno's ass."

"We've got to do something better than the women." I said.

"If we go anywhere," Lew said while rubbing his chin, "it's gotta have a tropical feel to it. I ain't going anywhere cold. I gotta go where it's warm."

That's when inspiration struck. Now that I think about it, it had to have been the beers - my clear mind would have never thought of this. As usual, Lew and I were thinking along the same wavelength.

Sterling Lewis has been my best friend since high school, but I've never called him Sterling. I always associated the name with a bratty rich kid. Don't get me wrong, his parents were very well off, but Sterling never flaunted or bragged about it, which is why I've always called him Lew. The nickname stuck; and to this day everyone knows him as Lew. We grew up in the same town and went through school together. However, by the time we got to college, we each went our separate ways. I went to The University of North Carolina on a track scholarship since my mom had grown up there and I already had a lot of family in town. Lew attended Ohio State University as a walk on for the football team. Lew's dad was an Ohio State alumnus. He ended up spending more time partying then practicing, and as a result his football career lasted only two years. But since football players normally worked the campus bars as bouncers, he was always let in first during the rest of his five-year college stint. Throughout college, we would see each other when we went home on break, but that was all. We pretty much fell out of touch. That changed about a year or so after graduation, when I got a call late one night from Lew. He told me about a business venture he was trying to get started and wanted to know if I was interested. Not really too attached to the job I had, I decided *what the hell* and moved back to the Midwest.

Lew and I moved into a condo together and worked out of it for the first year. Lew had recently quit the company he was working for in order to branch out on his own. He was trying to start a business out of his home until he got his feet on the ground, but he needed my expertise in the computer world. Between Lew's natural sales ability and my technical knowledge, it was a perfect fit. We design fountains and pools for both residential and commercial use. Well, fortunately for us, the business took off and now, a few years later, we have moved our office into a business district up town.

Since we've been through a lot as a pair, we can usually read each other like a book. Typically, each of us knows what the other is thinking, but despite that fact, we couldn't be more different. Lew is the best-dressed man I've ever met - he's got more clothes than most women, and they literally take up all the closet space in our place. Luckily for me, the clothing overflow usually finds its way into the closet in my bedroom - allowing me to become the second best dressed guy in our group. Lew is the only guy I know who could wear a different watch every day of the month -- he owns a drawer full. In addition to the watches, he's got one entire closet packed with shoes, mostly sandals of every shape and color. With jet-black hair, usually all moussed up and blue eyes, he's GQ all the way with the rugged good looks that women fawn over. However, Lew's a man's man -- great with the ladies and he knows how to have a good time. Lew simply has a knack for knowing where to be when those unforgettable moments in life occur. He's the biggest bullshitter that I know and can convince anyone in five minutes to do anything for him. Unfortunately, I'm one of those people. Whether we like it or not, Lew loves to be in charge, and therefore, he's an assertive son of a bitch that usually makes our decisions for us. And still, everyone who meets him and knows him instantly loves him. You are guaranteed to have fun with Lew around.

At that moment, I was just about ready to bust. I couldn't hold in my idea a second longer. "Boys...I got two words for you: 'Key West'. Think about it: sunshine, babes and the beach. Plus, Jimmy Buffett hangs out there."

"Tango, oh yeah! I'm in!" yelled Lew. For once, I had made a decision for the group instead of Lew -- and he liked it.

I turned towards Phil and spread my arms out wide. "Well Phil, what do you think?" I grinned.

"Hey, in my mind" Phil replied. "I'm already there."

A deal was struck that night. None of us would tell Reno what we were doing for his bachelor party. The only information divulged would be the need to request a week off from work. He would be told to pack lightly, to bring only summer clothes -- there would be no snow on this excursion. In addition, he would need no money -- that would be taken care of. We decided to plan the trip around Labor Day weekend. Now all we had to do was convince Phil's wife of the idea.

That conversation was what started it all. A week in Key West that none of us would ever forget. No matter how hard we would later try.

By the way, my name is Jay Murciak.
The guys call me Tango.

CHAPTER ONE

I woke up early that morning. As a matter of fact, after a sleepless night of tossing and turning, I decided it was hopeless to try and sleep any longer. The truth was, I couldn't sleep. I was too excited. It was four in the morning. Today was the day that our journey would finally begin.

After pacing around the house for a while and verifying that I had everything packed at least three or four times, I got dressed. I put on a silk flowered Hawaiian shirt, a pair of dark green cargo shorts and my sandals. A voice shouted out from the other end of the house. It was Lew. "Dude, get that twelve dollar car wash fired up out there."

"I'm on my way out the door right now" I replied.

After six months of planning and preparation, it was finally time to pick up Phil and Reno. I was carrying a small duffel bag with my clothes and essentials. Lew emerged from the house moments later lugging an enormous suitcase. He looked like he was ready to set sail for a year. I shook my head and laughed at the sight while I waited for him to load his bag in the back.

We had decided it would be best to document our travels on video. We arrived over at Phil's about an hour early; this gave us plenty of time to record some last words of advice before shipping out. Since it was my video camera, I turned it around, facing me, and started things off. "Well Reno, It's about time to let this journey begin." I smiled, as I stuffed half a bag of leaf tobacco into my mouth. After a long, juicy brown spit, I continued. "I got a couple words of advice for ya Reno. Relax. Take it easy. And let the good times roll." I yelled, as I clapped my hands, jumped up, grabbed a beer and slammed it down.

Next, it was Lew's turn to document his thoughts for the upcoming trip. He decided that he could not give a good speech without a little island music playing in the background. After all, he already had on his grass skirt and lei. So Phil helped to set the mood and loaded a little Caribbean music into the compact disc player. As the steel drums started playing, Lew delivered his monologue. "Reno; it's about time, a long time coming. You don't know what's in store for you; the travel log will give you some clues. I hope we meet some interesting characters along the way. You'll be cast away for about seven days; you won't win a million dollars. You'll come back with a sunburn and your wallet completely dry. But we'll have a freaking awesome time. So tune into the video later. In the meantime stay out of my grass skirt. Yeah, I'm out baby."

"Phil, we need a little advice for Reno on the upcoming trip" I hollered as I pushed *Record* on the video camera.

"Ummm. Let's just have an awesome time," said Phil. "How's that sound?"

At that moment the doorbell rang. The bachelor had arrived. He entered the house wearing a smile, designer sunglasses, a black Hawaiian shirt and a pair of Khaki shorts with sandals. "All right Reno, what are you thinking?" I questioned, as he waltzed through the door.

"Keep the video clean, Phil's gonna want to watch this with his family" warned Lew, as he grabbed an empty beer bottle to use as a fake microphone.

"Where are you going?" Lew questioned.

"I don't know" Reno said.

"Hey, where are we staying at?" Phil yelled from the kitchen. "I need to leave my wife a number."

"Where are you going?" Lew repeated, totally ignoring Phil's request.

"I don't know."

"Hey, where are we staying at?" Phil interrupted again, this time yelling even louder from the kitchen.

"I'll get with you smack - I'm in the middle of an interview." Lew hollered back. He rolled his eyes and then immediately resumed the questioning.

"Where are you going?" Lew repeated a third time.

"I don't know."

"Where do you think?"

"Somewhere in California." Reno finally answered.

"Somewhere in California...where...where do you think?" Lew insisted smiling.

"Well - I'd have to guess, by the clues I've received from you and Tango," thought Reno. "Somewhere in the southern portion of the state, maybe the San Diego region, where we can venture into Tijuana."

"Well, we hate to disappoint you Reno." I said, trying to keep him off track.

"Then again it could be Alaska..." Reno replied.

Apparently our secret was safe; Reno still did not know for sure where he was going. At least not yet. It had only been about a month since his fiancé had returned from the bachelorette party in San Francisco.

We had all stayed home and helped Phil baby-sit his kids, now it was our turn to leave. Fortunately, he was thinking we were sticking to the California motif.

It was nine-thirty in the morning, two hours before our flight would depart from the Kansas City International Airport. Time to head out. We got the suitcases, Phil's cooler, and ourselves loaded into my 4Runner. Lew turned on the radio, and we started our course towards the airport. Lew and I sat up front. Reno and Phil sat in back. "Damn Tango. This is the cleanest I've ever seen this car." Phil was always one to overstate the obvious. On normal occasions, my red 4Runner has up to six months of dirt on it. The silver alloy rims look black, and the inside looks like a sandbox.

"Must be that twelve dollar car wash I got yesterday," I replied. The truth was, my car had not been cleaned in over a year. This was a constant irritant for Lew, a man who has been known to wash his car twice in one day. It's all about looks with Lew. This was probably the foremost reason why I didn't wash it: I like to irritate Lew. As a matter of fact, Lew was the last one to wash the 4Runner a year ago when he got sick of looking at it parked next to his spotless Tahoe in the garage. It didn't help matters that one morning he accidentally brushed up against it wearing a brand new suit. I still haven't heard the end of his complaining about the grease and dirt stain that resulted in a thirty dollar cleaning bill.

"I didn't even know it was red," Reno said, continuing to beat the dead horse.

"Keep laughing assholes. The funny thing is, after I took it through the car wash yesterday, you know, to save me the trouble, the air conditioning started working and the antenna now works as well. It finally goes up and down again."

"Imagine that" Lew smirked. "I can't believe you've been driving this with the windows down in hundred degree heat all summer."

"However, let's keep the AC on low, just to be safe. O.K."

"Dude, no. It's ninety-five degrees outside," griped Lew, wiping the perspiration off his brow, while using his other hand to crank it up to high.

We had been shooting the bull for about ten minutes when Phil casually decided to change the subject. "Hey, I was watching the *Weather Channel* this morning…"

Lew and I looked at each other alarmed. Surely, Phil would have enough sense not to mention any of the specific details of this weather report. After all it was only a few minutes ago that Lew reminded us that one person in the car still did not know the final destination of the trip. To which, Phil had replied "Duh."

"…and the weather in Key West is supposed to be nice."

Lew turned around from the passenger seat to get a good look at Phil as I gripped the wheel a little harder, hoping Reno had not been listening. "Phil, the weather where?" Lew asked, looking him right in the eye, while telepathically trying to tell him to shut the hell up.

"The weather in Key West."

"Who cares about Key West, Phil?" Lew sighed, shaking his head back and forth while throwing his hands into the air.

"Well, Key West...Ohhh..." That's when Phil smacked his head with his hand and laughed.

"Well Reno, I guess you know where you're going now," I said.

At that moment I decided that the 'big fatty' I had in my mouth didn't taste so good anymore. Phil had just blown six months of secrecy and covert planning with one mindless comment. It was classic Phil. I reached into my mouth, grabbed the juicy brown wad, turned around and smacked Phil right in the chest with it. "We didn't even make it out of Kansas yet!" I yelled as the remains of my chew landed in Phil's lap, leaving a colossal brown stain on his new white, *Caribbean Soul* T-shirt.

Reno chuckled and informed us that he couldn't have even tried to play stupid after that. Well, thanks to Phil, the proverbial cat was out of the bag.

Phil then threw the wad of brown leaves off his lap onto the floor. "Hey, this will be cleaned up in another six months" he said shrugging his shoulders.

We continued to poke fun at Phil's expense as the car rolled down the highway. Phil, always a good sport and never one to take offense to our ribbing, took it all in stride. "So Phil, did your old lady give you any rules before we left for the trip?" Lew laughed, changing the subject.

Being single, Lew and I of course had no rules to follow, but we figured Reno and Phil would have a few, and it was to our advantage to know in advance what those rules were. That way when they got drunk in the Keys, we'd be sure to break them.

"As a matter of fact, I got three of them. Rule number one - 'don't get arrested'. Rule number two - 'don't break your marriage vows'." Lew and I started laughing. "Ya, ya, ya. Keep laughing smart-asses."

"So what was the third rule?" I asked.

"My final, and in my wife's opinion, the most important rule was 'no tattoos'." Phil replied. "What about you Reno? Did you get any rules?"

"I don't follow orders. I give 'em." He replied, his chest sticking out a bit. "All I was told, was to have a good time and don't let Tango or Lew talk you into doing anything stupid." Reno said.

Fortunately for us, Kansas City International is not a very big airport. The bar was located only three gates away from where we needed to depart. After a few beers, we finally reached the gate and noticed that the rest of the passengers had already boarded. We were able to enter the plane without delay. As we were sitting down and buckling in, the flight attendants stowed the cabin, closed the door, and started going over their pre-flight checklist. It turned out that the flight was almost empty.

"Hey, where are the stewardesses?" Phil repeated turning around in his seat to look behind us, "I could use another beer too." It had been a pretty quick flight and the alcohol had been flowing freely. As our favorite stewardess, made her way back to the front of the plane with four more beers, the captain announced that we would begin making our final descent into Orlando International Airport. A short while later we taxied across the runway and pulled into the gate. As we left the plane it reminded me of a wedding procession line, each of us receiving hugs from the flight attendants. With the first half of our flight itinerary complete, it was time to jump on the monorail and head to the main terminal in order to grab a quick lunch.

Now boarding all passengers for Flight 5025, non-stop Orlando to Key West. Please proceed to Gate 60, loading position H. "'H' as in 'Hotel', we're gonna be the first ones on baby!" Lew exclaimed as we led the way down the winding corridor towards the gate. As we rounded the blind corner, the tarmac came into view and there sat our chariot to the Keys: a thirty passenger Embraer Brasilia aircraft, it looked like the cheapest plane in the fleet.

Lew was already up the steps and into the plane. Reno and I followed. Phil was one of the last people to board. His face was ashen colored and he looked as if he might be ready to faint.

"Hey guys, I don't feel so good," Phil groaned while he struggled to fit into his window seat next to Reno. His large frame was definitely not the body style the engineers had in mind when they designed this plane. When he was finally buckled in, his knees were practically touching his chest. "Ohhh, being cramped in here is only making me feel worse," he moaned. Fortunately, I was seated next to Lew.

"Don't worry, Phil," Reno said reassuringly, patting him on the back, "It's a short flight."

"That's easy for you to say. I don't think my tolerance has been built up yet like yours. I feel like chopped meat," Phil sighed, his head lolling back onto the seat. Unlike our previous flight into Orlando, this flight was completely full. As a matter of fact, much to Phil's chagrin, we were still stationary on the runway when the flight attendant from the ticket counter stepped onto the plane.

"I'm sorry folks; we are above the weight limit for this flight. I'm going to have to request that two people deplane. I am offering three hundred dollars off a future ticket in exchange."

There was absolutely no response.

"I can go as high as five hundred dollars, along with complementary drinks and dinner…" the attendant pleaded. Apparently that was enough; as two passengers seated a few rows ahead volunteered to get off the plane. "Thanks guys. It will only be a few more minutes folks."

A few minutes later a middle-aged, very well dressed man entered the plane carrying a briefcase and reading *The Wall Street Journal*. He walked on the plane like he owned the joint. The strange thing was, the guy was overweight. He had to have weighed more than the combined weight of the two passengers that had left. The stewardess greeted him warmly with open arms and immediately prepared the cabin for takeoff. Just then, the door shut and we could hear the propellers starting.

"Who the hell is that guy?" Lew asked. "Two people left, so one could board? What's up with that? I thought we were under a weight restriction?"

"Must be the mayor of Key West," I replied. "I can't imagine they'd hold up this plane for just anyone."

The fasten seat belt sign did not go off soon enough.

With his barf bag already depleted, Phil bolted out of his seat the instant the captain turned off the seatbelt light. He climbed over Reno, and dashed into the bathroom. The funny thing was, he actually steadied himself by grabbing our mystery man on the shoulder -- much to the guy's dismay. While Phil was in the bathroom, Lew and I struggled to find out whom we had been waiting on runway for. But even with much prodding and Lew's charm, our stewardess would not reply. Oh well, at least Phil had pissed off the mayor, or whoever he was.

Seated in front of Lew and I was a guy and a gal, they looked to be about our age. If they were married, they were probably newlyweds; because during our wait, they were kissing the entire time before take-off. Now, however, they were simply content with holding hands and staring into each other's eyes. The guy was normal looking, and to say his companion was hot would have been an understatement. She was brunette and wearing a very revealing white sundress.

"So what are you two going down to Key West for?" Lew asked the guy, who was seated directly in front of him.

"We're on our honeymoon" he replied, breaking the trance between them long enough to glance back at us. "How about you guys?"

"We're taking that guy over there for his bachelor party." Lew replied, pointing in Reno's direction.

"Damn, all I got to do was go to some strip joints in Fargo" he replied grinning as his wife punched him in the arm.

"My name is Tango. This is Lew, and Reno is the one seated over there. Our buddy Phil is in the can."

"I'm Roger, and my wife's name is Cynthia," he said as he reached over the seats to shake our hands. "We live in North Dakota and thought we'd see some sunshine for a change."

"Hi." Cynthia said as she extended a hand over the seat towards me. I couldn't help but stare at the oversized rock on her finger. It turned out that Roger actually owned his own jewelry store. Well, he really inherited the store from his father, who had opened the shop up. As a matter of fact, that's how he met Cynthia. She came in one day with her fiancé shopping for wedding rings. And although she didn't even notice Roger, he instantly fell in love with her. It was kind of a love at first site deal, at least from his perspective. Well it turned out a few months later she returned back to the shop with the ring they'd bought. She confessed to Roger that her boyfriend had been cheating on her; and when she found out, she immediately called off the engagement. Roger, apparently not one to shy away from somebody on the rebound, jumped at the chance and asked her out on a date right there in the store. To his delight, she accepted and after a few years of dating he proposed, putting one of the nicest rings in his shop on her finger.

"So, do you have any big plans while you're down there?" Reno asked.

"No, we'll just be playing it by ear." Roger answered.

"Where are ya staying?" Lew questioned.

"*The Hyatt*." Cynthia replied. Just then the plane hit some turbulence. We were requested back to our seats.

Flying out of the clouds and away from the turbulence, no more than forty-five minutes after take off, Key West finally came into view. "There's A1A. Right there underneath the wing," I said as I elbowed Lew and pointed out the window. It was a beautiful site. The sun was shining over the ocean throwing a myriad of colors off the water. From our altitude, we could see the entire island laid out below us. Even from up here, the tropical colors showed themselves. The main island had a cluster of smaller islands surrounding the north coast, all covered in greenery with a circle of rocks or sand surrounding them.

"What an awesome sight," Lew said. The plane was banking to the right as we began our descent into Key West. We could see the island now had inhabitants, as the roads, bridges, hotels, houses and cars all came into view.

"I can't wait to touch down," I said. At that moment Phil returned from the lavatory, looking slightly refreshed. He informed us he'd feel much better once this sardine can landed and his legs were on dry land. None of us could speak; we were in total awe at the splendor of the island below. A few moments later, we were awoken from our reverie by the screeching of the planes tires on the runway. The plane had touched down in Key West.

We had made it.

CHAPTER TWO

As I stepped off the plane, the warm Florida sunshine instantly caused my skin to perspire, and the blinding glare resonating off the tarmac made me reach for my shades. The first thing I saw was the terminal entrance. Above it hung a simple message in tall, red letters: Welcome to Key West. The two story, pink and light blue trimmed building had to be the smallest airport terminal I'd ever seen. However, I could not have imagined Key West International Airport any better; it was picture perfect.

Lew, Reno and I were already waiting to get our photograph taken underneath the terminal entrance when Phil finally lumbered down the steps onto the runway; apparently he was still having a bit of trouble. The ground crew had rolled over a wheel chair, seemingly responding to the stewardess's request that one may be needed. However, a spectator would have thought Phil was either the pope or a returning war hero, because the moment his feet touched the asphalt, while waving off all attempts at assistance, he knelt down and kissed the ground. I even think I caught a glimpse of a tear rolling down his cheek. Phil had landed. "C'mon smack, get you're ass in gear and get over here," Lew yelled out. "I've got the perfect picture waiting." In the meantime, Lew had sequestered Roger to snap a quick shot of the four of us underneath the welcome sign. Just before the shutter snapped, Lew raised both his arms into his classic victory salute, I pointed my index finger in the direction of the sign, Reno grinned, and Phil... well; let's just say Phil was happy to be there.

We walked through the sliding glass door into the main terminal to the sounds of Bob Marley coming from the overhead speakers. The beating of the steel drums accompanying the reggae lyrics instantly placed us in a tropical state of mind. This had to be a good sign for the trip ahead; at least that's what we thought. As we walked outside to hail a taxicab, I noticed for the first time that, despite the bright sunshine, it had apparently just finished raining. From the looks of things, it must have been a downpour, there was standing water everywhere and it was extremely humid, as well as quite muggy. Hopefully this was not a sign of what the week ahead had to bear in terms of the weather. It was, after all, just leading into the peak of hurricane season. We had heard that a hurricane had just dissipated over Puerto Rico a few days ago, and some were saying it might head this way.

As I wiped the sweat from my brow, I noticed that Lew was already loading his bags into a van. I looked at Phil as we walked over to get into the taxi. At least the color had returned to his face. I put an arm around him and squeezed his lanky torso. "What time is it Tango?" he asked wearily, trying not to yawn.

I just wrinkled my nose and shook my head, "I'm taking off my watch. We're on island time now," I said smiling, while stuffing my watch into the side flap of my duffel bag.

Key West is a small island, just three miles wide and five miles long, but the airport was still too far away from our hotel to walk. I climbed into the back seat of the cab, while Reno and Phil took the middle seat. Lew had already grabbed shotgun. Much to our relief, the cab driver, a local for the past five years who both looked and talked like a weathered pirate, knew exactly where the *South Beach Oceanfront Hotel* was located.

As we zoomed down South Roosevelt, I tried to take in as much of the atmosphere as possible. There were parasails, wind surfers and water skiers to the left. On my right were rollerbladers, bikini clad women, and more tourists walking along the beach. Lew and the cabbie had been involved in a side conversation when I heard him ask, "You guys ain't gay, are ya? Lord knows, we got plenty of 'em down here. Key West has a pretty large gay district." Before we could answer, he followed that question up with, "Well if ya are, the Rainbow Pier and Aids Memorial are on you left side there at Higgs Beach. Clothing is optional, so enter at your own risk."

"Cool." Reno replied.

"So where is Louie's Backyard?" I interrupted. "I sure could use a Bloody Mary." The rest of the guys just laughed.

"It's just up the road here on Waddell, we'll be passing it in a second" our driver replied as he sharply turned the wheel to the left. Phil, caught off balance, almost tumbled out of his seat.

"What about Duval Street?" Lew interjected. "We need to know how to get there as well."

"Shit boys, your hotel is at the end of Duval. Just start walking North and you'll pass all the bars along the way. It'll take about a half hour to walk to the other end of the island. It ain't a bad walk." Just as he finished telling us this, we pulled onto South Street and within seconds were parked under the entrance to the hotel.

Our driver parked right next to the hotel office. He hopped out and began unloading our bags from the van. "How much do we owe ya?" Lew asked.

"Ahh, seven bucks each gentlemen" was his reply, as he waddled over towards where we were standing. He even walked like a peg-legged pirate. There were not too many other cars in the parking lot, only three as far as I could see. As a matter of fact, the hotel looked a bit dead, even for a Thursday night. I was beginning to wonder what kind of a place Lew had booked us at. Interrupting my train of thought, I felt the money being yanked from my grasp. He placed our money into the collection bag. "Here's a card, in case you need a ride later"

"Hey, we will," Phil replied taking the card.

"Appreciate it, we just might," Reno added.

"Yeah, well, to where most of the action is, it's a pretty good walk for ya out here. I know I wouldn't walk it."

There would not be a need for a taxicab in our near future; all of us were in good enough shape that a mile walk would not be a problem. Not to mention the fact that the seven-dollar fare would buy at least two drinks. We grabbed our bags and headed towards the hotel office. The office was offset from the rest of the hotel with a sliding glass patio door on either side. One set of doors opened up to the parking lot and the other set led to the hotel swimming pool. Looking through the sliding doors, you could tell that it was a nice sized pool with a couple of fish statues mounted to the second floor railing, continuously spraying water from their mouths into the pool. Papaya trees and other tropical shrubs surrounded the office, and you couldn't help but notice an abundance of cats strolling around. Some were sitting on cars, others were on the curb. Blocking the entrance was a tan cat basking in the remaining sunlight. Lew almost stepped on it as he opened the sliding glass door. The sign next to the door read vacancy, which explained the empty lot.

Reno and I approached the patio door Lew was holding open for us. "Well Reno, we made it," I said, slapping him on the back.

"Yes we did, and look at the view." The parking lot, at this point, was only about fifteen feet wide. Just on the other side of a concrete retaining wall was a beach leading out to the Atlantic Ocean. You could smell the salt water and hear the crashing of the waves as we stepped into the office.

"Hello." Lew yelled as he stepped over the threshold.

"Oh, hi," came a voice from the back office.

Lew walked up to the desk and removed his wallet from the pocket of his Polo khakis. "We need to check in, we've got a reservation."

"Just need your name," the office manager replied as he met us at the counter. It seemed he was concentrating very hard on not smiling.

"Real names or code names?" Lew joked.

"Actual names," was the curt reply. While Lew was busy checking in, Reno, Phil and I filled out the mailing list notebook, in order to get future mailings from the hotel. After checking in, we were informed that we had one of the best rooms in the entire hotel. It was room 228, on the second floor, overlooking both the beach and the swimming pool. We were given instructions along with our keys for the room and the safe. Lew led the way. We walked underneath the spraying fish and took the steps at the end of the pool to the next level.

"Our casa awaits." I said, as we walked up the steps and turned right towards the end of the hall where little black numbers indicated our room was located. Lew was already at the door, struggling to open it. "Show us the way Lew," I said. He was still screwing around with the lock. "Come on man," I yelled, growing more and more impatient.

"Come on Lew." Even Phil was getting a bit ancy.

"Don't use that safe key, use the room key." Taking my advice, he tried the other key and within moments the door sprung free. "Let's see what it's got to offer," I said, as Lew opened the door wide enough for the four of us to peek in.

"There ain't no champagne and roses." Lew smirked, as he stepped into the sweltering room. "Ooohh, it's hotter than a biscuit in here." He wasn't lying. The room was at least ninety-five degrees inside, with a relative humidity high enough to make a fish sweat. It was almost ten, if not fifteen, degrees cooler outside.

"Ooohh, a little bit muggy in here." I said, entering the room behind him. By this time, Lew was opening a sliding glass door that led to the deck in order to get some fresh air circulating into the place.

"Cripes. It's hot," Reno said, overstating the obvious.

I stepped onto the deck. "Nice view."

"Somebody find a freaking air conditioner." Lew demanded.

"Cool," Reno replied, as he entered the room.

"Hey, its right here." Phil said, making himself useful for the first time in a long time.

"Get that thing a cranking." Lew yelled.

As Phil got the air conditioner started, we left the deck and returned to the room to have a look around. We started by checking out the kitchen. It had everything: a sink, refrigerator, toaster, dishwasher, and the cabinets were stocked with all the dishes and silverware we'd need. The long kitchen counter that separated the eating area from the rest of the room had a few barstools positioned underneath it. "The room is hot. The fridge is hot. This ain't no *Hyatt*" Lew said as he slammed the door to the refrigerator shut.

I reached behind the fridge to insert the cord into the electrical outlet. "Well let's plug it in and get the fridge cold, 'cause I guarantee I'm the only one here who'll drink warm beer."

With the kitchen tour squared away, it was time to discuss the sleeping arrangements. The front room had two queen size beds adjacent to the bathroom. In front of the television cabinet there was a couch that converted into another bed. "I pity the suckers that have to sleep in that." Lew chuckled, as he looked at the pullout bed located directly in front of the sliding glass door.

Early on it was decided that our theme was survival of the fittest, so challengers get ready. The rules were simple; each day we were on the island there would be two competitions. The winner of the first challenge -- a sporting event held each afternoon -- would win the bed next to the bathroom. This bed was also the one that was also situated closest to the air conditioner, making it truly the most comfortable sleeping arrangement in the room. In addition to this prize, the winner of the afternoon challenge would get to decide what the second event that evening would be. The second challenge would take place at night, meaning we'd all more than likely be a little more crazy. The reward: the other queen-sized bed. The two losers would have to decide their sleeping arrangements for that night by themselves. The losing options were simple: either share the fold out; or, if the idea of sharing a bed did not appeal to the losers, then one of us would be sleeping on the floor. Reno had it easy that first night. Since it was his party, he was awarded the first place bed for tonight. Consequently, Lew, Phil and I would be battling later that night for the remaining places to sleep.

Feeling more comfortable in our surroundings, we decided to head out onto the deck and have a look outside. "There's the Atlantic," I said, as I opened the door and stepped out into the warm evening air.
The balcony, which held a wicker table and four white wicker chairs, was easily big enough for the four of us to lounge around. Our room, as promised, overlooked both the ocean and the hotel pool. There were two huge palm trees flanking both sides of the balcony, secluding us nicely from the rest of the rooms. "Dudes, I gotta make a call. Tango give me your phone." Lew demanded, momentarily interrupting us from our look around.
"Who ya calling?" I asked.
"*Tropical Tours*. We gotta make a reservation for tomorrow," he replied. Lew's sister and brother-in-law had recommended this mini-speed boat tour. They took the adventure when they were on a layover from a cruise last summer. I have to admit, from the brochure Lew had shown me, *Tropical Tours* sounded interesting. The pamphlet promised you'd drive your own boat, while a guide led you through the backcountry. There was also a snorkeling, swimming and sunbathing stop scheduled. It only took a few minutes on the phone and Lew had arranged the deal. "Dude's, we're set up for noon tomorrow - weather permitting. I booked us a reservation; we gotta be there thirty minutes ahead of time to get checked in. I also got the directions on how to get there - we're gonna need mopeds, it's on the far east side of the island." Lew instructed us as he handed me back my phone. The guy on the phone had told Lew to head up US 1 to the small bridge. They were located right there. It sounded easy enough.

"Hey Tango, can I borrow your phone to call my wife?" Phil sighed sheepishly.
For a guy on vacation, he sure seemed to be on a short leash. "Ya, I guess. What's the matter, you miss her already? Didn't you talk to her in Orlando?"
"Well, she's a little jealous of us leaving for this trip," he replied.
"Dude, we're on vacation. The only reason you should be calling home is if you're in jail...or dead!" Lew yelled. "Ain't that right, Reno?"
"That's my interpretation." Reno added. "I don't even think I'll be calling home at all." Just then, Reno took out the dice from his pants and started spinning them.

Our entire week lay out ahead of us.

A few seconds before we heard the flushing of the toilet, Lew cried out, "Whew, I feel five pounds lighter." He smiled proudly, as he exited the bathroom.

"My turn." I yelled, as I rushed into the bathroom from my spot on the couch. While I was in the bathroom, Lew decided for the group that it was time to get some beer and breakfast food for the week. He had seen a deli across the street from the hotel. Once we were outside, we could find a liquor store as well to stock up on alcohol for the week. No one argued. We needed to get out and stock our empty shelves with some food and alcohol. Besides, it had been about two hours since any of us had drunk a beer. We were starting to sober up by this point. As I exited the bathroom, it was apparent that they were waiting on me. I slipped into my sandals and we walked out the door.

"You got the key Lew?" I asked, before shutting the door all the way.

"Yup," he replied, as he showed me the key attached to his necklace. He was wearing the kind of nylon necklace that a lifeguard would attach to their whistle. "Here, you hold onto the spare." He shouted as he threw the spare key my direction.

I reached up and grabbed it out of mid-air. "No problem." I put the key into my wallet. By this time we had walked the short distance from our hotel room through the parking lot, across South Street. As we entered the air-conditioned deli, we noticed right away that they did not sell any beer. We would still have to find a liquor store after we stocked up on our groceries. The store was pretty small; therefore, it only took us a few minutes to get what we needed for the week. Lew had grabbed two jugs of Orange Juice, a box of brown sugar Pop Tarts, and a few granola bars. I walked up to the checkout counter with four bottles of red soda, a bag of powdered donuts and two frozen pizzas. Phil had a few boxes of cereal and a gallon of milk. Reno followed us up with some energy drinks, a couple bags of potato chips and red licorice. Looking at the spread of food laid out before us on the checkout counter, there was going to be some interesting meals the next couple of days.

As we walked out of the deli, the first thing I noticed was a flashing neon sign, hanging beside a drive through liquor store window. How we missed this heavenly oasis was beyond me. The glow from the orange sign was like a beacon guiding us home. We rushed across the street carrying our groceries and entered the store. "You got any cold beer here?" Lew asked, directing his question to the only worker in the store. A young Spanish kid, probably not even old enough to drink himself, was seated behind the register watching a baseball game on the miniature black and white television placed on the counter.

"No, I don't think so." He replied, in a thick Spanish accent not even moving his eyes off the small screen.

"Holy Shit." Lew interrupted, as he opened the door of the middle cooler. "They actually got Kalik here. The only time I've ever drank this was in the Bahamas. It's the best beer I've ever had and you can't find it anywhere in the States, believe me, I've looked. Grab that last case down there Tango." I complied, handing him my grocery sack, so I had two free hands to grab the beer. I'm always interested in trying a new beer. But just in case, I grabbed a case of Miller Lite as well, our old staple.

We returned to our hotel room, put the food and beer away and decided we were long overdue for our first toast in Key West. "Anybody got a bottle opener?" Lew asked. "These Kalik's ain't twist off."

"Here, hand them over to me. I know an old college trick." Reno said, tossing his dice across the kitchen counter. He grabbed a bottle and pressed the lip of the bottlecap against the edge of the counter. With the palm of his free hand he struck the top of the cap and the bottle broke free. The cap flew across the kitchen and landed harmlessly on the floor.

Lew handed him another bottle. "Neat trick Reno, now open the other three bottles" After the four beers had been opened, Lew divvied them out and we walked back into the living room.

"Gentlemen, raise a glass" I said, holding up a Kalik. "To our first night in the Keys." "Salute." The four bottles of Kalik's clinked musically against each other. Lew was right; this was some damn good beer. We popped in an eighties mix CD and after about an hour of reminiscing about the glory days -- while playing *'Who Sings This? Wrong... Drink a Beer'* – most of the Kalik's were emptied. It was about time to take a walk down Duval Street and grab some dinner.

As we were getting dressed, I happened to look over at Lew. He was standing in his underwear, lip-synching to his *Monster Eighties* music that was playing The Cure, *I'm in Love*. "Lew" I hollered over the music, "you gotta lose those whitey tighties." As GQ as Lew was, he still had his fashion problems; mainly the fact that he refused to wear boxers. "I'd rather go commando than wear those damn things." I laughed. *Oh well, to each their own,* I thought.

"Hey, what do you feel like eating tonight?" Phil asked us as we stepped out into the hallway.

"I say we head on down to Margaritaville," Lew replied, locking the door.

"Sounds good to me," I said. "Incommunicado's for everyone." The Incommunicado had become our official Buffett drink. I discovered the drink when I was at the Universal Studios Margaritaville in Orlando the previous summer. The boat drink menu described the Incommunicado the following way: *Close your eyes and imagine you're there. Captain Morgan Silver Spiced Rum, Absolut Vodka, Seagram's Extra Dry Gin, Margaritaville Gold, triple sec, cranberry juice, pineapple juice, sour mix and grenadine.* It sounded good to me at the time. I remember drinking one of the concoctions with cute chicks all around and volcano's exploding in the background and immediately calling Lew from the bar on my cell phone. It was after ten o'clock on a weeknight, and of course, I woke him up. Lew is not a late-nighter.

"What could be better than an Incommunicado at Margaritaville in Key West," shouted an excited Reno as we walked across the hotel parking lot. "My mouth is beginning to water just thinking about it."

It was pretty dark outside by the time we ventured out in search of Margaritaville. As we turned right onto Duval from South Street, we immediately noticed that we were definitely on the 'lifeless' end of the famous street.

"This side of Duval is certainly quiet," remarked Phil. Most of the shops on this end of the street were art stores, clothing stores or bed and breakfast establishments. Looking into the windows as we passed by revealed some of the most beautiful art scenes to be found anywhere. Sea life and beach scenes filled the canvases. The paintings looked real, and Lew was just about dying to dive in and empty his bank account in order to take a piece home. Fortunately for him, and his savings account, all of the stores were closed for the night. At this point of the island, there were just as many, if not more, art galleries than bars. The Caribbean colors of white-sand, blue-sky and green-nature were abundant everywhere. We were beginning to realize that in Key West, creativity and self-expression was definitely a way of life. It was a lot to take in on first glance. Making the job of searching for our destination a little more difficult was the fact that there were bums all over the place. The tropical climate seemed to be their breeding ground. Some were alone and talking to themselves, some would stop each passerby, and others seemed content just to hang around with a group of their peers inside a doorway or in an alley. For the most part, they were not begging, which made it easier for us to avoid them. After all, we were in Key West, probably the best place in the United States to be a bum.

By this point we had found ourselves smack dab in the middle of the gay district. This part of our walk only took up one full block, along both the East and West side of the street. I noticed that there were rainbows out in front of every business. A quick glance inside one of the bars revealed a sea of guys, bright lights and loud music. A glance across the street revealed a drag queen bar. There were pictures of beautiful men and women posted on the outside. A six foot tall blonde drag queen in high heels was hanging out front trying to lure in all passerby's. It looked interesting for some guys from the midwest, but we kept on moving. As we continued walking north, we finally started to get into the nightlife scene. Walking along, it was becoming apparent that this had to be one of the liveliest streets in America. Lining both sides of the street was building after building, each housing a different kind of eating or drinking establishment. Balcony's and decks were abundant with people and music. There were hundreds of choices. Each building had a quaint southern feel to it. The whitewashed look was prevalent. And everything about the place seemed to invite people in and prompt them to let their hair down. Plus, there were beautiful women all around, which made the task of looking for a place to eat even harder. I just wanted to run in somewhere and hug one of the well tanned, scantily dressed and physically fit women that were everywhere. Everyone seemed to be in a friendly mood. Key West is a docking point for many of the cruise lines and many of the people walking around were just tourists there for the evening. You could hear the different accents and foreign languages being spoken as you made your way through the crowd. Most of the people were in leisurewear. The Hawaiian shirt was the popular apparel of choice, with the T-shirt coming in a close second. Don't get me wrong; the tank top is well accepted, and we saw many of them as well. Almost every female that passed us by had her tummy exposed with a hoop in the belly button. Phil made the observation that most of the people we passed were adorned with multiple tattoos and body piercings. We must have missed the memo that said there was a two-tattoo minimum just to reach the island. It would be interesting to see if we would leave the island without one.

Becoming readily apparent was the idea that Key West is the end of the world for some. A variety of people come to the island for an assortment of reasons. Our reason, aside from celebrating Reno's bachelor party, was to experience 'Margaritaville', not the bar -- although we were presently starved -- but that place in your mind or dreams where everything is perfect. The sun always shines, the people are always happy, there is no business talk and your worries simply drift away. Every day is a holiday and every meal is a feast. This is a place where you can escape. The sun energizes the soul, nighttime elevates the heartbeat, laughter fills the air, and you end up talking for hours with the friends you brought along or just met. You fall asleep to the sound of the sea quietly rushing in and out and awake to the sound of seagulls and the smell of sea salt. That's why we found ourselves walking down Duval Street that night. It was all present here.

After maneuvering the next few blocks amongst the countless people that had started to litter the sidewalks, we finally saw our destination ahead. *Jimmy Buffett's Margaritaville Café* was a hot pink and neon blue Spanish style open-air café. Fortunately for us, it was pretty late for dinner. Although there were no spots available at the *Official Parrot Head Bar*, there were plenty of tables available for dining further back inside. We sat down at a table and tried to let the atmosphere of the place soak in. The lighting was dim. We were seated in wooden chairs around a hot pink table, located directly underneath an indoor palm tree with a bright green, stuffed lizard hanging from it. The inside of the restaurant resembled the scenery along Duval Street. It had an outdoor motif, inside the restaurant: it was as though you were seated on an outdoor porch without actually being outside. Above the entrance was a huge mural of a seaplane taking off. In addition, there was unique art hanging from the walls all around, mostly colorful renditions of Jimmy Buffett himself. Of course a Buffett tune was playing in the background, and we were seated at the table right in front of the stage - with any luck we could watch a band play as we ate. "Hi, I'm Denise, what can I get you guys to drink?" asked our waitress, a tall, skinny gal with her ponytail pulled through the back of her Margaritaville Key West baseball cap.

"I'll take four Incommunicado's, please Denise," Lew smiled.

"What are those?" Denise asked, looking frightfully puzzled. I said a short prayer to myself that she was new and simply unfamiliar with the drink list.

"They're boat drinks," I said, "You serve them in your restaurant in Orlando."

"Well I've worked here for over three years and I have never heard of them. Besides our menu is different from the one in Orlando. Each chain has its own distinct menu," she replied. At that moment my heart sank. She had caught me off guard. I didn't know what I wanted to drink now. To our surprise the mixed drink list was pretty scarce and none of the drinks on the menu really sounded that good.

"Do you have Kalik?" Lew asked.

"We got it in bottles."

"We'll take three Kalik's; give Tango a Key West Lager." Lew calmly informed her. "And let's start off with two orders of conch fritters for an appetizer."

She returned quickly with the drinks. As I read the label on my beer, I had high hopes for the local microbrew - the label stated that it was "a light, crisp, tropical beer." Let me put it this way: Key West Lager is no Kalik. It tasted like stagnate rainwater and I quickly ordered a Kalik to wash the horrid taste out of my mouth. Lew couldn't stop laughing. I had heard that in Key West the roofs were used to funnel the rainwater into cisterns for recycling purposes. They must have used this water to brew with; because that was the taste I still had in my mouth. "So have you guys decided what you'd like to eat?" Denise questioned while removing a pad and pencil from her apron.

"I'll take the conch sandwich with hush puppies and fries." Reno followed.

"Me too." Phil added.

"Sounds good to me, that's what I was going to order anyway." I said. "You want a conch sandwich also, Lew?"

"No, I don't want anything, I'm still a little too giddy to eat dinner right now," he replied grinning like a schoolgirl. He leaned back in his chair, with both of his hands behind his head. He glanced to his right. "Isn't that Roger and Cynthia sitting over there?"

"It sure as hell is," I responded after looking over in the direction he was pointing. The couple we met briefly on our plane leg to Key West was sitting at the far end of the wall enjoying a couple of drinks.

"I'll be right back." Lew said getting up to walk over there. The three of us weren't going anywhere. As Lew walked off, the band that had been setting up on stage began to play. They were decent; mixing a little Caribbean sound to an alternative rock beat.

About five minutes later Lew came back to the table, practically bumping into our waitress who was delivering the food. "Well, I was talking to them and they want to join us on the *Tropical Tours* tomorrow. Do you guys mind?" We all said sure. "Tango, give me your business card, so I can write down your cell phone number along with our hotel information, in case they need to get a hold of us."

"I can't wait to see Cynthia in a swimsuit," I mumbled between bites of my conch sandwich, while reaching into my wallet for a business card.

"That ain't no lie," Lew replied, pointing towards the stage. "These guys ain't too bad."

After Phil, Reno and I finished eating our dinner, we decided to have one last beer and listen to a few more tunes. As the band wrapped up their first set, we paid the bill and headed back outside. On our way out, we said goodbye to Roger and Cynthia. Lew reminded them to be at *Tropical Tours* by noon the next day. "Maybe, I should have had a sandwich," Lew said, as he rubbed his stomach. "I'm starting to get a bit hungry after all. Oh, well…I can wait until later."

"Hey, what do you guys feel like doing now?" Phil asked.

"Let's head further down Duval and see what interests us." Lew replied, while pointing straight ahead.

At that moment, Reno, who was looking at a scantily clad lady walk by, bumped right into a bum. He seemed friendly enough, so we started talking to him. He was shirtless, very tan, and had long, stringy, blond hair. "Hey, you guys want to hear a joke for a quarter?" he asked.

"Sure," I said, thinking that this ought to be interesting.

"It better be a good one though," Lew added.

"Come on guys - give me a motherfucking break, you're only paying me a motherfucking quarter, but I think you'll laugh you're motherfucking heads off." He yelled at the top of his lungs, specifically emphasizing the obscenities, while his arms spread out wide. He was as animated as a cartoon character. From the smell of his breath, he'd probably been drinking since last week. As a matter of fact, he was spitting as he yelled and may have gotten a little spittle on Phil, because Phil was backing off - obviously wanting no part of *The Joke Bum*. "O.K. Why was the blonde's belly button sore?"

"I don't know," I yawned.

"Because the motherfucker's boyfriend is blond too. Now give me a quarter." He held his dirty hand out, palm side up, awaiting his bounty.

"That sucked," I said, handing him a quarter.

"Come on at least tell a longer joke than that," Lew laughed, while slapping him on the bare back. "Give us another one."

By this time I had pulled out a dollar. "Tell us your best joke and I'll give you this dollar," I said as I snapped the dollar taught between the forefinger and thumb of both my hands.

"O.K. This is my best joke for one dollar. A blonde, brunette, and a redhead escaped from prison. They were running along when they came upon a dock. On the dock were three motherfucking gunnysacks. They could hear the motherfucking cops approaching, so the brunette suggested that they get in the sacks. So they got in the sacks right before the motherfucking cops arrived. A motherfucking cop kicked the sack with the redhead in it, and she said, 'Ruff ruff ruff!' He said, 'Oh, it's only a dog.' He kicked the one with the brunette in it, and she said 'Meow meow meow.' He said, 'Oh, it's only a cat.' Then, he kicked the one with the blonde in it, and she said, 'potatoes potatoes potatoes!'"

"Now that was a good joke," I laughed, smacking the dollar bill into his palm.

"So where do you suggest we go tonight. This is our first night in Key West." Reno asked. "It looks like you know the area pretty well."

"You guys have got to go to the *Upstairz Lounge*. The best motherfucking pussy on the island is inside," he smiled, as he leaned in to whisper to us. "I dropped two bills there last night."

"That sounds pretty good. Where is it at?" Lew asked.

"It's just down the street a few blocks, right above *Rum Runners*, on this side of the street. You guys will love it."

"Well, thanks for the advice. We'll see ya later," I said, as we started walking away. Strangely enough, Phil was walking uncharacteristically fast. He was already a block ahead of us. When we caught up to him, he explained to us that he didn't like bums and was pretty much appalled that we were talking to one.

Following *The Joke Bum's* directions, we found ourselves underneath the Jamaican colored sign of *Rum Runners*. On the South side of the bar there was a rickety white, wooden stairwell rising towards *Upstairz Lounge*. "Well boys, I didn't come all this way to stare at you guys. Lets go on up," Lew said as he took the stairs two at a time. The rest of us followed quickly behind. The top of the stairs opened up to a huge outside deck that went on forever, blending into the night. Our attention then shifted to the man guarding the entrance.

"What's the cover?" I posed the question to the rather large bouncer who had positioned himself between the door and us.

"Five dollars each, gentlemen," came the gruff response. We shelled out the money and held out the back of our hands to get them stamped before we were allowed to walk into the place. It took a second for our eyes to adjust to the lighting inside, but once they did, my, oh my...what a site. There was only one stage in the place and it was positioned on the opposite end of the room from the entrance. Up on stage was an older lady, sporting an enormous rack and a very thin G-string. Immediately to the left of the stage was another burly bouncer standing guard in front of a beaded doorway. A lit neon sign displayed the word: *Play Pen*, in hot pink letters. The bar was on the right. It ran the entire length of the club. Seated in front of the bar was a mixture of both patrons and strippers. There were small tables with black, cushioned chairs around them scattered throughout the rest of the room. A jet-black, leather couch ran along the remaining walls with smaller tables positioned in front of it. Most of the places to sit were full. The bathrooms were on our immediate left and as I glanced toward them, I couldn't help but notice that the stripper's dressing room was adjacent to the men's bathroom with the door left wide open. Inside were about ten gorgeous women getting dressed for their dances.

"Hey, there's a table over here," Phil yelled above the music, as he walked forward towards an empty table against a short transition wall between the bar area and the seating area.

"This will work just fine," Reno said as he sat down to enjoy the show.

As Lew sat down he ordered us a round of four-dollar beers. Meanwhile, I was preoccupied at the stage, introducing a few George Washington's to the lovely thirty-something lady who was about to wrap up her show. It was the best couple of bucks I'd spent in some time. Holding the dollars between my teeth with my back on the stage floor, I was getting quite a show as she grinded her body above my face in beat to the DJ's song. I could hear Lew whooping and hollering in the background, but that all changed as she mashed both of her grapefruit-sized breasts across my face and squeezed the dollar bill from my smiling lips. At that moment, I couldn't hear a thing. After collecting a kiss on the mouth, I hopped up and waltzed back to the table.

When I walked back to the table, the DJ's deep voice came over the speakers. "Let's have a hand for the lovely Paula."

"Boys, I think we're going to be spending both some time and money in this place," I grinned as I sat down to drink my beer. "Now let's find Reno a woman."

We decided that the best thing to do was sit back and scout the talent throughout the next few songs. During this time, our waitress told us that the *Play Pen* was a back room where semi-nude lap dances took place. Unbelievably, for only twenty dollars, touching was allowed and even encouraged while a patron was inside the *Play Pen*. We were determined to find Reno the best-looking woman in the club and send him into the *Play Pen* for a little bit of fun. "Now let's give it up for the talented and very beautiful, Sonya," the DJ's voice resonated from his crows nest booth behind us. That was the moment Lew spotted her, the perfect woman. She was a knockout. Sonya stood about five foot eight, had long brown hair, brown eyes, and revealed a perfectly tanned body with absolutely no fat attached. Her breasts were no more than a handful.

"What do you think about Sonya?" Lew whispered to me; never taking his eyes off of her. "I say after this dance we pay up and send her into the back room with Reno."

Trying not to clue Reno in on what was up; I just nodded.

Lew scooted his chair over to pose the question to Phil a moment later. No response. Phil was wearing a thousand yard stare. Lew tried again. Again, no response.

"Phil." Lew yelled. "I'm trying to ask you a question."

"Hey Lew, woah…" Phil replied, looking more annoyed than I can ever remember seeing him. "I'm taking it all in."

"Well…we'll just let Phil be," Lew said to me as Sonya's dance came to an end. Lew leapt up and walked over to the stairs on the left side of the stage. Sonya was busy collecting the loose dollar bills from across the stage, but eventually he got her attention and motioned for her to come over and chat. They talked for a few brief moments. Eventually their conversation ended and they came over to the table together.

"Mr. Reno, could you please join me in the *Play Pen*," she said, in an extremely thick accent. Her accent sounded like she may have been from Russia. She then sat down on Reno's lap and started running her fingers through his hair. As she started nibbling on his neck he accidentally dropped his dice on the table.

"Your friends here are very kind and have promised to pay for three dances. You're a very lucky man, Mr. Reno." She got down off Reno's lap and took him by the hand and led him into the back.

"Damn, that accent is sexy. I wonder where she's from?" I asked Lew, while we all stared at her ass, as she walked away.

"Beats me, but when Reno's done, it's my turn; so you better find yourself a women and join me back there for a few songs." He replied.

"That shouldn't be a problem," I responded. "How much do we owe you?"

"I gave her seventy bucks for three songs."

"Here's twenty five," I said as I handed over the money.

"What about you, big dog," he yelled over to Phil. "You still 'taking it all in'? Cough up some money for Reno's dances."

"Oh, Ahh…hey Lew, I'm out of money, man. I only got five bucks left for tonight. The rest of my money is back in the hotel. I have credit cards."

I started to laugh. It was classic Phil. "You mean to tell me you're not going to get any lap dances tonight?"

"Nah. I'll go back in that room later on in the week." He promised, or wished -- I couldn't tell which. We decided to give Phil a break; after all, he was a happily married man.

A few songs later, the rotation for the night was finished. Paula was at the front of the bar, seductively smoking a cigarette. I decided to join her and share some mindless conversation. The more I looked her over, the more I liked her.

"You guys are cool," Reno yelled, as he emerged from the *Play Pen*. He walked between the stage and our table, momentarily blocking my view of Paula. "That woman is beautiful, and God can she dance. I'm telling you almost anything goes back there. That's it; I'm going to buy you guys a round of drinks for giving me that pleasure. Thanks a lot." Reno had enjoyed himself. "Come on Phil, help me grab some drinks."

"You ready Tango?" Paula whispered into my ear from behind as I was trying to see what the rest of the guys were up to. She put her arms around my waist. "Why don't you leave these guys here and follow me. How's that sound baby?" How a man could resist a request like that was beyond me.

As I turned and wrapped my arm around her shoulder, I said, "I'm at your command. Show me the way." We started walking towards the *Play Pen*. The bouncer was already holding the beads aside for us to walk through. Lew had just entered with Sonya. As I walked through the beads, I finally saw what Reno was talking about. The room was rectangular in shape. Longer than it was wide. Along both of the elongated walls was a couch. Seated on the couch in random locations were other patrons receiving dances from their respective hostesses. Many of which, I had not seen on stage.

"You two boys sit over there," Paula ordered, pointing to the far left corner of the room. "Go ahead and take off you're shirts, but leave your shorts on," she added. The women took off their tops. This was definitely getting good. I stripped off my Hawaiian shirt. Lew was already shirtless, and seated on the couch. Sonya had just climbed on top of him. As I sat down beside him, Paula mounted me.

"So where are you from?" I heard Lew ask Sonya.

"I'm from the Czech Republic. I've been here one week." She replied.

"Do you know the rules?" Paula asked me, smiling seductively while running her fingers along my chest.

I was starting to get very, very comfortable. "You better explain them to me."

"Do anything you want within reason." She whispered while sucking on my earlobe.

"I think I can live with that rule," I replied grabbing a breast with one hand and her ass with the other. After a few minutes, I didn't even remember Lew was seated beside me.

I was enjoying the dance immensely, when I heard him yell out. "O.K. lets switch." With that command Paula got up and crawled over to where Lew was seated. Apparently that was Lew's big plan - a two for one special.

To my delight, Sonya took Paula's place on my lap. I quickly looked over at Lew, who was grinning widely. We gave each other a high five and then resumed the business at hand. Sonya looked and smelled wonderful. As she started dancing, I mentioned to her that I, too, was from the Czech Republic. Well, at least my ancestors were. "If I'd have known the women there were as beautiful as you, I'd have tried to get back to my roots long ago."

"Switch back."

At first I was disappointed to get Paula back, but I tell you, being an older, more experienced stripper, she definitely had much better moves. It didn't take me long to forget about Sonya. Besides, I like a well-endowed girl and Paula definitely fit into that category. Before I knew it, our two dances were up. We had gotten two songs for the price of one thanks to the switching. But as the second song ended, our six minutes of heaven were up. All Paula and Sonya wanted now was our money. Unless we wanted to end up broke like Phil, Lew and I had to end our stay in the *Play Pen* and retreat back into the lounge. These girls were beautiful, but two dances was our limit. I gave Paula forty bucks and a kiss. Lew had already paid Sonya and we were left alone to get dressed.

"Half wood always points the wrong way," Lew sulked, as he put on his shirt.

As I looked at him I couldn't help but laugh.

When we returned to the lounge, Reno and Phil were still at our table drinking their beer. The only difference was that Phil had an ugly Asian girl sitting on his lap. She was pale skinned and had an eagle tattooed across her entire back. "She's been sitting there since the last song," Reno said to us as we sat down. "She's trying to convince moneybags over there to take her into the PlayPen."

"Dude, she's butt ugly." Lew chuckled.

I looked over at Phil, he was grinning sheepishly as he sipped the remaining drops from his beer. "What's up Phil?"

"Oh, not too much Tango. Still taking it all in." He continued to look around, but refused to even make eye contact with her.

"You crack me up Phil." Reno chuckled. "You guys about ready to leave? Or, Phil, am I interrupting you?"

Lew stood up. "Yup. Let's see what else Duval has to offer tonight. Come on too tall; tell that lady you ain't got no money."

Phil immediately jumped on the chance to get the girl off his lap. "Nah, I'm O.K. with that. Let's go," he said, standing up abruptly; he accidentally knocked the stripper off his lap and onto the floor. Phil apologized to the girl and helped her up onto her feet. The rest of us were already heading out.

From the dressing room I heard a woman yell out. "Tango!" I turned around in time to see Paula walking towards me. "You weren't gonna leave without kissing me goodbye, were you? I hope you come back to visit me this week." I couldn't tell if she was serious or just trying to work more money from me later in the week. Not too worried about it either way, I grabbed her by the waist and kissed her anyway.

"Don't worry, I can guarantee we'll be back again." I stepped out the door and descended the stairs to catch up to the guys. "We've got to thank *The Joke Bum* if we see him. That place kicked ass," I said to Lew as we headed North, continuing our journey up Duval.

As we walked out, we simultaneously noticed we were missing one person. "Where the hell is Phil?" I asked.

"I thought he was right behind us," Reno replied.

"He probably went back to see if that Asian girl would accept five dollars for a lap dance," Lew laughed.

"I bet you five bucks he's trying to bum a cigarette from someone," Reno smiled looking for someone to take him up on his bet.

"Wait a minute, isn't that him?" Lew rolled his eyes as he pointed into a convenience store across the street. The only part of Phil you could see above the racks of food was his head. He was way in the back of the store, looking for something. "I'll go get him," Lew growled, as he ran across the street.

I looked over at Reno. "I wonder what he's buying in there. He's only got five dollars."

A couple minutes later Phil and Lew re-joined us. Phil was meticulously trying to open up a fresh pack of Camel cigarettes. The way he was fumbling with the package, you'd have thought he was wearing oven mitts.

"I didn't know you smoked, Phil," I asked him as we resumed the walk back down Duval towards the other bar.

"Yeah. I used to smoke all the time when I was in college. Now I only do when I get really liquored up and the wife's not around." He had finally managed to get the pack opened and was now struggling to light it with his new lighter. "Oh, yeah. I've missed these," he slurred between coughs.

"Wanna bet you can't stop with one pack?" Reno snickered.

I can't even remember the walk back towards our hotel that night. The amount of alcohol that I had consumed throughout the day had caught up to me. Before I knew it, my rum punch was gone and we were back in the hotel parking lot. I had reached my alcohol intake limit for the day. "What are we going to do for the other bed tonight, Reno?" I yelled out, as the hotel came into focus.

"I haven't decided yet, but let's walk down to the end of that wooden pier we saw from the balcony earlier. I have a feeling that the event will take place there." By this time Lew had put his arm around Reno and had started walking a bit faster, leaving Phil and I to bring up the rear. Lew was talking earnestly to Reno, apparently trying to coerce him into going a certain direction with the challenge. As we reached the end of the pier, it was blatantly obvious that Lew had decided what the competition would be that night.

Lew cleared his throat. "Get ready. Tonight's challenge will be to walk down the steps at the end of this pier and completely submerge yourself in the Atlantic Ocean." Before he had even finished talking, I had stripped off my shirt and sandals and was walking down the flight of stairs that led from the pier into the ocean. Lew was laughing hysterically by this point encouraging me to get in. I bounded down the steps and dove headfirst into the ocean. It's always been my opinion that nothing sobers you up faster than jumping into water, besides being pulled over by a cop. This night was no different. Instant sobriety - the moment my head went under. As I swam under the water I dove down to touch the bottom - it was only about eight feet deep at this point. Below the surface was complete blackness. The ocean was cold and had an eerie ring this far down. I did not have time to be scared. As I rose back to re-surface, I waded right through a thick patch of seaweed just seconds before I ran out of breath. I emerged with a vine wrapped around my face and a mouthful of saltwater. "The bed is mine," I yelled, pumping my fist into the air, while spitting a stream of seawater from my mouth.

"Not so fast." Lew yelled out. From the corner of my eye, I saw Phil lumbering down the stairs in his boxers.

"It's not going to be that easy Tango." Phil retorted as he gingerly inched into the ocean. It took a few minutes, but damned if Phil didn't submerge himself as well. Disgusted, I swam back over to the steps and joined Phil at the bottom of the wooden pier. As we waded down below, we looked at each other and shrugged our shoulders. "Looks like a tie," Phil said.

"Come on, Lew - you in or what." I yelled, looking up the steps at a very dry Reno and Lew.

"Sorry dude, it's between you and Phil. Come on back up. Reno and I will decide the tie-breaker."

As Phil and I walked up the stairs, Lew had grabbed Reno by the arm and was leading him back down the pier to discuss the tiebreaker in private. "Hey, why the hell is Lew deciding what we do?" Phil demanded. Although it was Florida, standing there dripping wet while waiting for the tiebreaker, I was starting to wish I had a towel to cover up with. At three o'clock in the morning, being in the water was definitely warmer than standing out on the pier.

"The tiebreaker has been decided. The first person to walk back naked to the hotel room wins the bed."

By this point, Phil had heard enough. "That's bullshit Lew - you're making up the rules and not even participating," he screamed angrily.

"I agree, to hell with you Lew. This is Reno's dance," I added.

Finally, Reno broke the silence. "Well then gentlemen, here's the deal. Walk back down into the water. Dive under and whoever comes back up with the most baggage in their hands wins. Throw you're catch on the deck and Lew and I will determine who the winner is. The only catch is, you got to be naked when you do it."

"Oh Cripes," Phil complained. He was still in his boxers.

I, on the other hand, was already naked and beginning to talk trash. "Come on Phil, you in or out? I'm not gonna stand here nude all night." Reluctantly, Phil removed his boxers and we dove into the Atlantic. I feverishly started flailing my arms out under the water, desperately trying to grab a hold of something…anything, for that matter. All I could come up with was seaweed; and that simply would not do. I swam down deeper, combing the ocean floor, beginning to run out of breath, but refusing to emerge empty handed. Just then my hand brushed against something on the ocean floor. It was the bottom step of the pier. My fingers wrapped around a thick rubber mat, laden with holes. I pulled with all my remaining strength, but it would not break free. I was running out of air, so I yanked as hard as I could one last time. To my delight, the mat broke free. It was about four feet long. I started swimming towards the surface, unfortunately as I broke out of the water, my arm was yanked backwards. The mat was still attached to the wooden pier. I reached back quickly with my other hand and held on tightly. By this time, Phil had already emerged and thrown his catch onto the deck.

"Phil, is that a handful of grass?" Lew was laughing so hard at Phil's catch that he had started crying. Phil was standing in the waist deep water at the bottom of the pier holding a single strand of seaweed wrapped around his right hand.

"That's all I could find," he feebly replied.

"What do you got Tango?" Reno yelled.

"Come on Tango, show us you're hands. Otherwise, Phil wins." Lew added between gusts of laughter.

"I got a hold of something here," I hollered back, as I tried one last time to yank the mat free, both hands still under water. Luckily for me, within mere seconds the bounty broke loose. I waded over to the pier gritting my teeth. In an exaggerated manner, I flung my treasure onto the landing. It was immense. Not only did I bring up the mat, but also attached to the end of it was a three foot long piece of lumber. On top of that, attached to the board was a heap of seaweed, barnacles and concrete. All together I would estimate the weight of my payload around forty pounds.

"Dude, that's half the Titanic!" Lew screamed out.

"Thank God - 'cause I ain't running naked back to the hotel room." A dejected Phil replied.

Since my cargo shorts were already soaked, I put them on over my wet, naked body. "Gentlemen, I'm not sleeping on the floor," I roared, as we started up the stairs that led towards our room. After we got back into the room, Phil and I put our wet clothes out on the balcony to dry. Reno was in the kitchen eating some donuts and drinking some of my red soda. I flopped down onto what turned out to be a very, very comfortable bed. I was going to do everything in my power throughout the next week in order to keep my sleeping arrangement. After much debate, Lew decided there was not a chance in hell he was going to share the fold-out with Phil. He decided he'd be better off creating a bed on the floor using the fold-out couch's cushions as his mattress. He set his bed up right in front of the bathroom and front door.

As I started drifting off to sleep that first night, the last thing I remembered hearing was Lew yelling out, "Reno, shut that freaking kitchen light off."

CHAPTER THREE

Let me put it this way, the next morning I did not wake up to the smell of sea-salt and the sound of waves crashing against the shoreline. After a dreamless night, in which I slept the slumber of a passed out drunken man, I awoke in a very comfortable bed to the unmistakable sounds of Reno and Phil snoring. I looked over at the alarm clock positioned on the nightstand between the two beds. It was 7:30 am. A rumbling erupted from underneath Lew's sheets. "Was that a wake up call?" I yelled, as I flung one of my pillows towards the floor, hitting him right in the face.

"No. But I think a mouse just ran by." He replied, laughing at his own joke.

I got up out of bed and lumbered towards the bathroom. "I've got to use the little boy's room," I said, as I stepped over him. When I was finished, Lew was still awake. "You feel like heading outside and walking around. See what this island looks like when the sun is out?"

"Sounds like a plan to me. Let's stretch our legs while these two knuckleheads sleep some more," Lew replied, as he got up from his makeshift bed. "I'm a little sore from sleeping on the floor anyway. Those cushions kept separating throughout the night. I lost track of how many times I woke up on the floor."

"Did you fall asleep pretty fast? I was out when my head hit the pillow." By this point I had put on my sandals and was ready to head out.

"All I remember was laughing when I fell asleep," Lew replied. He too, was now dressed, wearing a gray tank top, baseball cap, dark blue swim trunks and sandals. "Let's roll."

We headed out the door. "You got the key?" I asked before he could shut the door.

"Got it," he replied, while locking the door behind him. As we walked down the stairs, the splendor of the day hit us. It was perfect outside. Not a cloud in the sky, it was a comfortable eighty degrees. With a gentle breeze rippling through our shirts, we jogged across the pool deck. Not a sole was stirring outside, the only sounds we could hear was water splashing as it drained from the fish water fountains into the pool, and the occasional squawk from a seagull flying overhead. It was going to be an ideal day to be out on the ocean. We decided that it would behoove us to find a moped rental place as soon as possible; some way aside from a bicycle to help get around this island a little easier.

As we walked across the parking lot, our job was finished before it even started. Beside a wooden park bench, was a slightly larger than phone booth sized, white hut with a faded blue roof. In bold white letters on the weathered roof were the words: *Mopeds & Bikes*. In front of the hut, were about fifteen yellow mopeds.

We doubled back and walked toward the pier where we had our competition just hours earlier. By the time we had made it back to the wooden pier, the weather was starting to get a bit steamy. The sun was shining bright. This morning was no different from last night - the pier was still uninhabited. At the entrance, all of the teal and white lounge chairs were still stacked on top of each other. The thatched umbrella huts were positioned along the pier like lone palm trees. Apparently, not only were we the last ones on this pier a few hours earlier, we were the first ones back on it today. The boards creaked ever so slightly as we made our way to the end. "Dude, go back down to the bottom of the steps and raise your arms. I'll snap a victory pose." Lew said.

I carefully navigated the slippery steps. "To the first of many comfortable nights sleep," I replied, with my arms in the air, as he snapped the shutter. "Let's head back and see if those two have woken up yet." Just as we started walking back to the room, I saw something that made me stop in my tracks. It was a red and blue bold lettered sign, hanging loosely from the wooden pier. It read:

DANGER
SHALLOW WATER
NO DIVING   NO JUMPING
ENTER WATER BY STEPS ONLY

As we approached the old sign, I told Lew to stand guard while I positioned myself in front of it, gripping firmly along the edges with my hands. "This will look great in my office," I said, as I yanked the sign from the pier. It came off easily, especially since one of the screws holding it in place had begun to rot away. It was not a new sign, by any means. It showed the weathered look of being subjected to the elements for many years. It was mine now. Besides, I needed a little memento.

When we arrived back in the room, Reno and Phil were still in bed. I placed my newly found treasure next to the fold out. "Time to get up boys," Lew yelled as he snapped on the light. "Reno, Phil. Get your asses out of bed. You'll get enough sleep when you're dead." After a couple minutes of prodding, we were able to rouse the weary travelers out of their beds.

As they were getting dressed, the first coherent words out of Phil's mouth were: "Hey, where are we eating at? I'm starved." His next statement was: "Hey, nice sign." He had picked it up and was studying it carefully.

I walked over and grabbed it from him. "Don't get any ideas; I'm going to hang it in my office when we get back home." I propped it back up on the fold out and glanced over at Reno. He was sitting on the end of the bed, holding his head in his hands. As of this point, he had not yet said a word. Reno was not a morning person. "We don't know where we're eating at yet. Let's just head down Duval and find a place that looks interesting." I said. "The moped place opens at ten, so we can get our wheels after breakfast. You two ready?"

"Yeah, I'm cool" Reno mumbled. He was trying to comb his disheveled head of hair using his fingers. "But before we go eat, I gotta jump in the pool and get this smell off of me."

Phil nodded his head. "I agree. It'll be quicker than taking showers anyway. So you guys found a place that rents mopeds, huh?"

"Yeah, it's right across from the hotel." Lew replied, as he locked the door behind us. "Dudes, I grabbed the Nerf Football. We can play a little catch in the pool." We were all in swim trunks anyway, so taking a dip in the pool before breakfast made perfect sense. I know Phil and I still had the stink of the sea on us. On our way down the stairs, Phil grabbed my shoulder.

By the time we arrived back at *Why Not Rent a Scooter* to rent mopeds, the place had opened. A rich blue Key West Conch Republic flag attached to the front of the white hut was fluttering in the breeze. It seemed like everywhere you went on this island, the flag; which had a pink conch shell centered on a yellow sun with a flaming corolla, was flying. From the looks of things, we must have been the first customers of the day. The only person in front of the place was a blond guy with crew-cut hair, wearing a red Hawaiian shirt, khaki shorts and tattered maroon Converse All Star shoes. He was holding a pen and clipboard, marking notes as he inspected the yellow scooters parked out front. "Are you open for business?" Lew asked, extending his hand to shake, as he approached the guy.

"Sure am," came a very feminine voice. The guy was actually a gal. I could have sworn she was a he, was the look on our faces, as we walked up to inspect one of the mopeds.

"Well, me and my boys here need to rent four mopeds," Lew continued. "What's the best price you can give us?"

"Thirty dollars a day, a hundred and fifty per week, for the scooters. I'm assuming you want scooters, not mopeds. The price goes up fifteen dollars a day starting tomorrow, due to the holiday," was her response.

Lew tried to work the deal a little more. "We saw them for twenty-five dollars a day down the road."

Without even looking at us, she turned and headed back towards her air-conditioned hut. "I don't care if you rent them…or if you don't rent them."

Since Lew was doing the negotiating, he decided to pay for them using his credit card. Initially, all that was needed was a three hundred dollar deposit. We were told we would actually pay for them upon their return. As she started ringing the deposit up, Lew knew he was in for some trouble. "Oh shit," she said, as the modem from the credit card machine began to connect. "I accidentally added a zero to the amount. Instead of three hundred, I typed in three thousand." She had a very apologetic look on her face as she told Lew her dilemma. "If you don't mind waiting, I can back it out and do it again. It may take a while, but if you weren't talking to me, I wouldn't have messed this up."

Lew was clearly agitated. "We don't have time. Let's leave it at three thousand. It's not like anything will happen anyway." He signed the credit deposit slip reluctantly and said, "instead of twenty four hours, how about giving us a day and a half? We'll bring them back tomorrow at four o'clock and call it even."

"That's fine," she agreed, walking back outside to fill up the scooters with gas and go over a brief training session.

"Has everyone here already ridden a scooter?" She asked, as she looked each of us in the eye.

"Yeah," Lew replied.

"Yeah, I'm cool," Reno, responded. "It's been a while since I've ridden one, but I'm sure it will come back to me."

"Yeah," I lied. I had never driven one. I had ridden on the back of Lew's and other friends many times, but had never really driven one on my own. Being the guy who was always on the back of a moped, I had a vague idea of how to drive one.

"No," Phil answered

"Yes you have," Lew interrupted, shoving him.

"I mean yes!" Phil continued, catching on.

As we were lectured on the basics, we found out that the scooters had an electronic ignition with an automatic choke and each came with a basket attached to the back and a storage bin under the seat. Inside the storage bin was a lock for the front wheel. We were told to use it whenever the scooters were left unattended. She finally concluded her speech by informing us not to turn the handle grip throttle too fast when you started from a stop, and she reminded us to use both brakes to avoid toppling over the handlebars.

"Do we need helmets?" I asked, beginning to wonder what I had gotten myself into.

She actually laughed at me. "You may need them, but we don't have any." With that remark she started divvying out the scooters and recording who got what number.

Phil climbed onto his, then Reno. "I'll bet you twenty, that you lay out your moped before I do," Reno said to Phil as he revved the throttle, sending out a black cloud from the exhaust.

"Hey, you're on," Phil replied.

She marked off the next one on her clipboard. "Oh, number forty one is a quick one."

"I'll take that one." Lew yelled, pointing his finger in the air and abruptly walking towards it, much to my delight. A few minutes later I was given my scooter, number thirty-nine. Hopefully it was a slow one. As I adjusted my mirrors and familiarized myself with the controls, the other three guys had already done a U-turn onto South Street and were waiting on me. Reno was still revving his engine and actually attempting to do some wheelies in the middle of the street. Ignoring everything I had learned in the past ten minutes, I rotated the throttle forward way too fast, cranked the steering wheel hard to the left and kicked up a bunch of sand and dust as the wheels squealed and my scooter shot out from under me. Fortunately, I was holding on tight as I blew past the three of them like they were standing still and headed towards US 1.

Although Lew had contacted *Tropical Tours* the day before for directions, we still didn't really have a good idea where we were heading. All we knew was that we were supposed to drive down US 1 to the east side of the island until we came to a small bridge and then take a left. Well, we had been riding down US 1 for what seemed like an awfully long time. We had not yet found a bridge. I was riding beside Reno, on the safe side of the highway, when a box truck sped by us so fast the wake of wind he left in his path just about knocked us over. Lew was in the lead. I had no idea how far back Phil was lingering, and I wasn't about to turn my head around long enough to look for him.

"Dude. There's the bridge," Lew yelled, as he pointed towards the left. Of course, we were in the wrong lane. In order to turn left at the intersection, a double lane change would be required. The traffic was bumper to bumper. "Get over. Now." Lew veered to the left and easily slipped between two cars, I followed right behind. There was not enough time to see if Reno and Phil had noticed us. A car horn blared in my right ear and tires squealed behind me, as the car I had cut off came to an abrupt stop.
Lew was laughing as I throttled down the scooter beside him in the left turn lane. I looked behind me as Reno meandered up to the light. At that moment the three of us watched as Phil, still stuck in the outer lane, glanced over at us and waved as he rode past us. We could do nothing but hope Phil could catch up later.

Phil showed up about ten minutes later.

Tropical Tours, just off the highway, was a mere stones throw from the sea. The parking lot, aside from our four scooters, was abandoned. As we looked around, we saw a narrow wooden pier leading out into a tree-lined cove. Tied up to the pier were six small boats, three boats on either side of the pier, with small Nissan propellers pulled up out of the water on all but one. Five of the boats were white. One was lime green. The pier was empty, aside from Lew, who had by now wandered onto it for a snapshot. Adjacent to the parking lot were two run down shacks, one in front of the other. Each was gray in color, with a matching greenish-gray, tin roof. They were in desperate need of a paint job. The foremost building served as the check-in counter, office, and storage facility. There was diving equipment spread throughout the inside. Both garage doors were open; and the office that could be seen in the back, was very cluttered with all types of equipment thrown about. As we walked towards the check-in counter, we passed by a brand new soda machine. From the looks of things, aside from the boats, it appeared to be the only thing in working condition there. Reno leaned across the counter, straining to see if anyone was in the back. "I hope we're not too late. Do you think we're going to be helped?" he asked, as he slid off the counter and onto the sandy lot.

Just then a guy in a white T-shirt and red board shorts came out from the back office. He was carrying a propeller, a gas tank and some other spare parts. His arms, from his fingers to his elbows, were covered in grease. "You guys my twelve o'clock?" he asked, not skipping a beat as he rushed past us towards the pier. "My name is Bill. I'll be right with ya; I just gotta gas up the boats." He definitely looked the part. He had long, bleached blond hair, a deep tan, bare feet and a friendly, surfer smile. His face showed the wrinkles from many years spent sailing on the sunlit seas.

"Can we call you Captain Bill?" Lew asked.

"If ya want." Bill yelled back from the mouth of the cove.

Phil and I spent the next few minutes in search of a bathroom, we had drank a little too much throughout the morning in order to re-hydrate ourselves and our bladders were both completely full. We strolled around to the shack in back and found a dilapidated restroom attached to the side of the building, clearly put there as an afterthought. Just then, we heard a dog barking. It came running from around the corner and was heading right for us. Saliva was bubbling across its lips and its canine teeth were exposed. Frozen in place, I heard the snap of the chain-link leash, as the dog's neck was yanked back a mere two feet from where we were standing. The flea infested, dirty mongrel coughed briefly before returning to its barking. "Man that was close," Phil said, as we jolted into the bathroom. It was dark, dank and a bit smelly.

When we rejoined the others we found that Lew and Reno had already begun checking in. We had to sign a waiver form releasing *Tropical Tours* of any responsibility should anything happen to us during our adventure. I signed on the dotted line without even reading it. As we were getting fitted for our snorkeling gear, Roger and Cynthia pulled into the parking lot. Ironically, they had rented the same yellow scooters we were riding. After they parked them next to ours, a passerby might have mistaken *Tropical Tours* for a scooter rental place. "So do you guys mind if we add two more?" Captain Bill asked us, as he watched them approach.

"They're with us." Lew replied.

"Right on." Captain Bill said, handing us each a blue-netted bag. Each bag contained our fins, snorkel, mask and goggles for the boat ride. Captain Bill was not much for words.

Roger looked like he was ready to navigate an entry into the America's Cup. He was wearing a sailor cap, a dark blue Polo shirt and some yellow swim trunks. Cynthia looked outstanding. She was wearing a yellow bikini top and had on a pair of shorts over her thong bottom. The four of us were ready to get going, as was Captain Bill. Unfortunately, Roger had about a million questions in regards to where we would be going, how long we'd be gone, how much it cost, and what we could expect to see. He went on and on for what seemed an eternity. By the time he was finally done questioning Captain Bill, we all felt like we'd already been on a two-hour adventure. We were finally able to convince the two of them to finish up their paperwork. Captain Bill took off his shirt and said, "Follow me." The seven of us headed down towards the pier to pick out our boats and get instructions on how to drive them.

We were given a two-minute course in regards to the basic understanding of how the boats operated. It was actually pretty simple; you steered with the steering wheel and, unlike the scooters, hammered the throttle to take off. When the boat started hydroplaning, you backed the throttle off a bit and hung on. Captain Bill paused long enough to guarantee Roger had no other questions. "Now that you're all experts on how to operate the boats, let me go over my signals. I got two signals." Captain Bill put his arm in the position it would be in if you were making a right hand turn in your car without a functioning turn signal and had resorted to using hand gestures. "This means full throttle." He then put both arms out like he was hanging from a cross. "This means stop."

Of course, Roger had a question at this point. "Well how about using this signal if we need to turn around?" His finger was pointing straight up and his hand was rotating clockwise.

"Let's not have three signals. It's hard enough to remember two." I said.

"I only got two signals." Captain Bill replied, rolling his eyes. He ran his hands through his hair and paused for a few seconds. His hands rested on his hips and he simply stared at Roger. My guess was that he was contemplating what he had gotten into for the afternoon. "Now go pick out your boats."

"Is that green one yours?" Lew asked Captain Bill, pointing to the green boat tied up at the front of the pier.

"Nope, mine is the one tied up across from it. The fast one."

"Then that one is mine and Tango's," he yelled, excitedly running towards the lime green boat. Reno and Phil hopped in the one behind us. Cynthia and Roger chose the boat behind Captain Bill's - the one lacking a propeller, of course. By this time Lew had jumped into the driver's side, which was fine by me, I preferred to sit back and relax. I didn't want to drive anyway. Lew fired up the propeller, yanking hard a couple of times on the pull-string. Phil followed suit and ignited his engine as well.

"Wait a minute," Captain Bill hollered. "I got to put the propeller on this one." It only took him a few minutes to square away Roger and Cynthia's boat. With that task done, he hopped into his boat and led us out of the cove. We were told to let the boats idle until we reached the bridge. We were still in a 'No Wake Zone'. Captain Bill led, Lew and I were next in line, Reno and Phil followed us, and Roger and Cynthia brought up the rear. The adventure had finally begun. The sun was beating down and there was absolutely no breeze. We both put out hands in the water to cool off as we glided up the cove. Mangroves lined both sides of us as we headed out of civilization into the open sea.

As soon as we made the turn out of the cove and coasted our way underneath the bridge, Captain Bill enlisted the use of one of his signals. His right arm went into the air and before we knew it he was speeding away from us. Lew opened up the throttle and the little boat lurched out from under us. Upon takeoff the boat almost jumped straight out of the water. It took about a quarter mile before we actually started hydroplaning and by this time we were really moving. The boat literally flew across the ocean, skipping from wave to wave. We were following in Captain Bill's wake and Lew was feverishly spinning the steering wheel from the left and then back to the right in order to leap across the waves. The water was splashing into the boat at a torrential pace. Without the required goggles, we would have been blinded. The warm taste of salt in my mouth was a constant reminder of exactly where I was. I spun around to catch a glimpse of Reno and Phil to see that they were following in our lead, catapulting across the water. Far in the distance, barely discernible beyond the glare of the sunlight was Roger and Cynthia. Their boat was on a straight-line bearing and it looked like they were driving in slow motion. Captain Bill changed course and started heading towards what appeared to be a small island. When he got to within a few hundred yards his arms went out. Time to stop. We let the ocean carry our boat until it docked up next to Captain Bill's. Phil idled up as well. "Geez, those two are certainly taking their time." Captain Bill laughed, while pointing in the distance at Roger and Cynthia's boat. "Go ahead and turn off the engines while we wait on them."

While we lingered, we got to know Captain Bill a little bit better. He told us that he had spent some time in the navy and was stationed out of Fort Zachary Taylor, in Key West, for two years. During this time, he was an aquatic engineer and fell in love with the tropical island. He decided after he was de-commissioned from the navy to move the wife and kids out of Lubbock, Texas and into a house in Key West. He got this job as a boat and snorkel tour guide the first week he was back in town. He loved his life and his job. He had been here for six years now and couldn't fathom the idea of living anywhere else. As he finished his story, Roger and Cynthia had finally pulled up.

We sped around Key West for about forty minutes, dividing our time between the Atlantic Ocean side and the Gulf of Mexico side. We blew past a couple of cruise ships docked along the seaport. At one point, we were actually close enough to reach out of our boat and touch the side of one of them; much to the dismay of the cleaning crew dangling fifty feet above our heads as they scrubbed barnacles from the white paint. Captain Bill led us through the Navel Yard to see a World War II submarine that was housed there. Right before the entrance to the Navel Yard, he pointed out about twelve or so caves that opened into little caverns. The view of the caves was obstructed by another cluster of mangrove trees. I would have never seen the entrance to the caves if Captain Bill hadn't pointed them out. He said that back in the days when smugglers and thieves were the majority of the people taking up residence in Key West, those caves were where the old pirates used to hide out and stow away their loot. Once inside the navel yard, we cut the engines in order to get some clarification on the second part of the tour.

"What's that island over there with all the evergreens on it?" Phil asked pointing across the Navel Yard a few miles to the West.

Captain Bill squinted into the sun to see what Phil was asking about. "That island over there is called Christmas Tree Island. Back around World War II, taking a page out of the pirate's book, the Navy carved out even more caves inside the navel yard allowing them to hide submarines and navy soldiers. The rock and debris from this huge undertaking was deposited over there and after the project was completed it became its own island. After many years some rich northerners built vacation homes on the island and planted evergreens and spruces. Over numerous years, the trees have taken over. The locals refer to the island as Christmas Tree Island because it sticks out like a sore thumb next to all the palm trees. Lately, most of the vacation homes have been torn down and mansions have been built in their place. It's a very private island."

"Lets check out those caves, Captain Bill," yelled Lew.

"I would love to but they have been off limits for years and a buddy of mine was fined five hundred dollars for being caught in the area a few months ago. Sorry guys." stated Captain Bill. "Same goes for the pirate caves, which are technically on government property.

By this point, we were starting to get tired of the boats anyway, and were now in the mood to snorkel. The sun had started to bake, and we desperately needed a refreshing jump in the ocean to cool off. "So where exactly are we going to snorkel?" Reno asked.

"I'll take you there now. It's a shipwreck; there's some beautiful coral, and the place is full of sea life." Captain Bill sat down and fired up his boat. "Let's ride!" he screamed, as he hammered the throttle.

Reno, doing his best impersonation of a cowboy, 'Yee-Hawed', and pretended to lasso Captain Bill while Phil pushed their boat to the limit to catch up.

Before I knew what hit me we were skidding across the water at a break-neck pace, in a hot pursuit. I couldn't tell if Roger and Cynthia were still behind us or not, but Reno's lassoing might have confused Roger. For all I knew he and Cynthia were turning around.

We saw Captain Bill come to a skidding stop as he banked his wheel hard to the right and did a very impressive about face. As we re-grouped, he told us to throw out the anchors, which were underneath our seats, and handed us a rope to tie the boats up into a ring. There were a few other boats floating around the dive site, the most impressive of which were two Hobie Cat Sport Cruiser's. Each Hobie Cat featured white hulls sporting blue, green and magenta horizontal-cut sails. Both catamarans were positioned about a hundred feet in front of us and it looked like a family was on board with one member getting suited up for a dive. The other Hobie Cat contained about six gals in bikinis. We put on our snorkeling gear as quickly as we could and jumped into the water. The ocean was rather warm and incredibly refreshing. As we dipped our heads underneath it took a while for our eyes to adjust, but there about twenty feet in front of us and a mere five feet below us was unmistakably, the mizzenmast to the sunken Spanish Galleon. The ship must have plowed straight into the ocean floor since the front end of the hundred-foot keel was buried beneath the sand. There were some rocky caverns to the side that looked interesting. "You guys go ahead and explore the ship," Captain Bill said. He had grabbed a net and was holding a knife. "I'm going to be hunting lobsters for dinner tonight. "We'll meet back at the boats in about forty five minutes." He dove into the water and swam off in the opposite direction leaving us to investigate the remains on our own.

The floor of the ocean was only about forty feet deep where we were currently treading water and even from the surface the shipwreck was plainly visible. However, the ocean floor sloped away from us and at the far end of the shipwreck, an enormous coral reef had formed. Judging from the divers down by the coral, it would require air tanks to investigate at that depth. Having never snorkeled before, I spent quite a bit of time following Reno's lead. He had been trained and certified a few year's earlier at the local YMCA in preparation for a company trip to Hawaii. After gleaning as much information as I could in about ten minutes, I decided it was time to search the ship on my own. After all, I had learned not to breathe through the mouthpiece when I was under water and to spit in my mask to keep it from fogging up, what more did I need to know.

I had no idea where Lew and Phil had swum off to, but Reno was about thirty feet below me. I was determined to at least go deep enough to see some fish. As I dove under the water and started swimming towards the wreckage, I saw a shimmering gold beam out of the corner of my eye. Knowing for sure that I had spotted the lost treasure, I turned to look just in time to see Phil was right beside me. Unfortunately there was no lost treasure, instead I watched as Phil's wedding ring descended towards the ocean floor. "Shit" I yelled, realizing what I was seeing, as my mouthful of air bubbled up in front of my eyes. I made a feeble attempt to grab at it, apparently the water made it seem closer than it was, since I missed it by about fifteen feet. At that point I was screwed, I had to re-surface. I was out of breath.
"Damn it!" Phil yelled, as my head broke the plane of the water.
The other guys had also re-surfaced and were treading water a few yards away. "What's wrong Phil?" Lew hollered.
"Hey, I just lost my wedding ring!" We didn't waste too much time looking for the ring. It was hopeless. Phil was going to pay hell when he got home. Content that it was a lost cause, we decided to resume our exploration of the sunken ship.

There were all sorts of fish swimming in groups; displaying a myriad of colors. Reno yelled over to us that he and Phil had found an opening through the poop deck, and the four of us followed his lead as he swam into the galleon. I was the last to enter. As I swam into the vessel, an ominous darkness overshadowed me. I looked below and saw tons of bubbles surfacing from a group of divers below us walking along the ocean floor. Unlike the divers, we only had a few minutes to look around before we needed to re-surface, since we were swimming without tanks. I swam after the rest of the guys and saw that there was a hole in the wall of the room we were in. It led out to the main deck. When the time came to re-surface, we streaked through the wall, pushed off the main deck with our feet and shot to the surface. "Hell of a sight." I heard Phil say as I broke the plane of the water.
"I could stay here all day and investigate. Did you guys see the coral at the far end of the wreckage?" Lew added. He then took a deep breath and dove below again. Not wanting to push my luck, I decided to stay close to the surface and watch what transpired below. I was not disappointed. Lew had spotted an enormous sea turtle swimming by itself above the wreckage. He was in hot pursuit. As I watched on, Lew swam up behind the turtle, reached out, and grabbed it by the shell. The turtle, not skipping a beat,

continued to swim, towing Lew for about fifty feet before Lew finally ran out of breath. He emerged all fired up, shouting, "I just swam with a turtle!" Grinning from ear to ear, he made his way back over towards me.

Unfortunately, it was about time to hook up with the others back at the boat. Roger and Cynthia were already in theirs, and I could see Captain Bill climbing back into his, throwing two rather large lobsters into a bucket he had on the floor of his boat. Unlike Lew, Reno had seen enough and was starting to swim back, as was Phil. Lew looked over at me. "Tango, lets use up the rest of this film real quick." With that said, he dove back under the water. I quickly followed. We swam under as far as we could and snapped a few last shots. The split second that I snapped the last shot on my camera, I could have sworn the water dipped a few degrees. That was the moment that I made eye contact. There were two black shadows swimming in front of the hull. Almost instantaneously, I recognized the silhouettes. Two Bull Sharks were headed right at us. I had watched an entire week of shark documentaries on television a while ago and was able to recognize their short, blunt noses and a medium-sized second dorsal fin. I felt Lew tugging on my arm, but I couldn't swim. I was frozen in place. Lew's hand grabbed my arm, cutting off my circulation, as he literally dragged me back to the surface. "Shark!" I heard Lew scream, as we swam feverishly back towards our boat. Apparently Reno and Phil had decided to snorkel a bit longer after all - they were only a few yards in front of us. We practically collided into them as we splashed through the water. The four of us frantically swam in the direction the group. We had no idea if the sharks were following us or not. If I had been swimming in the Olympics, I would have won gold that day, because I beat everyone back and scrambled, as if my life depended on it, into the lime green boat. I looked across the water and saw that Lew, Reno and Phil were still about twenty feet out. Not more than ten feet behind Phil was the scariest thing I had seen in a long time. A dorsal fin emerged from the water.

"Hurry up!" I yelled. Lew had finally reached the boat and I pulled all two hundred pounds of himself into the boat like he was as light as a feather. I saw Reno climb into his boat as Phil let out a blood-curdling scream. I thought for sure he was a dead man.

"Help me in," he cried out, as Reno reached out towards him.

Reno's face was white; he was desperately trying to pull him on board, without falling back into the water. Phil outweighed him by at least a hundred pounds, but Reno's adrenaline kicked in as he yanked on both Phil's arms, hoisting him upwards. "Are you bit?"

"No man, it just brushed past me." Phil's voice was about two octaves higher than normal. "Scared the shit out of me though."

It was at this point we noticed everyone else in the vicinity was furiously swimming back to their own boats as well. It appeared there were more than just two sharks in the water.

CHAPTER FOUR

Can't you feel 'em circlin' honey?
Can't you feel 'em swimmin' around?
You got fins to the left
Fins to the right
And you're the only bait in town

Jimmy Buffett
Fins

Suddenly, our eyes darted towards the two Hobie Cats. Pleas for help seemed to be resonating from this direction. The four of us looked at each other and immediately decided to see if we could help. It was evident that Cynthia and Roger wanted no part in a rescue, and Captain Bill had already sped away in his boat to get some assistance. We raced over towards the catamarans to see what we could do. Reno and Phil went towards the family's boat, while Lew and I rushed over to the boat containing the girls. "What's going on?" Reno yelled out as they approached the first ship.

"Our son, Todd, is still down there!" the mother shrieked. "Our tanks are empty, we've been diving all day, please help us."

Just then, the father emerged from the water, gasping for air. He looked petrified. "I can't reach him without a tank. I saw him swimming over towards the coral."

Without a moment's hesitation, Reno and Phil sped off.

As we approached the other catamaran, to our horror, we found out that there were originally eight girls on board. The other two, Brooke and Kelly, were part of the group of divers we had seen earlier. Being the only men in the vicinity, we both felt obligated to try and help. Two of the girls handed us each a diving tank, another one came rushing over with an old fashioned spear gun, the kind that had a string attached to the spear. I grabbed the handle of the gun, figuring it would at least give us some protection from an attack. Just moments ago I had learned how to snorkel. Now, I was about to get a crash course on how to dive.

"Do you guys have any more tanks?"

I turned to see who was yelling. It was Reno. He and Phil were idling beside the Hobie.

"There's a boy down in the caves that needs help."

"We've got one tank left, but it's almost empty," one of the girls replied, running towards Reno holding the depleted tank.

"That'll have to do," he yelled, grabbing it from her. They sped away while Reno maneuvered to get the tank on his back. There was no time to worry about Reno, he was going towards the boy, so we went after the girls.

As we were about to drive off, one of the girls told us that Brooke and Kelly were last seen on the far end of the ship. We maneuvered the boat just past the wreckage. With the tanks strapped on and our mouthpieces inserted, I looked into Lew's eyes and said, "Fuck it. You only live once."

We fell back into the ocean.

According to Reno, the moment he dove into the water, he knew he had made a mistake. When he jumped in, he had failed to remember that he was about a hundred yards away from the sunken ship. He then saw a few shadows drift by, and immediately realized he had no means of defending himself from the sharks. Figuring time was of the essence; he swam as fast as he could towards the ship. When he reached the coral, he made a quick pass over it to try and get a glimpse of the missing boy. He couldn't see him anywhere. The kid must be hiding. The only crevice he saw was the one we had explored earlier that led into the poop deck. He swam towards the hole in the wall and looked inside. The cavern was empty. Desperate, he raced to the top again. Taking the mouthpiece out, he yelled towards the Hobie Cat. "I can't find him in the reef or the ship. Where would he be?"

The father cupped his hands around his mouth and hollered back. "Try the caves underneath the wreckage."

Lew and I dropped like rocks to the ocean floor. Not accustomed to using an oxygen tank, I was breathing much too fast, almost to the point of hyperventilating. We worked our way along the floor of the ocean, heading away from the wreckage. We started to kick up some debris from the ocean floor, which clouded the water a bit, but it didn't take too long to spot Brooke and Kelly. They were hiding in the ship about fifty feet in front of us. The cavern of the ship they were hiding in extended out towards the coral. A school of three sharks were circling above them. We slowly worked our way under them.

Reno dove back under. He swam quick, but not so fast as to deplete his air supply and made his way to where the cargo hold would have been located had the boat not smashed into the rocks. He had just about given up when he saw the boy. Like the father had suggested, he was hiding in a small underwater cave, beneath what was left of the wreckage. Just then, the air in Reno's tank ran out. Picking up the pace, he raced towards the cave. To Reno's delight, he could see bubbles racing towards the surface; an indication that the boy still had oxygen left in his tank. Reno slithered his way into the cave and for the next few minutes shared the tank with the boy in order to re-build his strength for the return trip.

By the time Lew and I had reached the girls, the three sharks had begun circling a bit closer. They were obviously starting to get braver by the minute. It was becoming difficult to see anything through the mass of bubbles being emitted from the girl's tanks. The sharks had begun swimming all around us. They did not seem aggressive at this point; just curious, when things suddenly took a turn for the worse. One of the sharks distinctly changed its course and set a heading straight for us. I was able to maneuver myself between the girls and the approaching shark, while Lew looked for an escape route and tried to get them to calm down. I pointed the dagger straight at its blunt snout. I about fainted when I realized the shark was not about to retreat. It headed right at me, its mouth beginning to open and its black eyes rolling back. I dropped down and squeezed the trigger, launching the spear right into its belly as it passed over me. Gripping tightly to the wooden handle of the gun, I held on for what turned out to be the ride of my life. The shark immediately began twisting and turning, trying to remove both the dagger and myself from its underside. Blood was pouring out of the wound. I kept my grip as it dragged me away from the others. I glanced over my shoulder to see that the other two sharks had picked up the scent of blood and had also given chase. The moment I looked back, the shark started convulsing ferociously. The end of the spear was ripped out of its belly. It smacked against my facemask, cracking the plastic. As water began to trickle in slowly, I had no idea where the sharks were. I let go of the gun, allowing it to plummet to the ocean floor.

After taking a few breaths of much needed oxygen, Reno looked into the boy's eyes, pointed up towards the surface and gave a thumbs up signal while breaking off a piece of wood to use as a spear. As they exited the submerged cave, Reno noticed that two other sharks had joined the lone shadow. They were still swimming in circles; however, they were now by the mainmast, a mere forty feet away. There was no time to delay; they had to get to the surface. Reno grabbed Todd's hand and they swam as fast as they could upwards. Fortunately, the sharks decided to ignore them, and they darted off in the other direction. Reno and Todd emerged from the sea, to the screams of joy from Todd's family. Phil helped them both into his small boat and took them over to the Hobie Cat. Utterly exhausted and gasping for air, Reno collapsed into the passenger seat.

To make matters worse, by the time I reunited with Lew and the girls, the cracked mask was filling with seawater. I stripped off the useless mask and let it fall to the ocean floor. Lew looked shocked, but immediately regained his composure and rushed over to lead the way. We cautiously started swimming along the reef back towards the sunken ship. It seemed that the sharks must have swum off in the opposite direction. The knowledge that I had just successfully defended some women in distress – very James Bondish style – gave me a boost of energy.

Lew and I feverishly swam towards the surface with the girls in tow. Just the Lew pointed behind me. Two of the three sharks emerged from the bloody dense fog and were swimming towards us again. Using the green bottom of our boat as a landmark, Lew and the girls had already begun their ascent. I was trailing behind. As the three of them broke the surface, Lew pushed the girls into our boat. Phil and Reno were there as well. So was Captain Bill. Phil and Captain Bill were each holding out a flare gun. As I hit the surface, I heard the two cannons go off. The last thing I remember was feeling the heat of the fire as it passed mere inches over my back and hearing the piercing sound the flares made as they punched through the water. I had passed out cold. They were shooting at the two dorsal fins that had emerged from the water.

Fortunately, Lew saw me go back under as he watched from safety. He grabbed me by the neck before I was out of reach and hauled my limp body into our lime-green boat. I awoke with my head sandwiched between a nice pair of breasts; belonging to the girl I was immediately introduced to as Brooke. Everybody was yelling and screaming. Todd's family and the other girls aboard the Hobie cats were ecstatic. We all started hugging and Lew yelled out, "Got through that feeding frenzy," as he and Phil exchanged high five's across the water. We delivered Brooke and Kelly back to their friends amidst a lot of thanks and hugs. We then headed back to rejoin Reno, Phil and the others in our group. Still feeling a bit light headed from the whole ordeal; the celebration seemed to be transpiring into a fog. It was about this time that the Shore Patrol boat arrived at the scene.

Eventually we bid everyone farewell and followed Captain Bill back towards the *Tropical Tours* cove. I used the time in the boat on the way back to unwind. The reality of the shark attack was beginning to sink in and I could not believe how lucky the four of us were. It was closing in on late afternoon by the time we cut the engines down and let the current push us underneath the bridge and into the cove. Lew and I had been following Captain Bill pretty closely. He turned around and was grinning madly. "You guys stay here, I'll be right back, I gotta check on something." With that he sped off through the 'No Wake Zone' and out of our view. He was flying back towards his office. We let our boat drift over to Reno and Phil. Roger and Cynthia had just coasted into the cove as well.

"Where'd Captain Bill go off to?" Cynthia asked, as she stood up in their boat to stretch.

Lew looked over at her; his feet were propped up on the dash. "He said to chill here for a while."

"I know I'm still trying to calm down." Phil replied.

"Me too," Roger said. "I was just seconds away from jumping into the water myself to help you guys."

As we let the Florida sun soak into our skin, I could feel my body relax. Then suddenly, I heard the whine of a motor shooting straight down the inlet into the cove. "Follow me!" Captain Bill yelled as he blew past our three docked boats.

"Dude, I don't think we need the extended tour," Lew yelled, as he kicked it into gear, trying desperately to catch up. Captain Bill turned opposite of the bridge and shot around a small island that opened up into the Gulf of Mexico. He headed straight out towards the sea. We flew by a bunch of houses on stilts, went past a few houseboats and eventually cut the engines above what looked like a huge sand bar. It was the oddest sight I'd ever seen. Right in the middle of what looked like the Gulf of Mexico, Captain Bill hopped out of his boat landing in water that only came up to his knees. After what we had been through, jumping back into the water was the last thing on our minds. We anchored our boats next to his, not quite ready or willing to get back into the water. I couldn't believe Captain Bill jumped into the water after what had just happened, but it was only three feet deep where we were now. He tried to set us all at ease by explaining the rarity of any shark sightings, and was now trying his best to change subjects. Captain Bill started grinning like a schoolgirl.

"I know you're all still freaking out about what just happened, but I wanted to show you something awesome."

We all just stared at each other, but the excitement of Captain Bill began to wear us down. Eventually we were all able to smile and even laugh again.

"So show us something," I blurted out. "We almost got eaten by sharks, what do you want us to do now? Wrestle some octopuses?"

"Yeah right, look you made it out alive, and now have one hell of a story to tell. Heck, I won't even charge you extra for that. Now, you guys know where we are right now?" Captain Bill looked at us, still smiling. No one answered. "Well, I just found this place. You're floating on a sand bar containing the largest number of live conch I've ever seen in Florida." With that said he bent down and picked up a huge conch shell. The little mussel inside extended both eyes out at us.

"Cool," Reno said. "These guys look harmless."

"We're in restricted waters right now. The conch is a protected species in the Keys. If a police boat comes around -- drop the conch." By this time Captain Bill had run down the length of the sand bar. He stopped and put both hands into the water. "But in the meantime, get a load of the size of these two queens," he yelled, proudly hoisting his find above his shoulders. The conchs were each about the size of a football. The shells were bright pink. This was exactly the kind of stress relief we needed. We spent the next half hour hearing tales about the conch industry and learning just about everything there is to know about the mollusk. One of the things we found out from Captain Bill was that the conch consumed in Florida is from the Bahamas since the conch in the Keys is protected. Lew, never one to miss a photo opportunity, took plenty of pictures of us holding the shells.

We headed back, unpacked the boats, and about the time we were getting ready to leave, Captain Bill said, "You guys are true heroes and what you did today was really incredible. Although I noticed that Tango and Lew never did get those girl's phone numbers."

"Whatever," I laughed.

"Anyway, how would you like to go to a Labor Day weekend bash tomorrow night? It's the biggest party of the year."

We all shook our heads, we were definitely interested. "Where is it at?" Lew asked.

"The party's held at Little V's Mansion, over on Christmas Tree Island, every Labor Day weekend. He opens up his entire mansion. The outside pool has a swim up bar, with another fully stocked bar inside the house. Waitresses walk around to cater to your every need. It starts at midnight and is by invite only. I might be able to get you guys into it, if you're interested - sort of a reward for saving those people's lives today." He paused for a minute and stood there looking us over, trying to get a feel for if we were still interested.

We were.

"Tell you what, meet me at Key West Bight, Pier Three, just off Mallory Square on Saturday night, I dock my boat there. It's in stall forty seven. Meet me there at eleven o'clock and I'll take you to the party."

"Why so late?" I asked.

"Don't worry, this party goes all night long. Trust me; you'll have the time of your lives."

We bid our farewell to Captain Bill and told him that we would meet him the next evening in order to catch a ride over to the party at Little V's. I wasn't really looking forward to the long trip back to the hotel, but I figured if I could survive a shark attack, then another thirty-minute trek on the scooter would be a breeze. The four of us, along with Roger and Cynthia, started our scooters and edged towards the highway entrance. It was rush hour and traffic was thick. There was little chance that we would be able to ride together in a pack on the way back. We came to a consensus that the only way we'd be able to get back anytime soon was to simply dart out into traffic individually when the opportunity presented itself and head towards Duval. Before we split up, however, the four of us exchanged handshakes with Roger and Cynthia. I told them to enjoy the rest of their honeymoon on the island, knowing that they would probably never forget the adventure we had shown them.

Lew was the first one out of the parking lot, gunning the engine of his scooter, as he immediately blended into the flow of traffic. To my surprise, Reno and I were actually able to merge into traffic simultaneously. Riding side by side, we crossed into the far right lane in order to turn back onto US-1. I didn't have a chance to look back and see if Phil had made his way out. But knowing Phil, he'd be taking his own sweet time. As far as I was concerned, Phil was on his own. I had enough to worry about as I struggled to become reacquainted with riding the scooter.

We had been riding for about fifteen minutes as we approached the traffic signal at First Street. Lew was only a few car lengths ahead of Reno and me. "Let's catch up with Lew and ride three wide," Reno said as we came to a stop. To the disgust of the drivers in the cars in front of us, we proceeded to maneuver the scooters between the two lanes until we reached Lew. We waited for the light to change.

Lew turned around to look behind him. "Where the hell is Phil?" he yelled, over the idling engines that surrounded us.

"I never saw him," Reno replied.

"You know Phil," I added, "he either turned the wrong way or is moseying along a few lights back, traveling at his own pace."

"That's what I'm afraid of," Lew said. Just to be on the safe side, we decided to pull into the first place we found after the light and wait for him to drive by. A liquor store parking lot a few blocks down the road fit our needs perfectly. Lew turned into the lot. Reno and I followed closely behind and pulled up to a stop beside him. We waited, and waited, and waited. About ten minutes went by, and there was still no sign of Phil. We had watched every car, scooter, bicyclist and walker stroll past as the light on First Street went through about five cycles. By this point, Lew was beginning to get a little irate.

"I repeat. Where the hell is Phil?" Lew yelled, as he started up his scooter. "This sucks. I tell ya what; I'm going to head back towards *Tropical Tours* and see where he's disappeared. I'll meet you guys back at the corner of Duval and US-1 when I find him." Seconds later Lew jetted across traffic and headed back in search of Phil. Reno and I waited a few more minutes; just to make sure Phil wasn't simply one light back, before we decided to continue towards the meeting place. It turned out we were only about nine blocks away from where Lew had requested we wait for him, but with stoplights and traffic, it took us awhile to get there. By the time we arrived, traffic had thinned out a bit and our only delay in arriving at the corner was that we had to wait on two ambulances to drive past us.

We pulled across the street and parked our scooters. We got off and walked back towards the corner. Standing there, we were able to get a good look down the street. Once again, we waited, and waited, and waited. After standing in the same spot for another few minutes, Reno and I were both starting to get worried. We could still hear sirens in the distance.

I looked over at Reno. "You don't think those ambulances we passed earlier were heading towards Phil do you?" My mind was starting to fear the worst. The only thing that I could think of was that Phil had wrecked the scooter. There was simply no other explanation. Not even Phil was this slow.

Reno stared right through me, keeping his eyes focused on the traffic. I could tell he was just as nervous as I was. He was playing with his dice. "God I hope not, his wife will be pissed if he winds up in the hospital. Of course, he may have just gotten a flat tire."

"I like that idea. I hadn't thought of that." I replied, already beginning to feel a bit better. The more I thought about it, the more I began to come to the conclusion that it was probably just something stupid and simple like a flat tire. "I know Lew told us to wait for them here, but I say screw it, let's head back up US-1 and see if we can find them. Worst case, we'll pass them if they're on their way back."

"If I roll these dice and they come up six or higher, we go looking for them. It sure beats standing here doing nothing," Reno replied.

I said roll.

Four and four rolled onto the dirt.

As Reno and I began our trek back towards the spot where we last left Lew, I kept thinking that any second now, we would pass the two of them heading the opposite direction.

I was wrong.

When we arrived back at the liquor store, I asked Reno if he had seen them. He hadn't, and neither had I. "What should we do now?" I sighed.

Reno scratched his head. "Let's drive back towards *Tropical Tours*, see if maybe they're having some scooter troubles." We eased back out into traffic and continued our journey. The further we rode without seeing them, the more nervous I got. I didn't know if it was hunger, fear, anxiety left over from the shark attack, or simply the intense heat scorching my body, but the knot I had in my stomach was making me noticeably uncomfortable. I was starting to feel sick to my stomach.

We only had to turn the bend before we would be able to see the intersection of A1A and US-1. I remember looking at Reno and wondering if my face was as ashen-colored as his was when we came around the curve. Because it was at that moment that the world seemed to be moving in slow motion as our worst fears came true. There were two ambulances parked diagonally across the intersection, along with more police cars than I cared to count. Red, blue, yellow and white emergency lights were flashing everywhere. There was absolutely no sound. The only sense in my body functioning was my eyesight, and I didn't like what I was seeing. I didn't even know Key West had a police department, but apparently the entire force had convened on this intersection. Both of the westbound lanes had been blocked off. Amidst the broken glass and yellow plastic fragments, the highway was lined with burning flares as three police officers directed the westbound traffic into the far left eastbound lane. There was a definite haze in the air from the flares and the humidity seemed to hold the smoke hovering above us.

Suddenly, my ears were filled with the sounds of traffic, burning flares, wailing ambulance sirens, and the police officer's whistles that screeched intermittently as they barked out orders. By this time, both ambulances had sped off in the opposite direction, followed closely by a couple of police cars. We had no clue who was inside. But, from the sight of the two yellow scooters that lay smashed in the middle of the road, I feared the worst. "I hope those weren't Lew and Phil's scooters." Reno said, his voice cracking a bit.

I didn't respond.

CHAPTER FIVE

Navigating cautiously through the roadblock, we managed to get over onto the sidewalk in front of the seaside yacht club. We parked our scooters and walked sluggishly towards the accident scene. "Well, let's see if we can get any information from one of those cops." I sighed, as we approached a young officer who was busy picking up the debris from the accident. He was holding a black rear view mirror from one of the scooters in his hand. His back was towards us and his feet were mere inches away from a puddle of red paint. Reno and I stopped dead in our tracks. It wasn't paint; it was blood – red blood.

"Excuse me, sir?" I asked, in a shaken voice. He turned around to face us; a long scar along his face automatically drew the attention of my eyes. The scar extended from just underneath his right ear, along the ridge of his cheekbone, all the way to the middle of his chin. Averting my eyes, I noticed his other hand was holding a very large ziploc bag. It was empty with the word 'Evidence' written across it in thick, black letters.

"I'm going to have to ask that you two step back up on the curb immediately." He pointed the broken mirror in the direction we had come from. "I can't have you disturbing this accident scene."

"We're looking for our two friends, do you know what happened?" Reno replied, as we ignored his order and continued walking towards him.

"Sorry guys, back up on the curb please," was his curt reply.

Not listening, Reno repeated himself. "Ahh, sir…I think our friends might have been in this accident."

"Look. All I know is that a couple of tourists were involved in the accident. Now please, turn around, get back up on the sidewalk, and let us do our jobs." He turned back around and resumed his investigation.

This conversation was going nowhere. Out of frustration I yelled, "How the fuck do we find out if it was our friends that were involved?"

That got his attention. The officer turned back around, threw the mirror down on the ground, shattering the glass, and walked straight towards us. Reno and I both took a half step back. Judging from the look he gave us as he approached, I thought for sure he was about to physically escort us away from the scene. He stopped in front of us, his arms folded across his chest, the ziploc bag clenched tightly between the fingers of his right hand. All I could think as he stood there was, *that scar looks worse up close*.

"The police station is in City Hall at 525 Angela Street. The chief went back there to interview a few of the witnesses and collect their statements. Maybe someone back there can help." He leaned forward and softly whispered, "Now for the last time, get off the street before I have you both arrested."

"Thanks," we both replied.

We walked back silently to the scooters. Neither of us knowing quite what to say. When we reached the scooters, Reno was the first to break the long silence. "So, you know how to get to Angela Street?"

"Crap, Reno. I was hoping you did." We were forced to go back and apologetically request directions to City Hall. Our young officer friend was not too thrilled to see us again, but at least he was able to, begrudgingly, provide us with the necessary information. Now that we had directions, it was simply a matter of negotiating our way back into the flow of traffic. Although rush hour was long over, the reduction in lanes going both directions had caused another traffic jam.

It took all of my remaining energy to simply turn the key in the ignition slot. I was both physically and emotionally drained. Although we had to get some information in regard to our friends' whereabouts, there was a small part of me that dreaded the trip to the police station. I kept hoping we'd see Lew and Phil along the way, so this nightmare would come to an end. But the further we drove, the closer I came to the realization that our two friends were indeed the victims of accident we had just left.

"I got a bad feeling about this" Reno said, as he looked over at me. The heat of the day was becoming unbearable, and even Reno was beginning to sweat a bit though his T-shirt.

"I know," I replied.

City Hall was easy to spot as we turned onto Angela Street. It was the first building I had seen in Key West that actually looked like it could withstand a hurricane. It seemed out of place, a concrete and brick structure, amidst the usual wooden decor of the island. There was absolutely no parking available anywhere out front. We were in a hurry, so we felt justified in parking illegally on the sidewalk. Not even bothering to lock up the scooters, we hopped off and headed inside. There was a large sign hanging in the lobby that listed room numbers for various departments, commissioners and committees. We scanned the small block, white letters until we found what we were looking for: Police Chief Robert Albertson: Room 103. A tiny placard on the far wall pointed down the hall for Office's 100 - 105. We started heading that way. When we got to the end of the hall we were forced to turn left around a corner. The Police Chief's door was on the right. Just as I reached out to open it, the door smacked me in the hand, not stopping until it had slammed into my nose. "Watch out," I yelled. Reno was laughing hysterically; I couldn't tell why since my eyes were now watering from the blow I had sustained.

"Where in the hell have you two been?" I heard Reno shout.

When my eyes cleared, I was standing face to face with Lew and Phil. "Damn, we thought for sure you two were dead," I said, as I gave them each a big hug. Phil looked very haggard, and Lew seemed upset. "What happened? We saw two smashed up scooters that looked just like the ones you two were riding."

Phil put his arm around me, leading us out towards the front door. "Let's find a place to sit down and I'll tell you two guys the whole story. Lew's already heard everything." We walked outside and found a couple of concrete benches underneath the shade of a few palm trees. I was never so happy as then to see my tall, lost friend. The four of us sat down as Phil leaned his considerable frame against the trunk of a lone palm and began to recount the events that had transpired since we last saw him that afternoon.

To the best of my recollection, here is what happened.

After we all got onto our scooters and got ready to leave *Tropical Tours*, Phil realized when Reno and I pulled out of the parking lot that he had left his sunglasses in the little compartment underneath the passenger seat of his boat. Captain Bill was in the middle of cleaning out the boats and, fortunately, had already found them. Captain Bill and Phil strolled back to the office and got to talk for a while. Phil actually met his wife; the next group of tourists had canceled, so Captain Bill was going to take her out for a late afternoon ride.

Traffic was slowing down a little, so Phil fired up his scooter along with Roger and Cynthia, who were still idling in the lot.

At this point, Reno interrupted him. "So Phil, did it ever occur to you that we might be worried about what was taking you so long? I mean, didn't you think we might miss you after a half hour had passed and you still hadn't even left the freaking parking lot?"

"Well, to be honest, I didn't even think about it." Phil replied.

Phil took a deep breath and continued.

Before they knew it, not only had the traffic lightened, but the highways were also pretty clear. Roger and Cynthia gave him a wave, and then they were off. Phil gunned his motor and sped out onto the road. As he glanced ahead, he noticed Roger and Cynthia were already stopped at the light. They were in the right hand lane waiting to turn onto the interstate. The signal had just tuned red on US-1, so Phil sped up in order to ensure he'd get through the light and not have to wait. He was still a couple hundred feet away when he saw the green turn signal illuminate. He had ample time to make the light, so he backed off the motor and decided to coast around the corner. Then out of nowhere Phil heard the distinct sound of tires screeching.

And that's when it happened.

A Lincoln Towncar had run the red light and was skidding right towards Roger and Cynthia. The guy didn't even hit his brakes until he had practically driven right over them. He must not have seen them turning, but even so, he definitely had blown through the light. The chrome grill of the Towncar struck Cynthia full force just as she was turning. She never saw what hit her as she was thrown from the scooter. While she was in the air, the front tires of the Lincoln rolled right over her bike, smashing it to pieces. Roger screamed out her name as the car, showing no signs of stopping, slammed into him next.

Phil instantly got tunnel vision; it was as though he was looking at the accident in slow motion. Both Roger and Cynthia were catapulting through the air. Roger's sailors cap shot like a rocket from his head. It floated through the air, landing out of harms way in the median. He came crashing down onto the hood of the car, taking the brunt of the fall with his head. Phil could hear the bones in his neck snapping as he watched him land. Cynthia wasn't so lucky, she was launched in the direction the car was traveling and got run over before he could avert his eyes. Phil almost puked. Her yellow bikini was barely visible from all of the blood. But, the worst part of the scene was the position in which she was laying. She wasn't moving. Her legs were severely mangled and both were bending the wrong way at the knee. Phil's eyes simply wouldn't look away. He didn't even remember how he had gotten where he was, but almost instantly, Phil realized that he was still driving in the direction of the accident. Phil was able to shake himself out of his trance in time to realize that if he did not do something quick, in a matter of seconds, he was going to slam into the back of the Towncar, which was now at a complete stop about fifteen feet in front of him.

Not wanting to be the third victim in this accident, without even thinking, Phil turned hard to the right. The front wheel of his scooter hit the curb; and he was propelled over the handlebars. He came crashing down onto the grass that served as the divider between the Gulf of Mexico and the front entrance of the marina or yacht club, or whatever it was.

"So what happened to your scooter?" Reno interrupted.
"Well Tango, when I hit the rocks, I saw a large object momentarily blot out the sun from of the corner of my eye. It was the scooter, and it was heading right for me. I barrel-rolled to my right and the scooter slammed into the grass a fraction of a second later. Before I was even able to think about trying to stop it, the damn thing slid right into the Gulf and sank like a rock into the water."

Lew jumped off the bench, his hands went into the air as he yelled, "Yeah, and guess who put down the deposit on that son of a bitch?"

Phil sat down on the dirt and sand, his back still against the lone palm and continued with his story.

He watched his scooter sink into the Gulf and then scrambled back up the embankment to see what was happening on the street. He noticed that the Lincoln had come to a stop. The motor was still running and although the hood was slightly dented, you would have never guessed it had been involved in an accident.

Roger was lying in the middle of the street about fifteen feet behind the car. He was face down and spread-eagled on the pavement. Even from Phil's distance, things didn't look good. There was a large pool of blood coagulating where Roger's face and the asphalt met. Phil couldn't tell if he was still breathing, but if he was, it appeared that he would drown in his own blood any second.

There was no doubt in Phil's mind that Cynthia had died. As Phil scanned the scene again, what struck him as odd was that there was nobody else around. There wasn't a car to be seen, the intersection was deserted. Phil couldn't believe no one else had witnessed this accident. Out of the corner of his eye, Phil saw something move. Before Phil had time to duck back behind the embankment, their eyes locked. Phil was staring right into the driver's dark brown eyes, and he was staring right back at Phil, grinning like a madman. Phil was scared to death and started praying that he didn't have a gun. Phil thought for sure he was a dead man.

He held out both his meaty hands as he shrugged his shoulders nonchalantly. He placed his chubby index finger up to his lips, like he was telling Phil to keep quiet. After what seemed like an eternity, pointing right at Phil, he nodded his head and winked. Phil got the message loud and clear: shut up or else. Then he rolled the tinted window up and sped off, kicking up a cloud of sand and dust as he quickly left the scene.

Just then Phil saw a few cars pulling up to the light at the intersection. Phil didn't know how long any of this took, but the light on US-1 was still red. To his relief, another car was approaching the intersection from the direction of *Tropical Tours*. That's when Phil heard a woman's voice scream out, 'Oh my God, somebody call an ambulance!' The Lincoln shot around the curve and sped out of sight.

"Did you get his license plate number?" Reno asked.
"No man, I didn't even think to. I guess I was in shock. I still can't believe what happened."
"Why didn't you run over and beat the shit out of him? From you're description, you could've kicked his ass. I mean, you could have at least restrained him until help arrived?" I asked. "What were you thinking man, you let the killer drive away?"
"I'll tell you what," Reno shouted, "for Roger and Cynthia's sake, we're going to get that guy."
"Easy Reno," interrupted Lew, "That dude will get his, that's why we're at the police station now."

"I don't know why I didn't do more," answered Phil, "It's like I couldn't get my legs to work. It was so surreal."

He continued on.

Phil felt like he was in one of those dreams where you're being chased, only you've forgotten how to run. He just stood there, not able to move, even after the guy had sped off, Phil was still rooted in place. A few car doors slammed to his left, causing him to blink. Phil shook his head and snapped himself out of the fog he was in. Finally, he was able to get his legs to work, climb back up the embankment, and rush over to see if he could help. The whole thing was over in no time.

He knew Cynthia was a lost cause, so he ran over to Roger. He was still laying face down in the street, the trail of blood leading from his mouth and nose had streamed over to the sidewalk. Phil couldn't believe there could be that much blood inside a person. It was bright red, except for some whiter stuff that had oozed out from his ears. Even as Phil knelt beside him, he still couldn't tell if Roger was still breathing, so he reached forward and put his fingers on Roger's neck to see if he had a pulse. Not wanting to press down too hard, for fear of causing more damage, Phil was barely able to feel a beat. Roger had a pulse, but it was very weak. He was really banged up; Phil could tell that at least one of his arms was broken. Both of his legs also looked pretty mangled, but Phil's real fear was that he had injured his neck when he landed on the hood of the Lincoln. Phil didn't want to inadvertently paralyze him by moving him onto his back, but he also knew that if he didn't turn him, Roger would choke on his own fluids. As Phil was debating whether or not to turn Roger's head, he started gasping and coughing violently. As Roger fought for air, his head lolled slightly to the side, enough to free up an air passage. Roger lay there moaning. Not knowing if he could hear or even understand what Phil was saying, Phil told him to try and keep still, help was on the way. The sounds of sirens were wailing in the distance. Within minutes, a blue and white, Monroe County Sheriff patrol car pulled up to the accident scene. Phil stayed with Roger, calmly talking to him, hoping he'd stay alive until the paramedics could arrive.

"So Lew, when did you find Phil?" I asked.

"Well, after I left you guys, I kept watching the oncoming traffic, so I knew I hadn't passed him heading the other direction. About the time I was coming up to the intersection, I heard some sirens behind me. I turned my head and saw a couple of ambulances coming towards me, so I pulled over to let them pass. I gotta admit, my heart started pumping as I began to think that Phil might be somehow involved. Fortunately, as I rounded the curve, I saw Phil as plain as day standing in the middle of the street talking to a police officer."

At this point Phil interrupted Lew and continued on with his story.

Phil hadn't seen Lew yet, but apparently he came up to the scene when Phil was giving his initial report to the Sheriff's Deputy. The ambulances had already arrived and there was nothing Phil could do to help. A guy and a gal had jumped out of the ambulance that was parked next to Roger. The guy rushed over carrying what looked like a plastic toolbox. The girl was pushing a stretcher, with a yellow backboard on top. She was holding a thick neck collar. They log rolled Cynthia onto the backboard and immediately went to work. The others focused on Roger, he must have been having difficulties breathing, because they inserted a trachea tube into him as he lay in the street. After that, they lifted him onto the stretcher and the girl started CPR, placing the bag on the tube sticking out of his neck.

They were putting Roger into the ambulance, when a police officer asked Phil if he had seen what had happened. Phil told him 'yes'. That's when Lew came up and they were escorted over to the Chief of Police. He introduced himself as Bob Albertson, and then asked us both to follow him back to the police station.

Once at the station Phil and Lew were led into his office. They sat down in front of his desk.

Phil was asked to provide a full name, address and telephone number. He had already pressed the record button on the tape recorder and reminded Phil that his statement was being recorded. Phil proceeded to tell him what he had witnessed, the same story that he had just told us. After Phil was done, the Chief hit the stop button. Phil looked over at Lew, not knowing if they should get up to leave or not. Chief Albertson opened one of his desk drawers and pulled out a cigar. Telling them not to get up, he spent the next couple of minutes looking for a lighter. He was finally able to find it underneath a stack of papers. He lit the cigar and took a few puffs in order to get it going and then leaned back into his chair, running his fingers through his wavy hair.

"We have a very good hospital and doctors here, so they will be able to take good care of your friends," Chief Albertson began. "You guys might as well just continue on with your vacation plans, and I will handle the investigation."
"Will you find the car?" Phil asked.
"I will find both the car and the driver. But it won't be easy. Let me explain the situation in terms you'll understand. First of all, Phil, you're the only witness. I mean, you didn't even get a license plate number, and your description of the felon describes about half of the male population on the island. It wouldn't do me any damn good to have you flip through the pages of our known criminals mug shots. The whole thing really just sounds like a simple hit and run. We'll take it from here."
He paused for a few brief seconds to let the point sink in. "Look, I've said too much already. The bottom line is that I'll get working on this case as best I can. I do appreciate the information and I know where you're staying. I'll get back in touch if I need anything more. Sorry guys." With that said, Chief Albertson showed Lew and Phil the door.

The four of us sat underneath the shade of the palm trees and let the tale sink in. No one said anything for quite a while. I snapped out of it as I heard Reno say, "Well, I say we go and find out how Roger and Cynthia are doing. After all, we're the only people they know down here."

"I hope they are doing ok," said Lew.

"So do I," I replied. I doubt we'll be able to cheer them up at all, but it would probably help them both to see some friendly faces. Any ideas where they took them, Phil?"

"I heard the paramedic say they were taking him over to the *Lower Keys Medical Center*. I'll go get some directions real quick and meet you guys by the scooters. Besides, I gotta take a leak anyway," Phil replied.

A little while later, the three of us straddled our scooters in front of City hall and waited for Phil to exit. He came out after a bit and told us that the hospital was actually back in the direction of the accident. "It's about a mile North of *Tropical Tours*, can you believe that?" We followed Reno and Phil, who were riding double on Reno's scooter, until we wound up right back at the scene of the accident. Only this time, you'd have never known anything had happened only hours earlier. All of the debris had been swept away and traffic was functioning just like normal. We pulled up to a red light and got into the turn lane as if we were heading back to where we started our day. We parked our scooters out front and walked in through the emergency entrance. As the automatic doors slid apart, the hospital aroma rushed out towards us. Reno walked up to the front counter and began to inquire about Roger's condition. He turned around and motioned for us to follow him. A nurse led us to a small conference room and told us that a doctor would be with us in a minute. There was a round table in the middle of the room, surrounded by six plastic chairs. We sat down and waited. When the doctor entered the room he sat down in one of the empty chairs and introduced himself as Dr. Zurich.

"Hey, how are Roger and Cynthia doing?" Phil asked.

Dr. Zurich took a deep breath and let it out through his nose slowly. "The female was pronounced dead on arrival. The male suffered a compression fracture, where his cervical vertebrae two, three and four were crushed. Beyond all of our best efforts, his trauma was so severe there was nothing we could do. I'm sorry fellows, we've already notified the family."

CHAPTER SIX

I went down to Captain Tony's
To get out of the heat
When I heard a voice call out to me
"Son, come have a seat"
I had to search my memory
As I looked into those eyes
Our lives change like the weather
But a legend never dies

Jimmy Buffett
Last Mango In Paris

I can't say that I was shocked when I heard the news. After listening to Phil's version of what had happened, it wasn't too difficult to understand that in a battle between a Lincoln and a scooter, the Lincoln will prevail every time. But still, it was pretty strange to think that two people whom we had just spent the better portion of our day with were now dead; so soon after we ourselves had just escaped death from sharks. Stranger still, the killer was at large, and it seemed like the police were just going through the motions in regards to their investigation into the accident. We had asked the doctor if there was anything we needed to do – should we call someone, things like that. He simply shook his head, no. Everything had been taken care of.

The four of us walked backed to the three scooters and along the way decided that the best thing to do, in spite of how we felt, was to take heed in Chief Albertson's words and simply continue on with our vacation.
"Dudes, I am really starting to feel guilty for inviting them to this gig in the first place," Lew sighed.
"Come on Lew, it's not your fault," I said.
"It was a pure accident, it could have happened to anyone," Reno interjected.
"I know, I know, but damn this sucks. It's going to put a damper on the whole vacation."
"We're doing our best by having Phil talk with the police," I replied. Not to be cruel, but when it boiled right down to it, we barely even knew Roger and Cynthia. We would have to be satisfied that we had done all that we could, and take for granted that the police would do everything in their power to find the guy. If we were able to help the cops out going forward, we would. However, it wasn't going to do anybody any good to sit around and mope.

Eventually, the decision was made to get something to eat. None of us had eaten since breakfast and since it was only an hour or so before dusk, we were all hungry. Lew suggested that we try *Crabby Dick's*. We had passed by the place at least four times already going back and forth today, and although it appeared to be a tourist trap, the location looked pretty good. Not surprisingly, the rest of us agreed and we followed as he sped off towards the restaurant.

"Half price appetizers upstairs" was the greeting we received from an older gentleman, wearing a red and white pinstriped vest. He was handing out menus to anybody passing by as we walked up to the front of *Crabby Dick's*. There was a giant red crab hanging from the roof line a couple of stories overhead that could be seen from blocks away, informing us that this was indeed the place to eat. Upon second glance, though, we realized that we were not standing in front of the restaurants entrance at all. We were instead facing the opening to the gift shop. You actually had to take the stairs straight up to reach the restaurant from the side. The facade was all white washed wood, and there was an extensive outside patio directly above our heads. I grabbed a menu and gave it a quick glance. It was loaded with all kinds of seafood and pasta dishes. Just what I needed in order to regain some of the strength that I had lost during the arduous afternoon.

Walking up the steps, alongside the gift shop, it was also apparent that we would not be eating anytime soon. Inside, there was a long line of people. We were promptly informed that there would be a bit of a wait before we were seated. Fortunately, there was still a bit of time left before Happy Hour ended, so Phil walked over to the bar and ordered us each a dollar draft. An advertisement stapled to the bulletin board beside the steps, claimed it was the coldest draught beer in town. I don't know if that was true or not, but who was I to argue, especially after an entire day spent outside in the tropical sunshine. When Phil came back wielding the four drinks, I quickly grabbed mine and allowed the chilled beer to flow freely over my chapped lips on its way down towards my empty stomach.

"You better slow down, Tango, we got a long night ahead of us," Lew said, as he took a sip from his frosty mug.

I looked at him and thought for a moment. "Don't worry. I'm not drinking more than two beers for dinner. I still gotta ride my moped back to the hotel."

While slipping the hostess a ten spot to expedite service, Lew asked if we could sit outside on the deck, since most of the people looked like they wanted to eat from the comfort of the air conditioning inside. A hostess than showed us a table outside. It was positioned against the railing, overlooking Duval Street.

We were shown our seats just as my beer ran out. I asked the waiter for another round and settled in to a chair. Our waiter, who cheerfully introduced himself as Jeff, quickly took our orders. He was overtly friendly, and, well, lets just say that we were all thinking that he was probably from the rainbow district. He joked around with us, trying to lighten the mood at the table, before he left with our appetizer order. Sitting underneath a spinning, white ceiling fan, we were able to watch the steady flow of people walk by as we waited on our appetizers to arrive.

It was turning out to be a beautiful night. The sun was just beginning to set as Jeff brought out our appetizers. The food smelled incredible. I was famished. Before we began to dig in, Phil raised a glass and made a toast to the memory of Roger and Cynthia. We touched mugs and took a drink. The spread of wings and conch in front of us dwindled quickly. Jeff came back and took our dinner orders. Each of us went around the table ordering a variety of fresh seafood, but before Jeff could walk away, Phil requested another order of conch fritters. We didn't know how long it would take to get our orders out to the table, and judging from dwindling supply of appetizers left in front of us, none of us wanted to risk being hungry while we waited.

"Dude, when our waiter gets back, we ought to ask him where a good place to eat breakfast tomorrow would be," Lew said, wiping sauce from the corner of his mouth. The wings and conch fritters were now completely gone.

"That guy won't know where to eat breakfast," I replied. Just after saying this, our third plate of conch fritters arrived. Moments later, so did our dinners. A huge plate of deep fried, soft-shell crabs was placed in front of me, rendering the remaining conch fritters useless.

"I didn't know our order would come out so quick," Lew said. Looking at our waiter he then asked, "So where is a good place to eat breakfast around here?"

"Are you looking for some place with a little atmosphere?" Jeff asked.

"Exactly," Lew replied.

"Well, I really enjoy eating at *Blue Heaven*. It's in the Bahamian Village at the corner of Petrona and Thomas Street. It's a great place to get a cup of coffee and the food is fantastic. I would recommend it to anyone, especially if you've never been there before. The experience is unique to Key West." He showed us how to get there on a map that I had stashed in my back pocket and left us so we could continue eating.

"Tango, when are you going to learn that gay guys always know where the best places are to eat and drink?" Lew smiled, cutting into his fresh swordfish. While finishing up dinner, we discussed what we should do the rest of the night. Everyone agreed that we needed to go back to the hotel to shower and change. Besides, Phil needed to call his wife. We were all interested in getting out and hitting a few of the more famous bars in Key West and putting this day to rest. The first place we wanted to go was *Louie's Backyard* for a Bloody Mary. After that, we'd simply see where the night took us. With dinner finished and the check paid, we bid Jeff farewell and thanked him for the advice on where to get breakfast the next morning. "Oh, one more question, can we go to Louie's Backyard in tank tops?" Lew asked.

Jeff's response was classic. His words, though short and to the point, became a recurring theme throughout the rest of the week, especially when conversing with the locals. "It's Key West."

"That's right, dudes," Lew said, giving each of us a high-five. "It's KW."

As we walked downstairs towards the scooters, Reno said, "You know, we forgot to do a challenge for one of the beds tonight."

"Damn, with everything that happened today, I completely forgot about that. That's fine. I already know what we're going to do. I knew there was a reason I packed the volleyball inside the scooter this morning. Dudes, it's time for a little beach volleyball." Lew ignited his scooter. "Follow me!" he yelled, pulling away from the curb.

Way too excited about playing sand volleyball at dusk, I gunned the engine and skidded away. The only problem was I had forgotten to sit all the way down. I guess the four beers, not two, I drank didn't help out too much. My back legs went flying out to the side and the scooter banged into a parked car. Not wanting to stop and see if I'd damaged anything, I climbed back onto the seat and sped off.

I heard a man on the street yell out. "That boy needs another cocktail."

Embarrassed beyond belief, I caught up to Lew. "Damn, that was close," I tried to look back to see if Reno and Phil were behind us, but the scooter started to wobble back and forth when I did. So I immediately turned and faced forward, not wanting to fall. Instead I decided to see if I could find them in my rear view mirror. I glanced down to look; my mirror was missing. Upon further investigation, however, I was relieved to see that it was simply dangling next to the front wheel. "Lew, I think I broke the mirror." We came to a stoplight. Lew looked at me and rolled his eyes.

"I'm never getting that deposit back," he sighed.

A few seconds later, Reno and Phil puttered up behind us laughing hysterically at my expense. "We don't need any more scooter accidents," Reno said.

"You guys are hilarious," I replied. The light changed and we continued straight to the beach volleyball court we had seen along the drive in from the airport. It was showtime.

The beach ran for miles along the Atlantic. We were at the extreme West side, and looking towards the East, the sand extended over the horizon. The parking lot was almost as long, and the beach was littered with sand volleyball courts, beach rental equipment sheds, lifeguard towers, palm trees and outside showers. The ocean was calm and looking out, you could only see a few white caps breaking against the beach. We practically had the entire beach all to ourselves; there were only a few people left walking along the shoreline.

"Get ready" Lew hollered as he ran onto the court. We separated into two teams. It was Lew and Reno versus Phil and me. We decided to play the best two out of three and then the winning team would separate and play a game of one-on-one to decide the overall winner. From the start, Phil and I had trouble moving in the sand. We were both pretty exhausted when the first game ended, with us at the losing end of a fifteen to two spread. I stood ankle deep in the warm sand, bent forward, with my hands resting firmly on my knees. I looked over at Phil. He was walking around the court with his hands clasped behind his neck. We were both gasping for air as the next game started. The second game went even worse. By the time Reno was serving for the match, we had failed to even score a point.

Phil looked over at me, sand was plastered across his chest and back, "Hey Tango, screw it, let's just end this game and get cleaned up." I nodded, and Reno's serve landed between us, securing their victory. As

Reno and Lew whooped it up and congratulated themselves on their volleyball prowess, Phil and I walked off the court towards one of the showers. I had never showered over-looking the ocean, while listening to the sounds of seagulls. This was perfect. Lew and Reno decided that they needed a break as well. The sun had finally set and the amber glow from the streetlights was the only illumination along the beach.

Just as the stink of the public restrooms facilities hit us, Lew yelled out, "there's no frigging lights in this bathroom, where are the urinals?"

A voice called out seductively in the dark. "Over here baby." The four of us did an about face so fast I'm surprised no one got whiplash. We didn't know who was inside that dark stall, but we weren't about to find out. Phil and I then focused on cleaning up, while Reno and Lew went back to the court to finish the challenge. We washed the sand off our bodies, and returned to the court in time to see the final points in a rather quick finale. Reno was now the one bent over, trying to catch his breath. Lew was making quick work of him.

"Two-on-two volleyball is a lot easier than one-on-one," Reno said, as Lew's winning serve landed in the far corner of the court. As if our day had not been disturbing enough, Lew had won the challenge. God help us all.

"Dude, get your stuff off my bed!" were the first words out of Lew's mouth upon walking through the door to our hotel room. The room had been cleaned, the beds were made, the couch was folded back up and even the empty cups from the night before had been washed. They were stacked neatly on the counter in order to air dry. Room service equaled that of most five star hotels. We were all impressed. "I'm talking to you, Reno, move it. I'll be sleeping in the good bed tonight." Lew was really very proud of himself. As a matter of fact he was glowing. He strutted around the room with his chest stuck out.

As we began to settle down, I heard my cell phone beeping. The sound always irritated me, because it meant someone had left a message, usually it was work related. I went to the counter to pick it up and scrolled through the display to see who had called. It showed that I had three messages, all from the same number. *Who in the hell called my phone three times while we were gone?* I wondered aloud. Just then the phone rang again, startling me. I answered. "Hello."

"Hey Tango," came a cheery voice from the other end. It was Phil's wife.

"Hey, I left a few messages, I've been trying to get a hold of you guys all day," she said.

"Is there a problem?" I asked.

"No, I just miss my hunk a hunk of burning love."

I was about ready to gag and quickly searched the room for Phil. I had heard enough. "Phil," I yelled covering the mouthpiece, "it's your wife."

Meanwhile, Lew had been looking through the CD holder, apparently in search of something in particular. I had been watching him out of the corner of my eye while I was on the phone. He kept scowling over at me. "What's up?" I asked, walking over towards him.

"Did you bring the Bob Marley disk?" he asked.

"Oh crap, I forgot it," I replied, walking past him on my way out to the deck. I needed to check on my shorts. "Well Lew," I said, holding up my only pair of shorts I'd packed, "on the bright side, my green cargo shorts are dry; I can wear them again tonight."

We spent the next hour or so, before going out on the town, trying to unwind. Phil was still on the phone explaining everything in excruciating detail that had happened to us today to his wife. There was about a case of beer left in the fridge, the boom box was playing and we were taking turns using the facilities, showering and shaving. Once again, we passed the time by playing *'Who Sings This? Wrong... Drink a Beer'*. The game was rudely interrupted when Phil, who had just finished about a forty five minute long distance, cell phone call at my expense, asked Reno to "rub a little aloe" on his back. It was going to take more than beer to get that image erased from my mind.

"Let's get out of here. By the way, try to control yourselves tonight; I got a great challenge cooked up for the remaining bed." With that said we took a pinch of Skoal and headed out for *Louie's Backyard*. "By the way, Tango, how many nights am I going to see you in that same outfit?"

"It's the only party outfit I packed," I replied.

"Those things are going to be ripe," Lew smirked.

We decided to ride the scooters over to *Louie's Backyard*. It was quite a hike from our hotel, and we didn't feel like wasting time walking there and then strolling all the way back down Duval later on. When we first entered the bar we found it to be a little too sophisticated for our taste. It was a big white colonial mansion that stood in front of the Atlantic Ocean. The foyer opened into a huge dining hall that had floor to ceiling windows, which let the eye wander to a deck overlooking he ocean. The room was filled with people eating by candlelight, and all of the men were wearing sports jackets. We turned around and headed back out the front doors, went back out to the sidewalk and stood there for a minute contemplating what to do next. We thought the bar would be a little wilder, since it had been made famous in a song written by Jimmy Buffett. Reno noticed a strand of illuminated ground lights strung along the fence lining the side of the restaurant. We followed the sidewalk, along the side of the house; in the direction the lights were headed and when we cleared the brush, could see paradise. There was a small inlet beach area to our right and Phil had to duck underneath a wood sign that read *The Afterdeck Bar*. As we passed beneath the sign, the ocean immediately came into view. We were standing on a large wooden deck that jutted out over the Atlantic. Small Christmas lights were affixed to the railings and a hint of music was playing. The place was beautiful, but the atmosphere was much more casual than what we had found inside. We settled into four, weathered wooden chairs surrounding a table overlooking the water. The breeze blowing off the ocean was amazingly refreshing, and we watched the stars glisten off the incoming tide. All our worries from earlier in the day began to wash away. Our waitress, a rather sexy brunette, was arriving with four Bloody Marys. She was wearing an outfit at least two sizes too small, showing off some very nice curves. As a result, my gaze was transfixed as she positioned the drinks on our table. I removed the celery from my glass, licking the tomato juice from the stem, and proposed a toast. As we sat there sipping our spicy blends, something caught our eyes out in the ocean. There was a solitary light bobbing up and down a couple hundred yards off of the shoreline, and we each seemed to notice it simultaneously.

"What the hell is that?" Lew asked, pointing in the direction of the light.

"Beats me. Is it a beacon?" I asked.

"Can't be, it's moving. As a matter of fact it's heading our way." Reno added. The four of us continued to watch the light as it held a steady course straight towards us. The wind was picking up and the strong smell of the sea continued to flood our nostrils. As the object approached closer, we were able to discern the image; it was someone in a black, wet suit. The light we had seen was actually a flashlight strapped atop the swimmer's head. The person was holding a pole in one hand; a net in the other, and was continuously dunking his head in and out of the water. It was the strangest thing that I'd ever seen. What kind of a fool would be swimming around in the darkness of night way out in the middle of the ocean? Just then our focus was diverted from the ocean to our waitress. She had returned to see if we needed anything else. Evidently, I was the only one who enjoyed the Bloody Mary. Phil requested a round of Kalik's.

"What's that guy doing down there in the water?" Lew asked our waitress, as she started walking away.

She looked out towards the sea and simply shook her head. "Just diving." She smiled as she walked away.

It was going to be a few more days until we were able to shake the Midwest out of our systems. To our dismay, we were still acting and talking like sunburnt tourists as opposed to locals. Hopefully, we'd be able to blend in better as the week wore on. We certainly didn't want to look out of place for Little V's party.

We finished our beers and decided that if we didn't leave now, we'd end up staying here all night. The ambiance of *The Afterdeck Bar* was outstanding, but once again, the nightlife along Duval Street beckoned us. We walked around the side of *Louie's Backyard* and turned underneath a huge tree that stood beside the restaurant's sign out front. As I crossed in front of the sign, something landed on the sidewalk beside me. It hit the concrete with a loud thud. "Was that a papaya that almost hit me?" I asked, as I bent over to pick up the fresh piece of fruit. Sure enough it was. Upon landing, the papaya had burst open and a juicy, star-shaped constellation was protruding from the top of the fruit. I took a bite and promptly spit it out. It tasted awful.

"Dude, that's a mango." Lew laughed.

I felt like I had a mouthful of ants, my tongue felt like fuzz. "Despite what you've heard, papayas and mangoes really aren't that good," I said, starting up my scooter. "I'll tell you one thing; we're not driving the mopeds back from Mallory Square. I'll meet you guys back at the hotel parking lot."

We were looking for the perfect location to spend the rest of the evening as we made our way down Duval. The first place we came to, tucked alongside *Willie T's,* was simply called *The Bar*. Entering through the front door, a long ramp led patrons straight to the bar. Walking up the sloped floor, I looked over the railing and saw an extremely worn pool table that sat unoccupied in front of a row of six tall glass windows.

"How about a re-match?" Lew asked. Phil and I, never ones to back down from a challenge agreed and promptly found out that neither the sand volleyball court, nor the green felt of a pool table was where we found ourselves most comfortable. We were beat somewhat handily in a best of three competition. I scratched on the eight ball in the first game. The follow up game saw Phil display his prowess missing every shot he took, easily making it another defeat. Quite frankly, who cares what happened in the third game. The most enjoyable part of the bar was the four, comfortable, theater style chairs that sat between the pool table and the bank of windows overlooking the street. Relishing the comfort we found from the plush chairs, we sat and drank what remained from our beers in surprising opulence. Lew and Reno continued to congratulate each other on another ill-conceived victory.

"This reminds me, Phil. You owe me twenty dollars," bragged Reno

"Hey, what twenty dollars?"

"The twenty dollars I bet you when we drove off with our scooter. Remember? I said you'd be the first one to wreck the scooter," answered Reno.

"Come on, that wasn't my fault. Where's your heart?"

"Pay up sucker," Reno continued, ignoring his pleas for mercy.

"He's got you there," said Lew, "and while you're at it, cough up three thousand. Your wife can wire you the extra money."

Sighing, Phil dug deep into his wallet and slapped a twenty-dollar bill onto Reno's happy hand.

I had heard enough and went off to find a toilet.

As Lew and I walked to the bathroom, he couldn't help but keep up with the verbal abuse from the pool game. I tried to turn the doorknob to the bathroom and found it locked. "That's strange," I said. "The door is locked."

"I don't know about you, but I gotta pee like a race horse," Lew replied. "I'm waiting."

We stood there for a couple of minutes before we finally heard a toilet flush. Seconds later the door opened and out stepped a little Mexican guy wearing a cook's uniform. The smell from within the bathroom didn't quite hit us until after Lew had shut the door. There was both a urinal and a toilet inside, and I had made a wise choice in saddling up to the urinal. Lew had been stuck with the abused toilet and let out a moan when he pried the lid open with his foot, almost falling over backwards in the process.

"Scoot over," he said moments later, "We're sharing the urinal."

The Bar had an unusual clientele. The crowd inside was a cut rougher than the rest of the bars we'd been in. A couple of biker babes walked past us sporting more than a few colorful tattoos on their arms and backs. While eyeing the two leather-clad blondes, Phil's statement shocked us all. "Hey. if I was still single, I'd have a tattoo," he said as he nonchalantly finished his beer.

"Why let that stop you?" I asked. "I saw a tattoo stand just past *Rum Runners* last night. How about getting one tonight? If you get one, I'll get one." I was trying to egg him on hoping that his wife's wishes that he not get a tattoo would be obliged that night. Never in my wildest dreams did I think he'd go through with it. "I'd be up for that," Lew added. "What about you Reno?" To my astonishment, things were starting to get a bit more serious. The tattoo ladies, now walking around with beers, decided to sit right next to us.

"Have a seat, ladies," was Reno's great line welcoming them.

Phil felt them out by adding, "Hey, there won't be two huge biker guys wanting to beat our ass for sitting next to you both, will there?"

"We sat by you big guy."

"He's a big dude all right, but it can't use it for a pool stick," said Lew, with a huge smile while moving towards the ladies.

"Big sticks are over-rated," was the other gal's response, eyeing Lew.

"Yes they are, at least coming from the smallest guy here. In height, that is." Reno backtracked as he realized what he had just said.

We all started laughing and exchanged small talk with the girls learning their backgrounds. They were both wearing tight tank tops. Our eyes shifted the conversation to their tattoos. They each proudly showed their paint. The ones on their backs, bellies and arms. Reno had to touch one of the girl's belly tattoos, and lightly stroked the belly button ring in the process.

"This ain't the Pillsbury dough boy," Lew said.

Reno replied, "She's sure laughing like one."

"Let's play doubles in pool, and if the boys win, we'll show you our special tattoos," was the challenge thrown out.

"What happens if we lose?" Lew asked.

"Then you'll each have to get a tattoo," was the response.

Lew surveyed the crowd. I was smiling and raised my eyebrows. Phil shrugged his shoulders, and we all knew Reno was in.

"Best two out of three?" asked Lew.

"Sure. So, pick your twosome. We're not that good."

Reno jumped in saying "Me and Lew are taking the boys to victory, and these tattoos better be good. But just to make things more interesting, lets add in a round of free drinks for the winners, and if we do win, we get to see you both kiss passionately."

"Is that a deal?" Lew asked.

"Deal," the girls smiled.

Reno and Lew extended their hands and shook with the girls. The bet was sealed. We swam with the sharks earlier; let's just hope these weren't two more.

The flip of the coin hit the table and rested on heads.

Lew decided to break.

It was starting off well. Both teams traded off shot after shot. The girls then bought four shots of whiskey. They touched glasses and proceeded back to the game. Phil and I just took it all in from the comfort of the theater chairs, and let me tell you this, the view was nice. The one girl had a beautiful resonating, multi-colored sun on her back and when she turned around, the Aztec design on her ring-filled belly button put you in a trance.

Back to the game, Lew and Reno were all high fives, as Lew hit the last striped ball in, and called an easy last pocket shot. The next game started off with Lew hitting in two from the break, but ended with the girls knocking in three in a row – including the black ball. It was now even, and the girls were flirting more and more with Reno and Lew. I had to break it up at one point and get them focused on the task at hand – the last game. Suddenly the girls scratched, and Reno grabbed the cue ball to line up an easy shot.

"Don't just take the sitting duck. Take a manly shot." Stated one of the gals.

Reno started to move the ball.

Lew yelled, "Reno, just take the duck and line up your next shot. We got a lot riding on this game."

But Reno was not listening, and shot towards the far right corner, missing his target.

"Dude, I'm gonna kick your ass. Start paying attention."

Reno just stood there, holding on tight to the pool stick, humbly taking the harassment.

The game went back to an even exchange of decent shots. The gals had three solids on the table, and the guys had two stripes. It was now Lew's shot. He hit the green striped ball into the side pocket and then missed his next shot. The girls' next shot smacked in and before they could celebrate the cue ball followed it in. Reno jumped back into the game and lined up his next shot. This one wouldn't be easy as solids surrounded it. Reno stared down Lew and the girls.

"Bet you ten bucks, you can't hit it clean," said the girl with the Aztec belly tattoo.

"Does it have to go in?" asked Reno.

"Nope."

"It better, Reno," yelled Lew.

Reno placed a ten right by the pocket and proceeded to take aim. He pulled his arm back and with an aggressive swing, hit the cue ball. It headed straight for the striped ball, but unfortunately hit a solid ball resting next to it. The solid ball rolled slowly in the direction of the eight ball sitting by the side pocket. Seconds later, the solid ball tapped the eight ball, sending it falling into the pocket.

"Friendly fire!" was the girl's response, jumping up and down hugging her teammate.

Lew and Reno were in total amazement and after some major consulting from the girls were ready to take their medicine.

Reno slammed the rest of his beer. "Let's go right now. After what we've been through, I say we get something that will remind us of what happened today."

"Are you girls coming or staying here?" asked Lew.

"Oh, we wouldn't miss this for the world."

So we all strolled north, then west down a side walk that opened to a small tattoo parlor off the back of the store-front businesses.

The funny thing was, the closer we got to the tattoo stand, the more and more Reno started talking himself out of it. Finally, with the help from Lew, he decided to get one on his ass cheek. Big talker. He didn't want to do anything that might upset his bride to be, mere weeks before the wedding. In the end, he opted for a tattoo that he could hide.

Reno was elected to go first; before he changed his mind, and it was the funniest sight I'd ever seen. You ever see that guy in the public restrooms that has his pants on the floor at the urinal? Well Reno decides to go buck naked, so his shorts were resting on his ankles. The tattoo artist rested a shaggy towel on his ass crack and went to work. This gave the rest of us time to pick out designs.

We had drank a lot so far, and I don't know if it was the alcohol that had taken over, or if we were all delirious from the sun exposure we'd received during the day, but I swear Reno's initial comment was making a lot of sense. I did need a memento to remind me of the past days events – and a shark tattoo was just the ticket. However, as I sat in the tattoo parlor's black, vinyl chair, and felt the needle puncture my skin, I was instantly sobered to the fact that there was no turning back. What had sounded like a good idea at the time was beginning to seem more and more like a tremendous mistake. Whatever it was that got me to this point, I knew it wouldn't help me out any when I tried to explain why it actually made sense to have a shark tattooed on my right arm. Lew was in the adjacent room with Tiffany, his newfound girlfriend. I could hear him chuckling and yelling out time to time. I looked over at Phil, who was seated in the chair next to me. I couldn't tell what the hell was being painted above his right shoulder blade, but the symbol looked either Chinese or Ancient Egyptian. "So Phil, what exactly is that tattoo supposed to signify?"

"It's the Chinese symbol for peace and tranquility," I picked it out with Cherrie, he replied, grinning ear to ear.

"Well, I know for a fact those are two virtues you'll be begging for, when your wife sees that black smudge on your back," I laughed.

Cherrie just kissed him on the forehead and stood there smiling.

When it was all over, we left the tattoo stand changed for life. Phil had his tranquillity symbol. I was now wearing a tiger shark. Lew had opted for a small sea turtle on his ankle, and Reno had a tattoo on his ass.

Feeling slightly re-born, the four of us exchanged pleasantries with Cherrie and Tiffany. They were meeting some of their friends east of Duval at some bar. We were determined to head up Duval making our way towards *Capt. Tony's Saloon* in desperate need of something to numb the pain. So we told them we would all meet up later. My arm was on fire, but I could tell I was not the only one struggling. As we strolled through the muggy night in search of some liquid refreshments, I caught the other guys more than a few times grimacing while they rubbed their respective body parts. Moments later, with a rum punch in hand, I pointed across the bar. "Well Phil, you feel lucky? Or can you only feel peace and tranquillity now?" Not waiting for him to answer, I continued on. "Let's head down to that center room and play some more pool." "No more bets though, Reno. You lost ten bucks and have a tattoo on your ass," exclaimed Lew.

Everyone agreed and we proceeded to enter what I have come to think of now as my Key West lair. You have to understand that *Capt. Tony's Saloon* is more than simply a drinking establishment. It is a way of life for many. As the inside jacket of the book of matches I found at the bar states: "The saloon is not just a bar. It's the personality of Capt. Tony himself. Capt. Tony is the spirit of Key West and when you go to his place for a cold one, be prepared for anything. He's not the type to sit back and rest on his reputation." To this day, when I think of Key West, I think of *Capt. Tony's Saloon*, but more specifically, I think of that lone pool table and the offshoot room where it was housed. The reason for this is simple. *Capt. Tony's Saloon* reminded me of my childhood.

Growing up, I lived in a makeshift bedroom down in the basement of our house. Although the basement was riddled with asbestos, slugs, snakes and spider webs, I quickly grew accustomed to sharing space with the washer and dryer on a cold concrete floor, surrounded by a bare rock wall. Being the oldest of three boys, it was either sleep downstairs or share a room with one of my brothers. I opted for the basement. I went to sleep many nights to constant droning of our dryer. I had to learn to fall asleep within twenty minutes, or I'd be awoken to the sound of the buzzer. The house I grew up in only had one bathroom, but my dad thought it was another living room. He was in there all the time. As a result, my bathroom became the sump pump in the far corner that I shared living quarters with.

"Smells like my old room in here," I said, as we stepped down the stairs into what can only be described as the worst poolroom in Key West. Not only was the table slanted, the floor was also leaning in the same direction. The sheets of plywood that served as a floor creaked and groaned under our weight. It was as if the entire room was sinking into the sand beneath. The walls were rotting from the effects of numerous floods. Even the thousands of business cards, left by travelers throughout the years, that adorned the wood paneling were mildewed. Lew would swear every time we found ourselves congregated in a corner of the room that he could smell urine. The concrete foundation was stained from graffiti drawn years ago. However, the four foot tall by eight foot wide, campaign sign that hung on the wall, looked as if it was drawn only days ago. The words were written in bold red and black letters: "Elect Capt. Tony Tarracino Mayor. Eyes that care." A picture of Captain Tony himself was painted beside the slogan, the lines in his face showed the signs of a lifetime of hard living. We found out later in the evening that quite a few years ago, some of the locals decided that the current politicians did not have the best interest of the people of Key West in mind. They had their own agendas. So the locals decided to band together and they elected their favorite bartender mayor. That explained the sign we were standing under.

The shadows hung heavy in the room, since the only light source was from a Budweiser fluorescent lamp dangling precariously above the table. One of the light bulbs inside the lamp was humming and it flickered every minute or so. "Reminds me of my old room," I repeated, as I breathed in the stale air deeply. I racked the balls in place on the table. Despite the karma I felt in the room, Phil and I continued to lose yet another round of pool. "Damn!" I yelled, when Reno sank the eight ball to give him and Lew the victory in the third game. We posed for a few pictures underneath the legendary campaign sign before we headed out to get some fresh air. I was beginning to remember why I had left home in the first place. The mildewed basement in which I lived for eighteen years simply stunk.

"Well boys, let's not get too comfortable. The night is still young," Lew replied. "Tango, you've been nursing that drink long enough. Let's head over to *Ricky's Cantina* and see what band is playing tonight and find some chicks, maybe we'll run into Cherrie and Tiffany." Before I had time to argue, he stepped off his stool and was beginning to walk away. The three of us followed, if not reluctantly at first.

Ricky's Cantina was hopping. The place was packed. There was indeed a band playing, and after listening to a few songs, we finally were able to weasel our way into a spot at the bar. The four of us huddled in the far corner next to three empty bar stools. The bar at *Ricky's Cantina* was the only one I'd seen in Key West with a bank of televisions on the wall. Just about every channel you could think of was playing. The shows ran the gamut of everything from sports to the Playboy channel.

"Yo Ricky!" Lew yelled across the bar, in the direction of the only bartender working the place.

It took a few minutes but Ricky finally walked over; wearing cut off blue-jean shorts and a red *Ricky's Cantina* T-shirt with a white palm tree on the front. He was a rather odd looking fellow. Although he looked our age, he was out of shape. The past few years appeared to have been spent partying a bit too long and a bit too hard. He had dark circles underneath his eyes, which were, of course, bloodshot. Let's put it this way, being slightly overweight, he was no poster boy for good health. Upon closer inspection, his most distinguishing characteristic, however, was his long, curly red hair. It hung down around the middle of his back and was jutting out from underneath his hat in every direction. As if the hair on his head wasn't enough, he had grown a curly, red goatee that put both Phil's and mine to shame. It was at least four inches long.

"Yo Ricky!" Lew repeated, shouting in order to be heard above the amplified incoherent screams of the lead singer up on stage.

"My names not Ricky, its Mark," he replied. A thirsty Lew had finally gathered his attention. "If I was Rick, I wouldn't be working behind the bar," he continued, smiling at us. "What can I get for you guys?

You look parched." Grabbing a wet towel, he removed the empty glasses that had been left behind, pocketed the loose change, threw down four coasters, and wiped the wooden countertop clean.

"Do you make a rum punch?" I asked.

"One of the best on the island. The ingredients to it are written right over there on the wall," Mark replied, pointing over his shoulder.

I quickly read through them. "We'll take four."

Although the place was full, Mark spent a good majority of the night at our corner of the bar. We were tipping pretty well since the drinks were loaded with alcohol. It was either the money or the gal sitting beside us. Either way, it didn't matter. Throughout the next couple of hours, over a few more cocktails, we swapped stories. We told him about the shark attack and then Phil recounted his story in regards to Roger and Cynthia's accident.

"So I guess that explains the fresh paint on your arm. Nice shark." He had grabbed my arm and was inspecting the artwork. After a few moments, he awkwardly threw up his right leg on the bar and pulled down his sock. "How do you like this one?" he asked, referring to the great white shark that was tattooed across his calf.

"I like it a lot," I replied. "So why did you have it done on your calf. It's kind of hard to see."

"Well, believe it or not, I used to be in pretty good shape." This comment elicited a chuckle from both Reno and Phil. "Anyway, a few years back I had gotten into an extreme sports phase and had tried it all. I mean I'd done everything from parachuting off bridges, rock climbing, extreme kayaking, and even cliff diving. But on a trip with a few buddies to Australia one winter, things got a bit out of control. We were doing some scuba diving in dangerous waters. For a while, things were going fine, a couple of great whites were amongst us, along with a few other types of sharks, but they were all pretty much minding their own business. That's when, for whatever reason, I don't know why, I decided to try and see if I could actually touch one of the great whites. It just seemed like the right thing to do at the time. Biggest mistake of my life. As soon as I reached out, the damn thing turned around and attacked me."

"Where did he get ya?" Reno asked. "On the arm?"

"Nope, I pulled back my arm and started to swim away before he got me. He bit my leg, just above the knee on the fleshy part of the thigh."

"No way" I screamed in disbelief.

"Do you have a scar?" Reno continued.

"I don't ever show this to people, but after what you guys experienced today, what the hell." Mark took a few steps back and pulled his shorts up over his other thigh. The flesh he exposed looked like it had been through a meat grinder. The skin graft they used to patch him back up was darker than the rest of his leg, and hairless. Just looking at it made my stomach drop; it looked horrible.

"So what are you guys in town for anyway?"

After finding out we were down for Reno's bachelor party, he gave us a drink on the house. He told us to make sure we visited the Bahamian Village. That area of town was close to where he lived and was his favorite place to spend time on the island. "You got to eat at *Blue Heaven* at least once while you are here." "You're the second person we talked to today that has recommended that place," Lew said.

Over-hearing the reason we were in Key West, the girl sitting next to me at the bar leaned over and whispered in my ear, while pointing at Reno, "I thought he was gay," she said. It took me a few minutes to stop laughing. She lit up a cigarette and offered me one. She was nice enough looking, wearing a light blue sundress, with curly blond hair and a deep dark tan. I figured this was my opportunity to get to know her a bit better.

"Nice tattoo," she smiled.

"Thanks," I said while rubbing my arm. I reached out to grab the cigarette. "Ya got a light?" This was going to be interesting. I already had chewing tobacco inserted between my lower front lip and gum, and I had not smoked a cigarette for a few years. But what the hell, I was going to enjoy having a pretty girl talking to me, while I was on a nicotine high.

She blew out a stream of smoke. "I was listening to your story about what happened today. You guys are heroes. I would have died if I had found myself that close to a shark."

I was busy thinking to myself that maybe I'd had enough nicotine in my system for one day, as I took another long drag from the Virginia Slim she'd given me. I hadn't really been listening to her and simply responded "Yeah".

She frowned. I realized that if I didn't recover quickly, I'd lose her. I remembered hearing something about being a hero so I just winged it. "Well, my buddy and I looked at each other and figured, what the hell, if those were our sisters down there, we'd want someone to help them." My head was really swimming now. As a matter of fact, the room had begun spinning as well. I blinked and stubbed my cigarette butt into the ashtray. Immediately, my nausea started to slip away.

We talked quite a while longer, but, unfortunately, I can't even remember what we talked about, let alone what her name was. During the time, Lew had ordered four shots for the band and had left the bar to personally deliver them to the band mates who were on a ten-minute break.

"You guys want a shot?" Lew yelled, walking towards the stage, while holding the four drinks in front of him with both hands.

The lead singer's voice boomed over the speakers; his microphone had not yet shut off. "We've had three already." After apparently being turned down by the band, Lew took the drinks and sat down at a table with two beautiful women. He had been eyeing them all night. While sharing his drinks, they began laughing and talking. Phil and Reno had also wandered off into the crowd. I could see Reno was on the dance floor, but I couldn't find Phil. Watching Lew work his magic out of the corner of my eye, my competitive juices started flowing. Unfortunately I was at a disadvantage. I found myself alone at the bar talking with a girl who's name I did not remember and was too embarrassed to ask for again.

I felt a tap on my shoulder. "Hi Tango." It was one of the girls Lew had been talking to. Up close, she looked like a model. She took my head in her hands and planted a kiss on my lips. After she was done, she looked at me and winked.

"Thanks," I smiled.

I heard her say, "I gotta go collect my reward" as she turned and immediately walked back to the table. The bartender brought over two green shots.

"That figures," I sighed, glancing Lew's direction as he raised a glass my direction.

"Boy, you seem pretty popular tonight," the girl sitting next to me, laughed. "It must pay to be a hero."

"I'll tell you what, I think I need another cigarette," I said. "Anyway, a kiss by you would have been a real reward."

"Oh really?" she smiled, taking the cigarette out of her mouth and placing it in mine. Blowing smoke into the air, she leaned forward and gave me a kiss on the lips that took the breath from me.

"Dynamite!" I yelled, "You put her a distant second."

Whoever she was, Beth, Brandy or Debbie just smiled.

By this time, Lew was out on the dance floor with both of his girls, he was sandwiched between the two of them, moving to the rhythm of the music.

"So, do you want to dance?" I asked her.

I saw her look back behind the bar.

"What? Do you need the bartender's approval?"

"Nah, don't be silly. I'd love to dance." Grabbing my hand, she led me out onto the floor. We blended into the beat – well, she blended in well, and I just followed her lead.

"Come on tangerine. Turn it up a notch." Lew yelled.

"What does tangerine mean?" my girl asked.

I haven't heard that in a while, I thought, but before I could even start, Reno, with a full glass in his hand jumped in out of nowhere and started dirty dancing with my dance partner. His hands were all over her, and then one of Lew's girls does the sandwich with Reno. All we could do was laugh. I took the opportunity to sandwich my gal between me and Reno and the four of us swayed back and forth. However, before I knew it, Reno did an about face and started dancing solo with Lew's gal. That left me alone once again, dancing with a girl whose name I didn't know.

I glanced over at the bar and noticed Phil was back. He was talking with the bartender. Suddenly, there was a big commotion, and as everybody takes a few quick steps back, I see Reno lying on his back like a cockroach. Beer had spilled everywhere, including all over the blouse of the girl he had been dancing with. But it seemed as though everybody had gotten a touch wet. Lew helped him up, and we laughed at Reno's expense. Our dance party ruined, we moseyed on back to the bar. All of the girl's went into the bathroom to clean up. We were all stuck solo.

As I saddled back onto a barstool, Phil sat down next to me.

"Hey Tango."

"What's up?"

"You've been hitting on the bartender's girlfriend."

I sighed. *Now I gotta start all over,* I thought.

By now, Lew and Reno had returned from wherever and were prodding Phil and I to leave because the girls Reno had spilled beer on had left after cleaning up in the bathroom. Mark recommended a strip joint called the *Red Garter* that was across the mezzanine from *Ricky's Cantina.* Upon her return from the bathroom, I told the girl that I'd been speaking with that I had enjoyed talking with her throughout the evening and thanked her for the smokes. For some reason, I reached into my wallet and handed her my business card. I told her to give me a call if she was ever in Kansas. I gave her a kiss and said goodbye, as Phil pulled me out of the place. He slapped me on the back and teased me about spending the whole night talking to that girl – when it turned out she was already taken. On the way out, we stopped and shook hands with Mark. He was still pretty busy and quickly said to enjoy ourselves during our stay in the Keys. "You know we will," I hollered over my shoulder.

"Dude, how much have you had to drink?" Lew asked on our way out. "She wasn't even that pretty. I had to send over a real woman to try to get him to leave the bar, and that still didn't work." Talking to Phil, he punched me in the arm.

"Not to mention, she was just talking to you to pass the time from talking to the bartender" Phil said.

"I don't want to hear it," I said. "And watch out for the shark tattoo."

"Dude, it ain't gonna smear," Lew said, punching me again, even harder.

"I know, but it hurts like hell."

Lew took this comment as a reason to punch me a third time.

Even Phil took a stab at me. "Yeah, at one point, I looked over at Tango, and there was an inch and a half long ash hanging from his cigarette." They were all laughing at my expense by now.

"Dude, at least you didn't get hit on by a guy while you were in there," Lew said, saving me from any more ridicule.

"What are you talking about?" Reno asked.

"Well, after those two girls I was talking to left, I got up and walked to the edge of the dance floor to get a closer view. While I was standing there this older guy was dancing next to me. He put his arm around me and whispered in my ear, 'I'm a sailor, and I just got into port'. It must have been a pick up line, but I wasn't buying what he was selling."

We all started laughing. "What did you say?" I asked.

"I said 'Good for you,' and walked away."

I don't quite remember when it happened, but somewhere between ordering a slice of pizza and beginning the long walk back to the hotel, all of the alcohol Reno had ingested began to catch up with him. He had been complaining non-stop about not feeling well and it was really starting to annoy me. Before I could say anything Lew yelled out, "The challenge for tonight is..."

"Oh God, I almost forgot," Phil moaned.

"What's in store for us tonight, Lew?" I asked.

"Follow me," Lew said. "Reno and Phil, it's about time you guys saw the Southernmost Point. Don't you agree?" He headed West off Duval and then South down Whitehead. The street was more residential and, much calmer. I remembered two things on that walk. One was Lew saying, 'Dude, we just passed Hemingway's House' and the next was standing in front of the concrete monument once again. Well, at least Phil, Lew and I were standing. Reno had sat down on the curb and was holding his head between his knees, trying desperately not to throw up.

"Boys, tonight's challenge for the last remaining bed brings us back to the ocean. Your challenge, should you choose to accept it, will be to walk down these rocks in front of the Southernmost Point in the United States and submerge yourself in the ocean. Then the first person to climb through that window in the concrete shack next to the Southernmost House wins." I knew Reno was out of this contest, so once again it came down to Phil and me.

"Hey, I'm sick of getting my clothes wet." Phil complained, but he started to edge over the ledge anyways.

I felt the tide start to swing my way. "Good thing I'm still wearing what I wore last night," I said as I hurriedly climbed over the edge, onto the rocks and yelled, only seconds before diving head first into the ocean. I was still wearing my clothes and cursed myself for forgetting to remove my only article of clothing worth any money at all: my sandals. I had just bought those sandals two weeks ago and they cost more than the rest of my outfit combined. Upon resurfacing I heard Phil complaining to Lew that I'd do anything to win that bed, so he may as well stay dry on the shore. The funny thing was, Phil was complaining while he was submerged waist deep in the water. Not wanting to complete only one half of the challenge, I swam back to shore and headed over to the shack. The entire shack was made out of concrete, even the roof. It sat adjacent to the two graves I had seen earlier. As I struggled to hoist myself into the small window, located about five feet above the shoreline, a terrible thought occurred to me. 'What if this was a tomb?' I lowered myself back down onto the rocks and took another look. It certainly could have been a mausoleum. That's when the catcalls began. "What's the matter Tango, you chicken?" Lew yelled.

"Maybe, I'll jump in after all," Phil added.

Well, mausoleum or not, I couldn't let Phil tie up the challenge. I leapt up towards the window. My elbows scraped against the ledge that I was propped onto. I stuck my head inside the tomb. Instantly a spider web wrapped its way around my face. There's nothing worse than to walk through a web, unless of course, you're inside a tomb when it happens. I tried to suppress my urge to scream. Figuring things couldn't get any worse; I wriggled my way in through the window. It was pitch black and with nothing but a hard floor to stop me, I toppled inside. I wasn't about to stick around and figure out what else was in here with me, but there was a strong smell of decay in the room.

"Aaaahhhh!" I yelled.

I could hear everyones voice outside, yelling back at me. I hung out thirty more seconds until I couldn't stand it anymore. I was staring to freak myself out. I immediately dove headfirst back through the way I had come in. I emerged from the shack, slightly scratched, but nonetheless victorious to a loud roar from the crowd.

"That's two in a row for you, Tango," Lew said.

"Looks like I'll be sleeping comfortably again tonight," I yelled, my arms spread out in a victory pose. A little blood trickled from my elbow and made its way along my arm, coming to rest fittingly inside the tattooed shark's mouth. I relished my victory the entire way back to the hotel and was even more proud of my accomplishment when my head fell comfortably against the pillows moments later. It had been an interesting day to say the least. A day that would haunt me for many years to come. I laid there staring at the ceiling recounting the days events and simply shook my head in disbelief. The sting of the tattoo was beginning to pierce trough the numbness of the alcohol's effect. My thoughts drifted to Roger and Cynthia and then floated over to Brooke and Kelly. Before I knew what happened, I was asleep.

CHAPTER SEVEN

Half baked cookies in the oven
Half baked people on the bus
There's a little bit of fruitcake
Left in every one of us

Jimmy Buffett
Fruitcakes

I awoke from my slumber, a comfortable one I might add, to the sound of my cell phone ringing. There's nothing like the feeling one gets while sleeping off a long night of drinking from the comfort of a soft mattress on a queen-sized bed. Apparently, Reno had decided to sleep on the floor last night, because those were his legs that I tripped over on my way to the counter to answer my phone. I glanced quickly at the display. It was a local number.

"Tango here." I said with a graveled voice that was barely audible. I cleared my throat. "Hello."

"Hi Tango, it's Mark." His voice was way too loud and it seemed as though a knife was being jammed into my eardrum, my head was pounding.

"Who?" I mumbled.

"Mark. The bartender from *Ricky's Cantina*. Remember?"

I massaged my temples and tried to recall who he was. "Oh yeah, shark attack, how could I forget you? So how did you get my phone number?"

"I just wanted to thank you for helping me get laid last night," he replied. "I got the number from Elisha."

"I don't know what you're talking about. Who's Elisha?"

"Remember that girl you were talking to at the bar last night?"

"Yeah," I yawned, while simultaneously scratching myself.

"Well, she was my ex-girlfriend. She's Elisha. Thanks for entertaining her last night because that kept her around."

"Whatever, to be honest, I can't even remember what we talked about." I looked over at Lew, who had sat up in his bed during the process of the conversation. He was rubbing his face. "Well Mark, thanks for calling man, but I gotta go, I just woke up and need to take a serious leak. We'll stop by *Ricky's Cantina* tonight."

"Tango. Wait. Before you hang up, I was calling to say I am heading over to the *Blue Heaven*. Why don't you all meet me for breakfast? It's on me. I'll pay."

"Sounds good to me," I said.

Not able to wait any longer, I was already heading towards the toilet. "Well, lets meet there around eleven o'clock. That'll give us an hour or so to get up and going. O.K.?"

"Catch ya later," Mark said.

"Later," I said, feeling better now that my bladder was emptied. "Rise and shine boys!" I yelled, re-entering the living room. "It's chow time."

"Dude, who the hell was that on the phone? Don't tell me it was Phil's wife again." Lew asked.

Lew and I weren't the only ones awake. Phil had pried himself out of the fold up and was in the kitchen looking for something to eat. Reno, however, was still sound asleep. It wasn't until the three of us had shaved, showered and were already dressed that the lump underneath the covers on the floor began to stir. It seemed to take an enormous amount of effort, but Reno eventually sat up.

"Good morning sunshine," Lew said, throwing one of the couch cushions over his shoulder towards Reno, hitting him right in the face. Reno yawned deeply and rubbed his sun burnt neck.

"So what's up?" Reno asked. He was now rubbing his face. "What time did we get in last night?"

"Late." Phil replied.

The three of us were settled in front of the television. Lew, controlling the remote, flipped through the channels. Reno took his time and slowly got dressed. Continuing a trend, he wasn't much for words this morning either. He did, however, mention that he had no recollection of anything that happened after we left the pizza parlor.

"You mean you don't remember walking past Hemingway's House on the way to the Southernmost Point?" Lew asked.

"Nope," Reno said. He was now dressed and looking for some juice to wash away the remains of the night. He settled for some red soda.

"Dude, you were sitting on the buoy when Tango jumped into the Atlantic," he replied.

Reno turned to face us, he looked confused. "I don't remember the buoy at the Southernmost Point. Was it floating? Anyways, are we eating this morning or what? I'm starved."

We laughed and decided it was time to ignite the mopeds and drive over to the Bahamian Village. Reno was not the only hungry one in the bunch. I too, was famished. Bounding down the stairs, we crossed the pool patio and, in order to get to the parking lot, took a short cut through the sliding door that separated the office from the pool. As we walked through the lobby, the front desk clerk stopped Lew.

"Mr. Lewis?" a voice from behind the counter asked.

"Yeah," Lew said, startled. "That's me."

"Two gentlemen came by looking for you and your friends yesterday. They said they were investigating a crime and requested the names and addresses of you along with your three friends. I wasn't going to give the information out, at least not without your approval, but when I rang your room, there was no answer. They showed me their badges, and were very rude. I just gave them what you filled out in the registry. After that, I was quite relieved when they left right away."

"That's fine," Lew replied. "My friend was a witness to a traffic accident yesterday. Two of the people we had been snorkeling with got killed."

"My heavens," the clerk gasped, his hand covering his mouth.

"The Police Chief said that he might send someone out if they needed any additional information from us. Thanks for the update." We followed Lew out through the other sliding glass door and walked over to the scooters. It was already hot outside; we were going to require some time in the pool later on in the day.

We walked up to the spot in the parking lot where we had left the three scooters. Resting against the back wheel of mine was a dark blue ball, with yellow and red flames painted onto it. At first, I thought it was a basketball, but when I bent down to pick it up, it was much too spongy to be a basketball. Closer inspection revealed it to be a rubber kick ball. I threw it down on the concrete and it bounced up over my head. It was in perfect condition. "This might come in handy later on," I said, placing it into the basket behind my seat. "Finders, keepers."

The Bahamian Village was one of the more unique neighborhoods we had visited thus far on the island. As if Key West wasn't strange enough on it's own accord, when you turned off Duval and headed southwest, underneath the flowered arch at Petronia Street, it was as though you'd left the island altogether and had landed in the middle of the Bahamas. Although some of the differences were obvious, such as the chickens, hens and roosters running around all over the place. They were clucking, pecking, cock-a-doodle-dooing and generally making a nuisance of themselves. But aside from the obvious, there were quite a few subtle variations. All of the street signs and shop windows were written in a different language, Bahamian, I figured, but since I can only read and write in English, it could have been anything. Another image that struck me as odd, when I scanned the street, was that nobody seemed to own a car that actually ran. There were, however, plenty of vehicles up on blocks, explaining the tons of bicycles parked in front of the houses. The bikes, painted in an array of colors, looked to be the only mode of reliable transportation available on this section of the island. We continued cruising down the street in search of what we now assumed must be an authentic Bahaman style cuisine awaiting us at *Blue Heaven*. Passing hand painted homes and businesses, we noticed that blue and white were the predominant colors. Everyone that we passed on the street seemed to be a refugee from the Bahamas; the women walked through the streets with baskets of laundry on their head, the children played shoeless and shirtless in the street and the men simply sat on the porches drinking coffee and playing backgammon.

After wandering through the streets of the village for quite some time, we finally found *Ricky's Blue Heaven*. We pulled up to the curb in front of the restaurant and parked the scooters; locking them, just in case, next to a rickety picket fence that stood about six feet tall. This gray fence was all that separated the street from the dining area.

The four of us walked around the outside along the sidewalk towards the entrance. The restaurant was not out of place. It looked every bit as run down as the rest of the establishments on the street. The exterior walls were originally painted white, but the dust from the streets had been baked onto the walls over the years and they now looked yellow. We passed what resembled a broken down old house, which served as both the gift shop and kitchen. Entering through the front gate, it was tough to tell if you were inside an actual restaurant or not.

A beautiful Spanish girl greeted us. "How many this morning, guys?" Our hostess asked smiling. She was wearing a green sarong with a black silk shirt that was pulled tight and knotted in the back. She was drop dead gorgeous.

"We're still waiting on a friend," Lew replied. "There will be five of us altogether though."

"Feel free to wait at the bar," she said, pointing to her right. The bar reminded me of something you would see straight out of a travel brochure. It was built out of bamboo stalks and palm tree leaves, and was shaped in a semi-circle. I noticed that to the far left of the bar, behind where you sat, there was a staircase leading up to a second floor deck. Built above the bar itself was an old-fashioned steel, water tank. It looked as though the gutters from the roof were positioned so that the rainwater was being funneled into the top of the open tank. I was hoping that this wasn't where the ice water came from.

Still a bit early, it was no surprise to find the bar empty. We each took a seat on a barstool and waited for Mark to arrive. The bar was separated from the actual dining area by a sand covered floor. The sandy area had everything that you might expect to find while on the beach. There were plastic buckets and shovels for building sand castles and a variety of other types of kid's toys. However, most unusual was the image of live poultry everywhere. At first I thought I was seeing things, but a second look validated that there were indeed roosters running wild amongst the guests. Even funnier still, at least a couple of the roosters were currently being chased by children. I watched and laughed as a boy about four years old gave chase, and ran right under a table of unsuspecting diners, almost causing an elderly lady to fall off the picnic bench she was sitting on. I looked around the rest of the yard.

"You guys want a Bloody Mary? I started drinking one at seven thirty this morning." I turned around and looked at the bartender. He looked like a biker with long hair, muscles, and just a hint of a bad attitude. He was sipping a Bloody Mary.

"No thanks," I replied. "I think we all got our fill last night. Speaking for myself, I gotta get some food in my body before I start drinking again."

He frowned at my reply. "Suit yourself." I caught him staring at my arm.

"Is that a shark tattoo?" Not waiting for me to reply, he rolled up his sleeve. "You want to see mine? I got a stingray." He was grinning, ear-to-ear.

We swapped tales about how we decided on our respective tattoos. The other three guys had heard enough and one by one they got down off their barstools and explored the scenery of the restaurant.

I felt a tap on my shoulder. I turned, figuring it would be one of the guys, and was surprised when I was greeted by a smiling Mark. Judging from the goofy grin plastered across his face, he hadn't been lying about getting reacquainted with his ex-girlfriend. The hostess was standing beside him and we rounded up the others, and were seated at one of the patio tables in the middle of the dining area.

"So did you guys find anything interesting while you looked around?" I asked.

"Hemingway's prize cock is buried over there," Reno replied, grabbing a menu.

"Yeah, and that outside stall over there says that showers cost one dollar, two dollars to watch," Lew added, pointing towards a bamboo shower that was over by the exit. "If you ask me, our hostess is starting to look a bit dirty; anyone besides Phil got a couple of dollars?"

Our waiter came by and took our orders. The seafood omelet sounded good to me. The rest of the guys ordered a variety of food and we sat back in our chairs, waiting for the meals to arrive. I felt something brush past my leg and leaned to the right just in time to see the rear end of a rooster dart underneath our table. Phil, who was sitting across from me, suddenly jerked his legs. His knees slammed into the table and caused his glass of water to knock over. My guess was that the rooster had continued along his course and had just buzzed Phil. He turned and watched the rooster run off.

"Hey, look at those chickens," Phil gasped, scooting his chair backwards to avoid a lap full of water.

"Dumb ass," Lew replied, "those are roosters." We were all laughing at Phil's expense.

"So Mark, you haven't said a word since we sat down. I'm not much of a morning person myself, but what gives, it's almost noon. Surely, you're awake by now." As Reno asked this, our waiter finally arrived with our orange juice. I was consciously making an effort to avoid drinking the water, still worried about its origins.

"Well Reno," Mark started, clearing his throat, "to be honest with you, so far I haven't been able to get a word in edge wise, I was just waiting for you guys to shut the hell up." He laughed and took a sip of juice. "Nah, seriously, I just wanted to treat you guys to lunch as a show of thanks. I don't know what Tango said to my girlfriend, Elisha, last night, but it worked. She decided to move back in with me and we agreed to try and give our relationship another shot. Not to mention, you guys left me one hell of a tip."

I interrupted him there. "Stop it, Mark, you'll make me cry."

Unfazed, he continued talking. "Unfortunately, Elisha had to leave this morning. Well, it's not really unfortunate, she's driving right back with her stuff, but that won't be until next week. What are you guys doing tonight?" Before any of us could answer, he said "If you're free, I can get you into the best party of the year. That is, if you're up for it."

"That wouldn't happen to be Little V's party would it?" Lew asked.

"Yeah, you've heard about it?"

"Lets just say we've already been invited, sort of second hand you could say," Lew replied. It was true that Captain Bill had invited us to go along, but there was still some concern on whether or not he could actually get us into the party, since we were officially uninvited. Mark's next comment put that issue to rest.

"My invite is golden. Trust me; getting you four into the party is not even a question tonight. I promise. Besides, I have more than enough room on my boat for you guys. The other bartenders are working the earlier shift, I don't have to get there until after midnight. What do you say? I don't want to have to ride all the way over there by myself."

"How can you be so sure that you can get us in?" I asked.

"Because I'm working the main bar at the party tonight."

I sat there, letting this sink in. I ran it over in my head, from all the angles and had to admit, the plan seemed flawless.

"Of course it will," Mark smiled. Just as he said this, our food arrived. We high-fived and got down to business.

The five of us enjoyed an exquisite brunch. The food was so mouth watering, that any attempt at conversation usually reverted back to a comment about how good our meals were. A few of the details for the evening, however, were hashed out during the course of the feast. Mark told us to meet him around eleven o'clock at the pier on the North end of the island. Ironically, it sounded like the same pier Captain Bill had told us about. Our plan was to call Captain Bill and let him know we'd secured another ride over to the party.

Before I knew it, our plates were empty, the check was paid, and we were getting up to leave. Outside, we shook hands with Mark. He had driven his Jeep over to the restaurant from his house and was now on his way to the bar to start working. "How far away do you live?" I asked, gesturing towards his Jeep.

"Not far. I live a couple of blocks south of here off Whitehead. I normally walk here, but I needed to run a couple of errands before work." We told him we'd catch up to him later on in the evening. Looking at the time, we still had a few hours before the scooters had to be returned. This was good, because Reno was starting to get a bit tired of having to share his scooter with Phil. Needless to say, Lew was dreading the scooter's return. He knew for sure that he was going to lose his deposit.

I bent down to remove the lock from my scooter's front wheel. The sun was already blazing through my cotton tank top. "So what do you guys feel like doing?" I asked.

"I'll be damned if we leave this island without a toe ring. I saw a shop yesterday called *The Toe Ring King*. Saddle up and follow me." As usual, Lew could be counted on to have a plan.

There was limited parking available along the storefront, so we had to settle for a spot in front of an old, brick cathedral. There was a group of about twelve bums sitting on the worn, concrete steps singing. As the group of bums finished the chorus to an old fifties tune, the title of which escapes me now, a couple of them left the steps and approached us, their hands extended out in hopes for a tip. Phil immediately retreated to the other side of the street.

"Give us a dollar, and we'll sing you a song," said the bum standing closest to us. He was wearing a black T-shirt and ratty blue jeans. His hair was cut into a stylish mullet, and his sideburns had grown into perfect lamb chops. He was short, fat and the stink of beer and cigarettes followed him.

"I don't want to hear any songs," Lew replied, smiling.

"Well then pay me a buck and you can take our picture," the bum suggested.

After snapping a few shots, the bums hamming it up for the camera, Lew pulled out a few dollars. He handed them to the short bum with the lamb chops. "I tell you what; for those two bucks, you and your friends here need to keep an eye on our scooters for us. We'll only be gone for about an hour."

"That's a deal," he said, greedily snatching the cash from Lew's grasp.

The four of us started walking away, when Lew turned around and hollered. "Dude, you also better watch that ball." He was referring to the kick ball that was still in my basket.

Another bum wearing nothing but a pair of cut-off jeans hollered back. "Well can we play with it?"

"Sure" Lew replied. "Just make sure it doesn't get lost." He turned around and we continued walking towards *The Toe Ring King*. The King's shop was located a couple of blocks over, but before we got there, we stopped and did a little shopping at a few jewelry kiosks. Outfitted with a variety of necklaces, bracelets, and beads for later that night, we headed across the street to shop for toe rings. I had visions of vast walls full of toe rings imbedded in my mind, as I approached the entrance.

A large wooden foot, with a ring painted on each oversized toe was holding the door ajar. Crossing the threshold, I was disappointed to say the least. The shop was about as big as our hotel's bathroom. The four of us stood shoulder to shoulder in front of a solitary display case.

We all turned around and headed back out. After we left, Lew commented, "she was not the King of toe rings."

We arrived back in front of the cathedral about an hour later. The bums were gone. Our ball was gone.

"They stole our ball!" Lew yelled. "That figures."

A bum we had not seen earlier was sitting on the very top step. He was crouched in the corner with his back resting against the wall of the stairs. It appeared as though he had just awoken from a not so restful slumber.

"Where did all of your buddies go?" Lew asked.

The weathered old man looked at us. "Who?" His voice croaked. He yawned and then proceeded to scratch himself vigorously. He actually had clumps of sand crusted into his beard, and was quite literally, the dirtiest person we'd seen thus far on the island.

"All the dudes that were here earlier. They were singing," Lew replied.

"Oh. They all left," he said.

We all looked at each other. "They stole our ball," Reno said.

We headed over to our scooters and Lew asked, "Dude, which way did they go?"

"I think they just went around the corner." He waved in the direction they had gone.

We saddled up and rode the scooters around the side of the church, in search of the missing bums. Lew was the first to make the turn around the corner. His scooter stopped immediately. As I caught up to him, I saw our ball sailing through the air. I figured there must have been a basketball hoop on this side of the cathedral. I was wrong. Flashbacks from grade school instantly resurfaced. There were eleven bums lined up against the wall, their backs pressed firmly to the bricks. The bum we had spoken to earlier was standing about twenty feet in front of the others. He had just thrown the ball. They were in the midst of a classic game of dodge ball.

The ball slammed harmlessly against the brick wall and rebounded back to the shirtless bum wearing the cut off blue jeans, just as Reno and Phil came to a stop beside Lew and I. We sat atop our idling scooters, too stunned to speak. Lew quickly got out his camera and snapped a few pictures.

"I guess you guys want your ball back," yelled the bum with the mullet haircut. He shuffled his feet like a depressed schoolboy, not wanting recess to end. I heard the groans reverberating in the alley from a few other remaining participants in the game. They were all just looking at us, with puppy dog eyes.

"No dude!" Lew shouted, clapping his hands. "We're playing." He turned off his scooter and rested it on the kickstand. Jumping off, he motioned for the rest of us to join him. We got off our scooters to a resounding cheer.

The short bum with the lamb chops approached us. He appeared to be the leader of the pack. Walking beside him was a bum who stood about seven feet tall, wearing the grungiest pair of cutoff blue jeans I'd ever seen. To call them blue was actually a lie, in reality they were cutoff brown jeans. He was wearing a grease stained, blue jean vest that was only slightly cleaner. The vest was unbuttoned all of the way, exposing his skinny chest. He had hair that hung down to the top of his ribcage and a mustache that was about an inch below his chin. He was wearing a blue bandanna in an attempt to keep all of the hair out of his eyes. "Hi, I'm Elvis," Mr. Side Burns said, his hand extended out towards Lew. "And this here is Ted Nugent," he pointed, with his thumb toward the tall bum standing next to him. As Lew shook hands with Elvis Presley, I shook hands with Ted Nugent.

"Ted, you look much bigger in person," I said, shaking his blackened hand. I was wondering to myself when the last time Ted had bathed, and had to consciously suppress the urge to wipe my hand off on my shorts. We introduced ourselves and turned around to introduce Reno and Phil. I had to laugh when I turned. Phil had yet to get off the scooter and he had an 'I can't believe we're doing this' look plastered across his face. Reno, a bit more receptive, had already put an arm around Elvis and was engaged in what appeared to be a serious debate.

"Come on, Phil. Get over here," Lew hollered. Phil begrudgingly got off the scooter and made his way over to introduce himself. Having already met Elvis and Ted, we found out that the bum with the mullet cut, was named Three Bears. Yankee, who was wearing a New York Yankees baseball cap, and Casper, who was dressed in white shorts and a white sailor's cap, were two of the others. I would be lying if I said that I remembered the names of the other five or six bums that were still lined up against the wall.

"It's been a while since I've played dodge ball," Reno said. "What are the rules?"

Casper spoke up immediately. "The boundaries are the left hand side of that car all the way over to the fence. You gotta stay between there with your back against the wall. Three Bears won the last game, so he has honors and is throwing. If he hits you, you're out. But if you catch the ball, then you get to throw, and Three Bears lines up against the wall with the rest of us still left in the game. The person throwing when the last guy gets hit, wins."

"Well, that's how I remember it. Let's go," I said, walking over to a spot against the wall. Reno and Lew followed my lead. It took a few seconds for Phil to line up; in fact; I think he was the last guy to pick a spot along the wall. However, as soon as his back touched the bricks, Three Bears threw a missile right at him. Phil ducked out of the way and was almost hit as the ball rebounded off the brick wall.

"You better watch yourself over there, Phil," Reno yelled.

After Phil's near miss, Three Bears next few throws didn't even come close to hitting anybody. His fourth or fifth throw, however, nailed Ted Nugent right on the head, causing his bandanna to fall to the ground. As if nothing had happened Ted just stood there, grinning.

"Hey Ted," yelled Three Bears. "You're out." He waved his thumb like an umpire calling out a baserunner

"I am?" he replied. I think it was safe to say that Ted had been hitting the bottle early today. Shrugging his shoulders, he walked off the court and took a seat on the sidelines.

Surprisingly, Three Bears was not in peak physical condition. After a few more throws it was evident that the velocity of his fastball had started to dwindle a bit. Just then, a thought occurred to me. I looked over at Reno and Lew, who were standing beside me to my left and yelled, "Boys get ready." Although Phil was on the extreme right side, he was still able to hear that the gauntlet had been thrown down. "The last one standing, out of the four of us wins the bed tonight." To my delight, Reno, Lew and Phil all agreed.

Hearing all of the commotion I had been making, Three Bears focused his next throw on me. My plan worked perfectly. Three Bears threw a wounded duck right at me. I caught it easily. It was now my turn to throw.

I smiled wide as I dribbled the ball between my legs from my spot touching the wall and turned to face the row of derelicts in front of me.

"You got nothing," one of the bums heckled at me.

"Bring it big man," another one added.

Not wanting to waste any time whatsoever, I proceeded to unleash hell. I rifled the ball in Lew's direction. He jumped to his right and the ball ricocheted off the wall and nailed one of the nameless bums right in the ankle as he tried to run away. Unfortunately, he'd had a bit of alcohol in his system and as the ball struck him, he was knocked off balance and stumbled across the parking lot. He tripped over a concrete curb and fell on the asphalt, scraping his leg in the process. When he regained his balance and stood back up, there was a long line of blood trickling from his knee.

"Whoa! That son of a bitch means business," Ted yelled, from his spot on the curb, slapping his knee.

"So much for a friendly game fellows," I replied. Elvis had seen enough and walked off the court. He stood next to Ted and started babbling incoherently about the police.

Lew was lucky on my first throw. He was not so lucky on the second throw. Aiming right for his mid-section, I threw the ball. For a split second, Lew froze. In my opinion, he was trying to decide whether to catch the ball or jump out of the way. When he realized it was hurtling through the air, heading right for his package, he opted to try and catch it at the last second. The ball slammed into his hands and fell to the ground. Lew was my first victim. Figuring Phil would be an easier target; I faked a throw in Reno's direction and instead threw it at Phil. Like a deer trapped in the headlights, he stood there watching the ball as it struck him in the chest. I focused my attention now solely on Reno. It took a few throws, and a couple of bums bit the dust in the process, but eventually a tired Reno took a hit, his dice flew against the wall in the process. I had successfully won the challenge. The bed was mine, but the game was still on. There were about five bums remaining, and they were nervous as hell about being hit, but excited at the same time with the thought of winning the game.

Four throws later, there was only one bum remaining against the wall. It was Casper, and let me tell you, he had moves like a ghost. It took me at least ten tosses to hit him, but, eventually, he went down like the rest. Today was my day. I was king of the dodge ball court. Having just finished posing for pictures with the participants of the game, we were debating whether or not to play a re-match when things started to get ugly.

Since leaving the court after being hit, Reno had been talking with Elvis and eventually Lew had joined them. I don't know what they had been saying, but suddenly Elvis yelled out hysterically, while pointing at Lew. "I know what you're doing. You're a cop!" He then grabbed Reno's shirt and screamed, "he's wearing a wire." Elvis viciously lunged forward, grabbing Reno's new shell necklace and ripped it off. Reno got a bit excited by all of this and proceeded to get into a scuffle with Elvis. It looked like more of a wrestling match than a fight when both Ted Nugent and Lew pulled them apart. A delirious Elvis Presley ran off screaming at the top of his lungs. He stumbled over to the side of the building, pushed open a green wooden half-door that was cut into the concrete and escaped into the darkness inside.

"Where'd he run off to?" I heard Reno ask Ted, who was standing next to him. "He just tore off my necklace."

"That's were we sleep man. It keeps us dry. Anyway, don't worry about him man, he freaks sometimes."

After that spectacle, we decided that maybe a re-match would not be the wise thing to do. I walked over to Casper and gave him a five spot for coming in second. Seeing this, Reno yelled out, "Cool, Casper has got your money." Hearing that, all but a few of the bums gave chase. Only Three Bears was left standing there with us. He was still holding the ball.

"So, do you guys want you're ball back?" he asked.

"Nah," Lew replied. "You can keep it. You'll get more use out of it than we will."

"Hey, thanks man," he grinned. "You cops rock."

Walking back to the scooters, I looked at Reno and Phil's bike. "Reno, your back tire is a little low." It was time to return the scooters, before we had another casualty.

Phil hopped on the back of Lew's scooter, to be safe, and we headed towards the rental place to return what remained of our scooters. "Dude, we just played dodge ball with some bums!" Lew yelled, giving me a high-five. We sped away from the curb, heading in the direction of the scooter rental lot.

To our delight, the same lady we had met yesterday was still working the scooter rental stand. Her disposition had not changed in the past day and a half; she was as grumpy as ever. The rental stand was overflowing with prospective customers in search of some wheels. Returning the scooters, with gas tanks that were practically empty, would have been a much bigger deal, had we not been missing one. The four of us placed the three scooters up on their kickstands and were immediately intercepted by the moped rental lady. She was frantically flipping through the pages attached to her clipboard. "Where's thirty seven?" she asked.

"It's a long story," Lew said, shaking his head.

"Well, I ain't got time for stories. Did it break down?"

"Nope. It's at the bottom of the ocean," Lew replied. "You got time for stories now?" Apparently she did. She handed her clipboard to one of her co-workers, and told him to take over for her for a while. Reno and I let Phil and Lew go off with the moped lady to try and work out an agreement on the compensation required to pay for the damages. They took a seat on an empty bench. Figuring that it might take some time, Reno and I went across the street to the liquor store. We needed to stock up on some beer for the remaining afternoon and evening before we took on our version of Bourbon Street.

Our plans for tonight included taking turns choosing a place to drink, with, of course, that person buying a round. Our goal was to hit as many bars along Duvall as possible. Once the drink was finished, it was the next persons turn to choose a new bar and a new drink. We wanted to hit as many bars as we could on the main drag, then set out on Mark's boat to get into Little V's party.

We left the liquor store with plenty of beer and snacks. Looking across the street, I was able to see that Lew and Phil were still negotiating, so we walked the beer back to the room and placed it all in the refrigerator. By the time we got back outside, Lew and Phil were standing across the street, waiting for the traffic to clear so they could cross. Lew didn't look too upset, that was at least a good sign.

"So what's up?" I asked, when they rejoined us. We were heading back towards the hotel room. The sun was directly above our heads and there wasn't a cloud in the sky.

"Well," Lew started. "I guess she took pity on us, if you can believe that. Phil went over the whole story again with her and ten minutes later, after he got to the part about the scooter landing in the ocean, he stopped. I thought she wouldn't be interested in hearing anymore, but she actually asked Phil what happened next. So he took another ten minutes and finished up the rest of his story. As it turned out, she had actually read about the accident in the paper this morning. That's when I asked her the magic question. 'How much do we owe you for the scooter?' She led us over to her stand and opened up a drawer containing a bunch of hanging files. She pulled out the one labeled '37', and thumbed through the documents inside. Grabbing a calculator from the counter top, she punched in a few numbers. 'Lucky for you,' she said. 'Thirty seven wasn't too new, I'll take nine hundred for her.' I slammed my fist on the counter and yelled, 'Come on, we just went through a tragedy here. Besides, that bike's not worth that much. I mean, I bought a moped when I was fourteen and only had to pay four hundred and fifty for it. And that one was Italian.' 'Yes, but these are Japanese,' she smiled. At this point, she pulled up a barstool to sit down, and placed the file on the countertop. 'So what do you propose its worth?' she asked. I told her I thought it was worth about five hundred. She said we signed papers stating full replacement if anything happened. 'I wish I'd have bought the insurance,' I said. Well, needless to say, Phil didn't have that kind of cash on him, so she slammed me for eight hundred dollars and took it out of the deposit." We were already inside the hotel room when Lew finished his story. "I think I would have rather bought breakfast this morning."

Looking around the room, we all laughed. Phil blurted out "Hey, it's KW."

"Cool. All the beds got made and cleaned today - except for one - the fold-out," Reno noticed as he grabbed a few Coronas out of the fridge and we sat down to try and decide what to do before we went out. I was sitting on the same bed that I slept in last night, and would continue to sleep in tonight. Reno was out on the deck, looking down at the pool. Suddenly he yelled for us to come out. My eyes settled on the exposed butt of a girl who was lying on a lounge chair. We had walked up the stairs in back of the pool when we came up to the room, and had missed this sight. The tanned beauty was wearing a dental floss, black, G-String bikini bottom. From my view, she appeared topless. To top it off, she even had some friends lying next to her.

"So, who's up for a swim?" Reno asked. It didn't take much prodding. Once we had finished checking out the abundance of women lounging on the pool deck, we quickly changed into our swim trunks and headed back outside.

The weather was turning out to be the most perfect day we'd seen so far. It was approaching ninety degrees, but there was still enough of a breeze to keep the air from becoming stagnant. The past few days spent in the sun had really begun to deepen the tan Lew and I had brought with us. However, the sun was doing nothing but increasing the burn on the other two guys. Reno and Phil were really turning red; both of their faces resembled cooked lobsters. I decided not to wear any sunscreen, but encouraged Phil to put some on. He had approached Reno, who was lathering himself up with a heavy helping of lotion. "Hey Reno, I need your help on some spots. I don't want people to see you rubbing it on my back down by the pool." I laughed to myself and left the room. I went down the steps and met Lew poolside. He was standing directly underneath our deck, about forty feet from where the ladies were tanning.

"Would you look at that," he whispered, putting on his sunglasses. My eyes scanned the pool. Yellow, purple and blue bikinied beauties floated on an array of colored rafts. It was as though we were right in the middle of a calendar girl convention. They were all modeling skimpy bikinis, and a few of them were wearing the thong variety. As we stood there waiting on Reno and Phil to finish rubbing lotion on each other upstairs, a large chested blond, wearing a red, white and blue bikini walked in front of us. She had a Kalik beer beach towel wrapped around her waist, and her bleach blond hair was pulled tightly in place, secured with a rubber band. "I'd like to pledge allegiance to that flag," Lew said, our eyes following her backside as she exited through the gate on the far side of the patio towards the private beach.

When Reno and Phil finally rejoined us, they were prepared. Reno had stopped inside the gift shop and had brought us each a raft.

Reno said, "I saw a sign that read; 'Floaties? Two dollars to rent or four dollars to buy, so I bought us each one. Besides, whoever ends up sleeping on the floor tonight can use them as a mattress."

I quickly blew up my yellow raft and slipped into the pool.

The pool, rectangular in shape, was very long, with the deep end taking up much of the room. The steps, from which we exited, opened out into the deep end. This end was littered with people drinking, talking, tanning and occasionally dunking each other. The shallow end was quieter. We had plans of just lying out in the sun for a few hours so we headed over to the shallow end of the pool. Settling onto our rafts, the only sound you could hear at this end of the pool was the water spilling from the fish head fountains above the pool deck. But as the time passed, we realized the other end of the pool started getting louder and louder. I propped myself up on an elbow and looked across the pool. There were a few girls hoisted up on some guy's shoulders playing a game of chicken. Reno, Lew and Phil were watching this as well. The sun was glaring off the water and the reflection was making very tough to see what was going on, so I decided to wade over to the side and exit. I needed my sunglasses; unfortunately they were back up in the room. I strolled up to the room, making sure I said "hello" to the gang at the opposite end. Once inside the room, I sorted through my gear, in search of my sunglasses. I always thought you couldn't wear sunglasses in the pool because the chlorine would ruin the lenses. That thought went out the window since everybody down at the pool was wearing his or her shades. I went to the bathroom, grabbed a thirty pack on my way out the door, and headed back towards the pool. As I walked up to the pool's edge, what I saw made me do a double take.

Across the other end of the pool, Phil had Reno up on his shoulders and they were playing chicken with a gorgeous red head that was up on some other guy's shoulders. My eyes scanned to the left and I spotted Lew. He was still on his green floatie, drifting alongside a short haired, petite, blonde gal wearing a sexy blue thong. She was lying on her stomach talking to Lew. *What the hell did I just miss out on?* I thought to myself. *A few minutes ago, we were on the opposite end of the pool doing nothing. I get back and the guys are in the midst of what looks like a Roman orgy.* I grabbed Lew and I a beer out of the fresh thirty pack and left the rest of the beer sitting out in the sun, by the side of the pool. Just as I had positioned myself atop my floatie Lew yelled out, "Dude, put that beer in a cooler."

"We don't have one" I replied. "It'll be all right, it's not that hot out here."

"No it won't" Lew hollered.

Phil and Reno, having just lost a game of chicken had swum over my way by this time to grab a beer for themselves. "Tango, the beer is getting warm," Reno said, pulling a couple more out.

"Thanks. That really helps." I mumbled, getting back out of the pool.

Just then, I heard somebody yell out "You can put those beers in the cooler over there. As long as you let me have one." It was the muscular guy, with the red head on his shoulders; he must have overheard our conversation. She had pulled her hair back into a ponytail, and watched me as I made my way across the pool. She caught my eye. By this time, muscle man had made his way over to the edge and was also getting out of the water. He had a Superman tattoo on his arm. "You can take my place in there" he said, while grabbing a beer for himself. He poured the remaining beer into his cooler and headed towards the stairs "I gotta take a leak." He didn't half to make me that offer twice. I dove in and swam over to the girl with the red ponytail. She was even more attractive up close and had an extremely athletic physique.

"Come on Tango, hoist her up. You guys are dead meat." It was Reno yelling at me.

"What's your name?" I asked as she climbed onto my back.

"Lynn" she said.

"Well Lynn, lets kick that little guy's ass." With Lynn up on my shoulders I strode over towards Reno and Phil.

"Shouldn't be a problem" Lynn replied. "They haven't won a match yet." As the game began, I held onto her legs securely. Lynn's thighs wrapped tightly around my head, tighter than a python in the Amazon tropical rainforest coiled around its prey. *I could die happy, if I could just turn my head around*, I thought to myself. After several rounds, we emerged victorious. A dejected Reno and Phil threw in the towel and got out of the pool to grab a couple of beers and relax. "Chrissy" Lynn yelled. She was talking to the girl next to Lew. "Come over and play"

"Yeah, come on over Lew." I yelled. Lew and Chrissy rolled off their floaties and swam over our way. Chrissy hopped up on Lew's shoulders and then took a drink out of Lew's beer. Lynn asked for a swig and she passed her the bottle.

"Don't forget about me" I said arching my neck to look up at her. All I saw was the bottom half of a perfect pair of breasts pressed firmly underneath her bikini top. The next thing I felt was a cold beer trickling over my face. Everybody started laughing, so I lunged backwards and dunked her under the water. As I stood back up, she was still hanging on with her legs and as we emerged from the water, I charged towards Lew and Chrissy. "Let's get it on," I yelled.

Fortunately for my sake, Lynn was the more athletic of the two girls and from the start was getting the best of Chrissy. Then things got a bit more interesting. Out of nowhere, Chrissy reached for Lynn's bikini top and tried to pull it off. She came up short, grabbing nothing but air. Lynn, on the other hand, was much too quick for her. Before I really knew what happened, Lynn had retaliated and I was the recipient of quite a view. The left side of Chrissy's bikini top was momentarily yanked down, exposing a perky, hand-sized breast staring right back at me. Needless to say, this sparked a much more vigorous fight, but before too long Chrissy was yelling out "Stop. Stop. Please...stop. I lost a contact lens. I can't see." Lynn and I weren't quite sure if she was faking or not, so we lunged forward just in case. Lynn pushed her effortlessly off of Lew and when she emerged from the water it was apparent she was indeed serious. Her contact was lost. "I got a spare pair back in the room. I'll be right back" she said swimming off towards the pool's edge.

"Grab some more beer while you're up there" I heard someone yell out.

"Do you need a hand?" Lew asked, as he swam after her.

"Sure." I couldn't tell if she had winked when she said this, or if she was simply blinking water out of her eye. Either way, the two of the then left the pool, dripping wet and headed upstairs.

Twenty minutes later, we were all lying around on lounge chairs, or drifting on floaties when the beer ran out. I was sitting next to Lynn as we shared a patio chair just trying to get to know one another. She told me that Chrissy was her roommate and they were vacationing down here with another friend. Pointing at the reason we had come down to the pool in the first place, the girl in the dental floss bikini, she introduced me to her friend Maria. Maria, who had a boyfriend back home, had been lying on her stomach the entire time. I noticed Reno had taken the empty seat beside her. It turned out that the three of them were in a room only five doors down the hall from us. The rest of the people were friends that were all staying at another hotel.

Just then Reno walked over. "Where the hell is Lew? I thought he was bringing back beer." As he said this, Lew and Chrissy emerged from the stairwell. Lew was holding a couple twelve packs.

"Hey, what did you do, go to the liquor store?" Phil asked.

"Yeah. Something like that," Lew grinned. After they grabbed their refreshments, Reno and Phil went upstairs to get some chips and cookies to snack on.

For the next couple of hours we laid out by the pool, half asleep, simply enjoying the company of some new friends. We talked for quite a bit, fed each other some Pringles, but eventually we decided to part ways and meet up later that night. They were all going over to the other hotel's pool to meet some other friends. On the way back to the room I couldn't stop thinking about Lynn. I was snapped out of my trance by Lew's voice. "Tango. Dude, your hair turned blonde." Looking at the mirror in our bathroom, the combination of chlorine and sunshine had indeed done a number on my normally brown hair.

Blonde hair was not my only problem. Somehow in the past few days, I had worked up an enormous blister on the heel of my foot. Needles of pain raced through my leg when I tried to put on my sandal. Grimacing in agony, I looked over at Reno, my eyes watering. "Reno, you got a Band-Aid? I got a hell of a blister, and I think my sandals shrank after that swim in the Atlantic."

Apparently Reno also had a few blisters on his feet. He told me that he wasn't used to walking in sandals so much and had brought some Band Aids just in case. He was presently seated on the closed toilet lid, inspecting his feet. To my heel's relief, he threw me a tin can packed full of bandages. I promptly placed two across the back of my foot in order to make walking tonight bearable.

A few moments later, all four of us were taking turns in the bathroom, getting ready to do Bourbon Street, Key West style. Phil was inspecting his new facial hair growth. "Phil, is that goatee growing in backwards?" I yelled, slapping him on the back.

Just then Lew walked past.

"So Lew, what the hell actually happened, when you and Chrissy left the pool?" I asked.

Lew said "Living in the Midwest, you never really get the opportunity to simply lie out and drink beers all day in the company of beautiful women in thongs with the ocean just a stone's throw away. And then, to be able go up into an air conditioned hotel room, still dripping from wet chlorine water." He drifted off momentarily lost in thought. "Guess what's better then that?"

"What?" Reno asked.

"Making out in an air conditioned room with a beautiful woman in a skimpy wet bikini."

"No way" I yelled.

"Oh, yes way, my friend" was Lew's response.

"Cool" Reno added.

"Tango, you may have gotten to see her tits, but I got to feel them."

"Hey, are you serious" Phil asked.

"Yeah. How did you manage that?" I asked.

"Well, I watched her fix her contact lens, and then we walked into the kitchen to grab some beer, but before the refrigerator door opened, we were both in each other's arms."

"Man that is awesome" Phil yelled.

"Yes it was. It was even better when I picked her up, sat her on the counter, and made out with her; only to be surrounded by legs" Lew smiled.

"That pisses me off; you won't be one up on me very long. I'm going to do you one better and guarantee I'll be naked with someone by the end of tonight" I grinned jealously.

"I got twenty on Tango that he gets naked with a girl before Lew does," Reno said.

"Well I'm just getting started" Lew replied. "You're on Reno."

"Sounds like we have a challenge here boys" Reno yelled out excitedly. "But I'll tell you what; I just met the only woman that could ever get between me and my future wife. Her name is Maria. She didn't say too much, and just laid there, but she was gorgeous."

"That's the best kind" was Phil's response. We all laughed.

"Hey Tango, you got honors, where are we drinking first tonight?" Phil asked.

"Well boys, have you ever seen the sun set over Mallory Square?" I paused momentarily, allowing the question to sink in. "Tonight you will."

CHAPTER EIGHT

But now that's just the start of a well deserved, overdue binge
Meanwhile back in the city certain people are starting to cringe
His lawyers are calling his parents
His girlfriend doesn't know what to think
His partners are studying their options
He's just singing and ordering drinks

Jimmy Buffett
The Weather Is Here, Wish You Were Beautiful

In order to witness the sun setting over Mallory Square, we departed the hotel room a few hours earlier than when we had left the past few nights. The sun still had a couple hours left before it would dip below the horizon and, presently, it was in full blazing glory. The temperature had shot up to around ninety-five degrees and, unfortunately, the breeze that had been blowing throughout the day had ceased. Having only brought two shirts, I was happy when Lew gave me a shirt to wear. The T-shirt was an early birthday present, and since it was both nicer and cleaner than anything I had brought with me, I decided to wear it tonight.

I can't remember ever receiving a present from Lew that wasn't based on clothing. If it weren't for Lew, I wouldn't own any clothes that were brand new. All of the items in my closet, are either hand me down's from my friends or came straight of the rack from Goodwill. Old habits are hard to break. Ever since I was a little kid, I can remember taking the one trip a year, usually before school began to the local Goodwill. My mom would stock up on as many second hand clothes as possible for my two brothers and me. Now that I think about it, this is really how Lew and I first met. You see, I lived in a three bedroom; ranch-styled house that had been built well over fifty years prior and only had three sides of fresh paint at any one given time. Lew lived a few neighborhoods to the East, in a brand new development, that was full of three car garages and well manicured lawns. I remember riding on the bus during one of those first days of high school, when everybody is still getting to know one another. I was one the first stops, whereas Lew was one of the last. The bus was basically full by the time he boarded. On this particular morning, I was wearing an outfit at least a decade too old. My choice of clothing on that day was not very popular with two older macho kids seated directly behind me. They had been badgering me for what seemed like an eternity. It was at this time that the bus stopped in front of Lew's house. Looking like he just stepped out of a fashion catalog, I thought to myself *This is all I need*, as I realized the only vacant seat left on the bus was beside me. He took one look at me, rolled his eyes, but sat down anyway. The bus took off, and the guys behind started in again. To my surprise, after incessant harassing, Lew stood up and defended me. This got the guys out of their seats and before I knew what happened, Lew and I were fighting for our lives. Needless to say, within the hour, we were sitting in the principal's office. Bloodied and sore, we received a week's worth of detention for the fight on the bus. We've been friends ever since, and thanks to Lew, my wardrobe got a little more life added to it from that day forward.

The T-shirt was gray with red and yellow letters on the front that read: *Full Moon Surf.* The letters were accompanied by a naked female surfer riding a wave. The only problem was that it was high quality; it was made from extremely thick and heavy material. I don't think I'd even made it past the hotel parking lot, when I felt the first trickle of sweat roll down my chest. By the time we had reached Duval, the perspiration on my forehead was beginning to drip as well. "Are we in Key West or the Amazon? It's humid as hell out here," I said, tugging at the collar of my new shirt, in an attempt to release some steam.

"It's hot Tango," Lew replied. He scanned the section of street that lay behind us. "Let's hop on the next pickup truck we see and hitch a ride down Duval." Lew's great idea, unfortunately never came to fruition. As we continued our walk through the rainforest, not a single pickup truck, or for that matter, any vehicle capable of carrying four extra passengers, drove past.

None of us really quite knew how to get to Mallory Square, but we figured it was located somewhere around the north end of the island. So what I gauged was about half way through our trek, was when my chest started to feel a bit cooler. In fact, every stride I took seemed to cool me down even more. I began to wonder what was going on when I looked down. To my utter horror, I had a sweatstain in the middle of my shirt about the size of a golf ball. I quickly scanned the crowd of people walking around us and was relieved to see that the guy in front of me had a few perspiration beads forming on the back of his shirt as well. Like fools, the entire walk thus far had been conducted on the east side of the street, where there was absolutely no shade. Looking at Reno and Lew, I was disgusted to see that they had hardly even begun to sweat. Phil, sweating as well, had worn a dark green, almost black, Hawaiian shirt. Even if he had perspired through his shirt, you'd have never been able to tell. Just then I heard Phil, who was at least ten paces behind the rest of us, yell out, "Let's move over to the left hand side of the street." We all simultaneously glanced across the street. I was relieved to see that the entire sidewalk was covered in shade. Lew, stubbornly looking for a truck to hitch a ride in, was the last one to join us on the other side.

Although we were now walking on the shaded side of the street, the humidity was still as thick as a can of tomato soup. That only meant one thing; the sweat stain that had begun to flourish across my chest was not going to dry anytime soon, at least not in this weather. I considered myself at least lucky to have made it this far without any of the guys taking notice. All of that was about to end, when I saw Lew dart into an Art Store. Following him, I stepped across the threshold to the sounds of a chime ringing and walked into the air-conditioned art store. I might as well have walked into a shower, I thought to myself, as my pores opened up and allowed the sweat to flow freely in the comfort of cool air. I wiped my brow and walked over to the painting that had attracted Lew's attention from the window outside. Without so much as a glance my way he said, "That sweat stain has gone down to your ass." Slamming the back of his hand against his knee, he was hunched forward and laughing uncontrollably.

Reno, over hearing this comment chimed in, "Tango, it looks like you're about to have a heart attack."

I looked down at my chest and saw that the sweatstain had grown to the size of a baseball and the expansion showed no signs of stopping. "It's this heavy shirt Lew bought me. I swear to God it feels like I'm wearing a turtleneck."

Reno continued grinning.

"The collar is tight as hell and I don't know what type of fabric it's made out of," I continued. "But I can tell you this; it doesn't breathe at all."

Reno, bored with me, turned and started to walk away.

"I really think it is more of a winter shirt," I said to his back. "Hell, I'm just glad we found some AC." Now that I'd acclimated myself to the store, my sweating had stopped - at least momentarily. The door chimed again.

Phil had finally arrived. He looked me up and down as he walked over towards us. "You feeling O.K., Tango?"

"I've been better," I replied.

A very well dressed man approached us carrying a glass of water in one hand. He handed me the drink and asked if there was anything we needed to know about the piece of art we were looking at. The painting was fantastic. It was a large piece, and an assortment of colors had been used to display the tropical scene. Lew, interested in purchasing the painting, asked what he would have to do in order to buy it.

"All you need to do is put down fifteen percent -- we ship for free -- you have one year to pay it off," the salesman answered.

"Well how much is it?" Lew asked.

"At fifteen hundred, you'd only need to come up with around three hundred right now. So what credit card do you want to use, and shall I wrap it up for you?"

Lew looked at the salesman and smiled. "Let's just say that the last time someone put a deposit on my credit card on this trip, things didn't quite turn out like I had expected. I really don't feel like repeating that misfortune." I handed him an empty glass as we walked through the store and returned to the blast furnace that had become Key West.

We hadn't traveled more than ten feet from the storefront when we almost tripped over a bum, whose legs extended onto the sidewalk. He was propped up, with his back against the white washed wood, and from what I recalled, he was one of the bums we had played dodge ball with earlier. Lew, who was leading the way, looked over his shoulder and yelled, "Where are the rest of your buddies? Do they still have our ball?"

Not even bothering to look up, he hissed at us, "You speak poison." A reply that elicited a chuckle from us. "Want to see a drug addict?" he continued. He then proceeded to place a big red pill on his tongue and swallowed.

"Hey, did you see that?" Phil, sputtered, "That's why I hate those bums."

Continuing our stroll down Duval, our attention was drawn to a huge black Bull's head protruding on the outside of the bar called *The Bull*. An older lady was standing in front of an alleyway entrance that led to a stairwell alongside *The Bull*. She was passing out little yellow slips of paper, about the size of a business card, for the *Garden of Eden*. "Gentleman, two for one upstairs," she said handing us what turned out to be a coupon. We each grabbed one and started to walk away. "Clothing is optional," she added. We stopped dead in our tracks.

Lew immediately turned around and approached her again. "Is there any cover?" he asked.

"We're a local bar."

"Well what goes on up there?" I asked.

"The usual stuff," she replied. "We're just a place where people can relax, have a drink, enjoy the outdoor atmosphere, and get naked if you like. There's body painting, if you're into that, and if you don't want to get undressed, that's fine too."

"Cool," Reno replied, placing the yellow card in the front pocket of his shirt. As we walked away, he continued. "I don't know about the rest of you, but that's where I'm buying a round later tonight."

By this time, we had reached the end of the road and were faced with a choice. Do we turn left or right? None of us knew, so we simply followed the crowd and hoped that they were all going in the same direction we were. Lew, never one to sit back and let things happen on their own, approached some guy ahead of us in a wild Hawaiian shirt that was so big it could have covered a small village. "Excuse me sir. Do you know where Mallory Square is?"

He turned around and simply said, "Follow me, I'm heading there." Our leader, being more than slightly overweight, slowed our pace to a near crawl as we tagged along beside him; even Phil began to walk ahead of us. Lew glanced down at his watch. Our escort, seeing this, interpreted Lew's body language to mean that we were in a hurry. "You see that lady in the fuchsia dress?" he said, pointing ahead.

"Yeah," Lew replied.

"The entrance to Mallory Square is beside her."

Lew, Phil and Reno all focused their eyes a few blocks ahead of us and to the right. I had no idea where they were looking and had to ask, "What color is fuchsia? Is it green?"

Lew looked at me and shook his head. "Dude, you just bought a fuchsia tank top yesterday when we were at Margaritaville."

"No way, that was a dark pink, almost red tank top," I replied.

"Well then, dumb ass, follow the lady in the dark pink dress." The lady in the pink dress had just walked underneath a large wooden sign that hung above the sidewalk marking the entrance to Mallory Square. As we got a bit closer, we were able to see that the sign read: "Welcome to Mallory Square. Where the sun sets, and the fun begins." Personally, I could not have thought of a better mantra for our evening ahead.

We stood underneath the wooden welcome sign for a few minutes and gathered our bearings. Hot, and still sweaty from the long walk, I focused all of my attention on finding a place to buy the first round of drinks. Maybe a cold boat drink would prevent me from sweating any more. However, as my eyes surveyed the red, white and gray brick boardwalk that was called Mallory Square, I was momentarily lost in its vastness. It was huge and extended out to the sea, as far as we could see. I was overcome by the inordinate amount of activity that seemed to be brewing along the oceanfront. There was booths set up all over the place and merchants were selling their wares: jewelry, artwork, literature, clothing and tourist trinkets. The crowds in front of the displays made it appear as though these shopkeepers made a rather nice living. The steady murmur from the crowd was partially drowned out by the obnoxious clamor coming from the direction of the Southernmost Bagpiper in the United States.

I left Reno, Lew and Phil, who had walked into the crowd and started browsing around at the different items for sale. I had to make a quick stop at an outdoor bar that was set up along the row of buildings that separated the square from the street. Searching for the guys --with four drinks in hand -- I noticed that in addition to the retailers, there were just as many street performers who had set up a show. Although the acts that these performers put on varied, there was one common denominator: at the conclusion of every show, a hat of some sort was passed amongst the audience that had gathered to watch.

I stumbled across the other three standing in front of an artist that had actually painted his entire body silver. This guy's specialty was to pose like a statue. With his body covered in paint, he might have been the only guy there who was sweating more than me. But he had a fan pointed right at him in order to keep from overheating.

After watching the tin man strike a few poses, we continued to move through the square, until we came across a large crowd that had surrounded a performer who had dubbed himself 'The Glassman.' The Glassman's forte was to lie down on shards of broken glass. While lying there, he called for the assistance of four audience members. Without hesitation, we offered to volunteer. To our surprise, were actually chosen to assist The Glassman with the finale of his show. I could not believe my eyes as I watched up close as The Glassman lay down on his stomach across the broken glass one more time. He then instructed one of his helpers to pour another five-gallon bucket, which was completely full of broken glass, across his back. He resembled a scene on a beach: when someone buries themselves in the sand, leaving only their head exposed. The only difference here was that The Glassman was face down, and instead of sand, he was completely covered with sharp glass, only his head was visible. He then requested a half sheet of plywood be laid across his back. With the finale's set up complete, it was now our turn to get involved in the show.

"Gentlemen," The Glassman began, "I want you each to step across my back, using the plywood in order to protect your feet from any injuries." One by one, the four of us stepped across the plywood and then back off, thus sandwiching The Glassman between the shards of glass. Phil went first, and then Reno, followed by Lew and, finally, I went last. The crowd was cheering wildly, and thinking that our job was completed, we began to walk back into the audience. I saw Reno and Phil high-five.

"Not so fast guys," I heard The Glassman yell out. He was still lying on the ground buried beneath the glass, but was now looking over at the four of us, smiling. "I have one more job for you. If you would, break out into groups of two." Following his orders, I stood next to Reno, making Lew and Phil the other team. "Good. Now I want you two guys to both step onto the plywood, from opposite ends, at the same time," instructed The Glassman. "I need you to meet at the middle, facing each other and just stand there. Hold each other's forearms if you need to keep your balance."

Looking at Lew and Phil, he continued on. "Once those two are in place, I want you two guys to join them, but I want you to get on the plywood at the same time, facing each other, from the other two ends." Reno and I started to walk towards him. "Now, this part is very important guys. Don't jump and do exactly what I say once you are on top of me. O.K?"

"O.K." we all replied.

Reno and I stepped up without any difficulties. Unfortunately, the same cannot be said for Lew and Phil. As they stepped onto the plywood, Phil's foot got hung up on the edge and he slipped. Lew however, continued to step up and when Phil slipped, the plywood tilted to Lew's side. Seeing this, Phil quickly hopped up to avoid having the entire sheet teeter to one side. When he did this, Phil's end slammed down hard onto The Glassman's shoulder blades. The glass shards crunched noisily beneath our feet. It sounded as though the air had been knocked out of The Glassman's lungs as he let out a muffled cry. The crowd gasped. I heard a woman let out a scream. I had a sick feeling that The Glassman was going to be sliced up pretty good. We stood on the plywood motionless for what seemed like an eternity, waiting for a command, or a sign that The Glassman was indeed still with us. Miraculously, one of The Glassman's arms worked its way out from the rubble and his thumb went up in the air. "I'm O.K.," he yelled out. The crowd cheered noisily. We stepped off in the reverse order we had gotten onto the plywood and watched in amazement as The Glassman stood up. He brushed pieces of glass from his body and, believe it or not, only had one small cut on his chest with a matching one on his back. Aside from that, he was completely normal, or at least as normal as a guy who makes his living lying on top of glass can be.

The tip hat was passed to Phil.

"Hey Tango, I don't have any cash," Phil said. "Could you put in ten bucks for me?"

Sighing, I shook my head and grabbed some bills from my wallet.

"Hey, these guys aren't bums. They actually work for their money," Phil said as we made our way over to another crowd favorite, The Tightrope Walker.

The Tightrope Walker's act was already underway by the time we took a seat in front of his stage. He was presently about fifteen feet above our heads and was walking back and forth across a tightrope that spanned twenty feet. He was working without the aide of a net: the brick patio was directly below him, and he was precariously positioned right on the edge of the water. The edge dropped eight feet, straight off into the ocean. Like The Glassman, he was looking for a volunteer from the crowd.

"Hey, I think we've done enough volunteer work tonight," Phil said. The rest of us couldn't agree with him more.

The Tightrope Walker ended up choosing a guy from the crowd who was visiting the Keys with his wife and daughter. His name was Dave. I, along with the rest of the audience, began to sense that Dave was a little bit nervous. It seemed as though he didn't want to do anything that would embarrass his family. He looked like the kid in high school gym class that was always picked last. Dave was now older, and this time he had been picked first. He was totally unprepared. Fortunately for Dave, his only job was to throw a tennis ball up for The Tightrope Walker to juggle; the only catch was that The Tightrope Walker was going to be juggling razor sharp machetes at the same time. The Tightrope Walker steadied himself above the crowd in the middle of the tightrope and began juggling the machetes.

"Listen to me Dave, when I give the command, toss me up the first ball." The blades of the machetes glistened off the sun as they flew through the air. "Now Dave," he said.

Dave was caught off guard. He tossed the ball underhanded and it barely cleared the tightrope at its highest peak, before it came crashing down against the brick boardwalk. The ball took two bounces and fell off the edge of the Square, landing in the water below.

"Dave," The Tightrope Walker began, "did that ball just go in the ocean?"

"Yes," an apologetic Dave replied.

"Fortunately I have two more balls Dave. Try it again on my command."

"I got ten bucks Tango, says he throws the next one in the ocean too," said Reno.

I shook my head and the bet was on.

"Now Dave," said The Tightrope Walker.

The Tightrope Walker had now donated two of his three tennis balls to the sea, and I was ten dollars lighter.

"Dave, sit down," The Tightrope Walker snarled. Dave looked visibly shaken and sat down next to his wife and daughter, a shell of the man he once had been. His wife put her arm around him, rubbing his shoulder in condolence. His daughter patted him on the back and frowned. The Tightrope Walker quickly scanned the crowd. Phil, who stuck out like a sore thumb at his height was the obvious choice. "You, in the dark green Hawaiian Shirt, get up here." I could hear Phil sigh, as he stood. "You know the drill, let's see if you can show Dave there how to get it up. By the way, what's you're name?"

"I'm Phil."

"Now Phil." Phil did not disappoint. He threw a perfect pass to The Tightrope Walker, who was now successfully juggling three machetes and a tennis ball. "Phil, now it's your turn to catch. On the count of three, I'm going to throw you the machetes." Phil smiled and shrugged his shoulders, the crowd started laughing. "Just kidding, Phil. Here. Catch." He harmlessly threw Phil the tennis ball and continued on with his act. For a brief second, I had a vision of the ball bouncing off Phil's hands and dropping into the ocean. But as I smiled at the thought of this, Phil caught the ball. Phil walked off the set to the applause of the audience. By the time The Tightrope Walker's act was completed, the sun was just about to set.

As a warning siren wailed, all performances were suspended momentarily so the crowd that had gathered at Mallory Square could pause to watch the sun set. On our way over to the sit on the concrete stoop that separated the ocean from the Square, Lew yelled out, "Dude's, there goes Ted Nugent." I looked in the direction that Lew was pointing and was just able to see Ted as he ducked out of view.

As my eyes scanned back towards the sea, they lit up a bit, and it wasn't from the setting sun. I nudged Reno in the ribs, "That guy in front of me has sweat through his shirt. I don't feel so bad now." Feeling a bit better about myself, I settled into a seat alongside the ocean, and watched the sun setting over Mallory Square.

Looking out across the ocean, we had a perfect view of a little island packed full of pine trees.

"I wonder if that's Christmas Tree Island," Lew said, pointing towards the island.

"I'll bet it is," Reno replied.

At that moment, the sun had just begun to dip below the horizon. The entire sky lit up, and the vibrant yellows, oranges and reds that the sun cast were reflected across the water in front of us. It was a magnificent sight: sailboats, cruise ships, and a vast amount of people. The clouds were massive and puffy, dancing across the sky. The thousands of others who had come to witness this event stood in utter silence. Occasionally, you'd hear someone say 'Wow' or 'Awesome', or something else to that effect, but the end result was simply a feeling of standing alone watching the most beautiful sunset I'd ever seen in my life. Legend has it, that at the split second the sun dips below the horizon, a green light will flash above the water. I must have blinked, because I never saw it.

Applause echoed throughout the square when the sun had finally disappeared below the ocean line. The halogen lights above the Square were turned on, and we took that as our cue to get up and get on our way. The four of us posed for a few pictures in front of the last remaining streaks of sunlight and decided we'd seen enough of Mallory Square. It was now Reno's turn to buy a round. As we left the Square I reminded the others, "It's a journey boys, not a race. Let Bourbon Street begin."

"Hey, where are we headed Reno?" Phil asked after we'd walked a few blocks.

"Let's go to *The Hog's Breath*," Reno replied. "Rumor has it that there's a bikini contest going on tonight." That was enough to rouse my interest. We snaked our way through the crowd that had gathered outside The *Hog's Breath* and positioned ourselves towards the only available spot inside -- an unused stairwell in front of the bar -- while Reno bellied up to order the drinks. This was not an ordinary bikini contest going on that night; it was a homemade bikini contest. Meaning that the participants, some of Key West's more attractive ladies, had to fashion their bikinis by hand out of ordinary, everyday items.

Reno arrived with our drink, a *Havana Hog Punch*, just as the master of ceremony was announcing the next round of contestants. We watched as beautiful women -- modeling everything from seashell bikinis to bikini's made out of duck tape and band-aids -- traipsed across the runway. "There's no way, we're settling for these seats," Reno yelled. "We need to get a closer view." As luck would have it, a table of women sitting next to the stage got up to leave. Hustling, but not spilling a drop, we quickly claimed their table for our own.

Had it not been for our pact to drink only one beverage per bar, we'd have tried to get involved in the judging of the pageant. But, unfortunately, tonight was Bourbon Street. We tilted our cups and drank the last bit of our *Hog Punch*, as Phil, Reno and myself got up to move on. Lew looked at us grinning, but still seated. "Dude's, the one-drink rule, just got broken. We're staying here for two, there's no way I'm giving up these seats so quickly."

As we settled in for another round, a gal sporting a coconut bikini graced the stage. A beauty with some very well placed whip cream followed her up. That's when Reno lost it. He was going crazy as the whipped cream goddess bent over and shook her ass right in front of us. The crowd was going insane, and I swear the place had begun to shake. Lew tried to egg him on, "Come on, Reno take a lick."
"Do I get a bed if I do it?"
"No."
"Screw it," he said, jumping up from his seat. Quick as a flash, his tongue took a scoop of the cream, leaving a bare spot on her left cheek.
I was dying, I was laughing so hard. Reno turned around, his mouth covered with white fluff.
Before he could sit down, a bouncer grabbed him by the arm. "Parties over, cowboy."
"Yee haw," Reno laughed, pretending to lasso his victim.

The rest of us got up as Reno was being escorted outside.
"Our first bar, and Reno gets kicked out," Lew laughed, "This is going to be one hell of a night!"
We reconvened outside. Little V's party promised to have plenty of scantily clad woman running around, and if luck would have it, perhaps we'd meet up later with a few of the lovely young ladies that we'd seen on stage. Reno and I yielded the floor to Phil.
"Your turn Phil," I said. "Where to?"
"Let's head on over to *Captain Tony's*," Phil replied. As we walked, I looked down at my shirt. The open roof atmosphere of the bar had done nothing to combat my sweatstain. It was still as large as ever; my only

solace was in the fact that it had appeared to stop expanding. I began to abandon all hope that it would evaporate anytime soon.

Still thinking about my sweatstain, I shook my head in disgust as we approached *Captain Tony's Saloon*. "I should have worn an undershirt; I don't think I would have sweat through two shirts," I said. The guys just laughed.

We found the musty poolroom inside *Captain Tony's* completely empty and decided to rack the balls to set up a game of billiards while Phil bought the drinks. Reno had just struck the cue ball to break the game, when Phil arrived with our next round of drinks. "Tequila Sunrise, an old college favorite," he said as he passed them out. "Reno and I used to drink these like water when we were in school."

As we sipped our colorful concoction, Phil and I continued to display the eight ball prowess we had shown over the past few days, and preceded to lose two more games back to back. At the conclusion of the second game, some music suddenly started playing from inside the bar. The song, if you could call it that, sounded more like the kind of stuff you hear reverberating from the speakers at a strip joint. Curious as to what was transpiring, we set our sticks down on the table and walked up the stairs into the main bar. There was a group of about twenty guys all huddled around a girl who had just stood up on top of her barstool. The crowd that had gathered was hooting, hollering and, generally, trying everything they could to egg her on. A few guys were whistling loudly, when all of a sudden, she reached up under her shirt and whipped out her white lace bra.

"That chick is taking her bra off," Reno yelled, slapping Lew on the back. "Cool."

In order for us all to see, she held her bra up with both hands above her head like a heavyweight champion showing off his belt after a fight. The crowd went wild. Reaching down to grab a staple gun from the bartender, she began to staple her bra to the ceiling. Looking up, I noticed that she had just added her bra to a collection of at least a hundred others. I can't believe I hadn't noticed before the slinky lingerie that hung from the wooden rafters above the bar. In addition to bras, there were colorful assortments of panties. As I drank the last of my Tequila Sunrise, I thought to myself, this would be an even better show if she decided to add her panties as well. Unfortunately, as I looked on, she reached down and grabbed a guy's hands so that he could help her get down from her perch.

"Well, that's something you don't see every day," Lew said.

"You got that right," I added. The after-taste of tequila was starting to get to me. "By the way Phil, let's not add the Tequila Sunrise to our list of drinks. I don't know how you and Reno could stand to drink those in college. That's the first and, hopefully, last one of those I'll ever wash down my gullet."

I don't remember how we got there, or for that matter what the name of the bar was that we were presently standing in, but the place was wall to wall with people. I do remember that Lew had absolutely insisted on buying the next round. As we waited on him to purchase the drinks, I looked around the unfamiliar territory. I knew we were back on Duval -- that much I did remember -- but I couldn't for the life of me figure out what bar we were in. The coolest thing this place had going for it was the lineup of slushy drink machines behind the bar. For that matter, as I looked around, it seemed that a frozen drink was the only type of beverage this place served. Lew met us with four icy concoctions. We had been waiting for him in front of an old video golf game and had decided to play a few holes. Our money inserted, the four of us played the front nine of a course in Scotland. Things were going great; Lew was bursting into expletives and slamming the machine after every shot. But then I accidentally bumped into my drink after a particularly long drive on the eighth hole. My red slush spilled out across the monitor. About five seconds later, the screen went blank.

"Why did you put your drink in front of the track-ball?" Lew yelled. I noticed that Reno and Phil were looking around to verify that no one else had noticed the machine was dead.

"I thought it was empty. Damn. I was having the round of my life, too."

"Let's go out onto the dance floor before someone notices Tango broke the game." Reno said

"Good idea," I whispered, following him over to the dance floor. The scenery was much better over here anyway. Everywhere we looked, young beauties were dancing and moving to the beat of the music. Reno was already out on the floor, dancing with a skinny blonde. I watched him as the girl he was dancing with yelled something into his ear. Reno just smiled and hollered something back. The next thing I knew, the girl lifted up her tube top and showed Reno a perfect pair of breasts. Reno, continuing to dance as if nothing unusual had just happened, grabbed a strand of beads hanging around the next of the guy next to him and placed them over her head. She already had her top back on, and aside from Reno, I may have been the only other witness to this. I felt an arm go around my shoulder. It was Phil.

"What's up?' he asked.

"See that girl dancing over there with Reno," I replied.

"Yeah."

"She just earned herself a strand of beads. And let me tell you, she's got a nice rack. But Reno definitely got a better view than I did from here." Looking around I couldn't believe Lew missed the show. Then he appeared a few minutes later carrying another drink to replace the one I'd spilled.

"Why don't you try holding onto this one, ace?" A few minutes later, Reno came off the dance floor with his arm around the recently beaded girl.

"We'll be at *Ricky's Cantina* dancing," she said, as she maneuvered from underneath his grasp and continued walking past us over to her friends.

"Gentlemen," he nodded, grinning from ear to ear. "Lets go follow those chicks."

"Not so fast, Reno," I replied. "It's my turn again, lets head on over to that bar with the Bull's head."

We arrived back at the establishment we'd stood in front of earlier in the day; the place where the lady had informed us that there was nudity allowed upstairs. The building we were standing in front of actually housed three bars on three separate levels: *The Bull* was on the lower level; *The Whistle* looked out to the street below; and *The Garden of Eden* lay open air on top. My initial thought was to enjoy a drink in *The*

Bull, but when we walked into the place, it was dead. So we headed up one flight of stairs to check out *The Whistle*.

The middle level was right up our alley. The bar sat square in the center of the room, surrounded by pool tables and dartboards. I walked up to the bar and ordered four Absolut and Lemonades. After paying for the drinks, I saw that another game of pool was raked up. Just as Lew was setting up to break, a dog ran up and jumped on him. The first thought that ran through my head was, 'what the hell is Lew's dog Lucky doing here?' Lew has a yellow lab, and from my point of view, they all look the same. Grabbing an empty cup off the floor, Lew threw it across the bar. The dog gave chase, and a fifteen-minute game of fetch was on, which thankfully, ended any ideas of another game of pool. We finally wore the dog out and decided to stroll onto the deck that ran the circumference of the building outside. There were quite a few people out here, and from about twenty feet up, the view down Duval was perfect. We watched as people milled about below us and absently noticed the traffic continuously flowing back and forth. The sheer number of mopeds, scooters, bicycles and cars that drove up and down the street was too numerous to count, along with the abundance of near accidents. Looking down below, Reno spotted the girl he had been dancing with at the last bar. She and her girlfriends were heading up the street in the direction of *Ricky's Cantina*.

"Cool, let's moon them," Reno suggested. Before we could make up our minds, he whistled loud enough to draw their attention. As they looked up, we quickly turned around and dropped our drawers. I heard some high-pitched screams, followed by a lot of laughter. Phil did not zip and slip fast enough; it was over before he could bare ass.

I, along with Reno and Lew, pulled up my pants and walked back into the bar. Looking at my empty cup, I questioned Reno, "Where to now?"

"Well, Tango," he began, "exposing my ass like that has got me in the mood for a little more nudity. Lets walk upstairs to *The Garden of Eden*." None of us argued his decision.

On our way up the flight of stairs, Lew spoke up. "When I open a bar, Lucky will be able to run free through it."

"You know," I said, as we exited the stairwell, "When I open a bar, naked people will be allowed to run free through it."

I felt my heart beating louder and louder with each step. I didn't know what to expect to find when we reached the top of the rickety steps, but The Garden of Eden was like no other bar I'd ever stepped foot in. It opened to the sky above and all along the perimeter was a thick forest of tropical plants, effectively blocking any view of the roof from street level. When the lady on the street said clothing was optional, she wasn't lying. I had expected to see a couple women standing around topless, but I had not expected to see upwards of thirty or forty people milling around completely nude. Looking over in the direction of the bar, I saw a guy standing there completely naked. "Where does that guy keep his money?" I asked Phil while we followed Lew over to the disc jockey's table. Lew was flipping through a catalog looking for a song to request while the rest of us continued to gawk.

"Why is the ugliest guy in the room always naked?" Phil asked pointing over at a guy lounged out on a patio chair.

"I don't know, but I'm paying more attention to the women walking around. Did you see that gal over there wearing a spray painted blue bikini?"

"She's not the only one," Phil replied. "There's a couple more over there wearing nothing but body paint."

About this time, an idea struck me and I gathered Reno and Phil and walked them over to where Lew was standing. "All right boys," I said. "Here is the deal. The first one out of you three that strips down naked in this bar wins the other bed tonight."

"Oh, you got to be kidding me," Lew whined.

"Nope," I smiled.

After a couple of songs, all three of them were shirtless. Phil had taken a slight lead by kicking off his sandals when Reno drifted over to the bar so he could buy the next round of drinks.

"Dudes," Lew tapped us on the shoulder. "I just requested *Slide*, by The Goo Goo Dolls."

"Hey," Phil said, looking in the direction Lew had just come from, "Doesn't that DJ look a lot like Jerry Garcia?"

The next song that played was Lew's request, and let me put it this way; I will always associate the song *Slide* with that night at *The Garden of Eden*. I had begun to wonder where Reno had run off to; when as the song started, I glanced back over my shoulder to see if he needed any help with the drinks. When I finally spotted him, that silly bastard was walking over wearing absolutely nothing but a smile.

"Reno. Where the hell are your clothes?" I heard Lew yell out.

"I threw them in a pile beside the bar. Here you guys are," he said, handing out the drinks. Personally, I felt a little uncomfortable standing beside a naked Reno.

I slammed the bourbon and coke he'd given us and walked over to the grass hut that was set up to do body painting. I watched as the artist airbrushed a couple of flowers across the belly-pierced, stomach of some lady. Fortunately, by the time I re-joined the others, Reno was busy getting dressed again.

"You ready to roll?" Phil asked me.

I nodded.

"Let's head over to *Ricky's Cantina*," he said, placing his arm around me -- more for leverage than anything else -- as we walked back downstairs to the street.

"You all right, Phil?" I asked, trying to assess his condition further. I gave him a quick look up and down. He still had his arm round my neck and the weight of his body was starting to wear me down as we strolled out into the refreshing night air. I mean, even though the guy is skinny, he is still almost seven feet tall.

"Never better," he slurred. I was feeling great myself, especially now that I'd noticed the sweat stain had finally disappeared.

When we arrived at Ricky's Cantina, the four of us collectively wiggled our way through the crowd and found that Mark was still working behind the bar.

"VIP Reservation," Mark yelled out when he saw us; he gave Reno a high five as we stepped up to the bar. He immediately cleared off a space for the four of us, and placed a little placard on the bar that actually read: VIP Seating.

It was Phil's turn to buy a round, but Mark just pointed to a board on the wall that displayed the ingredients to *Ricky's Cantina Rum Punch* and passed a few down to us. This round was on him. We then confirmed that we'd be meeting back up with him in about an hour and a half. He told us that he needed to run home first and get into the outfit he was given to wear for Little V's party. Just before he left, he started running through the crowd, wearing a patch over his eye, dancing to the beat of the music, wielding a large plastic ax and acting like an old pirate. He then handed Reno the ax and told him to keep things under control. Reno took that as his cue to run around the dance floor swinging the ax wildly at unsuspecting dancers looking for his lost lady. On more than one occasion, I witnessed him using the device to lift up the skirt of an unsuspecting gal. "Knowing Reno," I thought to myself, "we'll be lucky if we make it out of here without at least some sort of fight breaking out."

I happened to look over at the guy who was standing next to Phil. I knew that I had seen him somewhere before, but I couldn't quite place my finger on it. As he raised his arm to get the attention of Mark's replacement, it dawned on me. He was The Glassman.

"That's The Glassman," I yelled, pointing across Phil. We immediately requested a picture with him. Lew started questioning him about what he thought about living in the Keys.

"I'm a straight, single guy living in Key West. I go home with a different woman every night of the week - life is good." Clutching two shot glasses in one hand, he used the other to grab the waist of the beautiful lady that had been patiently standing beside him and walked off.

"You keeping an eye on Reno out there?" I asked Lew. By this point, Reno had worked his way up on stage and from what I could tell, was presently trying to convince the lead singer that the next verse ought to be a duet.

"Yeah, I see him, that dumb ass is gonna get himself in trouble if he keeps it up," Lew said. "Dude, wait a minute, isn't that Brooke and Kelly out there?"

"Who?" I asked.

"The two girls whose lives we saved yesterday. You do remember the shark attack, right?"

"How could I forget? Where are they?"

"Over there dancing," Lew pointed. He got up and walked towards them just as the song was ending. Running behind to catch up, we ran into them just as they were leaving the dance floor. As soon as they saw us, both girls let out a high-pitched scream.

"I can't believe we actually met up with you two again," Brooke said, smiling from cheek to cheek.

"We owe you our lives," yelled Kelly, as she gave Lew a big hug.

"Wow," proclaimed Lew. "I'm just glad things turned out the way they did, and we can all laugh about it now." He pulled away, a little, but was still staring into Kelly's eyes. Kelly had shoulder length blonde hair and baby blue eyes. She was gorgeous, petite and I knew Lew had a thing for blondes.

"So, Lew, any idea where Reno and Phil have gone off to? By the way," I looked at Brooke, "are you two here alone?"

Lew ignored my question, but it was answered when both Reno and Phil came over to us while Brooke was talking. "Oh no, we're here with two of our girlfriends. This is Morgan and Jennifer." She pointed to the other two girls who were now standing beside them. "They were on our boat too."

"We just can't stop talking about you guys and what happened, it's a privilege meeting you all again," said Jennifer.

All four of the gals looked similar, except Brooke. Brooke was the one I couldn't keep my eyes off. She had jet-black hair and dark olive skin. She was exotic looking.

"By the way, this is Reno and Phil," I replied. "Reno is the one that saved the young boy."

"You guys are animals, I can't believe you all did that," Kelly said, looking at each of us.

"They're freaking crazy," Phil yelled out with authority.

"Yes they are," was Brooke's reply.

"If you think the shark attack was something, you should have heard what happened to us on the way back to the hotel," I replied. Phil was way too drunk to speak at length, so Lew told them the story. The tale pretty much dampened the mood, but just then the smoke machine started and laser lights were dancing off the glass above, making us move the party.

We spent the next few minutes chit chatting and Lew explained to them what we were doing that night. They loved our version of Bourbon Street and offered to buy us the next round. The eight of us ventured back outside and we decided to let the ladies buy us a drink at one of their favorite bars on Duval, *Diva's*.

As we strolled down Duval underneath a cloudless sky, the moonbeams provided plenty of light. I was looking down at the sidewalk following the two silhouettes of Lew and Kelly that had now joined to become one. Kelly had her arm around Lew's waist and her head resting against his shoulder. As I looked up, he had put his arm around her and was barely talking above a whisper; they started to laugh. I was walking beside Brooke. Reno and the other two girls were following behind me, and Phil was a couple of blocks back, having a hell of a time just keeping up.

"So how long are you girls in town?" I asked Brooke.

"We're here through the end of the weekend," she replied. Taking me by surprise, she added, "We're staying at the *Marriott*, on the North end of the beach. Maybe you guys could come by later and see the place. It really is a nice hotel." I was even more shocked when she slipped her arm around me and gave me a kiss on the cheek.

My body reacted instantly and I wanted more than anything to scream, "Yes!"

I really had no idea what *Diva's* would be like. Not only had we not been there, I didn't recall ever seeing it. So I was honestly surprised when we entered the gay district and found *Diva's* to be done in a drag queen motif. I had my doubts at first, but as we sat down at a table and began to watch the entertainment on stage, a halfway decent Marilyn Monroe impersonator began to perform and I really began to enjoy myself. Midway through the show, Phil got up and left us. Not giving us any indication as to what he was doing, being curious, I watched him as he walked away. Now I don't know if he was motioned by the blonde Amazon that was standing at the bar to join her, or if he went up there on his own volition. Either way, he was saddled up to the bar next to a drag queen, every bit as tall as he was. The difference between them was that she had long blond hair and protruding breasts. They were laughing and I saw her motion to the bartender to load up another round for both Phil and her. She then broke out two cigarettes and lit Phil's.

The rest of us watched a few more impersonators, before we decided we had to leave. It was about a quarter till eleven and we had quite a walk in front of us to get to the pier on time. We had invited them to come along with us, but they told us no since they had promised to meet up with their girlfriends at another bar later that night. In the end, we arranged to meet them back at their hotel a few hours later for a nightcap.

We said goodbye to the girls and, of course, Lew made a big scene by picking up Kelly and laying her on the table for a long farewell kiss. Not being the showman type, I just gave Brooke a quick kiss on the mouth. As we walked off, Lew whispered in my ear, "at least they won't get hit on until tomorrow night."

Phil must have seen us get up, because he pointed an index finger at us, as if to say, "Just a minute." As we watched, the drag queen kissed Phil on the cheek and then gave him a big hug. Reno, Lew and I busted through the front door, laughing hysterically. A few seconds later, Phil walked out.

"What's so funny?" he asked innocently.

"You just got kissed by a guy," Reno said between fits of laughter.

Phil immediately went on the defensive. "What are you talking about? That wasn't a guy." He paused for a few seconds and then said, "Besides, I was looking at her chest the whole time, they had to be real."

"Well, if your eyes had ventured a tad higher, maybe you'd have noticed that the guy's Adam's apple was as big as a baseball." I said.

Visibly shaken, I heard him mumble, "I could have sworn that was a woman." From that point forward, Phil's condition deteriorated. We only had ten minutes until we needed to be at the pier and we were closer to the Southernmost Point than the north pier. It was time to run, or in Phil's case, lumber. Running down the street, the only real barrier that stood in our way was a puddle that spanned the intersection of Duval and Eaton. Already running, it was an easy obstacle to jump. However, Phil splashed right through it, getting mud all over his legs and shorts in the process.

A dirty Phil, along with the rest of us, walked onto the pier a few minutes late.

Luckily Mark had waited.

CHAPTER NINE

We're gypsies in the palace
There ain't no wrong or right
We're gypsies in the palace
And we're raising hell tonight

Jimmy Buffett
Gypsies In The Palace

The four of us staggered aboard Mark's boat. "Cool boat," I said, as I stepped onto the red carpeting.

"Thanks," Mark replied. "My dad bought this boat brand new back in the sixties. It's a Sea Ray and I've spent the last five years restoring it. All my extra money working at the bar has gone into fixing this boat. My main expense was buying the twin, two hundred and twenty five horsepower engines. After that, my remaining investment has simply been finding the time to do the restoration. You wouldn't believe how hard it is to find authentic replacement parts for this old boat." Looking around I had to admit that he had done a nice job. The jet-black paint of the exterior contrasted nicely with the crimson red interior and set the boat apart from any other I'd ever seen. It was a classic. It had six, vinyl bucket seats, and an abundance of space for the five of us.

Phil's ass had hardly touched the cushion of the right rear seat, when he said, "That last shot at *Diva's* really did me in," and passed out cold. Bourbon Street had got the best of Phil tonight. But at least he would have a while to sleep it off before we got to the main event.

"You mind if I drive?" I asked.

"Have you ever driven a boat before?" Mark questioned me.

I frowned. "Well no," I replied, "but there's a first time for everything."

"You can't even drive a moped Tango; sit down," yelled Reno.

"Not tonight," Mark said, firing up the twin outboard motors. I guess I'd have to wait for another day before I realized my dream of becoming Captain Tango.

We pulled away from the pier through a cloud of exhaust and Mark idled the craft slowly out to sea.

"I love the smell of exhaust and sea air," yelled Mark.

"I love the smell of napalm in the morning," mumbled Phil. We all laughed because we thought for sure Phil was out like a prizefighter when he hit the canvas.

We left the marina behind us and cruised around the crest of the island on our way towards the Southernmost Point. Once we had reached the southern tip of the island, we continued to drift until we were out far enough to clear the 'No Wake Zone'. Mark gunned the engines, and the boat leapt into the air.

Phil fell out of his seat and landed on the floor with a loud thump. This time he was really asleep. We whooped and hollered as Mark pushed the Sea Ray to its limit. At this pace we'd be there in no time, I thought to myself. Suddenly, however, he slammed the throttle forward, sending the nose of the ship crashing back down into the water. We looked ahead at what Mark had already seen. An endless line of boats, too numerous to count, were drifting slowly a couple hundred yards in front of us in a ragged attempt at a line. The inboard lights from a countless stream of boats, reflected on the water in shades of green and red. The stars were dancing in the sky, and the bright lights of the Key had been turned down to dim. We slipped into the line and followed the pack slowly over to Christmas Tree Island.

Mark informed us that Little V's place was on the opposite, or Southern, side of the island. His mansion, along with about seven others on that side of the island, was blocked from any view while standing on Key West. Looking across the sea from Mallory Square, Christmas Tree Island would have appeared to be uninhabited. Eighty-five miles away, his mansion stared right into the heart of Cuba. Mark opened up a cooler that he had stowed underneath the captain's seat and handed us each an ice-cold bottle of Budweiser. We had yet to set foot on shore, but from the sights and sounds coming from the island, I could tell this party was big time. Just then Little V's property finally came into view. My jaw, like those of Reno and Lew, dropped to the floor of the boat as we looked at the place.

As we rounded the island from the northeast, the rear of the grounds had come into view, and it was impressive. The home seemed to emerge right out of the hillside that hid it from our view while on Key West. The evergreens, both beside and above the house on the hill, enforced the illusion. His mansion had the Old World appearance of a classic Mediterranean home. Carved out of the rocky shoreline was a man-made beach. It had a private beach that was about fifty yards long. The top of the beach blended into a grass lawn where there was a large pit spewing smoke and fire. The aroma of smoked meat hung in the air. "Smells like Little V's roasting a pig this year," Mark said, as he breathed in deeply.

Further back towards the house, resting on the right hand side of the lawn was an elaborate water fountain. It periodically sent up streams of water, rivaling the fountains found in many city parks. In the midst of the giant fountain was a nude statue of the Greek goddess Venus. The center of the grounds was taken up by what looked like a colossal in-ground swimming pool, which was positioned both inside and outside of the home. We could also see a large waterfall and rock waterslide on one end of the pool with a grouping of smaller round pools – most likely hot tubs – on the other.

Little V's mansion was quite possibly, the most beautiful home I'd ever seen. Seven arched entrances around the patio yielded to the vertical columns and horizontal lines of an enormous deck above. The house was painted white, with a very subtle grey tinted trim. The roof was made of red clay. Well-positioned spotlights along the property's foundation cast up enough light to allow arriving guests to get a good view of the backside of the mansion. I couldn't wait to get off the boat and do a little bit of exploring inside.

There were already about a hundred people milling about on the grounds and the steady beat from the metallic steel drums had already started my shoulders swaying. We were headed for the first of four big docks at the far end of his property. All four docks were shaped like large T's and could easily accommodate plenty of boats. The last dock in line though, only had three speedboats attached to it. The rest of that dock was taken up by an enormous yacht; I could only assume that it was Little V's personal craft. The first dock we came to was full, and an employee wearing a very tight, black Polo shirt and tan shorts instructed us to proceed to the next one. There were a few slots left at the end of the second dock and Mark told Lew to throw a line to another guy manning this dock wearing the same uniform.

As we docked the Sea Ray, I overheard a lady stepping off the boat beside us say to her husband that the home, "was designed in the symmetrical Palladian style of architecture." Whatever that meant.
"Wow" was all I could think to say.

After securing the boat, Mark moved towards the rear to grab some supplies for the party. Phil was now standing up and acting like he had been awake for the entire ride over. I stepped up onto the rail and grabbed the hand of a uniformed employee for support as I jumped on the wooden dock. Lew, Phil and Reno were following right behind me. "Thanks," I said to the guy as I looked at him for the first time. He had a familiar long scar across his face. "Aren't you a police officer?" I asked.
"As a matter of fact I am. Actually, I remember you from the other day at that big accident," he replied.
"And that skinny guy was with ya too," he said, pointing at Reno. He waved his arm in the direction of Phil and Lew, "Are these other two guys the friends that you were looking for?"
"Yeah," I answered.
"Well, if I recall correctly, didn't you tell me that you and your friends were from out of town? How'd you get invited to this party?" the policeman asked.
My mind started racing. I was trying to remember what our cover was, but my brain was drawing a blank. Fortunately Mark stepped in and saved me. "They're with me Al; they're helping me set up the bar."
Al stood there, running his fingers along his scar; he rubbed his jaw and thought about this for a few seconds. "That's fine, Mark, if you say so. But I'm gonna keep my eyes on you four. You better behave yourselves tonight." We started to walk away when he yelled again. "Mark. Don't forget to leave your keys. We may need to move the boat later." Mark tossed him the keys and we continued walking off the dock.
"Thanks," I whispered to Mark as we stepped off the dock. "So are all of the guys in black shirts cops?"
"Most likely," Mark replied. Apparently Little V didn't want any problems tonight.

Once we left the dock, the scenery changed for the better. There were two picture perfect women, wearing black and white G-string bikinis ready to greet us. Wearing smiles, they placed a lei over our beads and steered us in the direction of the party. Looking around, I noticed that all of the hostesses and waitresses were wearing similar outfits. I'd never seen so many postage stamp sized bikini tops in one place in all my life. It was like walking into the Playboy mansion. I liked what I saw. "So where did all of the female help come from? I sure hope they're not cops."

"Nah," Mark replied. "Most of them are locals, professional gals."

"Mark" Lew yelled, as we stepped across the rocky shoreline and onto the beach. "What are those boats for over there beside the yacht?" Looking in the direction Lew was pointing, I saw that there were four little powerboats. The outboard lights were on and they looked like they were ready to depart at a moments notice.

"Little V lets the guests use those boats in case they want to take a romantic moonlit ride around the island. Since all of our boats are going to end up double, if not triple stacked, it's just easier to use those if the need arises."

A rocky path, lit by the amber flames from several staggered bamboo torches, led the way from the beach through the lawn and over towards the pool. By the time we reached the pool, the smell of smoked pork was making all of our mouths water. Looking across the fountain, I could see the charred body of an enormous hog basting against the red glow of the pit.

"Well, I'll catch you guys later," Mark said. "I gotta go to work. You guys enjoy yourselves. I'm not scheduled to quit until dawn, so we'll be here all night. Catch up with you all later." He winked and headed to the side of the pool. Lew and I both looked at each other and said, "looks like a late booty call to Brooke and Kelly tonight."

The four of us stood on the Bermuda grass that separated the beach from the pool deck. Directly between the rocky shoreline and the stone patio that surrounded the pool were two of the most incredible palm trees I'd ever seen. They swayed slightly from side to side in the gentle breeze. The trunks of both resembled the shape of a quarter moon and each tree bowed away from the other, in order to allow the house to be seen from the water. Eventually, I diverted my gaze and quickly looked around the grounds at all of the people. As it turned out, most of the men and women at the party were dressed exceptionally well, wearing items that you'd expect to find in a fashion magazine. In contrast, the four of us, wearing a variety of Hawaiian shirts, T-shirts and khaki shorts were beginning to feel a bit out of place. Everybody was laughing and in a festive mood. "Maybe I should have taken a shower tonight," I said to Lew as we walked past the pool and headed inside. Stepping underneath one of the arched entrances, we walked into the indoor swimming pool room. Looking up, I noticed that the ceiling was made entirely out of glass panels, resting on a criss-crossed network of wooden joists. The overall effect was that of an extremely large skylight. Mammoth columns formed a semi-circle around the pool and held the ceiling in place. A wall along the back, with two sliding glass door entrances, separated the rest of the house from this room. As we walked in, I glanced to the left and noticed that along this entire side of the indoor portion of the pool was a bar. The top of the bar was made from some kind of stone and the bottom half was all glass block. Turquoise neon lights, positioned under the countertop, cast a blue tint, giving the bar a translucent look. It was about fifty feet in length, and there were numerous bar stools positioned in front, all of which were presently occupied. Mark was working behind the bar, and we stepped up to order a drink.

"This place is absolutely phenomenal," I said to Mark, as I took two of the cups from his hand and passed them out to Reno and Phil.

"Wait 'til you see the inside," he replied, handing me the other two drinks. He then floated to the end of the bar to fill another order.

While we were standing around the bar, at least every few minutes a girl in a G-string bikini would walk by carrying a tray holding a wide variety of hors d'oeuvres. Starving, we all began chowing down and ate more crab cakes than I could count. With a mouthful of food, I tried not to smile as I watched a group of women get pushed into the pool by a couple of wise guys. I didn't know who had pushed them, or I would have thanked them personally, especially when a few of the girls surfaced topless. Seeing this, Phil started to pop back into shape. But instead of commenting on the girls, he immediately started complaining about being starved.

"I need some real food" he went on, "enough of this finger food. Hey Reno, let's motivate inside. Try and find the kitchen." Without so much as a 'goodbye, catch ya later', they left Lew and I standing there and walked through one of the sliding glass doors and entered the house.

"So what do you feel like doing?" I asked Lew.

"Let's go over to the pool and look at those naked chicks," he replied. I was easily convinced and we sauntered over towards the pool's edge. Upon closer inspection, the pool itself was every bit as impressive as the rest of the place. Countless tropical plants flanked the pool along the shoreline, however, the rest of the free-form perimeter allowed for poolside seating. After removing our sandals, Lew and I sat down on the bar-side edge and stuck our feet in the pool. The water was luke warm and crystal clear. The abundant underwater pool lights surrounded the perimeter and lit up the water like a Christmas tree. Looking down I could see all the way to the bottom of the pool, where an octopus made out of mosaic tiles rested. A group of about six girls were splashing and laughing amongst themselves a mere fifteen feet from where we were seated. At least three of them were topless. Watching us sit down, one of the topless girls yelled over in our direction.

"Nice shirt. I like the surfboard design." I looked down, half way expecting to see that a new sweat stain had emerged. Relieved to see that my shirt was still dry, I smiled and thanked her, telling her it was brand new.

"Hi there surfer, why don't you jump in with us?" she replied, winking at me. I felt Lew's elbow nudge me in the ribs.

"Ya Tango, jump on in," Lew said.

I looked closely at the girl. She was hot, and she was topless. My mind was already made up, but I thought I'd fool around with her momentarily before jumping in. "First of all," I began, "I'm from Kansas. I don't surf. Second of all, I'm not wearing any swim trunks." Needless to say, I was shocked when a couple of seconds later a pair of wet bikini bottoms slammed into my chest with a thud.

"Neither am I," she yelled back. I looked down, to find that my shirt was once again soaking wet. Only this time, I wasn't about to keep it on. I glanced over at Lew and simply shrugged my shoulders. He was already grinning.

Some girls that were seated by us, moved closer to Lew and started egging me on. "Come on surfer boy," they yelled. "Jump in." I was able to count at least eight naked people swimming, four of which were men, after a quick glance back into the pool.

"Don't expect me to join ya." Lew laughed, as I took off my shirt and shorts. Lew was dressed way too nice, his hair looked way too good and he was entirely too vain to follow my lead. Not that I really expected him to anyway.

"I don't," I replied as I slipped out of my shirt and shorts and jumped in. This elicited a shriek from the girls in the pool. "I do expect you to keep track of my clothes and hang onto my money clip. Keep my cash in your pocket." I threw Lew my wet boxers and swam underwater, emerging in the middle of the six girls. Before I could get my bearings, I had the original naked lady in one arm and a newly unclad beauty in the other. From the looks of things, I liked the odds. One gal whispered in my ear "you're the only straight guy in the pool right now." I was beginning to enjoy the attention of all the ladies.

A short time later, now completely acclimated to my new surroundings, I couldn't believe I was standing in about four feet of water, encircled by three naked women. We were drinking, laughing and in general having one hell of a good time. I looked over to see what Lew was up to and noticed that he had moved along the pool's edge closer to where the food was cooking. There were a few tables set up on that side of the pool and each housed a cooler underneath. Lew was sitting in a long line of guests, all with their legs dangling over the edge, submerged to their knees in the water.

Noticing the women's drinks were starting to empty, I drifted over towards the spot where Lew was sitting. The bar on the other side of the pool was packed, so Lew was my best chance at getting refreshments for all of us.

"Lew," I yelled, when I had reached the center of the pool, "how about rounding up my ladies and me a drink?"

I heard some guy yell out from the far corner, "yes, Lew, and don't forget about us ladies over here." We all laughed out loud.

I saw Lew motion with his fingers for me to come on over. I quickly swam the rest of the way underneath the water and broke the surface a couple feet from where the legs of Lew's female friend were casually treading in the water. He stood up and looked across the pool at the packed bar. "You got to be kidding me. I'm not about to wait in that line just so you and your naked harem can get a fresh one."

"Just grab us some beers out of one of those coolers," I said, pointing behind him. A few moments later, he returned with two six packs. He tossed six beers over to the guys and then handed me the other six cans. I was enjoying myself too much to feel guilty for making Lew get me the drinks, even when a few of the other guests along the pool mistook him for a waiter and started requesting similar beer runs. Laughing, I returned to my skinny-dipping lady friends. Being Lew, he took it all in stride, and before too long he was filling the role quite well as poolside cabana boy, passing out drinks left and right to anyone who walked by empty handed. He was becoming quite popular, and the guys even tried to give him a five-dollar tip, which, of course, he pocketed.

As with all good things, my time spent naked in the pool with the other beautiful people had to come to an end. It was announced that the flame roasted pig was finally ready to eat. The cooks had been barbequing it for the better half of a day, and the charcoaled skin was blackened from the smoke. They began carving and slicing slabs of juicy white meat, stacking it onto huge platters that were set atop the picnic tables spread out on the far side of the lawn. A buffet line was starting to form. Lew wanted to be at the head of that line.

"Tango, get over here!" Lew yelled out. I was quite hungry myself, and the smell coming from the smoky pit was enough to make my mouth water. I said goodbye to the ladies that I'd spent the better part of the last hour naked. One of them grabbed my butt as I swam over to see what Lew wanted. "Come on dude, get out. Let's get in line," Lew said.

"Did you forget something?" I asked. "I'm naked. Where are my clothes?"

"Relax. I set them over on the other side of the pool, beside the bar where Mark is working. Here, there's no time to get them now. Wrap up in this." He threw me a big rainbow-striped beach towel. It was the only colorful towel on top of a stack of at least thirty others. Rolling my eyes, I wrapped it around my waist.

"You couldn't at least have given me a solid colored towel? People are going to think I'm gay." I sighed. He tugged me by the arm and led me over to what became the front of the buffet line. I dished up a plate full of smoked ham, potato salad, beans, crab legs and conch fritters. We sat down at an empty picnic bench and ate as though we'd been starved for days. I don't know about Lew, but after I was done, I felt sober again and was ready to investigate the inside of the mansion. I got up to go find my clothes and grab us each a fresh drink from the bar. Walking over to where Lew had told me he'd left my clothes, I found nothing but sand. Mark came over and took my drink request. "Lew didn't put my clothes behind the bar did he?" I asked him before he turned to get the drinks.

"Nope, I haven't seen them. But nice towel," he replied grinning.

Just then Lew walked up. "What's up?" He had a fresh plate of food in his hands. He passed me a rack of ribs and kept a couple of pulled pork sandwiches for himself.

"My clothes are gone," I said.

"I can't believe anybody would want to steal them," Lew said. "If they'd have seen what that shirt had gone through tonight, I guarantee they'd have left that alone. Not to mention the fact that you've been wearing those shorts for days."

"Oh well," I replied. "Screw it; I like to be naked anyway." Cinching the towel to my waist, we grabbed our drinks and walked into the mansion, through the same set of glass doors Phil and Reno had entered a while ago.

Stepping across the threshold, we entered a palace. We were standing in what appeared to be the main foyer. Most of the décor inside was in tune with a Mediterranean feel; the walls were yellow, with gold and black accents, and the white marbled floor resembled the sand found along the beaches in the Old World. Golden suede couches filled what appeared to be a living room, with at least a dozen over-stuffed black and gold crested pillows. Some gray and black, floral printed, high backed chairs sat in the middle of the room. The furniture surrounded a huge glass topped coffee table and well-placed tropical plants, baskets of fruit and candlesticks topped with elaborate trimmings were everywhere. The room itself was very open, with a ceiling three stories above painted to look like the sky, complete with clouds. A stairwell on both sides of the room led to the second floor balcony that formed a horseshoe. The archways, iron hand railings and elaborate chandeliers created an entrance to the house.

Neither Lew, nor myself, recognized any of the guests mingling here, so we decided to see what was behind the doublewide walnut doors on the right hand side of the room. Although the doors were as thick and formidable as what you'd expect to see at a bank vault, the muffled sounds of a good time seemed to slip between the cracks in the doorframe. When Lew opened the doors, I knew this was the room we'd be staying in for a while, because the first thing I saw was Reno and some other guy standing shirtless playing pool with two beautiful women.

"Tango! Lew!" Reno yelled, his eyes lighting up as he saw us come in, "You guys want in on this action?" We walked over to see what was up.

"What action is that?" Lew asked, while taking a bite out of one of his sandwiches.

"Why strip pool, of course," Reno grinned. "I want you to meet Daisy and Valerie. They're lingerie models."

"I don't think I'm wearing enough to put up much of a fight," I said.

"No kidding," Lew laughed.

Glancing at Daisy and Valerie I noticed unfortunately, that they were not wearing lingerie, and appeared to be completely dressed.

"Doesn't look like you're doing too well," I said to Reno, shaking hands with the two models. Daisy looked more familiar than Valerie. I'm pretty sure that I'd seen her on the cover of a few magazines.

"Speak for yourself, Tango. I thought with all the pool I'd been playing down here, it was going to be easy to see some beautiful women naked. I still got a chance." He looked me up and down, his eyes scanning from my toes to my head. "So, Tango, what's up with the towel?" Reno replied.

"Long story."

It turned out that Reno and some other guy from Jacksonville were losing to the two models. Both were down to their shorts, while neither of the ladies had removed even a stitch of clothing. Unfortunately for Reno, he just wasn't that good at pool, at least not without Lew's help.

Lew and I sat down on a couple of bar stools and watched the game play out while we ate.

Just then Daisy walked over to our table and sat down next to Lew.

"Can I have a bite of your sandwich? I'm starving."

"I didn't think models ate," Lew laughed.

Daisy grabbed the half eaten sandwich on Lew's plate and took a bite. Licking her lips between swallows she said provocatively "No. We like meat." as she continued to devour Lew's sandwich. "So what's up with your friend in the towel?"

"Someone stole my clothes," I sighed.

"God only knows why," Lew said grinning.

Just then we heard a huge roar. Reno was jumping up and down hugging the guy from Jacksonville. Valerie had just sunk the eight ball without pocketing the remaining striped balls on the table. Reno yelled, "Cool. Now take off your shirts." Then both girls took their tops off, revealing just their white bras.

"Nice Calvin Klein bras," Lew said, pointing to the small CK in the middle of Daisy's breasts.

"Thanks" she replied.

Figuring he wasn't going to see anything more than a bra, Reno decided to end their game and steal some of our food. Not surprisingly, the girls decided to head out into the rest of the party. Lew, never one to miss an opportunity, went over to Daisy and whispered in her ear, before heading back to our group.

"What did you say?" Reno asked Lew as he rejoined us at the table.

"I asked if her panties matched her bra."

"And?" Reno inquired.

"You had you're chance to find out," Lew smirked.

'So where's Phil?" I asked, just realizing that I hadn't seen him since he and Reno left us some time ago.

"I don't know" Reno replied. "He was watching me play pool earlier. Come to think of it, I haven't seen him in at least an hour."

At that moment, a familiar figure walked through the entrance. It was Paula from the strip club a few nights ago. Carrying a large tray of mixed drinks, she was in the standard issue cocktail waitress uniform of a black G-string bikini. She looked fantastic, her breasts spilled out on both sides of the bikini top, revealing an abundance of cleavage. I couldn't keep my eyes of her as she delivered a round of margaritas to a group of folks sitting around the big screen television across the room. Done with that order, she headed our way. She was about ten feet away from us when she stopped dead in her tracks. A trace of a smile wiped across her lips. "Hi Tango, what the hell are you guys doing here?" she asked.

"Tango fell in love with you, so we've been following you." Lew replied sarcastically.

She replied, "No, I fell in love with him."

Lew grabbed some drinks from her tray and pulled out his wallet to give her a tip.

"No gratuities needed," she grinned, "my tip will be seeing what Tango's got beneath that towel later."

Before I had a chance to respond she continued on, talking beneath her breath, as if to herself. "You know, I thought I might see the rest of you guys around here somewhere."

"What do you mean?" Lew asked.

She sighed nervously, eyes darting back and forth across the room. In a barely audible tone, she whispered, "I just saw your buddy getting escorted upstairs. Only I don't think he was going up there on his own free will. He made quite a scene out there."

As Paula told us this, I saw Reno's jaw clench tightly. "What in the hell! How could Phil get into trouble?" Reno looked at Lew and then me. "Well, we've got to go find him. That's all there is to it."

The three of us got up, thanked Paula for the information and told her we'd talk to her later on after we got all this straightened out. As we walked past her, she grabbed me by the arm. "So what are you wearing beneath that towel?" she asked.

"Nothing but my birthday suit."

"Make sure you see me again before you leave tonight," she winked. I smiled back and grinned, but before I could respond, Lew grabbed me by the neck and dragged me away.

"Come on," Lew yelled at Reno.

"I can't find my shirt and shoes," Reno hollered back.

"Leave 'em," Lew hissed.

We left the room and stood at the bottom of the steps leading up to the second floor and looked at each other. I was basically still nude, except for my towel, Reno was wearing only a pair of shorts, but Lew looked perfect, in the same clothes he'd been wearing all night. His hair wasn't even messed up. Not knowing exactly what to do, or where to go, we simply ran up the flight of stairs and tried opening every door we came to. Reno was hollering Phil's name every few seconds.

The first door we came upon was unlocked. It opened into an empty bedroom. The second door was a hallway bathroom with some people inside snorting coke. We glanced in amazement – not at the drug use but at the decor. This was not your ordinary, everyday bathroom. The walls had been painted to resemble an underwater scene of kelp and sea sponge. Hearing the obligatory, "you want some?" we slammed the door and continued our search. Several other doors led to more empty rooms. Then we were facing two huge wood panel doors that were at the end of the long hallway. Lew got there first and found they were locked. Reno kneeled down and pressed his ear up to the door and we stood there silently waiting for a few seconds. You didn't need your ear on the door to hear the yelling that soon commenced. Lew abruptly pulled Reno away. We stood there, not even breathing. Then suddenly, there was a loud snap, followed by a muffled cry.

"This is bullshit!" Reno yelled, pushing me and Lew aside as he rammed his shoulder into the door. It didn't budge. Cursing again, Reno stepped back and although barefooted, kicked the doors as hard as he could. The doors slammed open, wood splinters flew off the doors hinges and sprayed across the floor. We were looking into another bedroom, only this time it wasn't empty. Phil was seated on a chair; both wrists were wrapped with duck tape behind his back. His mouth was also covered with tape and his shirt was dripping wet. Standing directly in front of him, now facing us were three thugs.

Phil's face was bloodied. In the few spilt seconds before blows were thrown, I saw Phil raise his eyebrows and even smile. He yelled something unintelligible through the tape, right before Reno ran straight into the room, screaming at the top of his lungs. He charged right towards the biggest of the three guys standing in the middle of the room and tackled him. I don't think Reno ever played football in his life, but he could have been an all-pro linebacker, with the hit he laid on that unsuspecting thug. The two of them rolled across the floor towards the right side of the room, stopping at the foot of the bed. When they came to a stop, Reno was on top of the thug, who was lying face down on the carpeted floor. Reno quickly grabbed the guy by the hair with both hands, picking his head and torso up off the ground. Pulling him over to the foot of the bed, Reno slammed the guy's head into the walnut footboard. A hideous cracking sound filled the room. All of this happened in about five seconds, Lew and I were still standing in the doorway.

Phil, spotting his chance to flee, leapt out of the chair and ran straight for the door. He darted right between the two goons -- left standing in the middle of the room -- and rushed past Lew and I, who were running into the room to try and back up Reno. Fortunately, the other two guys Reno had left for us were quite a bit older and not in the best of shape. Lew lunged towards one. The goon had a roll of duck tape in his hand and tried to punch him with it. But Lew blocked the blow with his arm and then smacked him in the face, sending the guy sprawling to the ground. All I was able to do was simply push my guy around, before Phil had managed to work the tape free from his hands and mouth and yelled out, "Come on, let's get out of here." With energy that came out of nowhere, I shoved the guy to the floor and stood on top of him, my bare foot pressed against his throat. Out of the corner of my eye, I could see Lew punching his guy square in the nose, causing a spray of blood on the white carpeting. I quickly looked over in Reno's direction and saw that he was still beating his opponents' head against the bed frame. When he finally stopped, the thug was unconscious and lay in a heap at the foot of the bed. Taking Phil's advice, I stepped off the old man's throat and started to leave. I heard Phil yell out, "Hey Tango" and turned to see the guy had stood up and was coming after me. He reached out and grabbed the towel that was tied around my waist, pulling it off. I did the first thing that came to my mind. I kicked him right in the balls. Needless to say, the old guy crumbled like a sack of potatoes and lay howling on the floor. Hauling bare assed out of the room, I joined Reno and Phil in the hallway. Seconds later, Lew came crashing out, closing the doors behind him. He held onto both doorknobs, with a knuckle white death grip.

"What the hell was that all about Phil?" Lew yelled, still pulling on the doorknob, ensuring that no one inside could get out.

"I'll explain later, we gotta get outta here though."

"Guys. Head to the docks and grab a boat," Lew yelled, still hanging onto the doors. Phil was already running down the stairs. By this time, the guys inside were pounding on the door, trying to get out. The doors kept opening a crack and then slamming shut as Lew held on tight. Reno had already bolted, and I looked at Lew wondering what to do.

"Go Tango!" he yelled. "I'll hold them off."

I turned to run down the stairs, realizing for the first time that I was stark naked. *I better run fast*, I thought to myself, bounding down the stairs.

When I got to the landing I snuck a peek over my shoulder in time to see Lew let go of the doorknob. The door flew open and the two guys inside went toppling backwards into the room. A split second later, Lew was running past me in the foyer. As I raced to catch up to him, I could hear the shrieks, both ahead of me and behind me, probably in response to seeing a bloodied Phil and me streaking naked. I didn't dare look back to see if we were being chased, but everything inside me said we were. Distinctly I heard someone shout, "Stop those guys." but I focused all my energy on pushing through the crowd of people and trying not to get caught in the process. Since we had been inside, a lot more people had arrived, and we had to shove our way through the crowd of people milling around between the pool and the house. Finally through the thickest of the crowd and running as fast as my legs could carry me, I caught up and passed the other three guys. As we sprinted past the bar, I heard Mark shout out something about my clothes. Ignoring him, I led the other three as we crashed through the garden in front of the beach and ran towards the docks. My mind raced, almost as fast as my legs, trying to figure out what to do. Then I remembered someone telling us that the speedboats tied up on the last dock were there for the guests to use.

That was our ticket out of here. As I hit the shoreline, I turned in the direction of Little V's yacht and collided into the cop with the scar on his face. Hitting him square in the chest, he bounced backwards a couple of steps. Not even thinking, I ran past him, stiff-arming him in the process, causing him to fall off the dock. "I thought I told you guys to behave tonight!" he yelled out, his fist pumping in the dark water, as I ran off. I was already jumping into the first speedboat I came to when he finished his sentence. To my delight, the keys were in the ignition. I turned them and the boat engines roared to life. Here was my chance to become Captain Tango, I thought to myself. I raced to the back of the boat and started untying the ropes when Reno jumped in and started undoing the ropes in front. Phil lumbered in next breathing heavily and Lew crashed into the boat seconds later. Putting the kibosh on my plans of chartering this getaway, Lew planted himself behind the steering wheel. He gunned the throttle and we sped away from the docks, running over a 'No Wake' buoy on our way out. The inboard lights were turned off in an attempt to conceal our getaway. We quickly vanished into the blackness of the ocean and night sky.

The four of us were silent as we sped away from the party. Once we were out of range, he slowed the small boat's engine down to a low idle. We could barely hear the motor purring over the sounds of the waves lapping against the boat. It was only at this point any of us dared speaking, and even then just barely above a whisper. We were looking behind us to see if anybody was following us. They were.

"What are we going to do now?" Reno whispered loudly.

"I'm going the long way around the island, hoping to throw them off track," Lew replied.

Almost as soon as he said this we heard the engines ignite on a couple of other boats, probably the remaining two that were tied up next to the yacht. Seconds later, we saw the distinct lights illuminate on both vessels. There were at least one, maybe two or three men in each boat, and they all were carrying floodlights that were shining back and forth across the ocean. Lew's plan seemed to be working: Both boats raced off in the opposite direction we were headed, back towards Key West. Relieved, we spent the next half hour circling slowly around Christmas Tree Island. Feeling a bit more secure for the moment, we were finally able to catch our breath and think about what happened.

"So Phil, what gives? What in the hell did you do to get beat up like that?" Lew asked.

Phil sighed loudly and then chuckled, "Long story, I'll tell you later."

By now, we had finally come full circle around the island and were starting to head back towards Key West. Lew kept the boat at a slow idle as we all continued to look around to see if there were any signs of trouble.

"There they are," Reno whispered. He was pointing in the direction of Mallory Square. Clear as day, we could see the two boats circling in the harbor beside Mallory Square. They must be searching for us in the marina where Mark's boat was docked earlier that night.

"Any ideas?" Lew asked.

"Well we gotta hide out somewhere," Reno replied.

"Lew," I said. "Do you think you can find those caverns Captain Bill showed us? The ones the pirates used to hide out in?"

"Good idea Tango. I can find them." He quickly banked the wheel to the left and we drifted east, staying as far away from the coast, and the bad guys, as we could. Once we passed the piers; it took us about ten minutes to reach the caverns we had seen a few days ago during our adventure tour. He pulled the craft into the first hideout we came to that looked large enough to house a small boat. Lew carefully navigated the boat through the rocky entrance and cut the engine once we were inside. It took some time for our eyes to adjust to the blackness within the cave, but once they did we were able to see the inside walls surrounding us on three sides. Phil pulled out his lighter igniting a large flame in front of his face.

"You got that thing at full throttle," I said.

He lit his cigarette, and then used the flame to get a quick look around. "I guess now is as good a time as any to let you guys in on what happened tonight," he said as he took a long drag from his cigarette.

"Well, first of all, thanks for the rescue. I thought I was going to be tied up in there all freaking night." He rubbed his jaw; obviously still tender from the beating he'd taken. "You guys are never going to believe who Little V is. I know I couldn't." He then proceeded to recount the events that had happened that evening. "I was watching Reno play pool inside, just kind of hanging back, you know, getting a feel for the crowd. As the game wore on, it was obvious that none of the women were going to be taking off any clothes, so I decided to head back towards the bar and get another drink. That's when I saw him."

"Who?" Reno interrupted.

"The guy from the accident. The fat guy that caused it."

"You're shitting me." I said.

"No man, that's what I thought, but I even rubbed my eyes, to make sure they weren't playing tricks on me. They weren't. He was standing in the foyer, laughing and talking to just about everyone that walked by. I asked a girl that walked past me who the guy was. She had just finished talking to him. When she told me he was Little V, I couldn't believe the irony." He stopped talking, wincing a little, and rubbed some more on his sore jaw. He laughed to himself again and continued on. "I tried to disappear in the crowd but, instead, as I headed in the opposite direction, I ran right into a waitress carrying a plate full of drinks. The drinks soaked the front of me and crashed to the floor. Everyone was looking at me – especially Little V. Our eyes locked for the second time in so many days, only this time I knew I was trapped. He nodded at the man standing next to him and before I knew it, I had three guys surrounding me. They dragged me upstairs into the bedroom, tied my wrists and sat me down on that damn chair. I couldn't believe it when they started interrogating me, asking me what I was doing here and things like that. I guess they didn't like my answers. After about ten minutes of intense badgering, Little V left and the other guys were telling me to keep my mouth shut, things like that, they put the tape across my mouth and really started laying into me. One guy actually smacked me a few times with the roll of duct tape. I was seeing stars, my mouth was filled with blood and my head was throbbing. Thank God a few minutes into it you guys burst in."

We sat in silence after Phil stopped talking. Nobody quite knew what to say. It was noticeably cooler in the cave and I became much more conscious that I was naked. Before I knew it, I was starting to shiver. I looked around the boat to see if there were any towels to cover up with. There were none. My teeth clattered for what seemed an eternity as we sat in the darkness and waited. Seconds became minutes and I swear the minutes dragged into hours. I think hypothermia was beginning to set in and just as I was wondering if it was possible to develop frostbite in the tropics, Lew cleared his throat, snapping me out of my self-induced trance.

"Let's get out of here," he said, starting the motor.

We cautiously headed back in the direction of our hotel.

"I'm thinking we park this boat around the corner from our hotel," said Lew. We all agreed. By this time, the first signs of dawn were appearing on the horizon as streaks of paler blues were smeared across the sky. Apparently, we had waited in the cave long enough, because as we crept out to the open sea, we couldn't see Little V's boats anywhere. Relieved, Lew increased the speed of the boat and we flew around the island. Driving past Fort Zachary Taylor and the Southernmost Point, I was finally able to feel a sense of relief, aside from the fact that I was still a little chilled. The long night was just about over. Lew docked the boat at the pier next to our hotels. It was the only dock around that could house a boat and, hopefully, it would blend in with the others. After tying the boat down, we walked up a flight of stairs, heading towards the gated exit. It was locked from the outside with a bolt. The fence was at least nine feet tall, made from rod iron with sharp little points on top. There was absolutely no chance I was going to scale that fence naked. It was simply too risky. *Just great*, I thought. The only way back to the hotel pier was to swim across the ocean. The same swim we had refused to do the first night on the island.

"What the hell," I said as I dove into the water. The other three guys quickly followed. Phil had begun to stiffen up so we each had to take turns helping him swim back to the hotel pier. Fortunately, the ocean was calm, and we managed to navigate the distance between the piers with relative ease. Emerging from the sea, I felt a hundred degrees warmer. Phil looked at my naked body and laughed.

"What's so funny?" I asked, beginning to take offense to his laughter.

"Remember that first night, when you said you wouldn't run back naked to the hotel room?"

"Yeah," I said.

"Well, it looks like you are now."

CHAPTER TEN

It's that kind of mornin',
Really was that kind of night
Tryin' to tell myself that my condition is improvin'
And if I don't die by Thursday
I'll be roarin' Friday night.

Jimmy Buffett
My Head Hurts, My Feet Stink and I Don't Love Jesus

We were all laughing with nervous unease as I ran, or should I say jogged, back to the hotel room. It felt good to laugh, but it felt even better to bound up the stairs and see the black, steel numbers identifying room 228. Still naked, I was very anxious to get inside and put on some clothes. This had to be some kind of record for the most time I'd ever spent outside in the nude. After standing alone by the door for a few brief seconds, I was joined by Reno. "Where's Lew?" I asked him, "He's got the key."

Reno backed over to the railing and looked down the stairwell. "He's walking out in the parking lot next to Phil."

I sat back down and shut my eyes, hoping to catch a bit of a rest before Lew and Phil got back. I could hear Reno doing the same, as he took a seat across from me. I was just about to drift off to sleep when I heard footsteps coming up the stairwell. I rubbed my eyes, suppressed the urge to yawn and stood up, stretching as I did. Becoming more and more comfortable being naked, my arms were above my head, with my fingers interlocked as I stretched my aching back. I opened my eyes, expecting to see either Phil or Lew standing in front of me. I was wrong.

"Ay mi dios!" screamed the cleaning lady. "Santo mierda!"

I tried to cover myself with my hands as the heavyset old lady continued to gawk at me. Shaking her head, she walked over to the supply closet located next door to our room. "Reno, you know any Spanish?" I asked. "Tell her we need our key."

"Ahh, perdido..." Reno paused. "Perdido...clave. Yeah, Perdido clave."

"What the hell did you say to her?" I asked.

"I told her we don't have our key and need some help getting into the room."

"You said all that with two freaking words?" I yelled.

"What can I say; my Spanish is a little rusty. But I'm pretty sure that's what I said."

"La respuesta es no" the cleaning lady said wagging her index finger at us. She walked into the closet, slamming the door shut behind her.

"What was that Reno, I didn't quite understand everything she said, but doesn't 'no' translate into 'no'?"

"Come on Lew," I yelled, "I'd like to get inside before the sun comes back out." A few minutes later, Lew and Phil finally emerged from the staircase. Tired from waiting and still a bit embarrassed after the run in with the cleaning lady, I was sitting on the wooden boards of the hallway floor, hoping I wouldn't pick up any splinters on my back side. "'Bout freaking time. Could you open the door please?" Lew was busy fishing around in his pockets. I watched as he felt inside both of his front pockets and then put his hands inside both of the back pockets. He quickly touched his neck, but all that was there was a strand of beads and a battered lei. "You gotta be kidding me." I sighed.

Lew looked shocked. He held his arms out to his side. "Dudes, I can't find the key. It must have fallen out of my pocket during the fight. Either that or when we were running away." He stood there rubbing his forehead. "Tango, you still got that spare key, right?"

I stood up abruptly. "Does it look like I got the spare key? Where do you think I got it hidden Lew?"

"Well since we're locked out, let's just go see if the girls are still up. We can bang on their door and crash there." Before I could even respond, Lew started walking in the opposite direction down the hall towards their room.

"No way, Lew" I yelled. "I'm naked. The only thing I want to do is get into bed and sleep. You can make out with Chrissy later, after you get this door open." This got Lew to turn around.

"Can you just go ask the front desk for a replacement key first?" He looked at each of us and finally realized that I was naked, Phil was bruised and bloodied and Reno was shirtless and shoeless, because he quickly changed his mind and said, "I'll go down and get a spare key from the front desk." He turned and left the three of us standing in front of our hotel room door. I could hear some seagulls squawking above the beach and looking out was upset to see the first streaks of daylight as the sun began to rise.

"He better hurry up, I don't want to get caught nude again out here with you two."

Out of the corner of my eye, I saw Lew start running. Turning to see what was going on, I watched in horror as he sped past the stairwell and stopped a few doors further down the hall. Just as I realized what was going on, he slammed both of his fists against the door and banged loudly, like a hard rock drummer conducting a solo. As quick as he'd stopped to knock on the door, he was even quicker about running away. As he jumped down the staircase, I realized that I better get something put on real quick. Any second now, there was likely to be a few women in the hallway, in response to Lew's barrage.

"Phil. Quick, let me wear your shirt" I yelled, hoping to at least cover myself up somewhat. No sooner had I pulled Phil's shirt over my head, when the girl's door opened. Fortunately Phil's Hawaiian shirt hung down to the top of my thighs, so it wasn't readily apparent that I was naked, at least not from a distance.

Lynn's head poked out from behind the open door. She looked the opposite direction from where we were standing first, but quickly turned our way. Focusing in on me her eyes grew real wide and she smiled. "What's all the commotion, Tango? What are you doing out here?" I noticed her hair was all messed up, she had obviously been sleeping. She was wearing a white cotton nightie that stopped just above her thighs. It looked great on her.

I started walking over towards her, slowly. "We're locked out. Lew banged on your door, screwing around on his way to get a replacement. I don't even know if the lobby is open, so he may not even be able to get one."

"Well, why don't you come on in? You can wait inside" she smiled.

"That would be great. Thanks." I continued walking towards her.

"You two can come in too" she said, looking over my shoulder at a shirtless Reno and Phil.

"Nah. We're cool." Reno replied.

As I approached the open door, I followed her eyes, as they looked down. "Tango, where are your pants?" she gasped.

I sighed, knowing this question would be coming. "It's a long story" I said as I crossed the threshold and entered the room. I heard her close the door quietly behind me.

"What did those guys do? Did they de-pant you?" she whispered.

"Something like that" I replied. The room was dark. I could see that Maria and Chrissy were still asleep. Chrissy was on the fold out and Maria was on one of the two beds.

"Here. Put these on. They should fit." She had handed me a pair of boxer shorts. "I wear then when I lounge around."

"Thanks." I stepped into the shorts. "Do you mind if I crash on the floor. I'm dead tired. It's been one hell of a night."

The last thing I remember was hearing her say, "You can sleep with me in my bed."

I awoke from a sound sleep some time later to an incessant knocking on the door. *It's got to be Lew*, I thought. Lynn's bed was so comfortable; I had fallen asleep the second I laid down. Unfortunately, at the moment, Lynn was not in bed with me, since she was once again answering Lew's incessant pounding. Lynn opened the door, and as I suspected, it was Lew. I heard him explain that he had finally managed to round up a spare key and our room was unlocked. At the sound of Lew's voice, Chrissy sat up on the fold out. Lynn slipped back under the covers with me and nestled in against my chest. Needless to say, I wasn't going anywhere.

I heard Chrissy whisper, "That doesn't mean you're leaving does it?"

"Not now." Lew grinned. "I was sleeping on the floor back at our place. But why does Tango get the good bed?"

At some point later that morning, Lew and I exited the love shack. The girls needed to get ready for the morning, and we were still looking for some more sleep. "I told you I'd be naked with someone tonight." I said as we walked back down the hallway towards our room. We both laughed as we opened up the door. Within minutes I was crashed out on my bed.

I bolted upright, still in bed. Somebody was banging on the door. Hard. It didn't feel like I'd been asleep too long, my head was pounding – or was that the door? Out of the corner of my eye, I watched Lew get out of bed and stumble over to the door. As the knocking continued, Lew opened the door. The chain only allowed it to open a crack. But through that crack I saw them both. There were two police officers standing in the hallway.

"Sir open up the door."

Lew complied. The two officers stepped across the threshold. "Everybody get up, slowly. How many people are in the room?"

"Four," Lew answered.

"Get where I can see you," an officer shouted as the lights in the room snapped on. His partner stepped behind us, as the rest of us rolled out of bed. Corralling us like a herd of cattle, before we even realized it, the four of us were standing by the door, with an officer on either side of us, blocking both our exit and our passage back into our room. "You guys stay put," the cop in the room, ordered, as he started to search our space.

I looked down and realized I had pink hearts on my borrowed boxer shorts. Nice. Real, nice.

"You got a warrant to do that?" Reno mouthed off.

"Shut up," the cop in the doorway replied.

"I bet you don't," he continued.

"Hey, I'll take that bet," Phil smiled.

"I said, shut the hell up," the officer yelled, interrupting their transaction. "Where were you guys last night?"

Lew spoke up. "We were at a party out on Christmas Tree Island."

"Try again guys, that's invite only," said the second officer, seemingly complete with his search. He resumed his position behind us. "Where were you really?"

"Dude, I swear to God, we were at that party."

"I guarantee the whole party will remember that Tango was there," Reno added.

"If I have to tell you to shut up one more time, you'll be sorry," the officer by the door scowled at Reno. He pointed at Lew, "you were saying?"

"Nothing," Lew said. "I don't know what more to tell you, we were at that party."

"So whose car is that out front?" the officer asked, changing the subject.

"What?" Lew questioned. We all had puzzled looks on our faces.

"Whose car is parked out front?"

"Dude, we don't have a car."

The officer by the door sighed loudly. "This is going nowhere," I heard him mumble. "Follow us, and grab your ID's," he said, turning around.

"Um, excuse me sir?" Phil was standing there with his hand raised.

"What now?"

'Hey, um, I lost my ID last night," Phil replied.

"So did I," I added.

"Well isn't that convenient. You both lost your ID's? Follow us anyway."

We were led outside, into the thick morning air. We followed them over to a big silver Buick.

"One last time guys. Whose car is this?"

"I think I can speak for all of us when I say, we've never seen this car before," I said.

"Is that a fact?" The officer who'd been questioning us paused, as if to add drama to what he was about to say. "Let me bring you guys up to speed. O.K.?"

We all nodded.

"We ran the plates on this car. It's been reported stolen."

"So? What's that got to do with us?" Reno yelled.

The cop gave him a cold hard look. "When we searched the inside, we found two sets of ID's and some clothing."

Lew and I exchanged glances, we were not quite sure where this was going, but neither of us liked what we had heard thus far.

"Anybody recognize these wallets?" He was holding one in each hand. Ripping the Velcro free on one, he pulled out a driver's license. "So which one of you guys is Jay Murciak?"

Phil blurted out, "Murciak? Who the hell is Murciak? Ha, ha you got the wrong guys."

I just shook my head. "You dumb ass, I'm Jay Murciak."

"Oh yeah, that's right. I forgot."

Smiling, the cop approached Phil, "so you must be Phil Kappell," he said handing him his ID. "Do your friends call you Einstein?"

"No," Phil replied.

"Look dudes," Lew interrupted, "We've obviously been set up. We've never seen this car before."

"Well that's very interesting," he replied. "You guys go to a party last night – an invite only party, two of you just happen to lose your ID's when you're there. This sound accurate so far?"

We nodded.

"Anyway, where was I? Oh yeah, a car winds up stolen last night, about the same time you guys are at this party, and then miraculously, it ends up parked in front of your hotel room the next morning. On top of all that, two wallets are found inside the car, Jay and Phil's, and there is a set of clothing that looks like any one of you would fit into."

None of us quite knew how to respond, but we knew we'd been set up.

"Now this is how it's going to go down. Detective Mahony over there is going to take down all of your information."

"Yeah, then what?" Reno asked. "Are we under arrest?"

"Not yet," he replied. "We're not going to arrest anybody at this point, we still need to check into a few leads and what not. We'll be getting back in touch later."

"Well how long will that be?" Lew asked. "We're planning on heading home in a few days."

"For now, you guys need to stay put. Don't leave the island, don't change hotels, in other words stay where we can find you."

"Hey, how long is this going to last?" Phil asked.

"No more than a couple of days, don't worry, we'll be back in touch."

After giving the detective our details, we returned to our room. We needed to figure out what we were going to do now.

"We've been screwed," Lew yelled as he opened our door. It hadn't been locked when we left, luckily, since none of us had grabbed the key. Sitting back down on the bed, I heard Lew go into the bathroom. "Dudes, get in here. Now."

Reno, Phil and I walked towards the bathroom. Standing in the doorway, I saw it. Stuck to the mirror, was an envelope. We squeezed into the bathroom and watched as Lew opened it.

KEEP YOUR MOUTH SHUT

It was four simple words; the letters all cut from various newspaper and magazine articles.

"Well that's cool" Reno said.

"Dudes, we got a serious problem."

"Oh shit," Phil yelled.

Reno and Lew sat down on bed across from me, and the three of us sat silently as we listened to Phil's conversation. He had just gotten a hold of his wife.

"Hey honey. I got one hell of a story to tell you..."

She must have been screaming at him, because he was holding the phone about three inches away from his ear.

"Honey, honey, calm down."

"Yeah"

"Yeah"

"Yes, I'll check into it right away."

"I know babe. I love you too. Kiss the kids for me."

"Goodbye."

Without so much as a glance our way, Phil opened up one of the counter drawers in the kitchen and pulled out the Yellow Pages. He flipped through a couple of the pages, apparently found what he was looking for and started dialing again.

"Who ya calling now, Phil?" Reno asked.

Phil simply frowned and held his hand, palm side out in our direction. And once again we were forced to listen to one side of another phone conversation.

"Hey, I need to check on changing a flight." He'd called the airport.

"I'm trying to fly out immediately."

"Dude, were you not listening to what the cops just told us?" Lew yelled out. "We can't leave."

Phil turned his back to us.

"Kansas City."

"I see."

"Are you sure that there's nothing else available?"

"O.K. Thanks."

"Goodbye."

He sat down onto one of the barstools and sighed loudly. His hands were rubbing his temples. "Well, no flights are available until after the holiday. He wasn't really speaking to any of us, he was just thinking out loud, but the rest of us definitely had our own opinions on the matter. All of us knew the stolen car was bogus, but we couldn't leave until our names were cleared.

"Phil, you gotta think this through. You might have a warrant out for your arrest if you leave before the cops get this car deal cleared up. We're already leaving in two days anyway," I reminded him.

Reno stepped in, "Yeah look Phil, we only got forty eight hours to kill. Let's just make the best of it. It's just a scare tactic."

Phil slammed his fist into the table, causing us all to flinch at the sudden sound. "Guys. I appreciate the concern, but this is pretty serious stuff. I mean Little V knows everything about me now. Not to mention this little detail of grand theft auto, looming over my head.

Lew spoke up next. "You know Phil. I've been thinking about that. How can you be so certain that Little V is the killer?"

"Because I've seen him twice now Lew" Phil yelled.

"I hate to be the one to have to point out the obvious, dude," Lew continued, "but let me be the devil's advocate. You drank a ton of alcohol last night. I mean dude, you passed out once, got up and kept on going. Think about it, your mind had to have been pretty fuzzy. Can you tell me for sure you know that Little V was the guy? Come on Phil, you knocked over an entire tray of drinks on the guys' marble foyer. Maybe you were being belligerent and the wrong people in the crowd got splashed with mixed drink droplets. Now that I'm thinking about it, you're lucky they decided to be kind enough to drag you upstairs before they laid into you. They could have done it right there."

"Well then, why were they continually telling me to keep my mouth shut – the exact same quote on the letter," Phil interrupted.

"Maybe you were screaming," I answered. I was beginning to see Lew's point and was now myself questioning the validity of Phil's identification of Little V as the killer. Like Lew had said, Phil was extremely intoxicated last night.

"Think about it Phil," Reno asked, "Did they ever say we know you saw them get run over? Did they even mention the accident at all?"

"No." He scratched his head and ran his fingers through his hair. "They never mentioned the accident once, now that you mention it. But, I know what I saw, and what I saw was the same guy from the accident."

Reno continued. "Come on Phil. How can you be one hundred percent sure about that?

"Exactly," I said.

"Maybe you guys are right. You know, I wasn't really up there that long before you guys busted in. And yeah, I'll admit it; I was a little bit tipsy last night."

Reno spoke up. "You know Phil, you could be right. Anyway, like I said before, we only got about forty-eight more hours in Key West, lets just stay away from any more trouble."

"I guess you guys got a point" he sighed. "Let's just not mention this to anyone. Just let the police do their thing." He stood up and folded the two pages a couple of times. When they were small enough, he slid them into his back pocket for safekeeping.

Lew started pacing back and forth across the living room. He was clearly planning our next move. "You know Reno, that all sounds good. 'Let's just make the best of it.' 'Enjoy ourselves before we leave.' But I got news for you all. We ain't staying in this hotel a minute longer."

"What?" I asked.

"Think about it dudes. Whoever the real killer is, Little V or not, he knows where we're staying. He got information about us from this hotel; addresses and all. I guarantee next time it won't be a folded letter shoved under the door. There's no point staying here any longer." He walked back over to the foot of the beds. "So, let's pack up and leave."

"Where are we going?" I asked, still not totally agreeing with this new line of thinking.

Lew simply shrugged his shoulders. "Who knows. Let's go grab something to eat after we pack. We'll figure it out as we go."

It didn't take long for us to pack up. Lew, who had never unpacked to begin with, sat on the couch and started flipping through the yellow pages Phil had left lying on the counter. He was searching for new lodging. Before too long, though, Phil was back on the phone with his wife, explaining to her our next move.

We took turns showering and gave the room a quick glance over, before we pulled the door shut behind us on our way out. Our destination was unknown. It turned out that every hotel in the vicinity of Duval was booked through the weekend. The earliest Lew could get us into anything was two days out.

The four of us found ourselves in the hotel lobby. Lew bartered with the hotel manager for a while, but was only able to get one of the two remaining days taken off the bill. All in all, it was a pretty even trade, but as we sat in the parking lot waiting on the taxi to pick us up, I can honestly say, I would have still rather stayed at our hotel; I was exhausted.

"Where to gentlemen?" It was the same taxi driver that had driven us from the airport, and I would swear from the smell, he was still wearing the same clothes. He hopped out of the van and pulled open the sliding door on the side and raised the back hatch.

It was a simple question, but the four of us stood there, not knowing what to say.

"Take us to *Ricky's Cantina*," Lew replied. He looked at the rest of us and added, "We need to talk to Mark, especially after the exit we made last night."

"Plus it's always free drinks with Mark," Reno added. "Maybe they got breakfast pizza?" We threw our bags back into the minivan and climbed inside. Our driver sped off.

We'd been in the cab for about five minutes when I had a revelation. "Why would Mark be working only six hours after tending bar at an all night party?"

"That's a good point, Tango," Lew said. "He wouldn't be there at this hour."

"Well now what the hell do we do?" Reno asked.

"I wish we knew where he lived." Lew said.

All of a sudden, it clicked. I remembered the conversation I'd had with Mark when we left *Blue Heaven* a day ago. "I know where he lives" I grinned. "He told me yesterday."

"Where?" Lew shouted.

"He told me he lived on Whitehead, a couple blocks south of *Blue Heaven*."

Lew shook his head. "How is that going to help us?"

"I guarantee his Jeep is parked out front. We find his Jeep, we'll find his house." I replied.

Our driver had been listening in on the entire conversation. "So what's it going to be boys? We still going to *Ricky's Cantina*?"

"Nope," I said. "Take us over to Whitehead Street. We're looking for a red Jeep."

"Sure thing guys," our driver yelled out. He swung the wheel hard to the left in order to complete a U-turn in the middle of the street. The abrupt change in direction caught Phil off guard. He must have been thinking about the note in his pocket, because he didn't even flinch when his head slammed into the window. Within minutes, we were creeping along Whitehead looking for Mark's Jeep. We were looking to the left and right without much luck. Things were beginning to look hopeless when we found ourselves surrounded on all sides by huge trash dumpsters, on a one-way alley that led behind an old apartment complex. We pulled back out onto the main street, and was just about to give up when we saw a red Jeep parked cock-eyed in front of a four-plex condominium. We piled out of the cab and told the driver to wait out front. We had a one in four chance of picking the right door, but if we each took a door, then we were guaranteed someone would find him. We split up and each of us approached a closed door. As we each walked up our respective sidewalk, Lew yelled out. "If we do find ourselves with a bed tonight, whoever finds Mark gets it." We all agreed.

Bang. Bang. Bang. Bang.

Lew's door opened first. An elderly lady was standing in front of him, wearing a heavy, blue cotton robe. It was cinched tightly, almost as taught as the hairnet keeping her curly white hair held firmly under wraps. "Can I help you young man?" her voice cracked. "Are you selling something? A vacuum perhaps? Mine is on the fritz you know."

Lew shook his head and said "No", walking away before the conversation dragged on any longer. "No dice," he yelled, as he continued along the concrete sidewalk. Putting his hands in his pockets he slowly started heading my way.

"Thanks for coming by," the old lady said to his back. He was already to the sidewalk.

I glanced over at him, as I continued knocking loudly on my door. Before I could glance back at the door, it opened, just barely more than a crack. A short brass chain attached to the jamb prevented the door from opening any further. "Hello?" the nervous voice of a female resonated from behind the door. She was speaking just barely above a whisper and was hardly audible from where I stood. I shifted my position on the landing over a bit, so I could get a glance inside. The stink of cigarettes pillowed out from the slit in the door.

"Does Mark live here?" I asked.

"Sorry, I don't know..." The door slammed shut before she even finished her sentence.

What didn't she know?, I thought. I stood there, scratching my head and looked over at Reno. He was standing on the landing next to me. No one was answering the knock and it was not looking good. Reno was just standing there, patiently staring at the floral wreath hanging above the address.

I jogged across the lawn and joined Lew back on the sidewalk that ran parallel to the condos. We walked over in Phil's direction. He was still knocking.

"Nobody home?" Lew yelled.

"I don't know, man," Phil replied. "No one has answered yet and I've been knocking for about five minutes now." Just then Reno joined us and said "no one answered at mine, but I don't think Mark would have flowers over his doorway." We were zero for three. Phil was our last and only hope.

"Dude, he's got to be here," Lew said. "His Jeep is outside. Try the handle."

We watched as Phil turned the doorknob. It was unlocked. With the door opened just wide enough for his head to slip through, Phil yelled out "Hey Mark. You in there?" He turned so he could listen. His ear pressed into the crack. Silence. "Mark!" he yelled again, "Mark?"

Just as Phil was about to give up, he heard someone cough. "Who is it?"

"I found him," Phil yelled, as he turned towards us. "Looks like I got the bed tonight."

"Who's there?" resounded loudly from inside. Even from my position at the bottom of the flight of concrete steps leading up to the landing, I could hear feet pounding as someone ran towards the opened door. Phil had forgotten to respond to the original question. The door swung open violently. Mark stood there, his eyes glazed like a mad man. He was tightly holding a wooden Louisville Slugger in one hand. His other, free hand was clenched tightly into a fist. "Oh cripes. You guys about gave me a heart attack." His body slumped forward in relief and the anxiety seemed to drain from him instantaneously.

"Sorry" Phil replied. We all started to walk into his house, as he gestured us past him with the business end of the bat.

However, before we could even make it through the entryway, Mark stopped us. "What the hell happened last night?" he asked rubbing his eyes.

"Dude. It's a long story." Lew began. "But before we go into it with any detail, we gotta ask you a question. Can we crash here for a night? We really need a place to stay, or at least leave our bags for a while."

"Sure. Mi casa, es su casa." I stole a quick glance Reno's way and just smiled. That was the second time since morning that we'd been spoken to in Spanish, only the previous time hadn't been nearly as pleasant.

"Thanks. Reno, Tango, go get the bags." Lew demanded.

"No way Lew, you get them," I replied.

"Sorry dude, I'm too tired," Lew grinned.

"Lets Ro Sham Bo for them," Reno suggested.

On my way back out of the condo I was cursing myself for not choosing rock. "Tango," Lew yelled out behind me. "Make sure you give the taxi guy a good tip."

Disgusted even more, I shook my head and jogged over to where the cab was parked. *I hope I have enough cash*, I thought, as I approached the van.

"So how much do I owe you?" I asked.

Our taxi driver was sitting in the driver's seat of the van, reading a book. His short, stubby legs were propped up on the dashboard. The meter was still running. I think he purposely let the dial click off another quarter before he answered me. "You guys staying here, are ya?"

"Yup."

He slammed his fleshy hand down to stop the meter. "Looks like that'll be fifty one, fifty."

"Ouch." I replied, pulling three twenties from my pocket. "You can keep the change, if you help me unload the bags."

"Sounds good to me buddy. Where we taking them?"

By the time we had all the bags stacked neatly inside the entryway, Mark and the other three guys had already sat down in his living room.

The room, which opened up from the entryway, was decorated sparsely. An old neon bar sign was surrounded by a couple of *Speedracer* cartoon posters, in an attempt at artwork, and there was a fichus tree shoved into a far corner. An entertainment center took up one side of the wall in the back of the room. It was loaded with stereo equipment and a large television. Every component was left on, but the television just had a blue screen. Phil and Reno were sitting on a futon that was along the wall to my right. There was a fifty gallon fish tank along the opposite wall that held water so green, you couldn't even see what was swimming inside the tank. The water line was down about five inches from the top of the tank, and giving it a second glance, I continued to doubt anything was alive in there. Mark had crashed into a beanbag in the center of the room. The cushioned seat practically engulfed his body as he lay half awake listening to Lew speak. Lew, who was sitting in one of two, very worn leather recliners, was wrapping up the events, as we knew them from last night. I sat down in the other recliner as Lew reached the part of the story where I was walking back naked to the hotel. It was at this point that Mark perked up a bit, and started laughing. Phil jumped in and explained about the package that was left for us this morning under our door.

"So did you guys call the cops yet?" he asked, hesitantly. It seemed as though he wasn't quite sure what to say.

"Nah" Phil said. "We just decided to take the notes advice and stay quiet. This leads us to why we are here."

"Yeah" I continued. "We didn't feel too safe staying at the hotel, in case the goons decided to pay a return visit, carrying a little more than just paper envelopes."

"So dude. Is it still ok that we crash here for a while?" Lew asked. "Now that you know our situation."

"Like I said; no problem guys. I got plenty of space. My room is upstairs, I only got one bed, but with any luck I won't be home tonight anyways. There's enough space above us in the loft to sleep two comfortably, I got a couple of small beds in there right now. I got the futon here, and there's the beanbag too. Besides, you'll never find anywhere else to stay on the island, this time of year. At least not for the next few days."

"Thanks" we all replied, feeling instant relief. We told him we were leaving in two days anyway and he agreed to let us stay at his place as long as we needed.

"So how did you find where I lived?" Mark asked.

After accounting my story, Mark interrupted and yawned loudly. "Oh guys, I gotta go on the clock at six tonight, and I really need some sleep. So if you don't mind, I'm gonna bail."

"That's cool," Reno said. "We're just going to stow away our bags and then head out of here until later tonight anyway."

"Go ahead and grab an extra key. There's one in the cabinet above the microwave." Mark said, as he got up off the beanbag. "I'll see ya tonight at the bar. The drinks are on me."

What a Godsend, I thought as I got up and walked into the kitchen to grab the key. I noticed another ring of keys sitting on the counter. One of the keys had Jeep stenciled across the base. I had an idea. "Mark, can we borrow your Jeep? It sure would make getting around the island easier."

"Sure," he yawned. "I'll get a buddy to pick me up tonight. Just bring it back with a full tank of gas."

Lew walked over and gave me a high five. "Good thinking," he grinned.

I heard Mark's bedroom door close. "Well guys. Drop your cocks and grab your socks. Saddle up, let's go get some grub. I'm driving," I yelled, as I headed out the front door. The four of us piled into the Jeep and I turned the key. The engine fired up and the Jeep sputtered loudly as I slipped the transmission into reverse and backed out of the grass. It shook violently as I put it in drive. Glancing at the gauges, I found out why. The Jeep was bone dry. We were running on empty.

CHAPTER ELEVEN

Sometimes the best map will not guide you,
If you can't see what's round the bend.
Sometimes the road leads through dark places
Sometimes the darkness is your friend.

Jimmy Buffett
Pacing the Cage

We limped into a gas station not a moment too soon. As I twisted the gas cap back into place, I noticed Phil had his head tilted back, nostrils pointing upwards. He was breathing deeply. "Are you trying to get high off the fumes?" I smiled, placing the nozzle back onto the pump.

"Can you smell that?" he asked.

The three of us simultaneously breathed deeply. All I could smell was gasoline.

"Smell what?" Reno asked.

Phil breathed in again. "That's definitely barbeque I smell."

"What the hell are you? A bloodhound?" I laughed.

"I'm telling you guys. I smell barbeque."

"Well where's it coming from?" Lew asked.

"Couldn't tell ya." Phil sighed. "But it smells good."

I walked around to the driver's side of the Jeep and grabbed the door handle, noticing for the first time that the entire driver's side door was white. Contrasting noticeably against the rest of the red exterior, I couldn't believe I hadn't seen it. "So Lew, did you notice the color of the door?" I asked as I settled into the driver's seat.

"How could you miss it?" he replied. "You know, it kind of reminds me of that car you used to drive when we were in high school. The foreign job that was white, with blue doors, a blue hood and a blue trunk."

"Not all of us could afford a sports car back then," I smiled.

My first car was a seventy-five dollar jalopy that was actually pieced together from the better of two junked out Datsun's. I bought both cars from a kid's dad, who was trying to take them to the dump. Not having a clue what I was doing, I spent the better part of a weekend, camped out in front of their house doing the restoration. When I was done, I drove off in a car that was two-tone, had no floor boards and not one of the seat belts would fasten. About three blocks out, the clutch burnt up. That didn't phase me. I kept that car for the next three years, putting on well over sixty thousand miles on an already past its prime engine. The beauty of it was, I sold it to another guy for twenty-five dollars – it had only depreciated fifty bucks in three years.

Smiling at the thought, I turned the key and fired up the engine to Mark's Jeep. With a full tank of gas I peeled out of the service bay in search of Phil's barbeque restaurant.

Like a pack of dogs following the scent of a rabbit, we chased the smell of smoked meat down the street. The only establishment we could find was a brilliant neon green shack. "This must be the place," Phil said, wiping a little drool from the corner of his mouth.

I parked the Jeep up on the curb and we hopped out. Walking towards the entrance, we stepped underneath a sign that read *The Green Parrot Bar*. A huge outdoor smoker was positioned behind a rickety wooden fence just a bit past the entrance. We also noticed that there was outdoor seating available by the smoker, so we decided to enjoy the early afternoon and settled into a table on the patio. Laced throughout the patio were Christmas lights that hung so low that Phil had to duck underneath them in order to get past.

The smoker must have been on all night long. It was noticeably warmer as we sat down. We sat there looking at the smoke billowing from the black iron contraption and realized we were sizzling ourselves. We were the only ones out on the patio. Phil stood back up and took off his shirt. We hadn't even seen a waitress yet, when Lew yelled out, "Dude, I'm going to barf, if I have to sit here and watch you sweat while I eat." I glanced across the table at a still shirtless Phil. Beads of sweat were trickling slowly down his chest.

"Hey it isn't getting any cooler out here," Phil replied, using his shirt to mop up the sweat glistening on his shoulders.

In disgust, Lew's chair scooted out from the table. "That's it, we're going inside. I'd rather starve than watch Phil sweat while I eat."

Stepping inside, a slogan painted on a sign hanging in the entranceway, beckoned "*a sunny place for shady people*." Some blues was playing from a jukebox by the pool table and a handful of people were seated at the bar. A thick cloud of smoke engulfed the room. Looking to the left, there seemed to be another room attached to the bar, almost as an afterthought. As I focused in on the other room, I saw that there were both tables and booths set up inside. "Let's go see if we can eat in there," Lew said.

No sooner had we walked into the room, when the cheerful voice of a waitress asked if we wanted a table or a booth. "We'll take a booth," Lew answered. Noticeably cooler in here, Phil did us the favor of putting his shirt back on. Our waitress handed us each a menu.

"So what do you recommend for someone who's from the home of barbeque?" Reno asked.

"How come everybody always claims they come from the home of barbeque?" our waitress smiled. "So where do you call home?"

"Kansas City," was our reply.

"Well, I've been told our pulled pork is very good. It's slow cooked, smoked slow and low in our smokehouse for sixteen hours." We each ordered a pulled pork sandwich and Newcastle Brown Ale on tap.

It looked like an entire hog had gone to its demise, judging from the amount of meat piled on top of the bun. I might have been hungry, but I wasn't finishing this sandwich. As expected, when it was all said and done, Phil was the only one who was able to devour the entire meal. He even washed it down with another heavy ale.

"You never cease to amaze me" was Lew's comment to Phil as we left the restaurant. None of us quite knew what we were going to do next, so we piled back into the Jeep and headed towards the blazing sun in search of some afternoon entertainment.

"How's that beach over there look Tango?" Lew yelled, pointing to my left. We were driving beside a sandy white beach littered with palm trees.

Not waiting for an answer Lew jerked the wheel hard to the left, causing us to swerve into a small parking lot. "What do you say we hang out here for a while?"

"A relaxing afternoon in the sun," I sighed.

We all hopped out and headed straight to the ocean. There were surprisingly few other people swimming in the vicinity. In fact, there were more palm trees than actual people where we were wading. "Dude!" Lew said, swimming up beside me. Reno and Phil were sprawled out on their backs attempting to soak in a few rays of sunshine. "I got an idea. You remember that game we used to play, Frisbee golf?"

"Sure," I said. It had been years since we had last played a game, but I could remember spending hours in Lew's old neighborhood, picking out trashcans, bumpers, light poles, mailboxes and whatever the hell else we thought we could hit with a Frisbee. We played it the same way you played golf, except we used a Frisbee as the ball. There were some days the whole neighborhood would play, and usually somebody would get pissed off because they'd lose their disk in a tree or on a roof top. "I don't think we got any Frisbee's in the car, man."

"We don't need them. We're going to play with coconuts, the beach is freaking littered with them. Speaking of coconuts, let's get those two involved." We headed out of the water and explained the rules of the game to Reno and Phil. They both thought it sounded good, so we each picked out a coconut and determined the target for the first hole. "Before we begin," Lew said, "Mark has got two beds up in the loft. Phil's already got one of them; whoever wins this game after nine holes gets the other bed." We all agreed.

An epic battle of coconut golf was well under way. After about six holes, it had become apparent that Reno – already down twenty five dollars in lost bets -- and Phil were simply along for the ride. Once again, it had come down to a confrontation between Lew and me. By the ninth hole, Lew and I were all tied up. Reno had chosen the setup for the last hole, a short par three. Lew had honors and tossed a perfect spiral in the direction of the hole, or in this case, palm tree. The coconut wobbled a bit and finally settled a few feet from the base of the palm tree.

"I am dialed in!" he yelled triumphantly.

Undeterred, I stepped up in the tee box and let it rip. My coconut flew through the air, heading right in line with the tree. At about the moment I thought for sure it was going to hit the target for an ace; I watched the coconut sail right on past, settling up about twenty yards past the tree. Lew threw up his arms in a victory pose and ran around giving out high fives to the small crowd that had gathered to watch. "It's not over yet," I scowled as I walked past.

"Nice shot," he laughed. "Why didn't you just lie up and play for the tie?"

Looking back over my shoulder I hollered, "I only know how to play one way. To win."

Two shots later, Lew had won. After the game was over, Reno and Phil started screwing around, playing catch with one of the coconuts. "Phil, go long," Reno yelled, motioning with his hand for Phil to run a deep fly pattern. He hurled the coconut high into the air; it was heading for the water. A running Phil dove headfirst into the ocean to catch it. If I hadn't been watching with my own two eyes, I would have never guessed Phil would actually catch the pass. However, a completely horizontal Phil snatched the coconut out of the air and came crashing down into the water. He emerged seconds later dripping wet from head to toe. He triumphantly planted a big foot into the sand when suddenly, he stopped dead in his tracks and his face turned ashen. Reaching around quickly, Phil slammed a hand into one of the back pockets of his swim trunks. He had just realized that the note from this morning was still in his shorts. It too was soaked. As he held the note in front of him, he nervously attempted to open it. The note disintegrated in his hands. All that remained was a soaking wet mass of pulp.

With the evidence ruined, there would be no sense in notifying the police after all. As the note warned, our mouths were forced to remain shut. "Man that really bums me out," a dejected Phil mumbled to himself as he walked past. His head was slumped and his feet were dragging across the sand. A few moments later, I saw Reno and Phil talking over by the Jeep, so I headed that way. Lew had made a run to the bathroom. As I approached the two of them, I was thrust into the middle of a heated conversation.

"It's not like you were going to do anything about the note anyway," Reno said, throwing his hands up into the air.

"I know, I know. It just pisses me off that now I have no say in things whatsoever." Phil yelled, punching his fist lightly into the side of the Jeep.

"What's going on guys?" I asked.

"Oh, Phil's having second thoughts about going to the cops" Reno replied.

"I thought we'd settled this earlier, Phil. Besides, why would we want to go back to the police station? We're accused of stealing a car, remember?"

"Yeah, yeah, yeah. It's just the longer I had that note in my pocket, the more and more I was contemplating going to the cops after all. It just seemed like the right thing to do. I mean I kept thinking that's what would be best for Roger and Cynthia."

At that moment, Lew happened to walk up to the Jeep. "It looks like a freaking wake around here."

"Come on Lew, that's not right." Phil snipped.

"Dude, sorry." Lew replied. "What's got into you?"

"Nothing."

"He lost the note in the ocean," I whispered.

Not knowing what to say, Lew simply shrugged his shoulders. "Well, it's done now. Nothing you can do to change it."

Opening the door, I stepped in and ignited the engine.

"What do you guys want to do now?"

As the Jeep rumbled down the road, I felt a hand grab my shoulder. Giving it a squeeze Phil yelled over the sound of the motor. "Hey Tango. Screw it. Take me by the police station first. I want to talk to the cops again."

I turned around and looked Phil in the eyes. "Are you sure?"

"Yeah, I'm sure."

"You're the boss," I said as I turned the wheel hard to the right in order to change our present course. Not too much later, Lew and I were sitting in the Jeep, watching Reno and Phil walk back into City Hall.

"Remember a few days ago when I said the cops in Key West didn't really do anything?" Lew asked. "I said they were just here to keep the peace."

I nodded.

"Well, I hope I was wrong."

"These guys have crossed the line. I'm sure Phil's doing the right thing." I replied.

It wasn't until we were leaving the lot that Phil and Reno let us in on what had transpired inside.

"There's not too much to tell you guys" Phil began. "Reno and I went in. Told them our address had changed, gave them all our phone number's, and then told them about the note."

"Did they seem interested?" I asked.

"Oh sure, of course they were more interested in pestering me about the stolen car, but eventually they asked to see the note. When I told them it had been ruined, their interest waned. Basically the cop told us that both investigations were still ongoing, and that Roger and Cynthia's family had been notified. But without the actual note, there was really nothing left that we could do to help them out with their case."

"Phil," Lew interjected. "Did you tell them about the possible link between Little V and the guy you saw kill Roger and Cynthia?"

"Nope."

"You know. We still got that boat. We could always return it and see if you're sober vision yields the same results," Lew added

"Are you nuts?" I yelled. "We barely made it out of that place alive last night. That's the last place I want to head back to tonight. Besides, we got a date with the ladies. You do remember Kelly and Brooke,` right?"

"Relax Tango. I wasn't saying to return it tonight. I'm just saying, you know. Phil, there's always that option available."

"I appreciate that Lew. Hey, that boats probably found by now anyway." Phil said.

"I'm with Lew, I say we drive that damn boat right back into his dock," Reno added, not letting the topic die.

"Oh, there's a shock," I mumbled under my breath. "Any of you guys hungry?" I asked. "There's a pizza place just up ahead.

With a couple of warm large pizzas from *Island Pie* settled in the back seat between Reno and Phil, we drove towards Mark's house. It was almost dusk.

Speaking of Island Pie, I needed to get ready for my date tonight with Brooke, I thought to myself as I turned into the parking lot of the condo.

After some time well spent freshening up in the bathroom, I was ready. I had a couple of slices of pizza inside me, I'd showered, shaved and finished up the rest of my business before the other guys had even had a chance to get out of their swim trunks. I grabbed a beer out of the fridge and went over to my suitcase to find a nice set of clothes to wear out tonight. When I opened my bag, it didn't look good. In my haste to get out of the hotel that morning, I had left the only collared Hawaiian shirt I had brought on a hanger inside the hotel closet. I couldn't wear the same outfit from last night that Mark had sitting on his counter. Brooke had already seen me in it.

Sneaking upstairs, I tiptoed into Mark's room. Catching a glimpse of my stealth self in the mirror, I wondered why I was being so sly. Mark was already gone. I headed over to his closet. Opening the door, I hoped to find something that I could wear.

"What are you doing Tango?"

I spun around quickly, my heart rate fluttering a bit. It was Lew. "Nothing" I replied, my voice cracking slightly.

"You need some clothes dude?"

I sighed. All this did was justify the reason he had packed such a large suitcase. "I don't know."

"Dude, you only got those green shorts and a waded up pile of clothes on the counter downstairs."

"Yeah" I sighed again.

"Suck up your pride. I got some clothes."

A short time later, walking up Duval, I caught a glimpse of myself in the reflection from a storefront window. I was wearing one of about five outfits he had let me choose from.

We still had some time to burn before we had to meet the girls at *Ricky's Cantina* and we didn't want to look too anxious. We drank and played pool in a few establishments in order to kill some time. Some time later, we found ourselves walking out of a joint that was across the street from the *Upstairz Lounge*. "Guys!" I yelled out. "Let's go see if Paula's inside. I'd like to thank her for tipping us off about Phil last night." The other three guys agreed, so we ran across the street and headed up into the strip club. Looking around the place, we couldn't find Paula, and after talking to a bouncer, I found out that she didn't start her shift until later that night. I took out one of my business cards and using a pen that was attached to the little table that the doorman worked; I scribbled a quick 'thank you' on the back of it. I also wrote 'call me', and handed the card to the bouncer, with a ten-dollar tip. "Would you mind giving this card to Paula when you see her tonight?" I asked.

"Sure thing buddy."

I walked back inside to find the other guys. "Dude, you'll never guess who Reno just spotted" Lew yelled out.

"Who?" I asked, now facing the three of them, all grinning with the exception of Phil.

"*The Joke Bum*" Reno laughed, pointing over my shoulder. Turning again, my eyes scanned the bar. Sure enough, there he was. *The Joke Bum*. Only this time, he was wearing a shirt and long pants.

"He must be getting ready to drop two bills," Lew laughed. "I'd join him, but judging from the time, we better head on out to *Ricky's Cantina*. The girls are probably already waiting for us."

Sure enough, when we got to *Ricky's Cantina* the girls were already waiting. They had been sitting at a small table just off the dance floor and had five chairs squeezed around it. As soon as we walked into the place, I spotted Brooke. Putting down her drink, she ran up and threw her arms around me, planting a kiss on my cheek. "I was beginning to think you had blown me off!" she yelled into my ear, trying to shout above the band that was on stage.

"Not a chance," I said. "Especially after the day we've had."

"What do you mean?" she asked, taking my hand as we walked over to where the others were now standing.

"You'll see" I replied. As I suspected, Lew was already discussing the events that had happened since we last saw the girls. Leaving out a lot of the details, it didn't take long for them to catch up. He told them about Little V's and then the note we'd received.

"Trouble seems to follow you guys," Kelly said, giving him a hug.

"It's all cool" Reno yelled. "So ladies, who are your friends?" Brooke and Kelly had brought along three other girls.

Frowning, one replied, "Don't you remember us from last night? I'm Morgan, this is Jennifer. You talked to both of us at *Diva's*."

"Oh yeah, I remember you all," Reno stammered, trying to recover but looking more and more like an ass.

"I think what he means to say is, who's your other friend you brought? She wasn't with us last night." I interrupted, trying to save Reno.

"That's Monica." Morgan replied.

"Nice to meet you, Monica" Reno said. Having blown any chance of hooking up with Morgan and Jennifer, Reno walked over toward Monica and struck up a conversation. That left Phil together with the other two girls, while Kelly and Brooke took Lew and I out onto the dance floor.

Once on the dance floor, I couldn't keep my eyes off Brooke. She looked fantastic. Dressed in a red strapless flowered dress that came up to her thighs, all of my attention was focused on whether or not she was wearing a bra. In fact, if you asked me today, I couldn't tell you what the other girls were wearing.

Eventually we found ourselves taking a break from the dancing and were back standing at the bar. Reno and Phil had been working Mark out of free drinks all night long, now it was our turn. While we were standing there, taking those first couple of sips from some kind of fruity blended drink, Kelly asked us what the plans were for the rest of the evening.

"Don't really have any," Lew said. "Why do you ask?"

"Well we heard about this bar. They're having a dance party tonight, where they're going to be spraying soapsuds on the dance floor.

"I heard about one of those deals before," I said.

"Sounds good to me," Lew replied. "Let's head out."

The nine of us walked down the street, each of us carrying one last drink, compliments of Mark. "Why was that bartender there so nice?" Brooke asked me.

"Because we're staying at his place now." I answered. "Maybe you'll see it later." I grinned.

"I hope so," she said, squeezing my hand.

Our destination was called the *Her-A-Cave*. It's one of those underground clubs that the locals only know about, and the tourists find by word of mouth, which was how the girls had heard about it. We were told it was just off the beaten path and was located behind a storefront off Duval. The place had been built from an old cave that pirates used as a hiding place for their loot, back in the days. We joined up with a crowd of people and all I could see was an old wood railing leading down cement stairs to the entrance. Once around the corner, it was apparent why the line was so long. There were two bouncers choosing who entered. We waited in line, heading down step by step slowly towards the bouncers and a rock entrance with a neon sign illuminating *Her-A-Cave*.

"This is just like Miami," Kelly said. "We could be here all night long, unless we look just right."

"Tango, it's a good thing I dressed you," Lew laughed.

Shaking my head, I replied, "This is something you never see in Kansas."

"Well ladies," Reno started, "it's time to turn on the headlights."

The girls simultaneously rolled their eyes.

"I got ten bucks says you can't get us in there, gals, " Reno continued.

We were behind a group of about fifteen people, most of which were guys. After a little while, half of them were still left."

"This is ridiculous," Lew said, staring to get irate.

"It's O.K., we're used to this," Kelly said.

"Don't worry, we'll get in," Brooke added.

Leaving the four of us behind, the girls all walked up to where the bouncers were standing.

"Cool," Reno mumbled under his breath. "Maybe now we'll get somewhere."

Just then, one of the bouncers held up his hand. "It's gonna be a while ladies."

"Pay up ladies!" Reno yelled out.

"But..." Morgan began, ignoring Reno.

"Look. It's packed inside. We're only doing one for one's. One in. One out."

Just then, Morgan yelled out, "nine people just left."

"Yeah, there they go," Jennifer added, pointing at a blank wall.

"No they didn't," the bouncer replied.

Taking a page out of Reno's book, the girls all simultaneously flashed the bouncers. Their backs were towards us, but the two bouncers definitely got an eye full.

"Oh. Ya they did," the bouncer said smiling.

Running back, the girls grabbed us and we all walked into the club.

Reno slipped Brooke a ten spot.

The place opened up into an enormous room. It smelled of an old cave. Enormous, cylinder, cement pillars surrounded the dance floor. The left side had a huge DJ booth encased in plastic and the bar extended along the whole right side. Everything around us was rock. The dance floor was packed and the suds were starting to spill out on the floor. After a quick run to the bar, we all walked onto the dance floor. It was like getting inside your washing machine, or going through a car wash with the windows open. There were two foam machines placed in each corner, creating a generous helping of non-stop bubbles. The entire dance floor was now overrun with suds; at the present time they were about calf high, but ten minutes later, they were up to my knees. Everyone was dancing and throwing bubbles when the machines went into overdrive. Pumping out more and more suds, the lights above our heads started spinning faster and faster. It was an incredible feeling. The bubbles glowed, the music was electric and quickly we were up to our waists in suds.

Kelly was wearing a white dress, similar to the one Brooke had on. We were all having a great time and believe me when I say that after a while on the dance floor; none of the girl's clothes left much to the imagination.

About an hour later, we were all soaked and all of us looked ready to leave except Reno. Having successfully alienated all of the other three girls by this time, he was over in front of the soap machine, grabbing handfuls of bubbles and throwing them on the female dancers. I think he'd already been asked a couple of times to stop. He was pushing the limits and was getting a little bit out of control, showing no signs of slowing down. Phil, having yet to step foot on the dance floor, was saddled up to the bar, nursing a cigarette. It didn't take too much to convince everyone that we wanted to leave, with the exception of the girl's friends. By this time, they had hooked up with a group of three guys and were not quite ready to leave. Fortunately, for Lew and me, the other girls didn't have any problems with Kelly and Brooke leaving. They said that they'd find their own way back to their hotel. This was even nicer, when we found out that Kelly had a car parked a couple of blocks away. She offered to drive us to Mark's house. Not wanting to walk, but more than that, wanting to spend more time with them, we jumped at the offer. *Things were starting to heat up a bit*, I thought as we left the club.

Walking back to the car, the combination of a faint breeze and slightly damp clothing fortunately made it a necessity to snuggle up close to Brooke. I had my arm around her shoulder, and she was grabbing me tightly around the waist. I noticed Lew and Kelly were also huddled close. I glanced behind me, in response to hearing Reno howl out. "Damn!"

Seconds later, I watched and laughed as he crashed down hard on the sidewalk. "What the hell happened Reno?" Phil yelled out as he jogged up to help Reno back onto his feet.

"I think I blew out my flip flop on the dance floor" he laughed. "Ouch. I was trying to walk with it broken, but I caught it on the sidewalk. How much further we gotta walk?" he yelled out. "I'm down to one good sandal."

"It's just another block from here" Kelly replied.

Reno, the drunken trooper he was, complained the entire way as he hobbled to the car. He had skinned his shoulder from the fall, but his main concern was the blown out tire.

"A three series? You got to be kidding me. How the hell are we all going to fit in there?" Reno yelled as the lights flickered when Kelly released the car alarm.

"Well I'm driving" Kelly replied.

"And I got shotgun" Lew said, opening the passenger door.

That left me, Brooke, Reno and Phil in back. We made sure that we worked it out so Reno had to sit in the middle. Brooke sat on my lap. Reno was all fired up, by the time we pulled away from the curb.

"You know, it would have been much more comfortable if this BMW was a five or seven series" Reno continued.

Lew yelled out "Reno what the hell do you know about BMW's?"

"My brother's girlfriend had one. I know all about them" he slurred. We all just laughed.

Finding Mark's house was a lot easier to do during the daylight hours, than at night. Everything seemed to look the same when it was dark out. Not to mention that our only landmark, Mark's Jeep, was no longer parked out front. We were cruising down Whitehead looking for the condo when it started raining, making our search even more difficult. We knew we had gone too far when we crept up on the Southernmost Point a few minutes later. Kelly turned the car around and we headed back the opposite direction. It had really started pouring. Water was slapping off the windshield making it almost impossible to see, even with the wipers on full blast. I had given up all hopes of finding the place a long time ago when the windows in back had fogged over. I had no clue where we were; it was up to Lew to find the place. Eventually he did; though it took another couple of passes. Slamming the doors, we ran inside. Our damp clothes were drenched by the time we were standing safely out of the rain in Mark's foyer.

"Mi casa es su casa" Lew said.

I was freezing. The air conditioning had been left on and the condo was cold enough inside to hang meat. I looked at Brooke and she was literally shivering. Grabbing a throw blanket off a chair, I sat down on the loveseat next to her and draped the blanket over us. She drew in close and hugged me tightly. I could feel her goose-bumped flesh press warmly against mine. It felt good. Her hair had fallen down over her eyes and using my free arm, I brushed it away lightly. She smiled. Taking advantage of the moment, I bent forward and kissed her.

"You two lovebirds want some of this pizza?" Reno yelled from the kitchen.

"No thanks" I laughed. "But we will take a couple drinks." While Reno and Phil were busy warming up pizza and making drinks, Lew turned on some music and the television with the sound turned down. He then went around and opened up all of the windows as well as the doors to the screened in porch. Kelly and he went out on the porch to listen to the sound of the falling rain.

"Reno" Lew said, just before he left to go out on the porch, "even though I won the bed upstairs, why don't you take it tonight?"

"Thanks Lew" Reno smiled, taking the hint. Moments later, Reno and Phil left the kitchen, dropped off a couple of drinks on the table in front of Brooke and me, and then headed upstairs. They turned down the lights as they left. The only light left illuminating the room was coming from the television.

I'm not sure what Lew and Kelly were up to out on the porch, but Brooke and I were getting busy before the sound of Phil's footsteps plodding upstairs had ended.

CHAPTER TWELVE

`Cause I've seen incredible things in my years
Somedays were laughter, others were tears
If I had it all to do over again
I'd just get myself drunk and I'd jump right back in

Jimmy Buffett
Landfall

Kissing each other, with the blanket thrown over us, it became too hot for clothing. I began to unzip her dress. To my horror, she was wearing a bra. I wrestled with that damn thing for what seemed like an eternity. She was wearing a strapless, two clasp version that was throwing me off my game. Plus, Brooke's passionate kisses were distracting, to say the least. Normally I would just ask the girl to take it off herself, but I was determined to unhook the contraption. After all, I was a Midwestern guy under the covers with a hot Miami chick, and I'd be damned if I was going to give up this easily. My head was swimming and Brooke's hands were gliding up and down my body, making it next to impossible to concentrate. The thumb of my right hand was behind the clasp, and my two forefingers were working the hooks. Finally the first clasp broke free, but as I was struggling to finish the job, she rolled over, pinning my right arm to the bed. I froze, faced with the undaunting task of trying to unclasp a bra with my left hand. With the circulation in my arm cut off, I focused hard on the mission at hand. The rain had picked up a bit outside and the steady beat began to divert my attention. The strikes of thunder were like a drum roll, willing me to succeed. With one last effort, the bra came free, falling gently to the floor. Thunder rumbled and lighting struck at that exact moment, the sounds echoing like someone triumphantly striking symbols. Somewhere muffled in the background, I heard the door fly open and felt the wind gush in. A few drops of rain sprayed on my bare back. Brooke moaned. Reluctantly, I broke free and looked over my shoulder in the direction of the open doorway. Thunder cracked and a bolt of lighting lit up the room. To my shock, I could see the outlines of a pair of silhouettes standing in the doorway. Startled, I propped myself up on an elbow and tried to look back a second time. The room was too dark to make anything out. "What's wrong?" Brooke asked. Lighting flashed again. My eyes focused clearly on two men wearing hooded ponchos. That was when the lights inside Mark's townhouse slammed on.

I stood up abruptly, inadvertently taking the blanket with me. Brooke screamed out. I turned my head to see if she was all right and noticed she was lying on the loveseat, topless and sundress-less. *God she looks good*, I thought, as I draped the blanket down over her. She sat up on the loveseat and clutched the blanket tightly against her chest. Glancing quickly around the rest of the room, I saw that Lew, and a completely dressed Kelly, had just arrived. I couldn't help but notice that Lew, trying to be sly, was checking out Brooke from the corner of his eye. The rest of us stood staring into the expressionless eyes of two hooded men. Dressed all in black, dripping wet, and bigger than an NFL lineman, they stood motionless, glaring right back at the four of us.

"Get your clothes on honey," one of them snarled, causing us to jump back a bit. His voice boomed out like a foghorn. "Where are your other two buddies?" The other guy standing beside him had yet to move a muscle and simply held his ground, flexing.

Reaching down, I grabbed Brooke's dress and handed it to her. She looked terrified. I winked at her and trying to reassure her, I mouthed, *its O.K.*

"We're up here," echoed the voice of Reno from above our heads. I looked up and saw both Reno and Phil leaning over the balcony railing. Still sleepy, Phil was rubbing his eyes. "What's going on?" Reno asked.

"We'll ask the fucking questions here," the silent one yelled out. "Who's BMW is that parked outside?" He took two quick steps towards us and stood there with his hands resting on his hips. His fists were as big as a couple of baked hams. Meanwhile, his partner started walking towards the stairs. He stopped when he reached the bottom of the stairwell and yelled for Reno and Phil to come down.

"It's my car" Kelly said weakly, as she raised her hand. Her face, like Brooke's, was as white as a ghost. She was standing with her legs crossed, like she had to pee. Lew, whose arm was around her, was trying to help her relax. It wasn't working, she was practically shaking.

"I suggest that you and your girlfriend get in it and leave" he said calmly, almost reassuringly. Kelly started walking very fast towards the door. Brooke, struggling to squeeze back into her dress, awkwardly zipped it up halfway, grabbed her shoes and followed Kelly's lead. When they had both reached the doorway, the guy by the stairs, yelled out "Wait a minute." The girls stopped dead in their tracks. Neither of them turned around, and I saw Kelly's back hitch up and down rapidly. She was beginning to cry. "If either of you two calls the cops, there'll be four dead guys left in here." Brooke screamed out and Kelly fumbled around with the doorknob, sobbing feverishly by now. Her shaking hands and the rain that had drenched the entryway caused her hands to keep slipping off the polished knob. Finally, they got the door opened and they ran out into the dark, wet night. By the time they reached the car, they were almost hysterical. In a scene right out of a horror movie, I watched Kelly try to open her car door. I could see her hands were shaking so badly that she couldn't seem to work the key fob. Just then, my vision was cut off as the front door slammed shut.

"You guys just couldn't let it rest could ya?" The goon with the foghorn voice was pacing back and forth across the room, while the other guy resumed his position by blocking the front door. He sighed loudly, blowing air through his teeth. "We've been watching you. We know you've been talking to the cops." He continued pacing. The four of us were watching him closely. Lew and I exchanged a quick glance. We were all standing in front of the loveseat. "I thought the note we left you guys was pretty clear?" The goon by the door chuckled to himself when he heard this. "What part didn't you understand?"

"We didn't say anything..."

"Shut Up!" the guy by the door yelled, interrupting Reno before he could finish. Seething, he stood there pointing his index finger at Reno's head.

Reno's words trailed off almost unheard as I watched the pacing goon stop mid-stride. In a long sweeping gesture, he reached his right hand inside his poncho.

He's got a gun, my mind screamed. Time seemed to stand still as I watched like a deer trapped in a headlight as his hand flew out from underneath the dark rain gear. He was holding something. It wasn't a gun; I felt the tension rush like a stream from my body. A folded up brown sack whistled across the room and struck Lew right in the middle of the chest. Caught by surprise it bounced off Lew's chest and fell to the floor.

"Pick it up," the goon said, smiling.

I watched Lew as he bent down and scooped it up the package. He held it in his hands, turning it over to inspect all sides.

"Open it!" came another roar.

Tearing along a perforation in the bag, Lew's eyes bulged out at the sight of what was inside.

"What is it Lew?" I asked.

"Its five grand," the goon answered, not waiting for Lew to respond. "I've got one for each of you he said, as he flung matching envelopes at me, Reno and Phil.

Ripping mine open, I was looking at more one hundred dollar bills than I had ever seen in one place. The envelope was stuffed completely full, with the stack of c-notes at least an inch thick. "Wow," I whispered, as I fanned the stack.

"Like I was saying, we know you've been talking to the cops. Maybe this will keep you guys quiet if they come around asking any more questions. I want you to think long and hard about this." He paused, trying to emphasize the point. "You guys really aren't that hard to find. This better keep you quiet."

Before I even knew what was happening, Lew had grabbed the envelope out of my hands. "Give me that" he said, tugging the money from my grasp. He went around and did the same to Phil and Reno. Standing there, holding twenty thousand dollars, Lew just stood there, grinning ear to ear.

"What's so funny mother fucker?" the goon by the door yelled out.

Not bothering to reply, Lew calmly opened up the top envelope and pulled out eight, crisp, one hundred dollar bills. He then walked over to the guy that had thrown the hush money at us and dropped the envelopes at his feet. "We don't want your money."

"Cool," Reno gasped.

"Lew, what are you doing?" I yelled out.

"Shut up Tango!" Lew yelled back, glaring at me. He turned back around quickly and repeated himself. "We do not want your money."

"So what's that in your hand?" the guy asked, bending down to collect the four envelopes.

"That's for the moped" Lew replied. "But don't worry, our mouths will stay shut. Believe me, you've convinced us already."

"The boss is gonna be pissed," came a quiet menacing voice from the door.

"If that's what you guys want," the other guy said, "fine." He waved the envelopes at us, smiled and backed up towards the entrance. "Who's to say the boss will even know they didn't take it?" He winked at his partner. Before we knew it, they were gone. Leaving the door wide open behind them, we watched as they jumped into a van and drove off. The rain had stopped and steam was beginning to rise from the street.

"It's going to be another sleepless night" Phil moaned, falling into the beanbag. It was the first time he had spoken since coming downstairs. Sighing loudly, he turned up the volume on the television. "Wow. I thought we were all dead."

I fell back onto the loveseat. Drained from the past few hours, I was debating whether or not to find out what was poking me in the ass. Eventually I leaned to the right and pulled out the culprit, a red lace bra. It was Brooke's. In her haste to leave, she had left behind a memento. I folded it up and shoved it into my pocket.

"Not bad, Tango. How far did you get?" Lew asked as he plopped down beside me. "Want a beer?" He had two in his hands.

"Thanks," I said, grabbing a cold one, while shaking my head. "I can't believe you gave back that money."

"Screw it. That was blood money. Trust me; we're better off without it." He winked, tipping the beer. "So dude, what happened out here between you and Brooke, before all the ruckus?"

I smiled and took a long drink myself. "Well, let me tell you, I had her dress off in no time. After a minor struggle, I finally managed to get her freaking bra off."

Lew laughed. "Dude, you always have problems with bras. What is it with you and the brassiere?"

"Yeah, yeah, yeah. Anyway, after the bra came off, my hands were roaming north and they were roaming south, and believe me when I say she was returning the favor. I was mere moments away from ecstasy when those two idiots barged in. If it wasn't for them, I'd be winning the challenge right now, instead of talking to you." I paused to take another drink, trying to wash away the pain of that last thought. "So how'd it go with you and Kelly?"

"Dude, we were out on the porch, dry-humping with our clothes on." We both started laughing. Just then, my phone rang. Reno, who was standing in the kitchen, grabbed it off the counter and threw it my way. It continued to ring. We all looked over at Phil.

"Hey, it ain't my wife," he yelled.

I pushed the send button. "Hello?"

It was Paula.

"Oh Tango, thank God you're not hurt. I didn't know what to think last night when I saw you and your buddies running out of Little V's. I was worried all day, but when I got to work, Greg gave me your note. Sorry it took so long to call you. I'm just so relieved you guys are O.K."

"Well it's been an adventure, the past day, that's for sure." I replied, not wanting to get too specific with her, especially since our last encounter was still so fresh in my mind. I noticed the other three guys were intently listening in on my conversation.

"Dude, who is it?" Lew asked.

Paula, I mouthed.

"Come on Tango, there's got to be more to this story than that. You guys were the talk of the party after everyone saw you getting chased out. I mean come on Tango; you were running around naked for crying out loud. What happened?"

"I don't know what I can tell you Paula."

"Did you guys steal something?" she continued.

"No, it's not like that. Well, actually I guess we did steal a boat" I laughed.

"Well then what is it?"

I could tell she wasn't going to let it die. "Paula, I don't even know where to begin."

"Well you can start by telling me exactly what happened after I told you about your friend getting dragged upstairs," she said.

So that's what I did, I told her all about Phil's beating, our fight with the thugs, Phil's rescue and then the escape. I even told her about the note we had found under the door at the hotel this morning. Like I figured, this story only served to confuse her even more, and it led to more questions. "So why was Phil singled out by Little V?" she asked when I had finished talking.

"That's what we keep asking ourselves," I replied. I didn't feel like getting into all of the reasons we had come up with so far. "Let's just say Phil thinks he may be linked to a murder he witnessed." I sighed, already tired from thinking about the last day and recounting the events.

"So where are you guys staying now?" Paula continued, changing the subject slightly.

"We're shacked up at a friend of ours. Maybe you know him; he worked the party last night too. His name is Mark, he was the bartender."

"What?" Paula screamed. "Tango, you guys got to get out of that house."

"Why?" I asked.

"I saw Mark talking to Little V last night," she said.

"So what." I said.

"I know Mark. Red hair and works at *Ricky's Cantina*?"

"Yeah, why?" I replied.

"Don't you get it?"

"Get what?" I asked, getting more confused.

"What's going on?" Lew interrupted.

"Yeah, what's up?" Reno added.

Frowning, I waved for Lew and the others to quiet down. "Paula, what are you talking about? You're not making sense."

"Tango, *Ricky's Cantina* is owned by Little V. He owns that bar and a couple of tourist shops, amongst some other illicit businesses." I almost dropped the phone. Dumfounded, I couldn't speak as I listened to her continue. "Ricardo Vargas is Little V. Ricardo is Rick. He owns *Ricky's Cantina*. Mark works for Rick. You put two and two together." She was practically hyperventilating as she told me this.

I tried to think clearly. Sighing, I snapped myself out of the fog and asked. "Paula, are you sure about all this?"

"I saw Little V talking to Mark after you guys ran out of the party last night. Tango, you've got to believe me. Get out of that house before they find you."

"It's too late Paula, they already have." I said, as I hung up the phone.

Setting the phone back down on the counter, I felt like hitting something, or more particularly someone. We'd been screwed over by a guy we had come to think of as a true friend. "So are you going to let the rest of us in on what the hell that was all about?" Lew asked.

"It's not good news guys..." I began. By the time I was finished recounting the conversation I'd just had with Paula, I wasn't the only one who was mad. Reno was furious.

"I can't believe Mark double crossed us." Reno yelled, throwing one of the pillows across the room. "This is not cool." What should we do now? I say we wait here and beat the shit out of him."

"Calm down Reno" Lew said. "Doing something like that will only add to our problems, it won't solve anything. It's pretty obvious what we need to do now."

"What?" Phil yawned.

"Well, we need to get out of here for starters. Come on guys, let's get packed up" Lew ordered. "Tango, call us a taxi."

In no time, Reno, Lew and I were standing on the front porch waiting on the taxi to arrive. Phil was inside taking his own sweet time. Lew looked down at Reno's feet. "Nice sandals" he said.

He was wearing a brand new pair. "Thanks. I didn't think Mark would mind."

By the time the taxi pulled up, we already had our bags loaded and were just sitting down inside when Phil came loafing out of the townhouse. He was grinning from ear to ear, even chuckling to himself. Giddy as a schoolgirl, he continued giggling as he sat down next to me.

"What's so funny?" I asked, staring at him. He was still laughing.

"Nothing. I'll tell you later."

The cab driver slammed his door. Putting the car in drive he glanced over at Lew, who was sitting in the passenger seat. "Where to?"

"Yeah, where the hell are we going Lew?" Reno demanded.

Turning around, Lew calmly replied, "We're sleeping with the bums tonight."

CHAPTER THIRTEEN

And the Wino and I know the joys of the ocean,
Like a boy knows the joys of his milkshake in motion.
It's a strange situation, a wild occupation,
Living my life like a song.

Jimmy Buffett
The Wino And I Know

Lew gave the taxi driver the directions to the old church. As the doors shut tightly, the aroma of the cab struck me like a bucket of cold water. The interior stunk of old cigars and cheap liquor. I couldn't find a comfortable position sitting in the middle of the back seat. The vinyl upholstery was ripped and a chunk of rough yellowed foam was rubbing against the back of my legs, causing them to itch. Our new confines didn't seem to bother Phil, his head was now pressed against the glass window and his eyes were closed tightly. He was still chuckling to himself as he tried to fall back asleep. I looked over at Reno, and he was snuggled up like Phil. "Hey Phil, what's so funny?" I asked, nudging him a bit. He didn't stir, so I poked him again.

Opening one eye, he peeked out at me and smiled. "Hey, I'll tell you later" he yawned. It wasn't soon after, that both he and Reno were sound asleep.

"Those guys could sleep anywhere." Lew said, turning around in his seat.

"Yeah, no kidding" I replied, scratching my legs.

He laughed. "I mean, we just got a death threat and they're back there sawing logs."

The cab slowed to a stop. Looking out to my right, past a sleeping Reno, I could barely make out the silhouette of the old church in the darkness. "You sure this is the right place?" our taxi driver asked. "It's pretty late, and I'll bet that place is locked up" he continued, as he parked the cab.

"Yeah, we're sure this is it," Lew replied. "How much do we owe you?"

The driver sighed. "If you guys are staying here..." he began. "This is my last ride for the night. Hell, I thought I was the only one up tonight anyway." He reached forward and cleared out the meter. "Just give me ten bucks and we'll call it even."

"Thanks," I said, while trying to rouse Phil and Reno.

"No sweat. I'd feel guilty charging you any more. It looks like you've had quite a night."

"Dude, if you only knew," Lew said, handing him the money.

The four of us were left standing in an empty parking lot. The reflection of the moon, in a standing puddle of water, cast up the only light around. Our cab had pulled away a few moments earlier and yet we all still stood there. Reno and Phil were rubbing their eyes.

"What now?" I asked.

"From what I remember, that green wooden door along the side of the church was where the bums slept. I say we go in," Lew replied.

"Are you nuts? Under the church?" Phil screamed out. "I'm not sleeping with them. Hey, this is insane."

"Calm down Phil. It's not like you're going to have to share a sleeping bag with one of them," Lew replied.

"Yeah but..."

"I'm with Phil," Reno began. "I don't like the sound of sleeping underneath there any more than he does. And I'm not even scared of bums."

"Hey, it's not that I'm scared of them. I just don't like them."

"Sounds like you're scared to me," Lew said. "What do you think Tango?"

"I don't even know what to think," I laughed.

Lew had heard enough. He started walking over towards the entrance without us, yelling "We escaped death once tonight, why not take a chance." Once in front of the door, he stopped and turned around to face us. "You guys got a better idea?" Before any of us could answer, lightning cracked overhead and it started raining again.

"Oh God," Phil moaned.

"Looks like our decision has been made for us," I said. "I'm sure as hell not going to sleep in the rain."

"Cool. I'm in," Reno yelled.

So despite our best judgment, we hustled over to where Lew was standing. The rain was already picking up. The three of us looked over at Phil. His head was hanging down. Thunder rumbled above us. As the rain continued to gain intensity, a dejected Phil walked slowly over towards the rest of us.

"No turning back now," Lew said, as he put his hand on the door knob.

"Don't you think we ought to knock first?" Phil asked.

Not quite having to get down on all fours, Reno, Lew and I were forced to squat down in order to enter. Phil, however, had to crawl. After we were all inside, the door slammed shut on its own. Without the aid of any internal lighting, it was pitch black. It took our eyes a few seconds to adjust to the lack of light; in the meantime, all we could do was rely on our other senses. My nostrils were immediately filled with the smell of puke and urine, and I got the intense feeling that we weren't alone.

"Anybody in here?" Lew shouted out.

Something beside us moved.

The four of us listened quietly, all we could hear was some loud snoring. Then we all heard the noise again. There was a scratching off to our right.

"Phil, get me your lighter," Lew said.

Seconds later, the dim light from Phil's full throttle allowed us our first glimpse of our new surroundings. We were squatting on a concrete slab that extended just a few more feet into the room. The concrete gave way in front of us to a pebbled rock surface. This surface extended to the walls; however, the entire room was surrounded by a ring of dirt, kind of like an outfield warning track. There were spider webs clumped in all of the corners. The room was triangular in shape, with the narrowest portion being at the entrance where we stood. The entire room only had about four feet of headroom, forcing us to continue to stoop, squat or crawl.

"Interesting," I sighed. Like the ashtray of life, this place was littered with empty bottles, paper and food containers. The trash was thrown everywhere. Breaking my train of thought was that same rustling noise again.

"What is that?" I whispered.

Lew cast the light in the direction of the noise. That's when I saw it. We weren't the only ones awake in here. Two beady red eyes glared back at us. It was a rat. Reno grabbed a rock and threw it in the rat's direction. Although Reno had missed his target, the rat scurried off into a dark corner.

"This sucks," Phil sighed,

Out of options, we were forced to call this dump our home for the night. The three bums sleeping in the far corner of the room, hadn't even noticed we'd come in. They were still snoring, and only one had even moved since our light had been flickering. More likely than not, they were sleeping off a long night of drinking or drugging. Heeding Phil's wishes, we set up camp at the opposite corner from where the bums were resting and the rat had run. Using our suitcases as pillows, we decided to try and make the best of it. At least we could get a few hours of sleep without getting wet. With the rain continuing to pound against the walls outside, sleep came easier than I would have thought.

Surprisingly, I slept pretty sound. I was awoken early that morning by Lew.

"Dude, you awake yet?" he asked, as he nudged me.

"Am now," I yawned. Opening my eyes, I was forced to squint. Light was shining in through the cracks in the rotting walls, and I noticed that the door had been left open. The room was hot and stuffy, the air was stagnant. As I sat up, I realized that I was drenched in sweat.

"Dude, it freaking reeks in here, and I'm sweating."

"You're not the only one," I said.

"We're going to stink like this place all day long." Lew replied. "Let's get the other two up and get out of here."

I looked over at Reno and Phil; they were both still cashed out. They were huddled up close together, sleeping like babies. Disgusted, Lew got up hacking and coughing. He grabbed an empty beer can and threw it at the two of them. The can clattered against the wall and fell harmlessly to the ground. Unlike the rat the night before; neither of them moved. Lew, shaking his head reached out and snatched a fast food cup with the lid still attached. He tossed it over in their direction. "Ooo, that had something in it," Lew gasped, right after it left his grasp.

Too late, we watched the cup as it sailed through the air, toppling end over end. A one in a million shot. The cup tagged Phil right on top of his head. The lid fell off and the chunky remains of what appeared to be a vanilla shake slid out slowly over Phil's hair. Phil immediately bolted upright. Making a bad situation worse, his head slammed against a wooden rafter. Screaming out in pain, his hands went up to his forehead. It took Lew and me several minutes to stop laughing, once we were certain he didn't get a concussion from the blow. Wiping the liquid from his eyes and wringing the chunks out of his hair he cursed at Lew repeatedly. It wasn't long before a bright red knot erupted on his forehead, above his left eye. Amazingly, Reno avoided the entire ordeal. By this time, he was inspecting Phil's head for damage.

"That might leave a mark," Reno said.

"Hey, let's get the hell out of here," Phil replied, rubbing his forehead.

Walking out the door, the brunt of the sun's force hit us. The rain from the night before had made the air as thick as molasses. There was a huge mud puddle to the left of the doorway. "Watch out for the mud," Lew smiled, "we don't want to get dirty."

"Yeah, we wouldn't want to get dirty," Phil replied. "Meanwhile, I got a day old shake in my hair and the stink of a sewer in my clothes."

"What time is it Lew?" Reno asked, as the four of us stretched our backs. Spending the last few hours hunched over underneath the church had not been kind to us.

Lew had both hands clasped above his head. As he brought his left arm down in an exaggerated swooping motion he yelled out, "Where the hell is my watch?" All that remained on his arm was the distinctive white tan line.

"Maybe it fell off," I said. "It might still be inside."

Not waiting around, Lew headed back inside. "Dude, it was on my arm when I went to bed last night," he mumbled, walking towards the entrance. A few minutes later he exited the hideout. "It's not in there," he yelled, visibly upset. He stopped dead in his tracks and slammed his hand into his front pocket. "Dudes," he screamed out, "My money is gone too."

"The eight hundred dollars from last night?" I asked.

"Yup" he sighed. "I put it in my front pocket before I went to sleep."

"I bet the bums stole it" Phil said. "Hey, I tried to warn you guys, but no, you wouldn't listen."

We checked our bags to see what else might be missing. Aside from maybe some spare change, everything else seemed to have been left alone.

Lew sighed loudly. "Well, it's a good thing I brought along a backup." Opening up a hidden compartment on his duffel bag, he pulled out a shiny silver watch.

"Only you would pack two watches" I said, as he slipped the backup onto his wrist.

"Hey Lew, do I still owe you for the moped?" Phil asked.

Laughing, we all forged ahead into the blazing sun.

"Where to now?" I asked.

This seemed to be a recurring question.

We'd been walking aimlessly, wandering toward the north end pier when Lew had enough. "What is so damn funny Phil?" Phil was once again snickering to himself as we walked.

Phil finally decided to let us in on what he'd been up to in Mark's house the night before.

"Hey, remember when I said I didn't need to go to the bathroom as often as you guys?"

"Yeah, so?" Lew replied. "Every two days, like a freak of nature."

"Well, I had to go last night when you guys were outside."

"Dude, big deal."

"I didn't use the toilet," he said between fits of laughter. "I went on his bed."

"No way!" I screamed.

"Cool. That sounds like something I'd do. Way to go Phil." Reno gave him a high five.

Finally able to control himself, Phil asked the next question; one that had been on my mind as well. "Hey, where are we going?"

"Follow me," Lew said, "I know the way."

At the end of our morning walk, the four of us carried our suitcases through the front desk and proceeded straight into the lobby of the *Marriott*, acting as if we owned the place. Air conditioning never felt so good. "I didn't think it would be safe to come here last night, since this is where the girls are staying." Lew began. "Just in case those goons were still following us." We knew two things heading into the hotel, one was that Brooke and Kelly were staying here, and two, we didn't know what their last names were. Finding them was going to be tough. Not quite sure why we hadn't gotten their phone numbers yet.

With an air of confidence, we continued right into the bathroom, so we could accomplish our ultimate goal for the morning. We needed to use the facilities in order to get cleaned up. It had been a rough night, and we all needed to freshen up. We were homeless, ridden hard and had been put to bed wet. I'm sure we looked like quite a sight, passing through the lobby: dust, dirt, rotted shake and all. We needed to focus on what we were going to do next: Settle our score with Little V.

Our plan was to walk over to see if the boat we had borrowed from Little V was still docked. If so, we were planning on returning it and ending this madness. Reno was more interested in confronting Little V, but that was still up for debate, at least as far as Reno knew. None of us really had much hopes of the boat still actually being there, but it gave us something to do for the rest of the day.

"Hey, you know, speaking of someone following us, did anybody else notice those two guys outside?" Phil asked, looking over his shoulder towards the bathroom door. "I think they've been tailing us since we left the church," he whispered.

"Phil, I was just joking," Lew sighed. "Nobody's following us."

"I didn't see anybody," I said, but in my mind I was almost visualizing what Phil had described. Reno simply laughed.

As we exited the restrooms, slightly refreshed -- at least as clean as one could get using a restroom sink -- I asked Lew, "What time is it?" for about the tenth time this morning. It was still a funny question.

"Yeah, real funny Tango."

Giddy, from a lack of real good sleep, we all started laughing. The sounds of our laughs echoed throughout the lobby, causing more than a few people to look our way. That's when I heard the screaming. Startled, I took a step back as four women jumped from a couch in the lobby and ran straight at us. I can't tell you how overcome I was when I saw that one of them was Brooke. She jumped straight into my arms giving me a big bear hug. Turning my body, with her still tightly attached, I could see that Lew was being mauled by Kelly. Their two friends, Morgan and Jennifer from last night, were talking with Reno and Phil.

"Wow. You stink!" Brooke said, fighting back tears. "It smells like you've been sleeping in a trash can." She was now smiling, that gorgeous smile, from check to cheek. As I bent over and placed her back gently onto the ground, I gave her a kiss on the forehead.

"What happened last night?" yelled Kelly, hugging Lew again. "It seems like lately every time I think I'm going to die, you two guys are around," she added, pointing over in my direction.

"Long story," Lew replied.

"You can say that again," I laughed.

"After you girls left, it was pretty much over. Just a bunch of idle threats," Lew continued. "Ricky's Cantina is owned by Little V. That's the guy Phil thinks he saw run over our two friends."

"Hey, I know he did it," Phil interrupted.

Rolling his eyes, Lew continued. "Well the bartender there, Mark, whose place we were staying at last night, he must have ratted us out to the thugs."

"We were so scared," Kelly said.

"Yeah. We didn't know what to do," Brooke interrupted.

"We thought you were in some serious trouble," Kelly finished.

"Nothing we can't handle," I smiled.

"Well, we can't stop talking about what happened last night. Neither one of us could sleep." Kelly said.

"I know how you feel. Sleeping on a dirty floor with a bunch of bums is not exactly the kind of thing I envisioned when they said they were taking me to Key West for my bachelor party" Reno said.

"Sleeping with bums? Where?" Brooke asked.

"A few blocks back, under a church," Lew answered. "We left Mark's, got a cab ride to the church and slept underneath."

"Why didn't you just come here? Or call us?" Kelly asked.

"Uh, yeah, we still don't have your phone numbers, plus we didn't want to lead them right back to you, in case they were still following us," Lew replied.

"Well I'm glad you're here now. I'm sure you all need to clean up. You can use our rooms," Kelly offered, already tugging at Lew's arm as she walked towards the elevators.

"Come on, follow us," Morgan said.

"We had just come down to the lobby and were trying to decide where we would eat, while we waited for our other friends." Kelly added. "Now you guys can join us."

"You all look like you had a rough night," Brooke stated, as she stared at Phil.

"Hey, that's an understatement," Phil laughed. The rest of us joined in and we were still laughing when the elevator doors slid shut.

However, in the seconds before the doors closed completely, I could have sworn I saw two guys put down a newspaper, that had been hiding their faces. They stood up and walked briskly towards the elevators. The doors shut as I wondered if these were the guys Phil had been talking about. "Did you see that?" I asked, looking at Phil.

"What?"

"Never mind, it was probably nothing."

As the elevator rose to the tenth floor, the girls told us that they had two rooms, but each only had one bathroom. Lew and I, of course, decided to go with Kelly and Brooke back to their room. Reno and Phil were going to use the other room. I breathed deeply. It felt like we were riding to heaven with four angels. They smelled like fruit punch and cotton candy. *Man I need a shower*, I thought.

Ting!

My thoughts were interrupted as the elevator came to an abrupt stop. When the doors opened, their other four girlfriends were standing there. They were all beautiful. Two of the girls were wearing sundresses, like the ones Brooke and Kelly wore, while the other two had on short shorts and clingy tops. Although our bed-head, wrinkled dirty clothes, and unshaven faces might have fit in fine with the bums last night, we must have looked like the four stooges. I was starting to feel uncomfortable. After some brief introductions, of which I'd be lying if I said I remembered any of their friends' names, Reno and Phil sauntered off with the four new girls. "Don't worry dudes, they won't bite," Lew yelled as we watched Reno and Phil look back at us as they walked away. They both smiled sheepishly and waved.

Brooke took me by the hand and led me down the long hall. Kelly and Lew were not too far behind when Brooke opened the door to their room and we walked inside. The room smelled like perfume and everything that is all girl, and the cool air conditioning was well received. I just laughed, shook my head, and followed her into the room. Lew came in right behind me; Kelly was still talking to Morgan and Jennifer in the hallway.

"I got to take a shit," Lew whispered in my ear as he walked past. Brooke had already gone into the bathroom, so it was just the two of us standing in the room.

"Now?" I asked, dreading the reply.

"Yeah, dude. But how can I, when there's going to be four hot girls on the other side of the door?" His face was beginning to show signs of panic.

"Help yourselves guys," Brooke said, as she exited the bathroom. She was holding some used towels and a few pairs of swim suits that she had pulled off the shower bar.

Not hesitating, since I was beginning to feel grimy standing in their room, I walked into the bathroom. Lew followed me up, saying "You could have left one of those bikini bottoms in here. Tango could have used it for a hair net."

Brooke just smirked and walked out onto the balcony. I turned on the fan as Lew shut the door.

Wasting no time, I reached inside the shower and turned on the water. Lew had already flipped open the toilet seat, so I stripped off my clothes and hopped quickly into the steaming shower. The combination of cool air conditioning and warm water instantly relaxed me. It was going to take a lot of soap to clean off all the grub that had accumulated on my body from the past night. I could only image what Phil was going through, trying to get the shake out of his hair. With a lather of soap working its magic on my skin, I poked my head out from behind the shower curtain. "There sure wasn't much to those bikini bottoms, was there?" I laughed.

Lew just looked up at me and shook his head, slapping himself across the face a couple of times.

I concentrated on washing my hair next. That's when I heard one of the worst sounds a person can hear when they're showering. The toilet flushed. My head was completely full of soap bubbles, when the scalding hot water pierced me like a knife on the back of the neck. Before I could scream my eyes bolted open, instantly burning them. Feeling like a slug that had just been salted, I jumped away from the water and pressed my chest against the far wall, when I heard it again. A second flush. "Stop it!" I screamed. "You're killing me!" I shrieked like a girl from the pain.

"Sorry dude, but I needed a courtesy flush." Moments later, I heard the door open and through the crack in the curtain and the wall that I was wedged against, I saw Lew walk out. Of course, he left the door wide open behind him.

It took a few minutes for the water to reach a level that was slightly below boiling. Only then was I finally able to rinse off the shampoo and finish up in the shower. As the water turned off, I heard the door shut again. The shower curtain was yanked back and a towel smacked me right in the face.

"Move out dude," he said, pushing me aside as he stepped in.

I resisted the urge to give the toilet a few flushes of my own while Lew was showering; but I figured that it would only prolong the ordeal. Lew was the kind of person that actually let the conditioner set on his hair for the entire five minutes that the bottle recommended. Once we were both clean shaven, showered and dressed, we rejoined the girls. They were all on the bed, watching some music videos. Brooke was combing her hair. Some eighties video was playing and the two of us stood there listening, starting to get our groove on. Looking up at us, Brooke smiled and said "Call your father now Kelly, they're all ready."

"Do you guys mind?" asked Kelly. "My dad said if we saw you all again, that he wanted to personally thank you both for saving our lives."

"Yeah, that's fine. I don't care," I said.

"Either do I," Lew added.

Kelly then ran over to the table, where the phone was resting. She dialed and then placed the phone next to her ear.

"You're calling his work, aren't you?" Brooke asked, as Lew and I walked over to the table where Kelly was standing.

Kelly just shook her head, holding up a finger. "Daddy! You'll never guess."

"I have both of the guys here with me in the room."

"We found them this morning in the lobby."

"Yes." She was grinning from ear to ear. It almost looked like she was about to cry.

"O.K." She sniffled.

"Here's Lew, the boy I was telling you about." She handed the phone over to Lew.

"Hello sir," Lew began.

"Yeah, it was pretty incredible."

"Uh huh."

"Well, we didn't think too much about it at the time. We were running on adrenaline."

He gave me a wink. "Yes."

"That's for sure."

"Yeah dude, we just showed those sharks no fear." He was smiling too, and just kept nodding and laughing. I had no idea what Kelly's dad was telling him, but they were getting along like a couple of old fraternity brothers.

Next thing I knew, I heard him giving the guy our home address. *That's weird*, I thought.

"Well, thank you sir. Do you want to speak to Kelly again?"

"Sure. My pleasure."

"I will. Nice talking to you too." He hung up the phone. Guess *he didn't want to talk to me after all*, I thought.

"What did he say?" Kelly asked excitedly.

"Oh, he just wanted to thank us, and Tango, he would have thanked you personally, but we got interrupted by his secretary. Something about a patient he was late to."

"Whatever," I sighed.

Lew walked over and put an arm around Kelly. "He told me that you were his only daughter and as a show of thanks, he was going to send us something from Miami. So I gave him our address."

"Maybe some Cuban cigars?" I interrupted, brightening up a bit.

"Who knows? Anyway, that was about it. He sounded like a real nice guy."

"He's a very successful doctor in Miami," Brooke informed us. "I'm sure you'll be getting something very nice." I looked at Morgan and Jennifer, who were still lying on the bed. They both were shaking their heads in agreement.

Knock. Knock. Knock.

Brooke opened the door. Looking over her shoulder I could see Reno, Phil and the rest of the girls were all standing in the hallway. Phil's hair was still dripping wet. He hadn't even bothered to blow it dry. They were both holding their suitcases.

"You guys ready yet?" Reno asked. "We're starved."

"Sure," Brooke replied. "Why don't you leave your bags in here, you can get them after we eat."

"That's cool." Reno replied, setting his bag down inside the doorway.

"Let's roll," Lew said, leading Kelly by the hand on his way out the door. He practically pushed Phil over as he was setting his bag down next to Reno's.

Wearing a fresh set of clothes and feeling much better about things, we decided to all grab brunch together. As we walked through the lobby, Lew mentioned that we ought to try and just get a room here for the night. Hearing this, Kelly immediately ran over to the front desk. "We're leaving this afternoon," she said, over her shoulder, "I'll ask if I can just extend our room one more night. We'll pay for it." Moments later she came back to where we were standing, all smiles. "It's all set up," she grinned. "You guys can stay in our room tonight."

"Thanks," we said. Lew gave her a big kiss.

Walking back out through the front door of the hotel we were greeted with a beautiful, ninety degree day. Although it was still a bit humid, the sunlight and the sound of seagulls were a welcomed relief. We all felt born again.

"Where do you want to eat?" asked Brooke. "It's on us."

"Cool. A free room and a free lunch, what more could we ask?" Reno replied.

I looked at Lew, Reno and then Phil. We all just smiled. I knew Lew would have a response to Brooke's question. "I saw this seafood buffet right over there this morning," he said, pointing off to his left.

"Hey, it's just past our hotel room from last night," Phil laughed.

"That sounds good to us," the girls replied. So the twelve of us all strolled across Duval, each of us chuckling, as we walked through the entrance to the *World's Famous Seafood Buffet*.

CHAPTER FOURTEEN

But livin' in the briar patch ain't what it appears
Sooner or later you gotta face your fears
I heard it from the parrot verbalizing in the tree
I heard it in the songlines of the aborigine
Off the see the lizard

Jimmy Buffett
Off To See The Lizard

I knew we were in trouble as the group walked past the buffet line on the way to our table. We were following our host, who was trying to find a table large enough for twelve. Looking down at the buffet, I strained to find even one item of seafood. Walking in through the front, underneath a banner that declared 'The World's Largest Seafood Buffet', I had envisioned piles of lobster, crab, shrimp and fish. What I saw in the stainless steel vats, which were sitting above flamed warmers, was spaghetti, rice, bread, soup, pizza and salad. Just about everything under the sun except seafood. It was as though the place had gone out of its way not to have any seafood on the buffet that day.

"This is no seafood buffet," I mumbled, as we sat down at the table. Our host had actually pushed two large, cafeteria-style tables together, and we were all seated, as the waiter took our drink orders.

Looking around the table, I noticed that Phil was missing. Turning around in my chair, I looked back towards the entrance. He was already holding two plates and had worked his way through one side of the buffet, with a biscuit hanging from his mouth. I started laughing.

Aside from the lack of seafood, brunch in and of itself was very pleasant. Everybody was in good spirits as we talked through our meal. Things were starting to look better; it was as though we had finally rounded the corner and were in the home stretch. We were enjoying a free lunch, a free hotel room for the night and beautiful women surrounded us. It just didn't get any better.

"You never did tell us about last night," Kelly said, between bites. "What was it like sleeping with the bums?"

I laughed, thinking about it. Whereas Lew, went right into the story. He told them all about our sleeping conditions from the previous night, concluding with the fact that he left the bums hideout, eight hundred dollars and one watch, lighter than when he had gone in. Kelly rubbed the back of his head, trying to comfort him.

"Come on Lew, it's not like you don't have fifty other watches at your disposal." I said.

"Dude, that was my favorite watch. It was sort of a memento. I bought that watch in Galveston Bay, when we were designing the fountains for that shopping center."

"I remember. That was one of our first jobs, at least the first one that we made a profit on."

"Yup, and that watch was what I spent my half of the money on," he sighed, really trying to soak up sympathy.

"Oh you poor baby," Kelly said, leaning over to kiss him on the cheek.

I rolled my eyes, and bit into an egg roll.

Moments later, I felt a tap on my shoulder. Turning around, I saw Phil. He looked worried. "There they are," he whispered, pointing across the table discretely.

My eyes followed his finger, and there they were. The two guys I'd seen in the hotel lobby. "Are those them?"

"I think so," Phil replied, still whispering. Sitting in the corner, near the entrance of the restaurant, were the two guys who Phil and now I thought had been trailing us since we left the church. Neither of them were eating anything, they were drinking something, and I swear, they were staring right at us.

"What's going on Tango?" Brooke asked, sensing our tension.

"I don't know, maybe it's a coincidence, but Phil and I keep seeing those two guys over there lately."

"I think they're following us," Phil said under his breath.

"Would you two ladies calm down," Reno said, he had overheard everything. "I swear, you two are paranoid."

Just then, a waitress a couple of tables behind us dropped a dish. As it crashed against the tile floor, Phil literally jumped out of the seat he had just sat down in. I quickly looked back towards the door, and the two guys sat at their table, continuing to stare, but grinning menacingly.

With the check paid and absolutely no seafood consumed, we pushed away from the table and began a slow walk outside. I glanced over my shoulder and looked towards the table where the two guys had been sitting. It was empty.

I was holding Brooke's hand as we walked, and was actually kind of disappointed. The girls only had a few hours before they had to get back on the road to Miami. As we continued our walk, I came to the realization that I was truly going to miss her. I gave her hand a tight squeeze and smiled. I brushed a strand of hair out from her eyes, which were now moist with tears. We had broken up into a couple of groups with Reno, Phil, Lew, Kelly, Brooke and myself walking a few blocks behind the rest of the girls. No one was really saying too much, until Reno yelled out, "Damn, this ain't a funeral procession." We chuckled a bit, but aside from Reno, nobody was in the mood to talk, and let's face it, Phil never spoke anyway. We eventually came to a point where it made no sense to continue on, the girls needed to head back to the hotel to get packed, and we needed to look for a boat. We exchanged names, phone numbers, addresses, emails, hugs and kisses. I put the girls vitals, which were written on a piece of paper that I could transfer into my phone later, into my pocket and gave Brooke one last kiss. As I watched her walk away, she snuck one last look over her shoulder, smiled and waved goodbye. I wondered if I'd ever see her again.

"Let's head down Duval, and see if the boat is still there," Lew said, interrupting my thoughts. None of us had any intentions of confronting Little V. really, we were just curious if the boat was still there.

"Hey guys, I'd really like to stop by a gift shop and buy my kids a present, before it's too late." We all turned around and looked at Phil.

"Now?" Lew questioned.

"If not now, when? It'll only take a second," Phil replied.

We found ourselves, moments later, shuffling between the cramped aisles of a tourist shop. Lew was busy scanning through a lineup of T-shirts, and I left him to join Reno, who was sitting on a wooden bench. As I sat down I heard Lew ask the storeowner how much the T-shirts were.

"Twenty dollars," was the reply.

"I'll give you ten."

"Where do you think this is? Miami? Get the hell out of my store." The owner came charging at Lew from behind the counter that held the cash register. A muscular man of Spanish decent with a neck full of gold chains, he was now cursing at Lew as he chased him out through the front doors. Reno and I were hardly able to control our laughter as we watched Lew hustle out backwards. Muttering a few choice phrases beneath his breath the storeowner returned to his post. Phil was waiting on him, looking as though nothing had happened. He was holding a medium sized stuffed animal. It sort of resembled a bear; it was white, with two black letters sewn onto its stomach 'KW'.

"Do you have a bag?" Phil asked as he paid the clerk.

"No."

"O.K. then." Phil tucked the stuffed bear underneath his arm and we went outside to see if Lew was still around. We found him looking through a storefront window a couple of blocks down.

"Your bartering skills could use some sharpening," I joked, as we re-joined him.

"Dude, I thought that guy had gone crazy back there, thanks for getting my back," he smirked.

"I had ten bucks on the Spanish fighter, I wasn't about to interfere," Reno laughed as he twirled his dice. As the giggles subsided, Reno spoke towards a more serious matter. "I've been thinking, if the boat is still docked there, I really think we ought to take it back to Little V's and settle the score once and for all."

"Are you nuts?" Phil yelled, clutching his bear.

"Think about it, it makes perfect sense, especially after what he did to us this morning with that car. I mean, damn, we borrow a boat, but get hassled for stealing a car? What's next? I for one, don't intend to wait and find out. I say we take the bull by the horns. It'll be like an act of goodwill on our part."

Phil was still not pleased. "No way" he muttered under his breath. "Besides I doubt that boat is even still there, I'm sure it's been spotted by now. We're just wasting our time."

"I got a five dollars says it's there," Reno said, pulling a five spot out from his wallet. "I'll even give you ten to one odds, Phil."

"Sounds good, that'll pay for my bear, and then some," Phil grinned.

"Well it's not like we got anything else better to do today," I said. "Don't sweat it Phil, nobody's going to beat up a guy hanging on to a cute teddy bear."

"Hold that thought," he smiled.

The plan seemed simple enough at the time, we continued along our current path, wondering if it would lead us back into the boat that had started this whole mess.

We crossed the threshold of another tourist trap, I had been glancing over my shoulder periodically, as had Phil, and as I turned around again to verify we weren't being followed, I saw them. The same two guys stepped out from the shop only seconds after we'd passed the door. "God damn, there they are again." I couldn't believe what I was seeing. They were standing about ten feet behind us, squinting into the sunlight. Not able to stand this any longer, I charged right over to them. "Why are you following us?" I yelled.

"What? What are you talking about?" they stammered. I couldn't quite place the accent, it sounded almost Swedish.

"You two have been following us all freaking day long," Phil hollered, pointing his finger at the two of them.

"Please, please, there must be some mistake…"

"There's no mistake, you son of a bitch, I've seen you and Phil's seen you."

"I'm begging you, we just got off a cruise ship this morning, I don't know what you're talking about."

It was at that point that Reno and Lew pulled Phil and I away. "You guys are paranoid," Reno muttered.

"Come on you two, snap out of it. This is ridiculous." Lew looked disgusted with the both of us.

A while later, sort of convinced that no one was really following us, we found ourselves behind our old stomping grounds as we walked along the side of a neighboring hotel. Passing alongside the dock, I glanced over at the swimming pool to see that nothing had changed since we'd left. There was another wild party going on in the pool – lots of bikinis and lots of splashing. "Are we sure we still want to do this?" Phil asked quietly. "I just know somebody is going to be waiting there for us."

Just then, Reno, a couple of yards ahead yelled out "It's there."

"I'll be damned," Phil muttered below his breath.

"Looks like you owe me five, Phil."

"Hey, I'll have to pay you later Reno; I spent all my money on the bear." Phil clutched his kid's stuffed animal a little tighter as we stood on the wooden deck."

"Let's just go over and make sure that is really the boat," Lew said, pushing us towards the dock gate, which unlike before was left wide open. "If it is, maybe we can make an anonymous call, let 'em know where it's at." I would have rather stayed at the pool and partied, but we were focused on the task at hand. As we strolled along the dock we passed an old fisherman polishing his boat. He grinned at us and tipped his cap. Reno saluted.

Our boat was one of the smallest docked amongst the forty footers and party boats. It looked suspiciously out of place, and on this occasion there were quite a few people milling about on the deck, just enough to make me feel uneasy about climbing back aboard. We tried to look inconspicuous as we stood on the dock, looming over the vessel. Inexplicitly, Lew jumped aboard. He was looking for the keys. I turned around at about that same instant, and out of nowhere, three big goons stepped out of the shadows and right onto the dock behind us. Before I realized what was going down, Reno was pushed onto the boat headfirst. Out of the corner of my eye, I watched as another grabbed for his gun, it was holstered at his hip. Phil and I submissively walked onto the boat – we were quick studies.

"You boys got some explaining to do. We're making a visit to Little V."

The ride over was pretty quiet; the four of us were sitting in the rear of the boat, while the three amigos sat up front. As we skidded across the small waves of the calm ocean, we occupied our time with some nervous chatter, trying to determine the best course of action when we landed. We all spoke under our breath, but with the crashing of the waves, it was hard for us, let alone our captors, to hear what we were saying. "So what do we say when we get there?" Phil asked.

"Don't worry Phil, I'll do all the talking" Reno replied.

"No, no, no" Lew and I answered simultaneously.

"What?" Reno shrugged.

"We sure as hell don't need you going off half cocked" Lew replied.

"Yeah, that's cool. I might just want to do my talking with my fists, and beat some ass" Reno smirked. "Besides, my back still hurts from sleeping with the bums. I mean, dammit, I had the bed won that night."

Phil, still not able to believe we were walking back into the lion's den, where he'd recently been beaten, just shook his head. "I'm not going to say a word."

"There's a shock," I laughed.

"Look dudes, we're just going to wing it. Follow my lead and it'll be all right" Lew assured us. Moments later we were easing our way past the back of Little V's place. The boat idled slowly over towards the docks, pulling along the beachfront. There were a few guys milling about on the grounds, it didn't take long for them to spot us. I saw a couple of them drop what they were holding and run over towards the docks, motioning for us to follow them over. When we got within earshot, one of them yelled out "How'd you get that boat?"

"Permission to come aboard" Lew hollered back, ignoring the fact that he wasn't even steering the vessel.

"Real funny assholes" was the response, "where'd you get the boat." We were slipping into a stall and the need to shout had passed.

"This is starting off well" Phil mumbled.

"What was that?" the guy asked.

Turning around I glared at Phil. "I thought you were staying quiet."

The three guys, who had escorted us over, jumped off he craft without even glancing back our way. We were left alone aboard the ship.

Reno threw one of the guys, who had run up to the dock, a rope, so they could help us finish docking. But instead of simply tossing it gently he threw it lasso style, hitting the guy right in the gut. The guy took a step towards Reno.

"Bring it on," Reno shouted, not backing down a bit.

"Hey, everybody, calm down, we're no thieves," Lew continued. "We're just returning this from the other night. We want to make everything all right."

"Getting better Lew, now you're starting to rhyme," I laughed.

The guy Reno hit was still upset; he made a reach for his side and revealed a holster. They were packing heat, a shoulder harness held a jet black Beretta. "So then why did you need an escort to find your way back?" he asked, patting the gun.

"We need to speak to Little V." Reno yelled out.

About this time another tall, skinny goon joined his two friends, positioned on the dock. We were still in the boat. As the skinny guy approached he said, "What a coincidence, V's been waiting for you." He then began talking into a shoulder-mounted walkie-talkie. I couldn't quite make out what he said, but I noticed he had a headset on. He stated nodding. "Roger that." He then took a few steps in our direction. "Follow us."

We walked along the path that led to the grounds. The skinny guy was leading the way and the other two goons were bringing up the rear. From the docks, we trekked through the green grass that flanked the pool. You could hear the water sloshing inside the pool's filters. We entered the house through a servant's entrance at the rear, however, before we were allowed inside, we were told to stop and wait for them to frisk us. As we watched Phil, the first of us to get frisked, Reno started laughing. "Phil, that's the most action you've gotten all week." Phil's face flushed and he accidentally dropped his bear.

Hearing this, the tall, skinny guy threw Reno up against the back of the house, planting his face firmly against the rough stucco siding. As he proceeded to frisk Reno, a little harder than normal, Reno started struggling. Unfortunately for Reno, he tried to knee the guy in the groin, as his hands went along Reno's sides. "Mother fucker," the guy yelled as his put a martial art move on Reno, body slamming him to the ground. In another move straight from an ultimate fighting championship, the guy dropped to the ground, slamming his bony elbow into the small of Reno's back. Reno screamed out. Lew and I glanced at each other, each of us starting to get a bit edgy. Almost immediately, the other goons stepped in and separated the two of them. "Boss wants them all in one piece...for now," one of the grumbled. Reno hopped up, and refusing to brush the debris from his clothes, acted as though he was the victim in the whole affair. "You're lucky your boys broke that up, I was just about to get wicked." He was bobbing back and forth, hopping up and down like a jack rabbit. From the looks of it, he thought he was Ali incarnated. Although stunned by what I had just seen, I was barely able to suppress a laugh. Lew was shaking his head.

Certain we were not carrying any weapons; we were finally allowed to enter the home. As opposed to the other night, Little V's mansion was eerily silent. I don't know if it was my imagination or what, but everything from the doors to the ceilings seemed much bigger inside. "Wait here." Reno's assailant ordered, as he walked through the double doors at the other end of the room. Moments later, both doors opened wide – seemingly on their own. We were told to enter.

Not knowing exactly what we were about to get into, the four of us waltzed into the room with our usual air of confidence; trying to act as though we owned the place. To my surprise, however, instead of following us in, the other two goons abruptly slammed the doors behind us. From what I could gather, we were standing in Little V's office. The only sound in the room was the circling of two bamboo ceiling fans over our heads, but despite their efforts, I still felt warm. For a brief second I thought the room might be empty, but that thought was squelched as I saw an enormous leather chair swivel around on its axis. An obese man, matching what I knew to be Little V's description, was seated behind a long mahogany desk. He was puffing on a cigar and drinking a dark liquor. *I know I've seen this guy before*, I thought to myself, I just couldn't put my finger on where or when, but I knew it wasn't the night of the party. He was a big man to say the least, and thinking about his 'Little' moniker made me chuckle to myself. He was dressed in all white and was wearing what I would have sworn were silk pajamas. His sleeves were rolled up and he sported a Rolex on one arm and a few thick gold bracelets on the other. The fingers on his left hand were lined with diamond rings. As I stood there familiarizing myself with the room, the tall, skinny guy made his exit out through a set of French doors to the left of where Little V was seated. Once again, the doors slammed behind him, cutting through the silence in the room like a gunshot. I jumped. "Welcome boys, would you like anything to drink?" His gravelly voice made my skin crawl. A ring of smoke exited his thick lips as he spoke.

"No thanks," Lew said. "This isn't a social visit."

Where have I seen this guy... "Yeah, no thanks," I added.

"We've got some unsettled business to take care of," Lew continued. "We left your place with a boat, but the cops have become confused and claim that we've stolen a car."

"Is that so?" Little V chuckled.

It's the fat man from the plane, my mind screamed out at that instant. "Lew," I whispered as Little V continued speaking. "It's the guy that held up the plane."

"What?" Lew whispered, as Little V continued to talk.

"It's the fat guy from the plane in Orlando," I replied.

"Holy shit, you're right" Lew said under his breath, as Little V continued talking. We were both left speechless as this realization sank in. Neither of us had heard Little V's response.

"I'll take a drink," Reno replied. I watched as Reno sauntered over to the bar and poured a tall glass of single malt scotch into a glass of ice. The bar was positioned on the left side of the room, in front of a bank of three windows. The view of the ocean through them was breathtaking.

"Good choice," Little V laughed, standing up behind his desk. "At two hundred dollars a bottle, you'll find few scotches can compare to its smoothness."

Maybe he's not so bad after all, I thought. "Maybe I will take a drink," I said, taking a step towards the bar.

"You had you're chance *hijo*." Little V replied. "Why don't you stay where you're at?" I stopped immediately and stood next to Lew. It was becoming obvious who was controlling the situation, and it wasn't us.

Getting up from his chair, Little V walked around his desk. He came to a halt in front of it and leaned back, his butt engulfed most of the available real estate that was on the desktop and he reclined on a small stack of papers. It didn't seem to bother him at all. Lew and I were probably ten feet in front of him. I could smell him from where I stood. He stunk of stale sweat. Reno was now sitting on a barstool and Phil was still at the doorway, clutching his bear. I hadn't realized it until now but he had never even walked into the room. Little V looked straight past Lew and I and was glaring right at Phil. "Do I look familiar to you, *hijo*?"

Phil stood emotionless, staring blankly at the floor in front of him.

"Have you seen me before?"

"Yes," Phil mumbled.

"Where?"

"At the scene of the accident a few days ago."

"Wrong answer *hijo*," Little V yelled. He bolted upright, jumping off the desk. Spittle flew from his mouth, the contents of his glass fell to the marble floor with a splash, and I swore he was going to squash the lit cigar he was holding. He started lumbering towards Phil. "Are you so stupid *hijo*, after all the events that have transpired over the past few days?"

None of us said a word. I noticed Phil take a step back, but he was out of space to maneuver. The double doors were closed behind him and his ass was pressed up against them.

"You come into my house uninvited."

"Actually Mark invited us the other night," Reno said, grinning. Proud of his comment, he paused to take a sip of scotch.

Little V stopped dead in his tracks and abruptly turned, facing Reno. "One more word out of you and I'll knock that stupid ass grin right off your face," he said softly. I could swear his eyes were gray. "I don't recall inviting you to my house today," he hissed.

Facing Phil, he continued. "You come into my house uninvited. Embarrass me in my own home."

"I'm sorry," Phil replied, his voice trembling a bit.

"You steal my fucking boat. Make a mockery of me and my men." He stopped to take a breath. "You think you're calling the shots?"

"No" Phil whispered.

"Shut up!" Little V roared. "You guys are fooling yourselves. I could have had you beaten, or dead, on my command." His face had turned bright red; he was sweating like a stuck pig. I thought his arm was going to fall off; he had been shaking it so much. At this point, he was nose to shoulders with Phil, shouting at him point blank. Phil just stood there, emotionless, stiff as a board.

I felt like my feet were nailed to the floor. I was so shocked at the abrupt swing the conversation had taken I was almost unable to comprehend what was happening. I do know one thing though, like Phil, I was nervous. This guy had the looks and sounds of a raving lunatic. *I hope somebody frisked him today*, I thought.

Pulling a handkerchief from his front shirt pocket, he ceased yelling, and wiped the sweat from his brow. His breath was coursing in and out of his chest; he sounded like a locomotive in overdrive. His chest rattled with each heave. "Let me ask you again, *hijo* – have you ever seen me?" He was panting.

Phil did not reply.

Out of patience, Little V reached out and grabbed Phil by the collar. Giving his shirt a tug, pulling Phil down to his level, he glared into his eyes. "You stupid, mother..."

Before he could finish his sentence, out of no where Reno kicked away the chair he was sitting on and hopped over the bar, spilling the expensive bottle of scotch in the process. "I know who you are," he screamed. "You're the coward who killed our friends...and then ran away."

"Coward!" Little V blasted, releasing his grip on Phil and turning in Reno's direction. Clutching his drink in a meaty hand, he wound up like a pitcher and threw it at Reno. The glass shattered into pieces in the far corner of the room, having missed Reno's head by inches. It had happened so quickly, Reno hadn't even had a chance to duck. Calming down a bit, Little V continued his rant. "The way I saw it, your friends ran the light and hit me. I wasn't about to stop; I had a multi-million dollar deal that I was already late for."

"Oh give me a break," Reno laughed. "That's the best you can come up with?"

"You barely even knew those two, but I know all about you guys. I've done my research. Have you?"

"No," Reno answered a little sheepishly.

"Well, that makes two stupid people in this room."

Little V took a deep breath and exhaled slowly, attempting to regain some control. He walked leisurely back to his desk and opened up a drawer. Lew and I exchanged glances. I looked back over at Little V in time to see him pull from the drawer a large buck knife, serrated on one edge. *We're goners*, I thought. Running his thumb along the blade, he strolled over to where Reno was standing. "Have you ever seen an animal gutted with a knife like this?" he grinned sadistically, while licking his lips.

"Not recently," Reno replied.

"Well, *hijo*, I like to use the jagged edge. It's a bit messier, and it will rip out the innards along with it. But it gets the job done." He was now standing menacingly behind Reno. His free hand was resting on Reno's shoulder.

I thought, *How can I stand by and see my friend get killed?* Everything was beginning to spin out of control. This was supposed to be a party weekend. For God's sake, Reno was getting married. Phil has a wife and kids. I had to do something. The situation was on the verge of becoming a bloodbath. "I know who you are." I blurted without thinking.

"Who?" Little V asked.

"You're the guy that held up our plane getting to Key West."

He shook his head. "Yeah, so?"

"So as far as I can see, you're a very important man on this island."

"Go on," he said, using his shirt to polish the steel knife blade as he spoke.

"Look, all we're trying to do is return your boat," Lew butted in. "I apologize for what happened at your party. At this point, all we need is a ride back to the island. Provided the police let us go, our plane leaves tomorrow. We'd get on a plane today if we could. I swear, after we leave, you'll never hear from us again."

"Two smart men...and two stupid men," Little V replied, pointing the knife at Reno and then at Phil. "I haven't decided, but it might be two smart men, and two dead men." He walked over to Phil; the blade of the knife caught the reflection from the windows. "One last time, *hijo*. Do you know me?" The business end of the knife was pressed against Phil's chest.

Phil, looking down at the ground, shook his head no.

"Get these fucking guys out of here." Little V shouted, grazing the point of the knife along Phil's chest. I saw Phil jump backwards, startled. He was inspecting the tear in his shirt when Little V's goons burst back into the room.

"A.J., Tiko, get these guys out of here," Little V said, as he hobbled back to his desk. He sat down hard into his chair and lit up a fresh cigar. Inhaling deeply, he sighed and snapped his lighter shut.

As the doors opened a pair of goons we'd seen before sauntered into the room, all smiles. It was the same two guys Little V had sent to Mark's the other night. These were the money men. They hadn't bothered to introduce themselves that night, but it became evident that Tiko was the guy who'd been doing all the talking at Mark's. "Plan still the same boss?" Tiko's voiced boomed.

"No Tiko, just take them back to the island."

I rolled my eyes, "Not these two," I whispered to Lew.

Reno gently placed his drink on the bar. Glass crunched beneath his feet as he stepped towards us.

"What about the cops?" Lew asked, as we were pushed towards the doors.

Little V spun around in his chair, his back facing us. I thought he had ignored the question. "If you show up at the airport tomorrow, no one will stop you," he replied under his breath.

We were escorted out of the room as quickly as we were led into it. Walking out of the house, the smell of chlorine from the pool hit me like a bag of smelling salts; my mind was instantly alert. No one spoke as we were ushered onto a bigger boat than the one we had pirated. The four of us were joined on board with A.J., Tiko and another guy, who was apparently the driver. Once again, I couldn't help but think the driver looked vaguely familiar. Pulling from the dock, I assumed we were being chaffered back to Key West.

I was wrong.

I should have seen it coming from the beginning. Almost immediately, Reno started getting lippy with the two thugs. He was telling them things like; "I'd kick some ass right now, if you guys weren't carrying guns." But it didn't end there; he kept needling them, taking jabs at everything from their manhood to their sexual preferences. I could tell it was starting to grind on both Tiko and A.J. as their jaws clenched with every comment. They began exchanging looks with one another. Roughly a half mile from the shoreline of Key West, the boat came to an abrupt stop. With the engines stalled out, we drifted aimlessly; the boat ebbed and flowed with the tide. *What now?* I thought. *I hope we're out of gas.*

"Boss said to get you back safe and sound to shore," Tiko began, "but this is as far as this ferry ride goes."

"Hey little man," A.J. said, motioning at Reno. "You're the first one off." Slowly taking his gun out, he pointed it at Reno. "Jump now or you'll be dead before you hit the water."

At this point Lew stood up. Trying his best to persuade our foes, he said "Come on dudes, how about driving us a little bit closer to shore. It's been a long couple of days."

Tiko calmly took out his gun and pointed at Lew's head. "You're next." Taking a couple of steps towards Lew he continued, "I swear, after the night of the party, a fucking boat chase, not to mention getting rained on all God damned night long, you think I'm going to give you cowboys a break?"

"Well, I was..." Lew started.

"Shut up," Tiko interrupted, he slapped the back of a leather seat. The noise made me jump, for a second I thought his gun had gone off. "I'm through with you guys." He pressed his gun against Lew's head. "Get off my boat and stay off my island."

"I'm counting to three," A.J. said. "The next sound after three will be a bullet leaving the chamber."

"Wait," Tiko yelled. "Put on your silencer."

Hearing this, Reno bailed before the countdown even began. Before Reno hit the water, Lew was following his lead. Laughing at the scene, the driver of the boat got up and headed back to join in on the action. For a brief second our eyes locked and I immediately knew where I'd seen him before. Unfortunately, I could tell by the expression on his face he recognized me as well. It was the guy I'd fought when we'd rescued Phil. His nose was still bandaged from where I'd hit him.

"Aren't you the one who slugged me in the nose?" He asked -- his voice a bit nasally.

"That's right," I replied.

Unable to suppress a laugh, he continued. "I grabbed your towel, and you ran away naked. Right?"

"Yeah, so?"

"So why don't you leave your clothes stern side then, hot shot?" He replied, quite happy with himself.

"What?" I gasped.

"Put your clothes on the deck, asshole. Now."

Unable to comprehend what I was doing, I quickly stripped off my fresh set of clothes, underwear and all. I jumped into the water, buck-naked. As I was in the air, I caught a glimpse of Lew laughing so hard he was choking. *How could he laugh at a time like this?* As my bare feet pierced through the surface of the water, my body quickly followed. The ocean water felt cold and murky against my goose-bumped flesh. My eyes were closed as I continued falling downward deeper into the water. Thoughts of seaweed, jellyfish and sharks made me feel uneasy. Paddling my way back up to the surface to grab some air, I blew out and re-surfaced. I could hear the rumbling of the boat leaving. Sucking in air, I breathed in a cloud of diesel fumes. I began treading water with Reno and Lew, knowing for sure a fish was about to become intimate with me.

I looked around as the boat sped away, and again, all I saw was Reno and Lew. Seconds later a stuffed teddy bear surfaced. *Where's Phil?*, I thought, as I watched the teddy bear bob up and down atop the ocean waves.

CHAPTER FIFTEEN

Well I have been drunk now for over two weeks
I passed out and I rallied
And I sprung a few leaks
But I got to keep wishing
I got to go fishing
I'm down to rock bottom again
Just a few friends, just a few friends

Jimmy Buffett
A Pirate Looks At Forty

Moments later, Phil emerged from the ocean, about a stone's throw away from where Reno, Lew and I were floating. His arms thrashed wildly, splashing up waves of water as he gasped for breath. By now his teddy bear had floated away from us and it was plotting a course to sea. Glancing over at us, you could tell by the look on Phil's face that he was about to be faced with a major life decision. Save the bear by swimming out after it, or save himself by swimming with the rest of us towards shore. He stayed in place, treading water for what seemed like an eternity; I could almost hear the wheels spinning inside his head. Of course by now, the rest of us had already started stroking towards shore. Initially, it hadn't seemed like we'd been dropped off too far from land, but despite how hard we swam, we just didn't seem to make any progress. We were actually losing ground, still fifty yards away from Phil by this point. The waves were getting choppier by the minute. All of us were having more success drifting sideways, charting a course that was parallel to shore, as opposed to making any real progress towards the island. Things were getting worse quickly and Phil still hadn't moved.

Trying to get my bearings, I spun around and was horrified when I realized where we actually were. Just to our left, sticking out of the water, were the flags that marked the spot where the Spanish Galleon had sank. We were right back at the scene of the shark attack just days earlier. My stomach sank.

"Holy crap, that's the shipwreck" I shouted, pointing in the direction of the markers.

The only difference this time around was that today, there were no boats, divers or snorkelers anywhere to be seen. *Let's just hope that the sharks had followed their lead and vacated the scene too*, I thought.

"This sucks," Reno yelled out. "We are screwed."

I hollered back at Reno, "What are you complaining about? This is all your fault."

Lew swam over between us and gave us each a look. Giving in to the apparent hopelessness of our situation, the tension began to mount.

The waves were really beginning to swell. I couldn't catch all that was said between Lew and Reno, since I was bobbing in and out of the water, but I could tell Reno was complaining about something. Concerned for my own safety I yelled back at Reno, "At least you've got clothes on. I'm freaking naked over here. And I'm petrified a fish is going to get intimate with me any second now."

"Come on dudes, focus," Lew hollered.

"Hey guys," Phil interrupted, just barely audible. He was pretty far from where we were drifting. "My legs are cramping up. I can't make it." His voice had crept a few octaves higher.

"This ain't no joke out here Phil," Lew replied, his hands cupped around his mouth. "You better start swimming."

That's when Phil went under, and turning to yell for Reno to help out, I noticed he was becoming a lost cause of his own as the tides had begun to push him away from us. Reno was now drifting with Phil's bear out to sea. *Things had gone from bad to worse*, I thought. Turning my head back around, I saw Lew had started swimming fast in Phil's direction to help him out and that's when Reno started screaming.

Oh my God, it's a shark, my mind shrieked out. Panicking, I frantically tried to swim towards land. That's when Lew started yelling too. I quickly glanced back over my shoulder and caught a quick glimpse of Lew holding onto Phil, waving his free arm feverishly back and forth, like he was trying to get someone's attention. His back was to me, so I looked further past him.

But before I could see anything, I actually heard it. The distinct sounds of a boat. It was like music to my ears. When I did see it, I could tell this boat was hauling ass right towards us, but more importantly, I could also tell it wasn't the goons coming back for more sadistic fun and games. I immediately did an about face and swam as fast as I could back towards Lew and Phil. I had lost sight of Reno. We all started screaming and waving our arms trying to attract some attention. As the boat approached Lew and Phil, it started to throttle down. I was still trying to swim in, but even from my viewpoint, I could tell it was crammed tight with people; there was no way they had room for the four of us on board. The boat slowed up and came to a drift beside Lew and Phil, everybody aboard was looking them over, practically scratching their heads trying to figure out what we were doing swimming in the middle of the ocean.

I started swimming their way.

"For the love of God, throw me a life jacket," Phil screamed out. Seconds later, a yellow life vest plopped onto the water next to him. "Thanks," he sighed, not even bothering to put it on, but instead slipping on top of it to keep him afloat.

As I swam up beside Lew and Phil, we all immediately began begging for a lift back to shore. The captain informed us that they were loaded up, but we could feel free to hop on the water weenie they were towing. My eyes lit up as I looked behind the boat, and saw an empty, yellow water weenie.

"Hop on up there boys," the captain hollered out. Not remembering, or for that matter even caring that I was completely naked I was more than happy to comply. He slowly inched the boat forward pulling the long weenie up next to us. Out of nowhere, Reno jumped up on back; he was grinning ear to ear. "Cool," he chuckled, "this beats the hell out of swimming."

"I thought you were a lost cause." I replied.

"Nope, I knew we would be saved by a boat toting a water weenie."

Lew, still in saving mode, helped push Phil on board. He plopped down in front of Reno, leaving the life jacket floating. As I swam over to grab the vest, Lew took the opportunity and jumped on our chariot next. Horrified, I realized that the only seat left was the one up front.

"Lew," I whispered, "scoot up, and let me sit behind you."

"No way dude, you're not sitting naked behind me," he laughed.

The women on board were going to get quite a show, I thought to myself as I climbed aboard. I quickly thought about putting on the life vest I was holding, but when I put an arm through it I realized the possibility of fitting into a child size vest was not going to happen. *No wonder Phil didn't slip it on.*

Almost immediately after hearing Lew's reply, the three women on the back of the boat shouted, "Why are you naked?" They were giggling to themselves as they spoke.

Reno and Lew were laughing hysterically. I threw the life jacket at the ladies, hoping to take their mind off the situation. It landed with a thud at their feet. I climbed aboard the water weenie, oblivious to the cat calls and laughter.

"Why are you naked?" the boat repeated.

"It's a long story," I replied.

Hearing my reply, a gal in an orange string bikini yelled back. "Long story? It doesn't look like that from where I'm standing." I buried my head in my hands as the entire boat broke out into laughter, along with my three supposed friends behind me.

With that, the captain shouted out, "Hang on to your hats cowboys." He gunned the throttle and the water weenie jumped out of the sea. I was beginning to wonder if our captain was drunk. He started turning the boat to the left and the right, causing the weenie to slam through the waves. Then I realized he wasn't drunk, he was simply giving us a good ride. I was holding onto the handles in front of my seat for dear life. As I grasped on tightly, all I could think was that we were the unluckiest and yet luckiest sons of bitches around.

With every bounce, my boys were taking a beating. As we raced ahead moving along the coastline, we almost went flying right past the hotel we were staying at for the night. "That's our hotel," Lew screamed out, to no avail. Nobody on board could hear us. I felt a tap on my shoulder, turning around, water slapping me in the face; I saw Lew bail, then Phil, and then Reno. I was the last one left on the big weenie. Following their lead I found myself right back in the warm water.

Surfacing this time, there was one noticeable difference; we were a mere fifty feet from the beach. Getting back on land would not be an issue. As a matter of fact, Reno was already walking the rest of the way in. Phil was right behind him and Lew was doing the backstroke to shore. But I just stayed put, for now I was the one facing a major dilemma. I was naked, yet again, and this time the beach was full of men, women and children alike.

"Come on Tango," Lew yelled out from the beach. "No sense in prolonging the inevitable." The three of them had settled into a row of lounge chairs. All I saw was the towels hanging on the back of the chairs. I quickly swam into shore and ran as fast as I could towards the towels. Hurriedly grabbing one, I wrapped up and sat down with a plop. Once again, the three of them were laughing at my expense.

"I'm glad I could be here to humor you," I smirked.

Between laughter, Lew replied, "Dude, if you could have seen the look on the face of those chicks on the boat when you popped out naked, you'd be laughing too."

It wasn't much longer, after the chuckling had subsided and the sun had dried our skin, that a waitress came over and asked if we needed anything.

"I'll take a pina colada."

"Tango," Reno sighed, "you can order a fru fru drink, but I just thought I was dead in the water, make mine a Jack and Coke."

"Me too," Phil replied.

"Make mine a double," Lew added. "You want to change yours Tango?"

"Nope, I don't do soda pop."

"You are a freak," Lew smirked.

"What can I say, I treat my body like a temple."

Happy still with my original choice, I was surprised, yet again, when the waitress returned. She handed me an entire pineapple carcass with all kinds of fruit, straws and umbrellas hanging out of the thing. It looked like a thrift store had exploded in my hands and it took both of them to hold onto it. I took a sip. The blended concoction tasted good, and that was all that really mattered. "Come on, enough with the laughing," I said between sips. They were still busting my balls.

We sat back, soaked in the rays and drank for quite a while after that. It just felt good to not be doing anything. I laid my head back, my eyes were closed, and like a bolt of lightning a thought flashed across my mind. *The girls numbers were gone.*

All of the information I'd gathered from Brooke earlier in the day, her phone number, address, everything was in my shorts that had been left on the boat. Not to mention, our hotel keys and my cell phone. Sighing, I look over at Lew. "I lost all the information on the girls and the key to the room. Where the hell are we going to stay now?"

"Don't worry about it dude, I got the other key."

"Thank God." I sighed. At least something had gone our way.

Chilling out a while longer, the heat of the day blended with the cool breeze that t he sunset was bringing. The beach was getting a little less crowded. Finishing up our last drink, we decided to head inside. The hotel was just behind us. Wrapping the towel tightly around my waist, I headed out.

"Ma'am" Lew yelled out to our waitress, "this guy is stealing your beachtowel."

"I saw him come out of the ocean earlier," she replied. "That one is on the house."

More laughter followed, I shook my head and continued walking.

My skin erupted with goosebumps as we crossed the threshold and entered the air-conditioning inside the hotel. Still chilled, we stood in front of the elevator doors. The doors slid open and we stepped inside.

"Which floor?" I asked.

"Ten." Lew replied, and I think this watch is douched, tapping on it feverishly.

Sitting inside our room, we took stock of our situation. It was our last night in Key West, Little V was off our case, and for a change, neither the cops nor the goons were trailing us. We really had nothing better to do than to go out and spend one last night on the town.

"Could we try and forget the insanity of the last couple of days?" Reno asked.

"Hell yeah!" Lew relied. I nodded in agreement.

"Hey, let's stick to beer tonight. O.K.?" Phil said. "I don't think I can take another night of heavy drinking."

We all agreed and slowly began to get ready for our last night on the island. This was going to be the first time in what seemed like a very long time that we could simply unwind and enjoy ourselves. I heard Phil in the background leave his wife a short message on the answering machine. "Another wild afternoon, but we're heading out for dinner and retiring early tonight, so I'll see you tomorrow afternoon. Love ya. Bye, bye."

God only knew what awaited us at the end of the night.

Refreshed, a few hours later we were exiting the cool air of the hotel in exchange for a steamy night. The sun had set a few hours ago, but the heat and humidity still clung in the air. Walking down Greene Street in search of Duval, Reno, looking up at the street signs almost ran into two people heading straight towards us. Fortunately, it wasn't a couple of bums. The guy yelled out, "Watch where your heading chief, the lady is delicate." The girl giggled as we all stood on the corner waiting for the light to change. Keeping my eyes firmly planted on the gorgeous lady standing beside me, all I had noticed was that the guy was tall, tan, and had long surfer-hair.

"You from around here?" Lew asked.

"Lived here my whole life." He paused and shook our hands.

"So you ought to know, being local and all. Where's a good place to hang out on our last night in Key West?" Lew continued.

"Well, we're just coming from *Schooner's Wharf*. Michael McCloud is playing tonight and things are starting to heat up."

"So why are you leaving?" I asked, "If that place is just starting to come alive."

"That's easy chief, this ain't my last night, and some folk have to work for a living."

That made sense to us, so we got directions, thanked him and started across the street. The light had just changed.

"By the way, what's your name?" Lew hollered back, turning around.

"Captain John Lamplighter, the doctor."

Hearing this I couldn't help but respond. "You don't look like an M.D., but it sure looks like you got what cures her."

"Oh, she's one hundred percent Key West all right, but there are tons of them where you're heading. Have fun chief."

A short walk later and we were entering *Schooner's Wharf*. The place was a little crowded, although it was still early in the evening. At this pace, it wouldn't be too much longer before the entire place filled up. We decided to sit out on the patio, overlooking the bay. All four of us settled into seats, aside from the fact that Reno fought with Lew for the spot next to a group of very good looking young gals. Their table was littered with plastic cups left over from Happy Hour, and their ashtrays were full from hours spent smoking. Phil wound up sitting next to Reno and Lew settled for a seat beside me. I had sat down next to some guy wearing a cowboy hat. *I hope this McCloud isn't a country singer*, I thought, glancing at the cowboy beside me. From our seats we had a perfect view of the night's talent. He was in the middle of a song when we sat down, and the one thing that I noticed right away was that he had a very distinctive voice. It almost sounded like he'd been drinking since noon, and his tone was slightly nasally, with a southern twang. I liked him immediately as I listened to him finish a song about Key West and how drinking was his favorite sport. He was playing an acoustic guitar and there was nobody else on stage, but he held the attention of the entire bar. In the short time since we'd arrived, *Schooner's* had already taken on a party atmosphere as McCloud broke into what seemed to be a local favorite. Everybody was singing, holding up their beers, laughing and whistling. The accent and language of the cowboy beside me was entertaining on it's own accord. He introduced himself as Jake, and told us he was from Australia.

"You out here on holiday?" Jake asked.

"Sure are," Lew replied, explaining our story. "Tonight is our last night."

"I see. I see. I was on holiday three years ago. Still on my last night, though. I never left." Jake said.

"We need to get Reno – the guy flirting with those two girls over there," I said, entering the conversation, pointing at Reno, "back to his fiancé; otherwise we would never leave."

"Who's the guy with you that could go duck hunting with a rake?"

"Oh that's Phil, we need to get him back to his wife also," I said, laughing at the metaphor.

"Yeah, he's a tall drink of water. You all drinking from the froth tonight?"

"We are," Lew replied. "But where are all the waitresses?"

Just then, Jake whistled and a waitress appeared from nowhere. "Pour it out from the tap for my four friends here Tammy." We all ordered, and had our drinks in no time, while Jake put it on his tab. "Good looking Sheila's in here, eh boys?"

"Yes, there are," we all barked in unison. Raising our cups, we toasted our newfound host and his two girlfriends. At this point Reno had even torn himself away from the gals to join us. Reno, it seemed, was coming alive more this night. He was talking with everyone. I think he was beginning to realize that this was his last night in paradise. Once back home, his reality would set in and all of this would just be some great memory.

"So, big Phil has a misses, and all the rest of you are single as a goat?" We all sat there shaking our heads and Phil had his left hand held high in the air. "Watch the lassies in here, many are locals, or down from the other Keys north of here. They're all ready to party though. Most in this joint aren't wearing any underwear." He whispered this last comment, but the two girls sitting next to him both grinned and shook their heads. Just then he started to edge up one of the gals skirts next to him. She quickly spun to the side, and pushed his hand away. "If I was a cat herder, this is the spot I'd pick."

"Dude, you've got some wild terms. You are a trip." Lew laughed taking a chug of beer.

"Well, I need to keep a little of my home here with me, but still feel as though I'm on vacation everyday," Jake answered.

We proceeded to drink for free as we continued listening to the talented McCloud strum on the six-string.

"So, Jake," I asked, "What do you do during the day to get all the beer money?"

Jake explained that he chartered many fishing adventures and received enough in tips to pay the bills, the rest of his pay was just gravy. Using this as an excuse, he then went into another story: "I was heading this charter, fishing for sharks, about two months back. We were out in the deep blue, strumming across the gentle waves, with this fellow roped into position. He was hanging onto the big stick when he leashed a brown shark. There were five blokes on board and we were all standing next to this big fellow chomping on a fat cigar, turning the crank. He was a bass fisherman from Iowa that had dreamed about shagging a shark, and that day he got his dream. So, he's working his ass off reeling in this shark, and the sucker is swimming around the back of the boat, then it shoots down giving this ol' bloke the buck ride of his life. And then, like a crack of lightning this big ol' fellow flies out of his seat and hits the water still hanging onto the reel. We all freaked and tried to grab onto him as he was dragged on by. It was not happening. I hit the deck and slid under the other blokes, opened the back hatch, and grabbed the belt in his pants 'cause the shark was taking him down to the deep blue."

"No freaking way," Lew shouted out, high-fiving Jake.

Hitting his stride, Jake continued on, he'd had the attention of about ten people by this point. "Everyone else helped me hoist him out of the water, and then he planted himself back into the chair, dripping wet but without a scar. This bloke proceeds to reel the shark back up, to only cut him loose after the fight. He wanted the kill, but he thanked the fish for the fight, and he threw his cigar and line back to the sea. It was the wildest time I ever did see."

We all sat there with our mouths open. Lew ordered the next round of drinks and leaned over to high five Jake again.

"I also got the biggest tip of my life from him after that ride. He even called and booked another charter next spring, wild people in Iowa."

"That son of a bitch should stick to bass fishing," I said.

"Si," was Jakes response. "So you all going to order some sandwiches, or ya just sticking to liquids?"

"Hey, we got an early flight." I spun around surprised to hear Phil speaking. "We need to retire ahead of schedule tonight. We're just sticking to beer."

"Oh laddie, that ain't going to happen. One of your own is opening the door with the lassies over there, and you got another two tan, single, mid-western accent blokes here all full of piss and vinegar. You're all here on your last night. You're gonna see the dew and dawn." Jake stood up and twirled his hat around. He excused himself, with a gal in each arm and walked away.

Reno had eased back into the conversation at the table beside him with his back to us; his newfound girlfriends had returned. Lew, Phil and I all just sat and drank, listening to McCloud singing about the Southern Zone and snacking on pretzels.

Later on in the evening, Reno came back over to our table, he'd been over at the bar with a large group of people for the past hour or so. "Come on, get up guys, these gals have been telling me all night about this cool bonfire party they're going to tonight. They're about to leave and invited us, well me, to come along. It's for locals only, but they say after all I've been through, I deserve to be treated to a true local party."

"Dude, did you mention us? Are we invited?" Lew asked.

"Oh, yeah, it's cool. Come on guys. This chick has been all over me, and she's hot as hell."

I didn't want to speak for the rest of the guys, but if we didn't go now, we would end up spending the entire evening here. "It sounds good to me Reno," I said.

"That's fine dude, we're in," Lew added. "But more importantly, does she have any hot friends?"

"Oh, she says there'll be tons of women there. You guys won't believe the things she's been telling me…"

He drifted off for a second, "Plus," he continued, back to reality, "she's got a few stripper friends."

"We're in," the three of us yelled simultaneously. Phil's knees hit the table as he stood up, causing a couple of empty bottles to topple.

"Well, finish up your drinks, these gals are ready to go!"

Passing Jake on our way out, Lew asked him if he'd heard about the party.

"I haven't missed one yet," he replied. "Maybe I'll see you blokes there." We thanked him for an amusing time, and the beers. Slamming the empties on the bar, we headed out, Lew paused to place some money in the coffer for McCloud.

Three gals I wasn't introduced to, along with Reno led the way. The entire walk to the beach was a blur; we were stepping though back alleys, zigzagging a route towards the Gulf of Mexico. All of a sudden the cement gave way to sand and before I knew it we were standing amongst a few small bungalows up on stilts. They were lining the shore. We bounded up the staircase that was attached to the third one. There were a few people mingling outside, with a bouncer-type guy standing guard at the entrance. Just as I thought, *man they've even got a bouncer at this party*, he nodded. "Hi, Heather." We nodded back at the guy, he nodded at us, and we followed Heather up the stairs. *At least I knew the name of one of the gals now*, I thought.

The place was dimly lit and it took my eyes a few moments to adjust. There was music playing in the background and the smell of smoke hung in the air. The room we were standing in was lit with black lighting, and a light fixture yielding every color in the spectrum illuminated the kitchen, which was attached directly to this room. As I looked around, I noticed the entire house was littered with bottles, both liquor and beer. There were empty pizza boxes everywhere. "I thought this was a beach party," I said, looking at Lew. "Where are all the hot chicks? We got the shortest hair in the whole house. There's nothing but burnt out hippies in here."

My question fell on deaf ears. Lew didn't know what to say and from across the room, we stood and watched as Reno, Heather and the other two girls were talking, laughing, high-fiving and shaking hands with the others. By the way he was working the crowd, Reno looked as comfortable as he would have been if he were at his high school reunion.

Out of my peripheral vision, I saw some motion in the far corner of the room. Looking closer, I saw a dreadlocked bartender, motioning for us to come over. Lew, Phil and I complied, strolling over to the makeshift countertop bar. As he poured us each a beer, he told us that all the action was outside. With a beer in hand, taking his advice we opened the screen doors that led out to the deck. The instant the doors opened, it was obvious that the party was indeed outside. The wrap around deck alone had upwards of fifty people standing on it. Tiki torches lit up the night. Hearing the crashing waves, and being pulled toward the soft light from the bonfire, we pushed our way through the mob and walked down the stairs onto the beach. As we approached what turned out to be a huge bonfire, people sitting on logs, wooden lounge chairs and blankets surrounded us. There was a guy playing a guitar, a few girls beating on tambourines and another guy playing a drum. Groups of people were singing, and there was a keg wedged in the sand. We pulled up three empty lounge chairs and sat down for the show.

"Now this is a beach party." I said.

As soon as we sat down, Phil announced that he had to pee.

"Now?" Lew asked. "Why didn't you go when we were inside?"

"Didn't think about it." Phil replied.

"Well, check up on Reno when you're in there," I added, as he walked off. He gave a half-hearted wave over his shoulder and never looked back.

A couple of beers and a few songs later Phil returned. "It's getting crazy in there," he said, pointing back at the bungalow.

"What do you mean?" I asked.

"For starters, the entire house is doing lemon shots, and then kissing the person next to them. Reno says he's on his eighth shot."

"Is he O.K?" Lew asked.

"He said he got tongue on the second shot." Phil answered. "From what I can tell, he hasn't stopped making out with Heather the entire night. When I pulled him aside, he told me that he'd never been hit on like that in his entire life."

"Really." I interjected.

"Oh, yeah, and he said that she's been telling him some wild shit."

"Like what?" I asked. Our ears were perking up.

"Things like, 'you can have me any way you want me tonight – no strings attached', and other stuff like that."

"What else was she saying?" Lew shouted.

"I can't remember. It was something really crazy though."

"Well, needless to say, Reno ain't sticking to beer tonight," I laughed.

The guitar player started playing an old time song, I couldn't quite place at first, though I'd heard it at least a hundred times before. When the crowd around the fire started singing the chorus, I realized, it was Don McClean's, *American Pie*. Midway through the song, everybody had his or her arms around each other and we were swaying to the beat. Somehow I ended up sandwiched between Lew and Phil; I was disgusted to see that both of them had a gorgeous girl at their side.

A lot of beers later, I strolled back from urinating in the Gulf of Mexico, and sat down solo again. Looking around, I was trying to decide if I had returned to the right spot. Lew and Phil were gone, but after a quick glance around I saw them on the opposite side of the fire. Finally realizing what was going on, I found myself in the middle of what appeared to be a game of truth or dare, duck, duck, goose. I had no idea how it had been started, but I quickly familiarized myself with the rules. It was pretty simple, if you were selected 'the goose' and then caught the person who had chosen you as you both ran around the bonfire before they could sit in your spot, then the reward was asking a truth of the loser or ordering a dare. If you failed to catch your opponent, then you would be the victim of a truth or dare.

After witnessing a fat guy mooning the group, and a busty gal flashing, there was a dark haired bombshell walking around the group 'duck, ducking'. To my delight, she planted a 'goose' on the top of my head. Like a shot out of a cannon, I jumped up and tore ass. Forgetting I was on sand and that I had been drinking all night long, I wound up face-planted firmly in the sand, three strides into it. Spitting out a mouthful of sand, and dusting my ego off, I slowly jogged the rest of the way around the group, taking my defeat in stride. Toying with me, she turned her back on me, as I positioned myself behind her with my hands on her shoulders, she asked me, "Do you want a truth or dare?"

Hearing Lew, Phil and the rest of the crowd scream out, "Dare!" I calmly said, "Truth."

She shook her head slowly, side-to-side and turning to face me, she said, "Nope. It's going to be a dare."

"So what do I have to do?" I asked.

"I dare you to pee on the fire."

The crowed erupted.

Pleading my case, I told her I had just gone only moments earlier.

"What's the matter?" she smiled. "Stage fright?"

I could distinctly hear Lew laughing loudly in the background.

"I swear, I just went." Ignoring my pleas, she commanded me again. "I just peed in the Gulf not more than five minutes ago." Shaking my head, "I just freaking peed," I muttered more to myself than anyone in particular.

That's when the chants started. "Piss on the fire." "Piss on the fire." "Piss on the fire."

So begrudgingly, I whipped it out, while cupping myself on both sides. I stood there for a few seconds; sweat began trickling down my back. I stood there motionless, willing myself to pee, when by the grace of the fire gods, a little trickle seeped out.

The crowd went wild.

That done, I bent over, wiped my hands on the sand and started duck, ducking myself. To make a long story short, two dares later, after having to kiss another man, and allowing a girl to pour a cold beer down my shorts, I decided to throw caution to the wind and 'goose' the hottest girl at the party. She was wearing shell-lined flip-flops. It was a guarantee, and it worked like a charm. Finally, it was my turn to get back. I decided to dare.

Strutting around like a rooster, I high-fived a few guys in the crowd. "My dare is two-fold," I announced, clearing my throat. "I would like for you to pick out another girl from the crowd." Complying with my demand, she proceeded to choose the girl that goosed me to start this whole ordeal. *Sweet*, I thought. I reached up and rubbed the shell necklace I was wearing for luck. "My dare has a reward. Whoever makes out with me the best, and by best I mean, most original, most improvisational; you know, whoever is into it the most, as judged by the crowd's applause, gets this necklace."

The crowd was silent, as if thinking this through.

"Now who wants to go first?" I smiled.

"I will." It was the girl I'd goosed wearing the shell sandals. "I mean, I guess since I lost, I'll go first."

"Great, what's your name sweetheart?"

"Amber."

Amber walked over very seductively and ran her hands up underneath the front of my shirt. Sliding around my shoulders and resting them in the small of my back, she pulled me close. As the front of our bodies pressed up against each other, she dropped her hands and grabbed my ass. Before I could gasp, she was rubbing every zone in my mouth with her tongue. Almost as quickly as she had started though, she was finished. As she pulled away the crowd clapped loudly.

Smiling feverishly, I tried to regain composure as my arch-nemesis stepped towards me. The girl who had gotten me into this whole mess seemed to be up to the challenge. Cracking her knuckles, she told the people standing behind her to move off the lounge chair they were using. Before I even got a chance to ask her name, she was on top of me like a lioness on a zebra. Throwing me down on the recently vacated lounger, she rubbed her chest back and forth, slowly and seductively across my face. As the bells in my head stated clanging, she mounted me on top, froggy-style and planted the best kiss I'd ever had in my life. I almost swallowed my Adam's apple. I couldn't hear anything in particular, just muffled sounds beating like a drum in the distance. Feeling like I was about to pass out, all I can remember seeing was her removing my necklace.

After that climax, the game disbanded and the group went back to singing and drinking. I didn't know what time it was, but from the streaks of light beginning to stretch across the horizon, I could tell it was closer to dawn than dusk. I was having some conversation with my dark angel, now clad in my seashell necklace. What we were talking about I could not tell you, but I'm sure it was something special when I was rudely interrupted. Both Lew and Phil were tugging on my shoulders, telling me it was time to go.

With that, she gave me a kiss goodnight. Not thinking, I told her "I'd be right back." I never even got her name.

Walking back inside, we headed upstairs. *Dreadlocks* was still tending the bar.

Reno was nowhere to be found. We asked the bartender where the skinny guy, with the all female entourage went. He said they had left a while back. Shrugging my shoulders, I started to walk back to the beach. *No sense leaving quite yet*, I thought.

Before I could reach the door, Lew hauled me in by the back of my neck. "Come on, Tango. It's time to get going. It's almost four in the morning."

We only had a few hours to get some sleep before we headed to the airport. Home was closer than I would like to think.

Along the route back to the hotel, the three of us chatted about the bon fire party, re-living it, even though it had just happened.

"Lew, you did what?" Phil laughed.

"I made it to third base with Amber, while Tango over there had an enlightening conversation with Beth."

Thinking back on it now, none of us really seemed all that concerned that we couldn't find Reno. The next thing I knew, I was in bed, back at the hotel. As the lights went out, Reno was still missing. I lay there wondering how it was that Lew and I were sharing the bed, while Phil went solo. To drunk to care, I rolled over and closed my eyes.

Bang.

I'm trying to sleep.

Bang.

Bang. Bang. Bang.

"Could somebody get that?" Lew yelled out. I bolted upright. I wasn't dreaming.

Bang. Bang.

Somebody was knocking on the door. Looking quickly around the room, I noticed Reno still wasn't back.

"What time is it?" I whispered to Lew.

"Quarter 'til six," he yawned.

Bang.

I started to freak out. "Who the hell is it?" I whispered. "Reno's still not here."

"Shit." Lew gasped, sitting up. "I hope it's not Little V."

"Or the cops,' I added.

Bang. Bang. Bang. Bang. The incessant banging continued.

How Phil could sleep through this was beyond me.

CHAPTER SIXTEEN

Island
I see you in the distance

Jimmy Buffett
Island

I looked at Lew, and he looked back at me. Shrugging my shoulders, I turned around and walked up to the door.

Bang.

My skin crawled, and I almost shrieked. Swallowing hard I turned the knob and opened the door, prepared to face almost anything.

"What's up?" yelled Reno, pushing his way past me as he stumbled into the room. His hand was wrapped up haphazardly with a roll of white gauze.

"Where in the hell have you been?" Lew asked. "What happened to your hand?"

"Yeah, where'd you disappear last night?" I added.

Mumbling something about cutting his hand last night, he tripped, and fell onto the fold out. I noticed Phil was still sound asleep. "Look," Reno said, placing his head in his hands, "I'm still drunk, I'm going on no sleep, and I got no clue how the hell I just got here."

Glancing at watch number three, Lew shook his head. "Dudes, we got an hour before we have to be at the airport."

"Thank God we never unpacked," I laughed. We woke up Phil and tried our best to keep Reno awake as well. Within minutes we were out the door and stepping onto the elevator. Hopping into a hotel shuttle, we dozed on the way to the airport. No one spoke, not even a peep. In no time at all, the shuttle pulled up to the curb alongside the airport entrance.

I couldn't help but look over my shoulder the entire time we unloaded our bags. All I could hope was that Little V was true to his word. Technically, we were leaving the island illegally and without the permission of local law enforcement, but as I glanced around, I saw no police. We had twenty minutes left to kill before our flight boarded. We sat down on some hard plastic chairs that faced the runway; we were ready to walk outside. Still a bit sleepy, I lounged back in the chair, trying to get as comfortable as possible. I could hear the early morning local news playing on the television across the room. Reno and Phil, both had their eyes closed, while Lew and I fixated our gaze on the television.

Looking more into the wall, staring into space, I heard: *A local entrepreneur in Key West, Ricardo Vargas was hospitalized late last night due to what was described as a heart condition. He's listed in critical but stable condition. Vargas known to many as a kind and generous...*

I looked over at Lew. "Ain't that a load of crap?"

I nudged Reno. "Did you hear that?"

He opened up one eye and grinned. "Yeah, I heard it. He got what he deserved."

Now boarding flight number twenty. Non-stop to Orlando.

We hopped up and made our exit, still shaking our heads.

I was trying to figure out what to do with the sign that I had acquired a few days back. All of our carry-on luggage fit snugly in the small overhead bins, but the sign was going to be a problem. I felt a tap on my shoulder.

"Can I help you?" It was the stewardess. I noticed immediately that she was damn cute, with long curly hair.

"Doesn't seem to fit." I replied, smiling.

"We're not full. Why don't you put it in a seat."

I looked around and noticed there was no one sitting next to Phil, who was once again asleep. From the row in front of him, I climbed over the seat and placed my cargo in the chair next to Phil. I strapped the seat belt across the front for good measure. Lew sat down with a thud in the chair next to me.

The plane taxied down the runway and took off with a jolt. We were traveling north away from this island. Lew and I were both staring out the window, watching the island below us get smaller and smaller; until it finally disappeared into an array of inlets and coral reefs, outlined by the blue-green sea. Our getaway to the southern zone at times seemed like a nightmare in a run away train, but now leaving this small island all in one piece, we looked through the small oval window and it all seemed so surreal.

I started laughing to myself. Within moments, Lew was chuckling too. The days had been filled with highs and lows, which neither of us would be able to explain to anyone, no matter how hard we tried. Not that anybody would believe what we had just been through. For some unexplained reason, just then Lew asked the stewardess for a stack of napkins. He handed them to me and said, "start writing."

I started jotting down every funny saying and weird situation we encountered during the whole vacation. As we went through the exercise, we were both battling constant fits of laughter. At one point I was even crying I was laughing so hard, tears running down my cheek. Wiping my eyes, I looked back at Phil, the butt of many one-liners we'd already written. He was totally out of it; still sound asleep. His head was almost touching the ceiling, and he was lying backwards with his mouth wide open.

Reno was sitting two rows back, just staring straight ahead. Too tired to sleep, I guessed. I decided to take the chance, while he was still awake to ask him again what happened last night. "So Reno, where were you last night?"

The constant sound of the propellers outside the plane was the only response.

"Reno? Do you have something to tell us?" I prodded some more.

A smile and a glance told us the whole story. With that, Reno laid his head to the window, and closed his eyes. He rubbed the bandage on his hand.

I looked at Lew, a smile, spreading across his face. "Lucy – you got some splainin' to do."

Reno just lay there idle, with a smirk on his face.

Shrugging my shoulders, I turned around and settled back in with the business at hand. Lew continued rattling off sayings and stories, things I'd completely forgotten, while I busily wrote down every word. *This would make one hell of a story*, I thought to myself.

Just then the stewardess walked past us and touched the Key West sign, to make sure it was still stable. Smiling, she turned around. "Now tell me the story about this sign that has a seat all to itself."

We proceeded to tell our tale, as she knelt down in the abandoned seat beside us.

Her face bright, her hair blonde, and a pretty smile spread across her face – she was the first to hear our story in short form.

A story that someday might be told to the world…

THE END

We'll see how easy sleep comes tonight...
We've got our own beds now.

"Southern Zone"

Some sing about Kokomo

Some sing about the Florida Keys

I just sing about getting drunk and swinging from the palm trees

I gave up the corporate life

Mending the relationship with me and the wife

Now I live on the beach

A boat drink is always within reach

With my feet in the sand I sometimes look to my left and my right

But now don't get me wrong, I sleep with the same lady (gal) night after night

Oh, oh The Southern Zone

Where the women's lips blister

But taste like ice cream cones

The thermometer stays fixed at ninety degrees

And you cannot find shade from any palm trees

No I do not miss the northern plains

Where the days drone on – They all seem the same

There may be four seasons

But only one is pleasing

Now I feel like I am on vacation everyday

Just sitting here strumming my life away

Oh, oh The Southern Zone

Where the women's lips blister

But taste like ice cream cones

The thermometer stays fixed at ninety degrees

And you cannot find shade from any palm trees

I love getting up early riding the schooner with the waves crashing

Standing there in a tank top with the sun blasting

I dream about being a pirate out at sea

Just my dog – Lucky and me

The sunsets here always draw a crowd

Everyone just gathers around

Then the bars fill up and I play until dawn
I stumble home waking up on the lawn

Times change but people stay the same
Walking around in bikini's, this place is never lame
There is an abundance of tattoos
An abundance of silicone
They walk hand in hand
The tourists just watch and stand
Out on the ocean the surfers hang ten
The local shop owners just want people to spend
I just walk around in amazement every day
Another sunset, another outdoor bar
Just getting ready to play

Oh, oh The Southern Zone
Where the women's lips blister
But taste like ice cream cones
The thermometer stays fixed at ninety degrees
And you cannot find shade from any palm trees